Spells in Waiting

by

Michaela L. Cane

A HellBound Books Publishing LLC Book
Houston TX

**A HellBound Books LLC
Publication**

www.hellboundbookspublishing.com

Printed in the United States of America

Michaela L Cane

Spells in Waiting

Chapter 1

David found himself scowling, his hands clenched into fists and braced against the wall behind him, as if simply grounding himself might make this conversation end sooner. In the dim light of the hallway, he could only hope that his partner couldn't see how jittery he was beneath his skin. But Josh was staring at him as if he could. As hard-lined as his partner was, and nearly as tall, David forced himself to stare into his eyes without flinching, and to keep his mind off of the human element at the heart of this conversation; that wasn't what this was about, not when this confrontation had come so far already.

"You don't think this is crossing a line, even for us?" Josh's voice was pitched low, betraying the fact that he was just about ready to let the witch go—that was, if his partner's plan was the only way of going forward. Slightly less experienced, he was also the less calm of the two for the moment, and David knew that could only work to his own advantage. Josh was giving away his anxiety with his hands jammed deep into his pockets, tense with annoyance that they were having this discussion at all, let alone again.

Distracted, David Fredricks went back to watching the witch as he spoke, noting the fact that she was fighting against her bonds even though it had to be clear to her that she wasn't getting out of them, and that the two of them were there and ready to catch her all over again even if she did. Hell, maybe she was doing it for their benefit, he thought now. Regardless, their ranch house was centered on 10 acres, all their property; she had nowhere to run to easily, whether she realized it or not.

David asked his partner, "You got any other ideas? We've had her a week and people are still dying; this bitch mother of hers stays on schedule, there'll be another body by tomorrow morning. You saying her feeling safe and cozy here is more important than the average joe carrying on with his fuckin' life?"

"She's not exactly *safe and cozy*," Josh Devlin retorted, the old scar along his cheek twisting with the stress of the words. He looked to be the scarier of the two of them, he knew, from the scars he'd brought home with him from Iraq, but every day it seemed like he was learning more and more that his partner was the more hot-headed, and the more dangerous, of the two of them. And he was right—the witch was far from comfortable, and his partner knew it.

For a week, the 25-year-old witch had spent roughly 20 hours out of each day tied to the chair in their interrogation room, getting breaks only for the bathroom and brief meals she generally spent standing up, warned that speaking would sacrifice her food. She'd been teased with more substantial meals, and showers—and bribed with both, as well as her own safety and freedom—and she'd been slapped more than once, back-handed by David when he was frustrated with her, and when his partner hadn't been around to suggest that physical violence on a witch who, they had to face it, might not have done a damn thing wrong herself, was itself a step too far. And now David was suggesting quite a bit more, but his argument was hard to refute. The witch's mother was, without a doubt, killing people, and disappearing faster than they or any of their colleagues could track her.

And their kidnapping her daughter hadn't gotten her attention either; it seemed, Josh thought, like the witch they were hunting cared slightly less about her daughter than he himself did. But the government had contracted them to find her, by any means possible—it was their job, after all—and they'd yet to let their boss down. They made good money, taking the time to find criminals that the government didn't have the time or the persistence to track down when an investigation started dragging on, or when crimes were coming too fast and required outside help. Witch, vampire, terrorist, mad scientist...whatever, they were criminals, and they had to be caught, one way or another. Right?

"Look, if she talks, I stop. Unless *you* want to..."

"Hell, no," Josh bit back at his partner, grimacing. Then a thought struck him. "You've done this before?" he demanded.

David glanced back to the witch, seeming to hesitate for the first time since the conversation had begun. They'd had it yesterday also, and this question hadn't come up. He looked back at the man in front of him, his partner of some three years now. The conversation was easier to have when he wasn't looking at the girl.

"I've threatened it," he finally answered.

"And meant to go through with it?"

David shrugged. That was the question, wasn't it? Had he meant to go through with it? He'd never had to decide. And in the past, he'd been threatening criminals—women who could potentially lead him to the rest of their circles, to other people who'd committed crimes and were still being hunted by the government. He'd never threatened it against a witch, or someone like this who wasn't actually involved in the crimes being investigated. But then again, they'd never had a serial-killing witch who didn't seem to be showing any rhyme or reason to her kills, either. There was no way to predict her actions, so the only path forward seemed to be getting a clue as to where they could find her in her down-time, and the woman's daughter was what they had to use. She was *all* they had.

Reasoning aside, though, it was easier than it should have been, maybe, to contemplate what he was thinking, given *this* witch's appearance.

At 5'3, she was shorter and curvier than what might have normally been considered his type, but she had a moxie to her that he liked. If she hadn't had her shoulder-length hair dyed goth-girl black, which made her look a fair bit older and less attractive in his opinion, he would have called her gorgeous. As it was, she was pretty enough for him to be curious about the feel of more of her skin than he'd yet seen. What it would be like to touch her when he wasn't slapping her or man-handling her back and forth from their window-less bathroom. She was well-proportioned, small and curvy as she was; and he liked her curves. Her face was round, sporting a small, perfectly formed mouth and fierce blue eyes, and she wore a light-weight sweater that hung loose, showing off her curves, along with boot-cut jeans that he'd thought about taking off of her more than once. Especially when they'd offered her warmer clothes if she'd tell them something—anything—about how to find her mother. Her feet were bare, and had to be freezing, and he didn't think the sweater offered much warmth...but none of their bribes had mattered to her, because of what they were asking.

That was the crux of it. They were looking for her mom, and if anybody could understand the drive to protect family, it was him. That didn't mean he'd let her off the hook for it, though. If she wouldn't give them any information, short of them taking more drastic action, then drastic action seemed like the right call.

"Look, Josh," he started again, nudging his partner further into the hall so they could talk more freely. "You don't want us to hurt her, and I get it, man, but we're out of options. What else are we supposed to do? It's not like she's a kid. She knows what her mom is and how the world works, and how the birds and the fuckin' bees work. Personally, I'd rather take this track than beat her to a pulp. Besides, she'll tell me something before it goes that far; what I'm talking about is basically just threats."

"And if she doesn't give in like you think she will?" Josh pressed him, looking back through the doorway at the squirming girl, and checking despite himself to make sure that the gag was still firmly in place—they didn't need her trying to spout spells, even if the concoction they'd been forcing down her throat each day ought to have depleted her powers nearly to nothing by now.

David shrugged, thinking about the last body they'd seen that had been the handiwork of the girl's mother. The man, a father of three, had been killed while gardening, his throat slashed from behind while he'd been bent over a patch of fucking cucumber. He hadn't even seen his killer coming, but she'd been caught on the family's motion-activated security camera, and the man's wife had found him. His kids had been in her car, behind her, and seen the slumped over body. The witch had never even met him, not any more than she'd met any of her other victims from what they could tell, but he'd been her type.

Nobody could tell David that another family should have to be put through that, and that someone harboring that type of a killer deserved any mercy. However nice Lauren had seemed when he'd met her at the bar to pick her up, however pretty she was, however much he might like her...she was the one standing between him and the killer who'd taken that man and more than a dozen others. With that in his mind, he answered, "Then nothing changes, and she's fucked, and we go to Plan C."

"Plan C being? And it's more like Plan F at this point, anyway," Josh grunted, his eyes still on their captive. She was pretty, he thought, in a sort of awkward goth fashion, but nobody he'd have paid any attention to in a normal setting. He thought David would have, though, which was what made him wonder if his partner was taking this step too fast, too eagerly.

"We'll figure it out. If nothing else, this breaks her down some, lets her know we're serious. We've barely hurt her yet."

Josh shook his head. "Bruises on her arms, I'd bet, and blood showing up on her lip every time I leave the room? You've hurt her plenty. I don't know that this is going to make a difference, all she's already ignored. And this..."

The scowl David gave his partner was response enough, and Josh cut himself off. All these years of fucking and splitting, and David had yet to force anyone into bed with him—no matter how much of a tease they might have been—but there was a small part of him that just wondered if it was only because he'd never had real reason to, and if he'd always been just convincing enough for it to never come up. If there was ever a 'real reason', he reminded himself. But he was sure, truth be told, that the thought didn't bother him nearly as much as it should have, now that he was contemplating it. Beat another guy to a pulp for doing it, sure—he'd done that more than once. Act like the big brother to a girl who'd dealt with it—he'd been there, too, and sometimes taken those girls to bed afterward. This was just the other side of the coin that he'd been bound to come to eventually, he had to figure.

"This is...it's *wrong*, man. You know it and I know it."

"Maybe so, Devlin, but we both also know that *she* knows how to get in touch with her mom and is holding out on us. We're not asking her to lead us to her. We're asking for a fucking address or phone number; her track record ought to tell this brat that that'll give her mom a fair chance. And we're getting *nothing*. We either break her, or all this time's been for nothing and we're back to square one, a new dead guy showing up every other day." David watched his partner think about the options, and he knew he couldn't disagree.

"It's gonna be on you, man," Josh finally said. Much as he usually hated putting the pressure—or the blame— for a step in a case on a colleague, let alone his own partner, he couldn't take part in this, even if he could admit that it might be the only way. At least for the moment, he couldn't think of anything else to try short of physical violence. And wasn't his partner right, that this track, however underhanded and wrong it might be, was better than the sort of torture they usually reserved for hardened criminals? It wasn't like she was a kid, or married, for that matter.

"She would have told us if she didn't know anything, and she hasn't denied it once. Not once. She knows how we can find her mom, I guarantee," David said quietly, flexing his fists in frustration. This hadn't been his first choice of a move, after all. His first choice had been that chat over a beer, that they'd had after first bringing her to the house and told her who they were. If she'd just made the right choice then, they wouldn't have been having this conversation.

"You convincing me or yourself?" Josh asked, but he followed the question with a glance inside and then a sigh. "You do what you have to. I'll get today's dose now, and then I'll let you know if I track down another lead."

"Besides another body," David answered to his partner's retreating back.

"Besides another body," Josh agreed, without turning around.

***

Lauren held her breath as the two men left the doorway, stalking in separate directions. Their conversation today—this morning? this afternoon? tonight?—had felt different, like more was at stake, and she was glad to see them go. They wouldn't be gone long, though—they hadn't bothered to shut the door behind them, and that could only mean that at least one of them would be back sooner than later. She wasn't sure what that could mean, given that they'd just taken her on a bathroom break, just before this last conversation.

Watching the door, and the hallway beyond, Lauren

shifted her shoulders, lifting herself slightly and trying to relieve the burning pain that the underwire in her bra was causing—there wasn't anything to be done about it, but after a week of wearing it, and with ropes tying her to the chair and pushing it into her further, it seemed like it hurt more with every passing hour. More and more, though, she was trying not to show any discomfort when either of the men were around. She needed them to give up, and just let her go...or find her mom in some other way. That would be fine, too, at this point. And then, she was sure, they'd let her go. They had to, right? With the prospect of at least one of them returning, however, she found herself steeling herself yet again for whatever might be coming next.

It was safer when they were both around, when it wasn't just David and his back-hand, but then again, it was Josh's guilt-tripping that had actually been tearing her up more. Maybe it was the classic good-cop-bad-cop routine, but it was getting to her. She wasn't to blame for her mother's horrors, but Josh Devlin was good at making her feel like she was. And who knew, she wondered—now that these men were involved, and available to put an end to the violence, maybe she *was* partly to blame, just for not saying anything. Every time she closed her eyes now, she could picture the family members Josh had described to her—the kids who'd lost their fathers to her mom, the women who'd lost their husbands. At first, she'd been thankful that the men didn't show her pictures of the families, but anymore, it didn't seem to matter—she'd imagined them clearly, over and over again, and everything from their family vacations to their spelling tests spilled through her imagination when she let her guard down. Her mother had taken away good fathers from families that had been picture-perfect, destroying families so that their misery would match hers, if in a different fashion.

And Lauren *could* have told them how to find her mom, after all. But her mom wouldn't stand a chance, Lauren reminded herself, tugging experimentally on the ropes around her ankles and letting her wrists rest for a moment. And these men wouldn't have any reason to let her go if she did tell them anyway, so what was the point? They'd have her cold on obstructing their investigation, and maybe she wouldn't be in as much trouble as her mom was, but she'd still end up in jail. Plus ...her mom was her *mom*. With this crazed dementia—this single-minded focus that had recently taken hold of her, pushing her to kill without restraint—Lauren wasn't sure that her mom would notice the agents and fight back, given that they weren't old enough to be her prey. She was only going for men in their fifties—not that that narrowed down the field of prey all that much.

So maybe Lauren was fighting back for nothing; not speaking, with nothing to gain.

But horrible or not, the woman was her mother, and she was Lauren's only bit of family.

With this thought, Lauren took another deep breath and began twisting her wrists once again against the ropes binding them to the chair. It seemed like they were tighter each time David tied them, but at least she had some hope, since they weren't the cuffs that Josh had insisted on putting aside once her wrists had started forming real cuts from the metal; now, they hurt like hell, but ropes could fray, and she did have the protection of her sweater sleeves. As if David Fredricks cared, she thought to herself, twisting at her bonds all the harder. Still, she'd take his lack of concern over Josh's reasoning any day of the week.

She was trying to lick around the foul-tasting gag at

her cracked lips when Josh came back in, carrying another beaker of the blue goop they'd been forcing down her throat. The first four days had brought two doses each day; now they were down to one per day. Of course, she realized upon seeing it in his hand, that's why they hadn't closed the door. Didn't they know her powers had long since been damped down to nothing by the stuff? What was the point in continuing with it so steadily? Already, the stickiness of it trailed down her chest from her chin, into the V of her sweater and lower. The wetted paper towels in the bathroom hadn't done much good without her being able to change clothes or take a real shower—by now, she couldn't escape the chemical smell of it, and it burned in her stomach once she swallowed it each day.

But she'd stopped fighting it. Better the burning in her insides than the stinging stickiness that stayed on her chin and throat for hours, after it had been spilled on her skin while Josh forced it into her. So today she let Josh pry her dry lips apart from the gag again, stick the end of the glass beaker between her lips, and tilt her head back. She swallowed when he poured it into her in two separate, choking doses. But she kept her eyes on him the whole time, accusing and angry. She could cooperate without being broken.

"Sorry," Josh said without any irony, having tilted her head back for a third time to make sure she got the last of the concoction. If the agency was right, her powers wouldn't just be weakened after another few days went by—they'd be gone. He didn't feel guilty about that, though he felt a twinge of guilt over the fact that they'd told her it was temporary; they at least could have let her know that she had something to fight for in trying to keep it out of her system. He might not have been fighting either if put in her place, if he'd thought the effects were short-lived. *She's a witch, you ass*, Josh reminded himself with annoyance as he tucked the glass beaker into a pocket and double-checked that all of her bonds were still intact. *Stop feeling sorry for her.*

She'd managed to loosen the rope around her left ankle, so he re-doubled the bond and tightened the knot before he stood, ignoring the annoyed groan she let out in response. And maybe David was right, he had to think—because that groan she'd let out had only been annoyed, and not nearly desperate. She thought she was safe enough with them, it seemed. And the last time he'd talked to her that morning, it had almost seemed like she was relieved somehow. David had said she'd seemed nice at the bar, and truth be told, he thought she probably was nice, and just had the wrong mother, and the bad luck to be a witch. Maybe their bringing her in for questioning had let her off the hook of trying to stop her mom herself. It wasn't the first time the thought had occurred to him, but it didn't change anything.

When he left, he didn't close the door behind him, knowing his partner would be coming by for her soon enough. By then, he planned on being at the opposite end of the large ranch house; he didn't want to know anymore than he had to about what came next. Hell, maybe he'd even go into town.

Chapter 2

David paused in the doorway, reminding himself that he'd made up his mind already as he looked in at the girl tied to the chair. *The witch*, he corrected himself mentally. She had her eyes closed and was rolling her neck back and forth in circles, not struggling with her ropes for the moment. Like this, she looked more like the girl he'd flirted with to get her outside of a bar, who'd looked younger than she'd looked lately, and almost too innocent to be the girl they'd been seeking. But her license had confirmed it. She was Lauren Merriweather, daughter of Phillippa Merriweather—the witch who'd killed 17 men and counting over the last few weeks, spread over four states and without any apparent connection to her or her daughter.

He'd give Lauren one more chance to talk, though,

even if his partner had made him promise her gag wouldn't come out without both of them being present.

When he got within five feet, Lauren's eyes shot open, her head snapping up as she straightened in her seat and automatically tested her bonds. She was tired, and sore, and had hoped it would take longer for David to come back. She'd hoped to sleep and try again to forget about what was happening for a while. This time, though, he approached differently; he didn't look angry, as he usually did, and he wasn't stalking. Instead, he looked almost resigned.

For a second, she wondered if it meant that he was about to let her go, and then she realized it probably meant the opposite—that they'd given up, yes, but that meant they were going to kill her so that she couldn't go running to her mother. With the thought, her eyes widened, and she pushed her toes against the floor, trying to force the chair backward and away from him. Her feet hardly reached the floor, though, not bare as they were and tall as the chair was, and she stilled when he loomed over her and rested each of his hands on her wrists, pushing them down against the armrests.

"I'm going to give you one more chance to talk to me like a rational little girl, and then we're going to try something you're not gonna like. Are you listening?" he asked her quietly.

He hadn't approached her like this before, Lauren realized. He hadn't seemed so ...dark. She nodded jerkily when he repeated his question.

"Now, I'm going to remove this gag, and I've got a bottle of water here if you want some. If I even start to suspect you're concocting a spell, though, no more conversation. You got me?" the man asked, pressing harder on her wrists to get his point across.

Again, she nodded.

He retreated and closed the door to the room before returning to her and walking behind the chair, where she felt him tugging at the knot of her gag until it released and pulled away from her mouth with his hand and a few of her hairs. She watched him tuck the cloth into one of his pockets as she licked her lips, and then gratefully accepted the mouth of the water bottle he held up for her. After two gulps, he pulled it away, and she forced herself not to beg for more; it wouldn't get her anywhere, she knew.

"Now, I'm not going to ask the same questions I've been asking, but maybe you'll confirm some other matters for me? Get the communication going?" David asked her, crouching down in front of her but keeping his hands to himself.

"Okay," she whispered, hearing her voice emerge as a rasping croak. She coughed but didn't allow herself to look at the water.

"Okay," he agreed. "The men your mom is killing, are they random, or does she know them?"

She thought for a moment but didn't see how the information could help him. "She doesn't know them," Lauren answered quietly, keeping her blue eyes on his brown ones for any clues.

"No connection to you or your mom that you know of?"

She didn't pause this time, and simply shook her head.

"As far as you know, she's working alone?"

Lauren was pretty sure they already knew she was—the man was testing her or teasing her. "Yeah," she nodded, finally flicking her eyes from his to glance at the water bottle.

He caught the gaze. "You want to ask *me* something now?"

Why was he behaving like this, when he'd been the violent one all week? It was scaring her, making her simply want him gone. Suddenly, she wished his partner were around also, or instead. This might have been the man who she'd enjoyed flirting with at that bar, but something was wrong. "Can I have some more water ...please?" she asked, forcing a calmness into her voice that she didn't feel.

Instead of answering her, David uncapped the bottle again and allowed her two more swallows. This was the first time she'd had her thirst sated since they took her, outside of the times when she'd palmed up as much water as possible from the bathroom faucet.

"Anything else?" he offered as he placed the water bottle down.

"Are you going to kill me now?" she whispered, and his gaze jerked back to hers, his hand nearly fumbling the water bottle as he set it back on the floor.

"That's what you're thinking?" he asked. "No, we ain't gonna kill you," he told her, his voice softening with the answer. "But you're not going anywhere until we find your mother, no matter how long that takes. So you'd be better off helping us."

She examined his gaze, and believed him, but didn't know what that meant for how he was acting today. The calmness was getting to her. This was more what she expected from his partner. Getting nowhere, she gave a small shrug that was aborted by the bonds around her abdomen and arms; she could only move so much.

"When's the last time you saw your mom?" he asked after a pause.

"In person?" she responded. "The holidays, a few months ago."

"And did she tell you she was about to go on the mother of all killing sprees?"

Lauren stared at him, grimacing freely now. "You think that's funny?"

His turn to shrug.

"She didn't tell me anything," Lauren finally answered. "She seemed ...herself."

"And that means what?"

Lauren stopped herself from saying more. Anything more, and she wasn't sure how much she'd reveal. Could she stop at saying her mom was conceited, self-absorbed, and hated men? Then, would any of that be news? And when would he ask when they'd last *spoken*, forcing her to stay quiet or reveal that they'd talked on the phone just the day before she'd met David at that bar, and that during *that* conversation Lauren had begged her mother to calm down and stop killing. And her mom had seemed crazy, again, like she had all those years ago. The stress from that call had been what had pushed her into the bar, into David, in the first place.

And how much of that would David believe anyway?

"Look at me. What are you thinking?" he asked her, reaching up and turning her chin forcefully so that her face looked directly into his again.

"Nothing," she shook her head. "I'm just ...I'm tired."

His lips twitched, and he shook his head. "If you don't find something to tell me that's going to help us, you're going to be a lot more tired. When did you last speak to her?"

Lauren bit her lip, wincing at the feel of her front teeth coming down on a dry crack in her lower lip, and thinking she tasted blood from it. She only shook her head in response; she could do that.

David leaned back, resting his ass on one of his heels and considering the girl in front of him. She was scared, he knew, and he wondered now if she was as scared of the woman she was protecting as she was of him and his partner, or the law in general. "Are you scared of her? Your mom?"

"I'm scared of what she's doing," Lauren whispered back before she could stop herself.

"Not scared she'll hurt you?" David pressed, eyeing her.

"No."

"You know I will, though."

Lauren stared back at him, wondering what the point of this was. Hadn't they gotten it through their heads yet that she wouldn't give her own mother up? Couldn't they understand that? "Yeah, no kidding," she finally said, when it was clear he wasn't saying more. She forced bravado into her expression, and asked more loudly than anything she'd spoken so far, "So?"

David shook his head as he stood and came to the back of her chair, where he reached down to force the gag between her lips and then tied it up tightly behind her head. She fought him, and then shook her head as he worked at the tying, but he tugged it harder in response and doubled the knot. It had been a mistake to take it off of her, he thought now.

Standing in front of her again, he could see it biting into the corners of her mouth more than it had before. *Let it.*

Kneeling in front of her, he rested both of his hands on her knees and gripped them, watching her eyes widen as he squeezed once, twice, and a third time. Not hard enough to hurt, but hard enough that she felt the weight and the size of his grip on her, so that she knew he had physical control of her. Then he moved his hands up, inching along her thighs and pressing into her jeans as her legs jerked against the chair legs in response to his touch. Still, he kept his eyes on her face and his expression blank. He felt her tense and try to pull back from him, deeper into the chair, but she had nowhere to go. He moved his hands slowly, squeezing and gripping her as he went, every inch, watching for any sign of surrender in her face as he enjoyed the feel of her toned thighs trying to come together, and failing; flexing his grip on her, he waited for any murmur to hint that she was changing her mind—she gave him nothing but fear, and stubborn resolve. He'd actually thought, when he was playing this out in his mind, that this alone might be enough. That he'd get this far, and she'd break.

Lauren watched David's hands moving up her thighs, feeling the heat of his skin even through her clothing. Her pulse was speeding, pumping with the adrenaline brought on by his presence, and she was starting to feel her body react in other ways, as well. Her body was heating up, responding to him and to the situation and to the look in his eyes. She could only tell herself not to panic, that this had to be another threat, another tactic, another way of getting to her. And she couldn't let him see or feel how her body was responding to him, either, she reminded herself—how the very core of her was heating up, and thrumming, wanting him even closer despite every iota of reasoning in her head.

When his hands reached her upper thighs, he let his thumbs come to rest on her crotch. He let his right thumb slide up and down along the crotch of her jeans, along the seam that had to be running right over her pussy and felt her shiver in response. She couldn't close her legs against him, not with the ropes holding her to the chair legs. He moved his left hand, tracking the skin along the waist of her jeans as his left thumb toyed with her zipper, pressing at it so she'd know what he was thinking, exactly where his hand was.

He looked to her face, seeing that her eyes were

glued to his hands, her whole body tensed. He moved his right hand up, keeping his thumb rubbing against the inner seam of her pants and pressing inward, but rubbing with his whole hand now. His left hand moved up, over, and gripped her waist hard enough that she jerked her gaze up to him, so he saw that her eyes were watering. And then she jerked them closed, shivering.

He knew that shiver—he was turning her on, despite the situation and despite the bonds; in fact, all that had started it, he was sure now.

He'd suspected all along that she was submissive, from the way she'd reacted to him in the bar, to his forwardness. She'd tensed but leaned into him when he'd put his hand to the small of her back and ushered her to a table without asking; she'd flushed with arousal when he'd insisted on ordering for both of them at the bar, speaking for her, and when he'd called her 'baby' instead of using her name; and her eyes had gotten wide, and glittered, when he'd jokingly said he wouldn't take out any handcuffs 'til their fourth date—she'd been biting her lip to keep from smiling. And more telling than anything, he'd felt her tensing and shivering all week now, when his skin touched hers as he was tying her ankles or her arms, and when he'd looked up to see that fear wasn't nearly always the first emotion on her face. She might not like pain or the situation, but she was turned on by being controlled, and bound before him, whether she liked it or not. She was turned on by him, whether she liked it or not.

In fact, David was sure that she hated that her body was responding to him, despising the fact that she was aroused by his having her in this position, but he was just as sure that it didn't matter; he had every ounce of power over her, and there was a part of her that was aroused by every bit of it.

And there was a part of him that was glad that she wasn't giving in yet, even if he wouldn't have admitted as much to his partner.

With the length of his thumb still pressing on the seam in her jeans, David let his other hand skim over the ropes holding her abdomen to the chair back and land at her right breast, his fingers expertly finding and circling her nipple through her sweater and bra while his palm rested on her sweater. He could feel her breath catching and hitching beneath his fingers as he spoke, forcing a hardness into his voice. "You know what's coming now? You understand, Lauren? 'Cuz this is the next step. If you're not going to give us the information, I'm going to take you to my bed and make you scream until you will. You understand that, *little witch*?" David asked, feeling her trembling and allowing himself to be turned on by it. Allowing himself to pretend that this was pretend.

He pressed into her with both hands and she gasped through the gag. "You understand me?" he repeated to her.

Shutting her eyes against his, she nodded. He pressed his hands into her skin again, into places that she hadn't let guys touch her in the past—even if he didn't know that—and she jerked her eyes open in response. She hadn't expected this, not for a moment, and she wished for the first time that she could lie, cursing her mother for the first of the spells she'd thought fit to put on her own daughter, all those years ago. She didn't allow herself to think of the second spell, which had kept her from allowing a man to touch her like this until now. And she didn't allow herself to think of how wet she was, beneath this man's hand, or how much pleasure was intermingled with the pain in her body at the moment. She couldn't think about how she'd been thinking about him that first night when they'd met, or even of the way she'd thought of him the next day, here in this same room, before she'd realized how serious they were about holding her for information.

"You going to tell me what I want to know now? Location? Phone number? A way to find her?"

I can't. Lauren shook beneath his hands, wishing she could turn her body off, and she shivered as she felt his whole hand press again against her crotch, the side of it sawing up and down her thigh. She hated herself, feeling the wetness in her panties, and another tremor through her body that this time started from her breast was the last straw in forcing tears from her eyes; she hadn't wanted to let them see her cry anymore.

She forced herself to nod her head jerkily when he asked again if she understood.

David let himself relax when he saw the nod; he'd known this would be enough, as he'd said. The threat had been enough, and she might hate him for it, but that was fine; they'd have what they needed to end things, to end the killing. He pressed his hands once more into her, holding his presence, and swallowed down into his gut the mercy he wanted to show her. He couldn't turn gentle on her yet; he needed to know where her mother was first.

"And you're going to tell me what I want to know," he said quietly, the threat still audible in his voice, he was glad to hear.

I can't believe this is happening, Lauren thought, tremoring. She didn't bother putting off the answer, though—he'd just ask again. She forced herself to shake her head in the negative, her eyes clenched shut.

His hands came away from her body suddenly as she heard him grunt with disgust. There was a moment when his hands weren't upon her, and she thought he was done, that his words had been empty, and then ..."Stubborn bitch," she heard him mutter as he fiddled with the bonds at her ankles. Was he really taking her to his bed? Should she just tell him? *I can't—he'll kill her. She's my mom.* Lauren repeated the mantra to herself, her eyes closed, as she felt him untying an ankle and then retying a single rope around it, apart from the chair, and tying that rope to her other ankle before he released her other leg from the chair. *He won't do it. He's just trying to scare me.*

David stood and went to the back of the chair, and Lauren kept her eyes closed, but she tested the ties at her legs—sure enough, her legs were tied together so that she could walk easily enough, but not kick, just as they'd been when they'd taken her to the bathroom or their kitchen. She felt him releasing the ropes around her abdomen, but kept her eyes closed, and then he was releasing her wrists and she automatically clasped her hands to them, rubbing at the skin through her sweater. The feeling in them hadn't left this time, as the ropes hadn't been tight enough for that, but even the touch of her own hands was a comfort. She knew better than to attempt to remove the gag, but she took as deep of a breath as she could from around its fabric, and then opened her eyes to look up.

David was standing a few feet in front of her, his head cocked to the side with a look on his face that was ...hungry, she realized. It wasn't the violence and the frustration that she was so used to seeing from him, though there was some of that, too. But standing still as he was, he looked like he was all muscle—like a fighter who was anxious for what was coming.

"You gonna stand?" David asked her.

They'd progressed over the course of the week. At first, she'd fought everything, and David had manhandled her in nearly every moment she was away from this blasted chair, but after a few days, she'd stood and walked between the two men—relatively calmly, she realized now—when they escorted her to the kitchen in those first few days, before they brought cold, meager meals her way, or when they'd taken her to the bathroom. After a few days, they hadn't had to touch her at all, but to prod her past an occasional doorway.

Now, the chair itself felt like a comfort.

She shook her head. If he wanted her to move, after the way he'd just touched her and talked to her, and considering what he'd just promised, she wasn't going to cooperate. These men had seemed like decent people until now—they'd been hunting a murderer, after all, even if the murderer was her mom—and maybe fighting for another few moments would make him reconsider, she had to think.

David was on her in a moment, though, his hands on her sore biceps as he pulled her to her feet and then turned, forcing her in front of him.

Chapter 3

As he marched her through the hall, pushing his body into hers from behind as she kept trying to stop, to stall, he reminded himself that this was a witch who was protecting another one—one who was murdering innocent people who'd done nothing to her, or to anyone else as far as he and Josh knew. Innocent as Lauren might have seemed in the bar before he'd convinced her to come out to the parking lot for a smoke, and before Josh had appeared to help him ambush her into the Mustang, there wasn't anything innocent about her. And what he was doing now—it was just another form of interrogation, and it had to be done. Better than beating her so that she had real lasting injuries, he figured, reasoning with himself silently as he lost patience with her again and shoved her forward hard enough that she landed on her knees, after having skidded to a halt in front of him for the tenth time in as many steps.

He went to one knee beside her, his hand on the nape of her neck to keep her in place, and growled into her ear, "You're not making this easier on yourself."

Drawing back at the anger she heard in his voice, she cringed down from his grip, having no idea that what she'd heard was as much directed at himself as anything.

When he yanked her to her feet again, she let him walk her forward until they came to a stop at a door they'd passed dozens of times over the past week. When David opened it, she saw a sparse, impersonal room that had to look like half the guest rooms in the world—basic desert landscapes on the walls and a bed in the center of the space with light blue sheets and a blanket that was pulled to its foot—but the pictures turned downward to hide their faces, on the bedside table and a dresser, were what made her panic. She spun against him hard, her whole length going up against the muscles of his chest and his legs, and when he stepped back in surprise she stumbled past him, catching her hands on the wall to keep upright.

Two steps out of the doorway, his forearm wrapped around her neck and pulled her backward into his chest where she froze, gasping for air through the gag that had muffled the few sounds she'd made in the struggle. Tears squeezed out from her eyes as she started squirming against his grip, but he just stood there, behind her, holding her.

David let her struggle against him, wearing herself out. Her driver's license claimed she was 5'3 and 154 pounds; she felt smaller than that to him, on both counts. It wasn't any effort at all for him to hold her, and since she couldn't separate her legs enough to do more than kick lightly at his calves with her bare feet, and her hands were occupied with gripping his forearm against her throat, there was no chance of her hurting him in return or getting an upper hand—even if she had had some awareness of how to fight, which she clearly didn't. She was helpless, and they both knew it; she just hadn't accepted it yet.

When she'd all but stilled and he'd gotten tired of her nails digging into his forearm, he turned roughly and forced her into their guest room, slamming the door behind them.

Lauren breathed in deeply as David's body pushed her toward the bed. He let go of her at the same instant as he shoved her forward so that she landed face down on the sheet, hands spread to catch her fall, and he was on top her in the next breath, rolling her over and upward. Before she knew it, he'd cuffed her right hand to the corner bedpost and shifted overtop of her to grab her left, his legs straddling her stomach; the cuffs had already been in place, waiting for her wrists. She simply hadn't noticed them. When she felt the steel click around her left wrist also, she'd never felt so helpless, and she couldn't stop herself from shivering. Suddenly, she was incredibly cold.

He was beside the bed then, and she pulled her knees up, her legs tightly together and her bare feet tensed against the mattress below her, all of her body but her legs pressed hard into the sheets and shaking. She looked to him, and saw he was standing and watching her, looking larger and more muscled than she'd ever realized he was when they'd only been flirting in that damned bar.

Had it just been a week ago when he'd asked to buy her a drink and she'd been joking with him? When she'd wondered what it would be like to have him kiss her, and whether it was crazy to think about making out with him in the parking lot or letting him think he'd get further than he would? When it had occurred to her for just a moment—only a moment, she swore to herself now—that he could be someone special? When she'd thought, over drinks, about letting him push her against the tavern's back wall and kiss her until she couldn't breathe, and couldn't step away? When he'd called her 'baby' and pressed his hand into her back like she belonged to him, and she'd thought for a moment that she did?

She'd been so stupid.

David stood beside the bed examining her, watching her squirm like his hands were all over her already, though his arms were crossed against his chest. He wanted to let her think about what could be coming. And then he'd loosen the gag, and if she told him what they needed to know, that would be it.

She'd tell him, he told himself again. This heightened threat would be enough. But if he re-tightened it, so be it. Truth be told, he'd thought about having her like this—just like this—when they'd been at the bar. He hadn't been able to help himself, the way she'd been looking at him and the way she'd looked with a drink at her soft lips. The idea of forcing her up against a wall and holding her wrists against it above her head as he'd kissed her had been an easy jump from the way she'd shivered and then relaxed against the pressure of his hand. Having her cuffed to a bed now, albeit fully clothed ...it was easy to imagine that this was all a game, and that she'd agreed to play. It wasn't the first time he'd had a girl bound and gagged before him, aching for him to drive her crazy—it was just the first time it had been without consent.

Wiping the thought from his mind, he decided she'd had enough time to contemplate what was coming her way. He took off his button-down—slowly—and then hung it on the back of a chair before he turned back to her in just his t-shirt and jeans. Taking the thinnest of the pillows from the floor, he forced it beneath her head; if this was going to go further, he wanted her watching everything he did.

Then he sat at the foot of the bed, out of reach of her feet if she should decide to attempt a kick, and methodically removed his boots and his socks before standing again to remove his belt, and then going to the head of the bed and standing there again with his arms crossed as he forced a leering grin onto his face—and he pushed down the resulting disgust he felt with himself when he saw her visibly cringe at the sight of it. *She's as responsible for the last four deaths as her mom is,* he told himself, leaning forward and overtop of her, putting his hands on each side of her head as he sank in and faced her, his expression fading into a half-sneer. *If she'd talked to us that first night, just a mile away from that bar when we stopped and had a beer, and offered her one, she'd never even have seen this house, and we'd be on to another case by now.*

And besides, he reminded himself, *she's a witch, too. She's probably done a helluva lot worse than what I'm contemplating.*

Lauren couldn't look away from him. She flinched back into the thin pillow as he leaned in closer to her, his eyes on hers. In a moment, he'd jerked the painful gag away from her mouth, dragging it over her jaw and chin so that she was sure it left friction burns, and he'd covered her mouth with his. Without thinking, she opened her mouth to scream, and his tongue flushed into her mouth, pushing at hers. Nobody had ever kissed her like this, like she belonged to them and they could explore her or force her to breathe or not breathe on their terms; it was a punishing kiss that she couldn't breathe through and couldn't have engaged with if she'd wanted to.

She gasped for air when the man above her pulled his face away from hers and realized suddenly that one of his fists was behind her head now, clenched and tangled in her hair, his weight rested against his other hand, propped on the bed beside her face, his chest leaning against her own. She blinked, finally untensing her head and just letting it rest on his fist; he didn't seem to be letting go.

"You understand what you've got comin' to you, little witch?" he asked her softly, and she lay still and tried to figure out what the tone in his voice meant. She couldn't.

Finally, she simply shut her eyes against his gaze and said, "Please, don't."

"I don't have to do anything. You tell me what I need to know, this ends, and you walk out of here tomorrow without anybody else laying a hand on you."

"Tomorrow?" she returned.

He shrugged. "Or the next day. We'll need time to ...act on the information." David stared hard at her, looking for a flinch. He didn't add that they needed time to give her the last few doses of the mixture they'd been feeding her. To both him and Josh, it had seemed safer that she not know it was permanent—even as a threat, it could do more harm than good, Josh had felt, pushing her to force herself to throw up or attempt some desperate spell-weaving after all. David thought she would have already done the last if she could, but also didn't think that telling her anything at all at this point, real threat or not, was going to do a damn bit of good. She was only responding to action, he was finding, and at this point he didn't really expect her to give in until he had her sweater off. She'd give in then, he was sure, if he kept up his act, making sure he pretended to himself that this was consensual, just a game, so that he'd act like it was real. He was almost sure she'd give in when he cut her sweater off of her.

Lauren was still breathing heavily, distracted by the sudden realization that she could actually feel this man's heartbeat as he leaned against her. What was wrong with her?

Suddenly, angrily, she bucked upward in her bonds against him, pulling against his hand that still held tight to her hair. She'd just wanted her chest further away from his, and she didn't know what he saw in the quick burst of attempted movement, but he didn't seem surprised. He did move upward a few inches—getting more comfortable above her, it seemed. "Would you give up a family member?" she demanded of him.

David stared down at her, his hand tightening cruelly in her hair once again as he suddenly doubted that she'd give in at all; unbidden, rage came through him, that she was forcing him to do this to her.

He pushed back the rush of anger and leaned down against her, feeling her flinch away from him even as he caught her lower lip in his teeth and tugged hard, biting down so that he suddenly tasted blood, which he hadn't intended. The taste shifted him sideways and out of her view until he was breathing hard on her neck, and then he moved up to her ear. With his teeth, he tugged at her earlobe and enjoyed the sound of the gasp he received; it hadn't been one of pain, though it might have been laced with shock.

After a moment, he moved his hands to her neck and untied the gag so that he had access to her throat, reaching back to stuff the dirty fabric into his pocket before he brought his lips back up, and then he kissed along her neck, enjoying the sound of her gasping, and the feeling of her caught breath as her muscles flexed in response to him laying against her. He put one of his hands on her arm, running it back and forth lightly just to remind her he could, and let his other hand go back to her hair as he ran his lips over her skin, teasing it with his tongue.

"It doesn't matter what I'd do, little one," he whispered into her ear after he'd taken another moment to regain control of himself. "You're the one tied to my bed. I'm the one in control. This is on you." Finished talking, he moved his lips to her neck, sucked, and then bit down lightly before mouthing and nibbling from her ear down to her shoulder, nudging aside the neck of her sweater and her bra strap as he went. He could feel it in her, that every touch to her neck and her shoulder was sending chills of arousal through her body.

He listened for any sign that she was attempting a spell, or ready to give up, but all he got were whimpers and an occasional 'please, don't.'

She felt his hand unclench from her hair and relaxed her head back helplessly, trying to block out the sensation of his hands against her forearms, his lips against her shoulder. It wasn't doing any good. He knew what he was doing, and she couldn't stop her body from responding to him, broadcasting its response through quivers, and then she let out an inadvertent moan when his lips turned gentle on her shoulder, so that she bit her lip to hold it back, to remind her of where she was and what was happening. More than scared now, she felt humiliated, terrifyingly aware that he knew exactly what he was doing to her. His body held her still beneath him, his hands on her arms and holding her flat to the bed as his lips and his teeth teased at her skin.

Suddenly, David let go of one of her arms and

reached down, to the waist of her jeans, and then snaked his hand up under her sweater and along her abdomen. Now she was struggling harder below him again, squirming. He leaned up as his hand reached her breast and he watched the fight in her face; he admired it, but it didn't change anything.

"This is your last chance, sweetheart. And then I'm gonna gag that pretty mouth of yours again so that your screams don't get too loud."

She closed her eyes and shook her head, sure that he didn't mean it. This *was* the same guy she'd been flirting with a week ago, who'd had that endearing smile and made bad jokes. Sure, he was an alpha—anyone could see that when he walked into a room—but that didn't mean he was a rapist. He was making threats, and trying to trick her, but he *wouldn't* go that far. She knew he wouldn't, that her judgement couldn't have been that far off. After all, wouldn't he have done it days ago, if that was his intention? Why wait? And why procrastinate and tease her so much if he was willing to go through with his threats? No. She knew he might tease her some more, and he might humiliate her, and this might be the worst week of her life ...but she knew he wouldn't actually rape her. He'd just ...threaten it. And no matter what he did, she wouldn't give in. She wouldn't let him coerce her into giving up her mother, or into giving up herself to him. She wouldn't give in to him, no matter what her body wanted. She told herself this, over and over again, and then she opened her eyes and flinched back at how dark his gaze was. His grip tightened over her breast and she gasped again, tears returning to her eyes.

"David, please. Don't do this. I haven't done anything wrong, I swear."

"You don't think protecting a murderer is wrong?"

Lauren closed her eyes. "She's my mom, David. You have to understand—"

"Nah, little witch. I don't have to understand a damn thing, except that you're standing between us and her." He leaned down into her, putting one hand against her forehead to hold her down so that she couldn't bounce upward against his own forehead, should she think about it. He pressed her into the bed so that her neck arched back into the pillow and her eyes widened as he put his lips to her ear again. "And another thing, baby, you can call me 'sir.' You got that?" he growled, and then he brought his lips to her neck and bit down, sucking, making sure to leave a mark that she'd keep feeling as he kept going with her.

He felt her shudder and nod against him, her breath suddenly hitching again, hard. She was trying to hold it together, it seemed, and shut down anymore tears from coming. He had to admire it.

He sat up, pulled out the gag from his pocket, and began untying the knot in the gag so that he could replace it more easily and hold her quiet; she wasn't going to break unless he went further, and he didn't expect any spells, but he didn't want his partner to hear her wailing and change his own mind either.

"Please, D...sir, please, don't. Please," she begged him again, shaking her head helplessly as he forced the gag back into her mouth. It stank of the blue potion, and he told himself they'd get her a new one later, even as his dick throbbed at hearing her address him as *sir*. He didn't tie the gag as tightly as he had last time, though. This time, it was tight, but not so much that it was cutting into the corners of her lips; he'd be able to make out words, and he'd know it if she changed her mind. And he'd stop, he told himself. It didn't matter that his cock had been hard as a rock since he'd dragged her in here, or that he'd been thinking about this non-stop for more than 24 hours now, since it had occurred to him that this might be the only option. It didn't matter that he couldn't remember when he'd last been this hard, or had a girl this enticing tied to his bed; he'd stop if she gave him what he wanted—that was the deal he'd made with her, and himself.

He yanked her feet down toward the foot of the bed so that her legs lay flat on the mattress, and then he sat atop her upper thighs, letting his weight push her down into the middle of the sturdy bed as he let his pelvis push into hers. His dick throbbed against his jeans, and he wondered if she could feel it through her own jeans; he could sure as hell feel it begging to get at her. He took his pocket knife from his back pocket and felt her flinch below him when she saw it. "I'm not gonna hurt you...with this," he added as an afterthought, letting his eyes rake over her upper body. Then he turned his attention back to his hands, and brought his knife to the hem of her loose sweater.

Stretching the soft fabric with one hand, he let the knife cut into the hem of it, and he held it up as he moved the knife along until it was split down the front, all the way up to the neck, displaying the lacy light blue bra it had been hiding. She lay frozen beneath him. Her breasts were round and white, as full as he'd imagined and only half-covered by her bra; he let himself be hypnotized for just a moment, by her hard nipples peaking over their cups, and then he traced their outlines before tugging the cups of fabric down so that the whole of the bra's intended coverage was crushed beneath her breasts. Staring at her hardened nipples, he pushed aside the sweater's ragged sides so that he could see her hourglass figure shaking, rising and falling with heavy, scared breaths.

Next, he took the knife to one side of the garment's neck, and began carefully cutting away the left sleeve, making sure to avoid her skin as he stretched forward to cut away from her outstretched arms, pulling fabric toward him to meet his blade with her wrists still cuffed to the sides of the bed. In a minute's time, what was left of the garment had been thrown to the floor beside the bed, and he for the first time saw the marks he'd left along her upper arms. The skin was peppered with bruises, especially around her elbows, with larger ones circling her biceps and upper arms.

Seeing the ugly marks on her pale skin, he felt a sudden guilt stab through him; Josh was right that he'd been hurting her all along. These were from *his* hands. And unlike the hickies that were already forming on one side of her neck, these hadn't brought her any pleasure at all, wanted or unwanted. They'd just hurt her. Seeing her eyes were still closed, he let himself hold up one of his hands, just over her bicep, and saw the way that the circling bruise matched up with the size of his hand, and his grip.

I'll make this up to her, he thought absurdly, before he bit back the apology he'd been about to make. He'd been about to apologize for hurting her, but considering the situation—he couldn't afford to, and it would have rung as more ridiculous than sincere anyway. It didn't matter that he was sorry; this was what they'd come to.

David closed his eyes and rested his hands on his own thighs, doing his best to ignore the shaky breathing of the girl below him and his own ready dick; he took two deep breaths. This wasn't about him or her, he tried to tell himself, and she could have ended it at any point.

Opening his eyes, he stared down at her and let himself ignore the bruises. His eyes on her face, looking for surrender, he traced his hands up her abdomen, along her sides, and let them rest on her full breasts. The lace cups had been easy to pull down to just below her breasts, pushing them up and together with the lower band of the bra and the crushed cups. He used the knife one more time to cut the bra straps at her shoulders, but he left the bra as a prop, to remind her of how vulnerable she was.

Lauren forced herself to keep breathing while David stayed still above her. She didn't want to open her eyes. She didn't want to see whether he'd put the knife away yet or know what was in his face. She didn't want to look down her body and see his bulging jeans, that she could feel, pressed tightly against her own, throbbing, and making her more embarrassingly wet with each moment that passed. She didn't want to see any of it. And then she felt him shift above her. She felt his thighs slide heavily lower on hers as he leaned down, and then one of her nipples was in his mouth, the breast gripped hard in his hand as he pinched and angled it for his lips, and her other breast was being tugged and groped by his other hand, his rough fingers expertly tugging at her nipple and tracking in circles.

For the first time, she felt one of his nails as it traced along above the nipple just as his teeth grazed her other, and she gasped through the gag as her eyes jerked open on instinct and her chest heaved below his weight, intensifying the pleasure of his mouth and the pain just below, where her bra's underwire had long since formed bruises. *Please, make him stop*, she thought desperately, wishing she knew a way to dull her senses, or even pass out. His fingertips kept tugging and she felt his crotch thrust against her thigh, hard, as his teeth bit down lightly on her breast, and she yelled into the gag, bucking against him; she couldn't take it. She couldn't take any of this.

David held her lower body still with his legs and let himself devour her breasts, ignoring the noises she made above him; he enjoyed driving women crazy, like this—just like this—and the taste of her sweat with her hard nipples pressed into his mouth and his hands was all he was thinking about now. He let himself go, squeezing hard and sucking, his teeth working against her skin until finally he was out of breath, and her crying was distracting, though he'd felt the pleasure running through her body, and heard her gasps coming in time to what he'd been doing; he wondered if she'd realized that all of the sounds coming from her lips had been mewls of pleasure, urging him on.

He let each of his hands come to rest on her breasts as he went back to her neck, licking and nuzzling, and then drifting down over her clavicle to the center of her breasts, until his chin stopped with her bra strap. He kissed her then, as gently as he could make himself, and let himself rise up above her, and he saw she was watching him now, her cries slowing now that his hands and lips had left her, for the moment. Finally, he let go of her breasts and reached beneath her, unhooking the strap and pulling the bra away. He wasn't prepared for what he saw when he did.

After a week of her wearing the bra non-stop, what must have started as simple lines against her flesh had formed into angry, dark marks, long bruises with raw centers and clear sores beneath each of her breasts, nearly a whole line of skin broken from where the wire had been grinding into her all week. He gently lifted one of her breasts with his hand, and examined the line beneath it, stopping at an angry sore and feeling her flinch at his touch when his finger came near it; he realized he must have been grinding the underwire and the fabric of the bra into the bruises and sores when he'd been mauling her a minute before; that's why her crying had escalated with the pleasure, and not when he'd first cut away the sweater and thought she should have been more upset. He looked up, and for the first time noticed lighter, but similar bruises with sores at their centers, at the apex of both her shoulders—they'd been covered as they formed by her sweater, or hidden by her bra straps when they'd peaked around the fabric.

He took a deep breath and looked up at her face, grimacing; these had probably been causing her more pain, for days, than anything he'd done. They'd probably distracted her from every word he or Josh said for days. With the bra gone now, she was looking back at him, and all he saw in her face was exhaustion, and relief. That bra had been a fucking torture device after she'd been wearing it for a few days straight he suddenly realized.

He shook his head, staring again at the angry lines below her breasts that circled around her sides, over her ribs, and which he was noticing only now. "Jesus, kid, you couldn't say something? Or just take the damn thing off when you were in the bathroom once it started to hurt? How stubborn are you?" She closed her eyes against the questioning, and he saw suddenly how ridiculous his questioning was. What would he and Josh have said if she'd come back from the bathroom without her bra? Short of her telling them she was injured, which she must have guessed would have led to them taking a look for themselves, what would they have thought? What would they have said, or *guessed*? David could guess how he would have reacted—he would have seen it as a come-on, however it was meant, and made fun of her. And in her position, that implication would have been the last thing she'd have wanted; she must have decided the pain was bearable, compared to her other options.

David leaned forward, reaching to the bedside table's drawer. He felt her shuddering below him as he pulled open the drawer and sifted through the contents. *There it is.* He pulled back his hand with a bottle of Aloe that he'd seen there earlier; he'd find something to help with the healing later, but he figured this ought to cool the skin and give her a little bit of relief until then. Uncapping it, he squirted some of the green gel onto his fingers and touched them first to the sores at her shoulders where the bra's edges had been cutting into her skin, seeing confusion in her face as he did so. He shrugged in response before sitting up and back and squirting more of the gel from the bottle.

"We didn't mean for this to happen," he told her quietly as he began at a sore on her left side and then moved to below her breast, tracing heavy helpings of the gel onto both the raw cuts and the sores as he went, conscious that these could have caused a serious infection if they'd kept her here for another week and never seen them, let alone treated them. He'd do more for them later; he couldn't now, he was so far along. More time spent nursing her would risk undoing all of the threats he'd offered, and still hoped would work before he took things much further. Meanwhile, his dick still pulsed as his knuckles brushed against her breast and his thumb moved below the cuts, along the smooth skin of her abdomen; maybe the kindness he was showing her now would convince her to give in, he thought. Otherwise, he'd gone too far to be done with her now. And although a part of him wished he felt differently, he didn't want to be done—even with this discovery glaring at him.

Lauren felt the Aloe easing into the sores beneath her breasts and closed her eyes with the relief of it. She guessed there was actual broken skin, and not just bruising, since he was bothering with it; she hadn't realized, though she should have guessed at it perhaps, based on the mounting pain. She didn't care why he was doing it right now; she was just thankful he was. For the moment, she could even forget that he was the first man seeing her unclothed, touching her and taking her breasts in his mouth—all that mattered was the sudden relief of the gel, taking away some of the sting she'd been feeling. She let herself relax fully, for the first time in what seemed like days, as she felt David lift himself from her body, and then she heard him moving across the room, and running water. Maybe it was all over.

David turned back from washing his hands in the attached half-bath and went back to the girl on the bed, coming to the side of the mattress this time and leaning down over her. He wanted to give her another minute, to catch her breath, but he let himself rest his left hand on one of her breasts, feeling her jerk back at his touch when he did so; still, he was careful to keep the side of his hand from rubbing against the sores beneath it. He leaned down to her neck, the side he hadn't touched with his lips before, and began lapping at her skin, kissing, and enjoying the salty taste of her sweat, and the way her breathing was beginning to change again. He bit down lightly this time, feeling her shiver beneath his hands and enjoying it, and then leaned into her ear.

"Time for the next step, darlin', unless you're going to change your mind," he whispered, his voice raspy. She whimpered, and pushed back from him, but didn't signal that anything had changed.

Now he removed his t-shirt as she watched him, her eyes wide, and went to the foot of the bed. She'd pulled her legs up again, and he took out the knife from his back pocket once more before gripping one ankle and pulling. He planned on leaving her ankles bound by the short rope that was already there; he didn't want her kicking him in the head in the next few minutes, if she could gain the control and foresight to try.

It took longer to cut through the jeans than it had her sweater, but he perched on her ankle and had no trouble keeping her still as he cut upward, from one ankle hole on to her waist-line. He left her panties, for now. The next leg went faster, and he cut her once along her calf accidentally, in rushing to be done, but then her jeans were left in two unhelpful pieces of denim fabric, and he'd thrown them to the floor in a moment. She'd been still throughout the cutting—frozen, in fact, in reaction to the sight of the knife and how close it was to her skin—but she began shaking her head and begging through her gag as soon as the jeans were torn away, leaving her in flimsy lace underwear that matched the torturous bra he'd discarded earlier.

He reached for this lace now and traced the edges before pressing two of his fingertips against her soaked crotch as if to point out what she was waiting for, and then he tore it from her body in a quick swipe, the fabric splitting easily with the force of his grip. He didn't ask her now whether she'd changed her mind; he was too anxious to taste what was coming. She'd get another chance, if she might still want to change her mind at that point.

Losing his own jeans, he breathed a sigh as his dick gained the freedom to tent his boxer-briefs, and grinned when he saw her eyes go wider and heard her muffled protests; he wasn't worried at the moment about the emotion that was there—he was going to enjoy this part, and he'd be damned if she wasn't going to enjoy it also. Changing his mind about what he wanted next, he fished the knife from his jeans and swiped it through the rope that had kept her feet from separating by more than 10 inches or so until this point. He saw her mouth had formed a silent 'no' of distress under the gag and that she was shaking her head back and forth, pulling at the cuffs around her wrists.

Even as she began squirming upward and away from him, frantic to be somewhere else, he'd knelt at the foot of the bed and grabbed hold of her ankles to still her, and then he was pulling her back down to the center of the mattress by her legs, leaving himself in between them, holding her hips beneath him to keep her still.

She was soaking wet. Holding her knees down to each side of him, he admired the slickness of her cunt, spread open below a carefully trimmed patch of light brown pubic hair that pointed right to what he wanted. He hadn't touched her center, other than that moment through her panties and before through her jeans, and yet he could see from above her that she was burning up with desire, dripping for him. He looked up at her eyes, and knew she realized what he was seeing. She wasn't making a sound now, just breathing heavily and watching him. He inched forward, one of his hands coming to her pelvis and pressing down. Her legs were shivering at each side of him. He let go of her other leg, keeping her steady with his knees and his hand on her pelvis, and moved his hand toward what he wanted.

Slowly, he pressed his thumb deep into her hot slit and saw her close her eyes, shuddering and gasping in reaction. Warm slick moisture greeted him, pulsing around him and coating his thumb in a moment, and his dick jumped as his breath hitched. He hadn't realized she'd wanted it this badly, or been this turned on, and the knowledge of it pushed everything else from his head. She was all his. He pushed his thumb further in, out, and then in again, and then pulled it back out and tasted her sweetness, pressing his other hand against her pelvis for the reaction he wanted as he did so—her eyes to open, and to see him tasting *her*, and her eyes grew larger when they did.

She whimpered unintelligibly beneath the gag as he slicked his fingers along her folds, but this was a whimper of desire, not pain or fear, and he kept offering a rhythmic pressure he knew her body couldn't resist, and then his thumb dipped in again, and out, and he slipped his hand away and leaned up over her, putting his thumb to her lips as his other hand pulled sideways the gag and allowed his thumb's entrance.

"This is what you've got for me, baby. You can't say you don't want this, little witch," he told her, grinning as she whimpered again and shivered beneath him, tasting herself from his own hand.

Lauren knew she was dripping with desire, but she tried to ignore it, as she'd tried to ignore the taste of his thumb when it found her tongue; his hand went back to her pussy for a moment, and then his lips found her neck again and she gasped, letting his finger slide all the way inside of her mouth for a second time, coating her tongue in her own fluid and telling her clearly that her body was begging for this man to fuck her, whether her mind wanted him to or not. But she wanted him to, she realized, desperately, and wouldn't have been fighting if not for that damned spell...

He can't. He can't. He can't. She repeated the mantra to herself suddenly—even with his lips on her neck and his hand cupping her face, his thumb against her tongue—she had to keep promising herself that he wouldn't actually go so far as to fuck her; she'd told herself before that he wouldn't get *this* far, that her jeans would never leave her body, but this was all she had to fall back on, this false promise. It didn't matter if she wanted him or what would happen if he did...because he wouldn't. He couldn't. That was all. She couldn't lie to him, or give up her mother's location, and so she was only left with promising herself that what *he* was promising wasn't going to happen—he was just threatening her, pushing her to believe him so that she'd give up her only family.

He raised himself above her, and she breathed deeply with the relief of his weight being gone from her, but then he moved back down the bed to where he'd been before.

All thought left her head when his hands pushed her thighs apart as far as her muscles would allow, stretching her open before him, and his mouth came down on her center, lapping at the excess moisture that had been dripping from her and then coming down...*there.* Her clit screamed with the pressure of his tongue just before he began sucking at it greedily, and she gasped, shaking beneath them, her heels pressed into the mattress and trying to push away. The pleasure was so much, more than she'd ever felt, and then his tongue was pushing at her slit, coming inside of her again and again, thrusting. She felt him shift his body over one of her legs to keep it to the side, and then his hand was groping her ass, squeezing and gripping her as his mouth worked at her pussy, licking and sucking, and she couldn't breathe.

Focused on the taste of her, and on the sound of her biting back pleasure through her gag, David let his teeth come down on her clit so that she screamed above him with the sensations as two of his fingers slicked through her folds, back and forth, rubbing at her as her pussy pulsed against his hand and her whole body all but vibrated with the sensations he was forcing upon her, her body thrusting up against his mouth and his hands as she bucked against his attentions.

Only when the most violent trembles of her body had slowed, and when he could hear her gasping desperately for breath instead of calling out with release, did he raise his head from her center and wipe at his mouth with the back of his hand. He'd already made her his slut, and now all he could think about was being inside of her. The way she'd just come for him, he was desperate to have her—to have all of her underneath him—and he wanted to stretch her open with his dick while she screamed up at him; it was all he wanted.

He'd kept himself from pushing into her with more than one finger at a time, wanting the pleasure of feeling her having to get used to him all on her own once he pushed into her—as wet as she was, he knew it wouldn't be a problem. Now, he slipped his thumb back inside of her and inched up along her body, her breathing heavy beneath him. She wasn't squirming anymore, but there were fresh tears on her cheeks that he ignored as he rubbed his thumb again along her lip.

"You taste delicious, little witch," he growled against her cheek before shifting to the side of the bed and standing, "and you're mine now."

Pulling a condom from the same drawer he'd opened earlier, he held it up for her in one hand while he lowered his underwear with his other hand and let it fall to the floor, displaying his proud dick for her sight and leaving himself as bare as she was. He didn't think for a moment that she'd say no now—that would come later or not at all at this point, but most likely when he demanded a second round after the first and she was finally able to see past her own desire. He'd let her rest, but not for long enough to recover, and he knew she'd give in then, sore as she'd be. She wanted him just as much as he wanted her right now. But he asked anyway, watching her start to shake again with awareness even as her body still trembled with the intense climax he'd just given her. "Last chance, little one," he said, praying she'd stay stubborn, and repeating in his brain, to himself, that this was pretend, just another role-playing—because he had to. "Are you going to tell me, right this second if I remove your gag, exactly what I want?"

Lauren watched him stroke his cock beside her, and it jumped beneath his hand; it was bigger than she'd imagined one could be, long and thick, and she couldn't imagine it would fit into her—a girl nearer his height, maybe, but her? Her brain was racing, searching for escape, and suddenly she realized that he'd meant what he'd been saying all along, and she panicked.

Jerking upward, she shook her head violently, trying to dislodge the gag, pulling at the cuffs at her wrists as hard as she could bear. She was still short of breath and trembling, but he had to understand that he couldn't—he just couldn't. Even if both of them wanted it, as they both so clearly did...he just couldn't. She'd explain that. She jerked again, pulling violently at the cuffs, and suddenly he was on top of her, straddling her abdomen and stilling her arms with his grip, his dick pulsing against her stomach, prodding her, and reminding her what was coming, and how big he was.

"Lauren, you listen to me," he growled. "You stop this with information, that's it. You understand? Those cuffs'll hold. You're only hurting yourself at this point. You give up, or you don't. One way or another, your body's already given in," he finished, pressing down on her arms and watching her expression, and feeling his dick twitch slickly between them, threatening.

Lauren closed her eyes and shook her head. He didn't understand, and it was too late to try to make him believe her. If he took her, she'd never get over him; her body would keep wanting him, and only him. *That* had been the second spell her dear mother had cast on her daughter—meant to be a safeguard to make sure she waited to give away her virginity until she was married. Meant for her soulmate, or at least a partner for life. Meant to be insurance that Lauren would never get bored of the man she chose, or he get bored of her, with the sexual electricity between them, left from the spell. Her mother had, apparently, never envisioned anything like this, or a first time with a man who offered pleasure, but not love; she'd only wanted to make sure her daughter saved herself for Mr. Right.

If David Fredricks went through with this, he might move on as if nothing had happened, but Lauren would never even have a chance to recover or be happy with someone else; her body would keep wanting his, wanting that first coupling to be repeated...the spell would ruin her life.

And now Lauren was shaking beneath David, wanting him. He was right—her body was already begging for it, dripping for his cock even if she could look at it and think it was far too much for her to take; her pussy didn't have that reasoning, and her body was ready to accept him. All of her but the smallest strain of logic wanted to pretend that spell didn't exist, and relish the way he was making her body feel. The tears came more desperately now, and she bit at the gag with her teeth until his hand left her arm and stilled her jaw, hard, holding her face frozen beneath his gaze.

"You listen to me, Lauren. I'm out of patience. My *dick's* out of patience, and your pussy is begging for me to fuck you in two. The only way to stop what's coming is for you to tell me, clearly and once and for all, where mommy dearest is. You do that, fine. Otherwise, I'm going to *take what I want*." David breathed in deeply, forcing himself to keep sight, for at least a moment more, of what was at stake. "Are you going to tell me where your mom is? Yes or no," he added, when it seemed like she was about to panic, once again.

He watched her lips form a 'no' around the gag, and he watched her shake her head, and he nodded; it was what he'd expected, for now, after the way she'd responded to him already. She wanted him. He couldn't even be sure her protests were real anymore, he told himself, wet as she was—maybe she'd wanted this all along. And he was a man of his word...but he also wanted to be sure. He'd really never thought it would come to this.

He pulled down the gag, and waited as she licked her lips, finding her voice. "David, I can't tell you what you want to know. But this...please, don't."

"Don't?" David leaned into her closer and captured her mouth with his. She wasn't fighting him now. He pushed up, meeting her eyes, and traced her lips with his finger. "You want this, little one; you could have stopped me before I started."

Lauren shook her head, looking up to the ceiling. She could feel his heart beating again, and his dick pulsing against her, and she closed her eyes to try to center herself, to try to remember why she was fighting at all. "It doesn't matter; it's a bad idea. You don't want to do this," she said quietly, but then she felt his hands tracing up her side, and then to her cheek. Instinctively, her face leaned into his palm, and she shut her eyes with the embarrassment of it.

His lips moved to her ear, and lapped at her earlobe before he whispered, "You want me to keep going."

Lauren felt herself nodding against him. Right now, with his hands and his body pressing into hers, she couldn't barely remember what she'd been fighting for. He was threatening her with pleasure, and as long as she'd avoided the spell and planned to avoid it forever...why not give in now, she thought suddenly, and then go back to avoiding it. No matter what, he wouldn't gain the information he wanted. None of it mattered, she insisted to herself suddenly, and met his gaze. When he kissed her again, she didn't fight it, and when his tongue came into her mouth, she accepted it, pushing her body up against his, her mother's spell all but forgotten.

When he stood, it occurred to her again what she was giving in to, and she realized that there were tears on her cheeks again, but she bit back from saying anything. There wasn't anything to say, was there?

Standing, David pretended not to see the fact that fresh tears had come to her eyes when she'd been kissing him back. Whatever they meant, he'd find out later; whatever had changed in her, she'd just been kissing him back, pressing her body into his like a lover. He again picked up the condom he'd left in the drawer earlier, just in case, and ripped it open, and then he slid it along his jumping cock.

She was stiller than she'd been when he'd come to the foot of the bed before—waiting now, it seemed— and it wasn't any trouble for him to pull at her ankles and spread her legs as he knelt before her, watching her dripping pussy open beneath him.

Pressing his knees up into her thighs to keep her open, he stationed the head of his cock at her pussy and allowed it to penetrate only barely, just to hold its place, waiting, and he felt her start to gasping and shivering once again; he was anxious for the moment when she'd simply give in, completely, no longer making him doubt himself, and when she'd break beneath him instead of fighting herself as he still thought she was doing, even if she wasn't saying anything or protesting at this point. But she looked scared, and he guessed it was because she hadn't taken someone of his size before; he could see in her face that she wanted him, though, and she still wasn't saying anything. He leaned up over her and placed one of his hands lightly over her mouth so that her eyes widened before him. She could breathe, easily, but he wanted to better muffle the scream that he guessed was coming.

He let his hand rest on her mouth, propping himself up on his elbow above her shoulder, and snaked his other hand under her soft, round ass. He felt her shiver again at his grabbing her, and his blood thrilled to the submissive streak he kept feeling in her, and the way his blood responded to it. His dick was hard, begging for her, and he knew what they both wanted.

David leaned his head down beside hers and whispered, "You're ready for me to own you, little witch, like it or not," and then, brutally, he let himself use the full force of his hips and legs to thrust all of the way inside of her body with one lunging motion as his hand pulled at her ass to bring her pussy jolting up against him so that he bottomed out for just a moment. She was wet, and so incredibly tight, and warm, and gasping for it, and he yelled with the effort and the pleasure of it as she screamed into his hand, her tight warmth engulfing his dick, finally.

But he'd felt like...he'd felt like he'd gone *through*...like he'd *broken* through. *Fuck. Fuck. Fuck.* David froze above her with his breath caught in his throat, his hands planted against her mouth and her ass, and his cock buried in her to the hilt, pressed all the way into her, pushing all the way in. Now that he'd stilled, he could feel the whole of her pussy pulsing around him and impossibly tight, his dick buried into her folds. It felt fucking amazing, but it didn't change what else he'd felt with that first lunge. He clenched his eyes shut and was painfully sure that he hadn't just imagined pushing through something—he'd broken through a ring of a barrier. She'd been a virgin.

David forced himself to stay still, feeling her gasping for breath beneath his cupped hand that had loosened its grip after her initial scream, allowing her breath if she could find it. His weight had been on her, and he lifted slightly from her chest to give her more air, feeling his dick jump inside of her in response and willing it to still as she gasped in pain beneath him, reacting to it all over again. He realized this wasn't just the normal pain of a girl getting used to his size—this was a girl who was having to get used to the pain of having been broken and now being full of a hard, demanding cock for the very first time.

"Breathe," David told her, "just breathe." *Why the fuck didn't she tell me?* he wondered, watching her. *Fuck, but I wouldn't have pushed her like that, not if I'd known she might not have been...fuck. How much of what I just did was a first for her? Why didn't she fucking tell me?*

Lauren hadn't expected the pain of it—the heartbreak, the fear, yes, but not the pain, not with how wet she'd been, and how badly she'd known her body had wanted him. And she hadn't expected him to push, so quickly, and without warning—all of a sudden, he'd just been there, inside of her, tearing her apart. Filling her. He wasn't even moving now, and still she felt like he was actively tearing her apart, like she was splitting open beneath him as if her whole body were centered on her pussy. It hurt—God, but it hurt. There'd been a stinging, and now it *ached.* And he wasn't even moving;

he was just telling her to breathe, repeating the mantra above her. God, but it hurt.

David forced himself to focus on the present moment, and on calming the girl beneath him. If he'd known ...but it was too late to think about that now. He hadn't known, and what was done was done. The best he could do was to ease her through this. Stopping would only mean that the pain she felt now would be all she'd remember of sex. He almost wanted to stop, to pull out slowly and walk away and finish himself off, and try to forget this had happened, but he also knew—even as he hated himself for knowing it and for telling her like the calm bastard that he was to 'just breathe'—that if he did that, if he forced himself to stop now and not touch her again, the pain she felt now that was pushing tears from her eyes was what she'd think of first when she thought of sex, until she tried it again ...if she ever tried it again.

He made himself breathe, taking his own advice. He couldn't change the fact that he'd pushed her, coerced her to the point where he'd essentially raped her, she'd been so reluctant when he'd begun, even if she had stopped saying no to him, and he couldn't change that he'd taken her virginity in this way, but he could make sure she understood that the pain would pass, and make sure she felt the pleasure her body had been waiting for, and even demanding.

So he stayed still above her, telling her to breathe and counting in his mind, willing his dick to stay still while her body got accustomed to him. It was still as hard as before, turned on all the more by her response and the tight heat of her. So he stayed where he was, buried in her, and felt her warmth pulsing around him as she gasped, crying. He pushed himself to listen to the sounds she was emitting, making out through her gasps—'it hurts, please'—he realized, a pang going through his chest. He was glad her eyes were clenched shut; he didn't want to look at them.

Carefully, he leaned sideways, and breathed into her neck, instinctively working to distract her body from the trauma. Slowly, he kissed her, lipping and sucking at her skin lightly. His right hand left her mouth to run gently up and down her side, gripping her only lightly as his fingers played on her smooth skin, and his left hand left her ass and came to her hip, holding her, and waiting for any sign that she was getting used to his size, his dick still throbbing inside of her and waiting to have its way.

Lauren was so focused on the pain that it took her a moment to appreciate that the whimpering sounds she heard were her own—words, mixed with desire and pain and pleasure so that she couldn't tell them apart. And he ...he was still so hard inside of her that she was afraid to breathe with the pressure of it all. Her neck was tingling with David's breath still, and she couldn't focus on any one part of her body—all of it, lost in pleasure and pain, from the confusion of the cuts beneath her breasts that stung with their sweat to the nipples above them, one of which was being tugged by David's fingers, sending shivers through her that trembled under David's hand on her hip.

And David was still inside of her, and he was moving also now above her, pulsing within her, and her pussy was clenching along with him, readjusting and ...holding onto him. His lips were on her neck, his hands on her arm and her breast, and his weight felt ...it felt like it was supposed to be there, was what her body was feeling, even as her mind was crying with the realization of what she'd just given up, and how, and what it meant. Tears were still coming out of her eyes, and she wouldn't open them, but she felt her whole body shivering with desire beneath him so that a low moan escaped her lips.

"That's it, baby, that's it. Don't think about it. Give in to it. Relax; breathe." David's words were murmured into her ear between his kisses; she hadn't realized until now that he knew how to be so gentle with her, and her body was responding in kind, reacting and trembling, having left behind the violent adrenaline of earlier. That had been one type of pleasure; this was another.

All at once, she realized that the ache in her body had dulled, so much, to the point where it was bearable; tired of waiting, her pussy clenched suddenly around the man above her with Lauren's realization, and she heard him groan in response.

"You're ready for me, aren't you? I'll take it slow," he promised gruffly into her ear, and she felt her head nodding against him of its own volition—she wasn't in control of her body anymore, if she ever had been.

David felt her pussy squeezing around him in rhythm with the throbs of his dick and began moving slowly above her, in and out, in and out, leaving her body until only the head of his dick was still buried in her warmth and then sliding back in, as gently as he could make himself. He worked to force himself into a rhythm above her, taking it as slowly as he'd promised. His fingers gripped her hips, guiding her motions below him, but she'd instinctually started allowing herself to follow the lead of his cock as it kept pressing in and then out, her body moving up and then back, and clenching him when he pushed all the way in, relishing her wetness.

Soaked in sweat, he let himself bite down on the warm flesh of her breast, and his dick jumped when she gasped, and he sped up, pumping hard into her and feeling her body respond to the heightened pressure he was putting her under. He moaned aloud when he felt one of her legs instinctually wrap around his thigh, pulling him into her. When he found his way to her mouth again, her lips welcomed his mouth, his tongue, and everything his kiss offered, the pleasure of his body on her and his presence chasing away everything else.

She could barely breathe, for wanting him, and she allowed all of her desire to broadcast through the kiss, long past begging him to stop; she wanted him above her, forever, taking away every other thought.

David took his time, feeling every inch of Lauren's body as he kissed her and pumped back and forth, pushing her to climax around him. By the time she began trembling beneath him with the beginnings of another shattering orgasm, he was close to exploding from the pressure of holding himself in check for her benefit.

He leaned down to her heavily, more sweat dripping from his brow and collecting between their bodies, and his eyes met her desperate blue ones, hooded with pleasure and confusion as she gasped for air. He wouldn't let up now, though. He rested his lips against her shoulder, groaning with the pleasure of sinking all the way into her body yet again, and then he allowed himself to speed up for a final time, thudding against her as she moaned beneath him, and when he came inside of her a minute later, he called out just as she did, screaming into her skin with the pleasure of the release, and then grunting against her as his cock continued jerking into her, her pussy pulsing with pleasure around him and clasping him.

He let his full bodyweight collapse overtop of her finally, his hands seeking out her hips automatically and grasping them in something like affection before he sighed, grunted, and pulled away from her as she let out a whimper in response to the sudden emptiness that she hadn't known to expect.

David lay beside her, catching his breaths and his thoughts, trying to block out the wrongness of what he'd just done to the girl tied beside him, her breath still recovering from an orgasm and her raw wrists still cuffed to his bed. It took minutes, for him to pull himself back into order, and by the time he had he could feel that her trembling beside him had turned to gentle shakes, signaling that the pleasure of everything had given way to realization, and crying.

He rolled from the bed, cleaned himself of her blood with a towel and tossed the condom, and then he pulled his jeans on without ceremony, noting that her body was as soaked with sweat as his own, a new, small bruise forming on her waist from where he must have gripped her too roughly at some point, though it didn't come close to matching the anger of the bruises on her arms or the angry welts below her breasts, or the hickies on her neck. He hadn't let himself take a girl's virginity before, knowing he'd never be sticking around, and the presence of blood on the sheets, and on her thighs, was something he tried not to think about.

By the time he'd dug up the key to the handcuffs and was moving to her right wrist, there were still tears coming from her eyes, and her face was soaked with them and sweat, but she wasn't nearly sobbing; she was resigned now, beyond any panic she'd felt before. He turned off his brain to the sight of her, doing what he needed to in order to take care of her in the moment and bring her back to herself.

When the cuff released her right wrist, she curled to her left, balling into a loose fetal position as David reached for and then released the left cuff, and she lay there while he moved around the room. She kept her eyes closed, blocking out the world, and thinking about the spell her mother had cast upon her, only because she'd broken curfew by going to a movie with some boy she could barely remember. This was what she wanted to forget. If she could only just remember the pleasure of David's touch that her body was now memorizing, holding in with the power of the spell, then maybe none of it would matter.

Finally, Lauren was beyond thinking, focused on calming her breathing, and blocking out what the day had brought, and how wrong she'd been. She'd given in to her own desire by the end, but now that the pleasure had been replaced with thoughts of her mother's spell, she was left wondering helplessly what she'd set herself up for. The fact that she'd never see David again after another day or so was all she could think of, and here she'd allowed herself to be connected to him by giving in to a few moments of pleasure. Coerced or not ...she'd not been fighting him by the time they'd come to the point of no return, and she couldn't help thinking that he would have stopped if she really had, or if she'd told him she was a virgin. She'd seen the shock on his face. He would have believed her, she thought now. Dazed, she no longer knew what to think, or how to even focus, her head was spinning so fast. She could have stopped this, she was realizing now, and that was bringing on a whole different kind of grief and regret.

Lauren didn't fight David when he pulled her into a sitting position on the bed and kissed her cheek, or react when she glanced down and caught sight of the blood against the white skin of her thighs before he wrapped a blanket firmly around her and pulled her easily into his arms, picking her up and cradling her against his chest. He'd removed the gag with the cuffs, but he still hadn't said anything, and she hadn't made a sound.

David hefted her in his arms, shifting her as needed to open the room's door and move into the hallway. He went as gently as he could, realizing she had to be sore, at least, and headed to the nicer of their two guest bathrooms, which wasn't attached to the room she'd been in. Inside, he sat her against the wall, still curled in the blanket, on the edge of the double sink's countertop, and dug beneath in the cabinet for supplies he knew had been left behind by a more willing visitor.

Finding the tray he'd known was there, he looked over the contents; shampoo, conditioner, bubble-bath crystals, body soap, shaving gel. Anything she could need, but for a razor.

He glanced to Lauren, who still hadn't looked at him or moved from where he'd placed her.

Moving beyond the nearby curtain, he started running water into the rarely used soaking tub, sprinkling in half of the bath crystals at his disposal. When the tub was half-full of hot water and bubbles obscured the surface, he returned to Lauren, noting that she hadn't moved an inch. He eased her from the counter, onto her feet, and guided her beyond the curtain. He stopped with her at the edge of the tub and looked away from her and the bath as he gently pulled at the blanket that had been wrapped around her. He felt more than saw her step jerkily into the tub and curl against its back, and they both waited in silence for it to fill. He asked if the temperature was fine as it did, and she nodded without looking at him, and they waited.

Finally, with the tub filled, David reached forward and turned off the faucet. He'd been holding his breath, he realized as he cleared his throat. "A friend of ours left behind some of her things on her last visit—she wouldn't mind if you used them," he added, picking up the tray and setting it down to get Lauren's attention, and he stood when she gave a slow nod in acknowledgement. "Alright...I'm gonna...leave you alone. I'll find you some clothes, get you something to drink," he said gruffly as his gaze focused on her swollen lips, and then he turned to draw the curtain closed behind him, trapping more of the steam.

He turned, at the last minute before he left, and added, "I'm sorry, kid. If I'd known...I'm sorry," he added quietly, knowing the words weren't helping either of them, and hating himself all the more because he could feel his dick still stirring in his jeans, wanting more of her.

At the door, he stopped at her voice, coming shakily from behind him.

"Lancaster County. The old Reed farmhouse ...an hour, maybe, from where you found me."

David turned back to the curtained tub, thinking he'd imagined her words completely. *What the fuck?* he wondered. *Now?*

He stepped back toward the curtain but stopped himself from looking in. "You said ..."

"She's in Lancaster County. There's an old blue farmhouse that's abandoned. She's been there for a month; they call it the Reed place." Lauren's hoarse voice broke on the last phrase, and she coughed into her hand, hating herself and her mother and David and Josh all at once. She could hear David's confusion when he spoke again, and felt her tears starting up all over again, but they didn't change the fact that she just didn't care anymore. Even once her powers came back, everything would have changed; her powers would never reach the strength needed to counteract one of her own mother's spells.

"You're telling me now," he said slowly, speaking through the curtain.

Her answer was just as simple, and just as true, she realized when she said it. "I didn't hate her until now." It wasn't fair or right, that she'd reserved hate even when her mother had continued murdering, but somehow she had, always thinking it was some mental break, some temporary psychosis she could break her out of. Confronted now with the reality of this spell that her mother had placed on her own daughter ...it suddenly hit her how selfish, and how horrible, her mother was when it came to the practice of being a human being. She was cruel, and she was a murderer, and Lauren no longer cared about protecting her from herself. She had enough to deal with in her own life now.

David didn't say anything more, but stepped back from the curtain, already fishing his phone from his jeans. He and Josh couldn't leave—not with Lauren here and a few days' worth of her doses still to go, to make absolutely sure she couldn't turn into a black witch and follow in her mother's footsteps—but there was another team waiting that was near to the farmhouse, if it was where Lauren said it was, and they could have the witch dead before the night's end.

He'd ask Lauren about what she'd said later, about hating her mother only now, if he could get up the nerve to speak to her at all.

Behind him, Lauren let herself fall back against the edge of the tub sobbing, barely hearing David's exit from the large bathroom. It didn't occur to her to get up and run, or hide, or try to find a phone, or do anything at all beyond sit in the tub and try to wash away *everything*. That was all she wanted and knowing that David didn't even realize the half of what he'd just done ...she only felt more desperate to try to forget that so much had changed.

Chapter 4

For the third morning in a row, Lauren woke up with David's name on her lips. It had been two weeks since his partner had driven her away from the ranch house, but while the men had promised she could go back to her normal life—and seemed even to believe what they were saying—her life had only continued its spiral downward. Already, she suspected this would be the fourth day in a row where she couldn't bring herself to do any schoolwork or try to make up for her missed class-time. In graduate school, the week she'd spent away from the university shouldn't have broken her—her classes only met once per week, after all—and with her mother's death in mind, her teachers had been more than willing to give her an extension on papers and projects. It had helped, of course, that Josh had emailed them on her behalf that she was ill, just after they'd taken her.

But the extended deadlines were coming up now, and things just ...weren't working.

As she had on every other morning for the last two weeks, she first lit some incense before she started coffee brewing, and then she headed into her make-shift office; it was really just a corner of her studio apartment, set off behind a folding screen, but it served the purpose of shutting her off from the world while she studied or worked basic spells on the table beside her desk. Breathing in, she began murmuring scrying words softly, her fingers pressed to the sides of the mirror she'd left out the day before. She was desperate to speak to the youngest witch from her mother's coven—the one woman among them she'd counted as something of a friend—but this was the only way she knew to contact her besides simply showing up on her doorstep.

She'd thought the other witch might come to her mother's funeral, hastily planned as it had been, but none of the coven had showed. Lauren knew they'd likely had their own rite of mourning, and their own wake to celebrate her mother's life, but their absence had still hurt. She'd all but grown up in their shadows, after all, and little affection as she had for them, they were something akin to a family. On the other hand, she knew it was hypocritical for her to criticize the way they chose to mourn; she'd barely mourned at all, herself, and had been involved in her mother being caught to begin with. That had been a long time coming, though, she realized now, and it had been years since she'd felt close to her mother, or anything like she thought a daughter ought to feel.

A full ten minutes after settling in to attempt a scrying, Lauren still felt nothing. There was no effect coming from her words, and no inkling of the power she'd used to feel swimming in her blood, always below the surface and just waiting to be called. There was nothing.

Standing and heading into the kitchen, still dressed in nothing but her tank top and shorts, she poured herself coffee as her mind went back to what Devlin and Fredricks had told her, before she'd been brought back here. She hadn't believed them at the time. How could they have the makings of a potion to take away power that was genetic to her blood? Everyone had some power, after all, if they just learned to access it, and even if the men had been able to mute her affinity for magic, and what she'd learned, she should still have been able to access the power inherent in human blood, and in her DNA. She refused to believe that they might really have taken away her power for good; she'd never heard of such a thing happening.

But thinking about that conversation invariably took her to thoughts of David, and his body on hers. The way he'd made her feel. He hadn't touched her again, as long as they'd kept her over the next few days. Instead, the men had given her a small guest room with its own bathroom, the space nearly identical to the one where David had taken her. She'd stayed there, locked in, while they visited only to bring her food or that blue goop, which they'd claimed was for their safety. They'd given her ointments also, that had gone a long way toward healing the welts her bra had left, and warmer clothes—little kindnesses that she'd wanted to refuse, but had accepted anyway, too tired to do otherwise. It hadn't been until hours after the last dose, when Josh Devlin had been waiting for her to pack up the extra clothes they'd bought for her so that he could bring her home, when he'd told her she was no longer a witch.

David had been standing in the background at that

point, waiting in the hall as if he was going to say goodbye, and the flatness of his expression had been what went furthest in telling her that his partner was telling the truth. Or, at least, telling her what they believed to be the truth. At that point, she'd thought about telling him what more he'd done to her, and telling him why she couldn't meet his eyes for even a moment ...but she hadn't. She'd been determined to leave with what remained of her dignity, and deep down, she'd felt sure that her body would stop remembering his as soon as she was out of his sight for a few days, and that it would remember where its power lay.

Instead, her powers had stayed dormant, and her body had stayed alert to thoughts of David Fredricks. She dreamed of him almost every night and hated herself for it.

Waiting for her oatmeal to cook, Lauren couldn't help looking at the lone business card clipped to a magnet on her fridge. Josh had given it to her, telling her he had 'regrets over how things went' and that they 'owed her', should she need anything; this, after releasing the blindfold she'd had on for the duration of the drive. She'd thought about tossing the card in the trash but hadn't quite been able to make herself do it— or rather, she'd thrown it away repeatedly, but always picked it back up and put it back on the fridge soon after. All it had was Josh's name and a phone number. *Shady as it gets*, she thought to herself again. It didn't matter anymore whether she threw it away, though; she'd long ago memorized the number.

***

After three hours of trying to focus on research, Lauren finally gave up. Theoretically, she was supposed to be working on a thesis related to natural medicines and recent studies on the toxins discovered in a river basin in Brazil. She'd always planned on parlaying her powers into the frantic and ongoing search that scientists were engaged in, seeking natural remedies that could aid treatments for diseases requiring such a breakthrough. With her affinity for sensing the powers of plants, and for instinctively knowing what to do with what the natural world offered, it had seemed like the ideal path she could use for channeling her powers into something good, and for making up for her mother's craziness.

This was why she'd studied environmental science and ecology to begin with, and why she'd wanted a graduate degree to move forward. But without her powers? She'd be just another graduate student flunky who barely understood the chemistry and the math, apprenticing herself to larger-than-life scientists in hopes of making a difference without going all the way toward getting a PhD, which was the last thing she wanted. Without magic, she didn't have a leg up, and whether or not she'd be able to make a difference in the field was anyone's guess if she only got her Masters, as she'd planned, but it was doubtful. And if she did go for a PhD, whether or not there'd be enough of a field for her to make a difference in, once she had the degree in hand, was an even bigger question, the rainforests were disappearing so quickly. So, that brought her to the question: what was the point? She wasn't a natural when it came to science, and whatever funding would have gone to her would be better spent on someone else if she didn't have her magic to aid her work.

Tired of second-guessing herself, she decided to get a bath and try to forget about everything for a while. Between thinking about her mother's recent death and the arrangements she'd had to make, and then her research, and being distracted by thoughts of David every time she turned around, it seemed like she was constantly stressed and exhausted. Since it was Wednesday, her one day where she didn't have to be at the university and was expected to just be working from home, she told herself she could afford the luxury, if it would just allow her an hour's escape from worry.

Sinking into the water was what she'd needed, she realized as soon as she'd laid her head back. Her apartment had a chill since she'd been trying to lower her heating costs—March in the Midwest meant it was too cold to not have the heat on, for now—but the bath and the steam were comforting, and it was easy to close her eyes and drift away from the world that, lately, had felt more like a prison.

Lying back, she let her mind wander, and tried to picture herself in a rainforest, sunbathing by a river. She thought of a trip she'd taken to Costa Rica in high school, to snorkel and study the ecology of its rainforests, and imagined herself back there, on the coast, baking in the sun in a bikini and exhausted from being out in the waves. It wasn't hard to do—with the heavy warmth of the steamed air and the hot water around her, she could dream up the sound of the waves, and even the face of the boy she'd developed a crush on during that trip. His name had been Henry, and they'd had a fun flirtation. He'd been tall and dark, and talked a lot about getting tattoos once he turned 18, and the girlfriend he had back home. They hadn't even kissed that summer—it had been fun, for her, to just flirt, and she'd had no desire to come between him and a girl he was planning on getting engaged to.

Now, though, she allowed herself to imagine him coming up to her while she lay on the beach, putting his hands on her and kissing her neck, and the way that would feel. Her mind in her fantasy, she let her hands wander. One of her palms went to her chest, and she ran the oily bubbles of her bath over her breasts, around her suddenly hard nipples, pinching them and thinking of other fingers doing the pinching, through a bikini on a tropical beach. Her other hand wandered lower, down to between her legs, and pressed in rough circular motions above her clit, the heel of her palm pressing down on her pelvis. Then she pressed one of her fingers just inside of her pussy; even with the surrounding water, she could feel her natural juices heating up with the motions and the memory.

She'd been thinking of her crush's hands, and what they'd look like on her body. She'd had her mind on the sensations, enjoying them, and now in her mind she tried to look at Henry ...and suddenly, instead, she saw David, above her on her tropical beach, smiling down at her with that dangerous grin on his chiseled face.

Lauren jerked up, splashing water outside of the tub and grabbing the porcelain sides for support. She'd been about to come ...thinking of him. She hadn't even realized it, but her mind had pulled him into her fantasy, and let go of any pretense. Sitting straight up in the tub, her hands holding onto the sides, she realized that the hands she'd seen in her fantasy hadn't been Henry's at all—they'd been rougher, and there'd been a scar along the knuckles of one of them, and a steel ring on one finger. They'd been David's hands from the get-go, she realized, her heart sinking as she pictured them again in her mind and shivered with the thought. She couldn't even force herself to fantasize without involving him. She'd thought she could walk away from her mother's spell, even if she wouldn't get the same pleasure from another's touch; that's why she'd given in. She hadn't realized his memory would keep haunting her like this.

***

David hovered over Lauren's number, once again. He'd gotten it from her that first night they'd met, when she'd thought he was just another guy at a bar and before they'd gone outside. He'd thought about erasing it every day since—when she'd been tied up in their ranch house, and then after they'd let her go. Three weeks since he'd gotten the number, and he was still thinking about it. It wasn't like he could, or would, call her. How could he, given what he'd done? He hadn't even gone with his partner to get her out of the house, it had been so hard to face her.

"You ready?"

Josh's voice had come from the doorway to his suite; they both tried not to enter the other's territory unless directly invited. Each man had a full, decked-out suite of rooms in the basement of the ranch house—once you left the house proper and came downstairs, you hit two doors, one with Devlin's name and one with Fredricks'. If they wanted to hang out or needed to talk about a case, that happened upstairs. A full kitchen was the only thing that the downstairs areas lacked, in terms of traditional housing, but each had a fridge, each mostly filled with beer and water. Upstairs, along with the kitchen, there was their generally empty interrogation room, a single-room gym for working out, a large office with a stacked gun case, and three guest rooms, along with a large common area and a pool table—their primary common luxury item.

Now, David called back that he'd meet his partner in a minute, and then gathered his gun and his government ID. He might not need either, and probably wouldn't, but he'd just as soon have them and be prepared for whatever came up.

They'd closed their most recent case that morning, arresting a man who'd been 'embezzling' samples of dead smallpox from the lab where he worked, apparently in the hopes of figuring out how to engineer a live strain from the dead ones. Nobody was sure whether he could have done it—it wasn't supposed to be possible—but it would have been absurd to take a chance on giving him the time to try. Devlin and Fredricks had spent the last week following him, biohazard gear packed into the trunk of Josh's Mustang and waiting, as they'd trailed his every move until finally he'd taken them not just to the storage facility where he was keeping samples, but to the warehouse where he'd set up a makeshift lab.

The whole thing had been nerve-wracking. Give him a serial killer or a vampire any day, over a virus-engineering scientist. David wasn't even sure he would have gotten into this line of work if he'd ever considered that bioweapons could be involved, smallpox or otherwise. If any case's finish had ever called for a drunken night on the town and a random hook-up, it was this one.

Upstairs, he followed his partner out to the Mustang and stowed his gun in the glove compartment, along with his ID. It was Josh's turn to drive and to choose the location.

"You know where you want to go?" he asked Devlin.

"Pizza good with you? Then on to the Kennedy Street Pub?"

"Good with me."

Raph's Pizzeria, their go-to pie place, was only a few blocks from Kennedy Street, and right in the main thorough-fair of town. It'd be easy for them to split up if they wanted to, one of them taking the car and one of them taking a girl to a hotel or getting a taxi, and it would mean only parking once. In the nearest town, that made a difference.

"You planning on meeting up with that scientist chick?"

"I called her," Josh answered with a grin. The woman who'd been smallpox-scientist's first assistant had painted a dark enough picture of the guy that he'd become their main suspect almost from the moment they'd learned his name, but the signals she'd sent to Josh had been just as clear. "She's working tonight, but we're gonna get together tomorrow, grab dinner at Pinacelli's. Suitably impressive?"

"Suitably impressive," David agreed, thinking that she'd been so into his partner, she might have settled for McDonald's. The fancy Italian fare would knock her socks off, literally.

As things turned out for the immediate night, though, they didn't get beyond Raph's Pizzeria. The place was crawling with coeds who were themselves suitably impressed with two men in suits who happened to be slumming it at a pizza hotspot. Not two hours after arriving, David was heading out the door with a redhead who was simmering hot, leaving his partner to decide whether or not he wanted to grab a taxi later or hook up with one of the barely-legal sweethearts at the bar, just a night before he'd have a date with someone who, no doubt, he'd have more to talk about with.

The ten-minute drive to the ranch took only seven minutes, and then David was leading Marissa downstairs to his rooms. She was nearly as tall as him at 5'10, leggy and curly-haired and brazen. She'd said she was studying elementary education, although she hadn't seemed too sure of that. She'd been a lot more sure that she wanted to come home with him.

Watching her sprawl backward on his bed, David

couldn't help thinking that this girl was as far from Lauren as he could have gotten, had he tried. She'd come onto him and Josh both in the bar, bringing over a pitcher and two of her girlfriends to their table almost as soon as they'd sat down, and batting her eyelashes like they were hummingbird wings. She had a 23-year-old model's body that was hard to resist—skinny, toned, and perfectly tanned.

Stripping, he made a show of undressing himself as her eyes got bigger, watching him as he went down to his underwear. He knew he wasn't as young as her, but his muscles made up for the age difference. He stood over her for a minute, letting her foot trail teasingly up his thigh as her eyes stayed on his six-pack and what showed beneath it, and then he knelt overtop of her to unbutton her dress and pull it apart to reveal her figure, which was just short of being too thin. She wasn't wearing a thread of underwear, which didn't entirely surprise him. He brought his lips to hers, pushing his tongue into her mouth as one of his hands found her right breast and covered it. She had B-cups, maybe, and he squeezed her in his hand until she gasped beneath him, both of her hands going to his shoulders and gripping hard so that he felt her nails in his skin.

He moved forward to her ear as she pressed her head sideways into the bedspread, baring her neck to him, and he whispered, "Watch your nails, darlin'," realizing as he said it that he wasn't sure of her name.

Sucking at her neck, he trailed his hands along her skin and then gripped tight to her hips and brought her up hard against him so that there was only the material of his own underwear between her pussy and his straining cock. He felt more than heard her grunt with the pressure of it at her opening, and then he rolled sideways to get rid of this last piece of clothing. As he did, he watched her untangle herself from her own open dress and then slide onto the floor, landing on her knees.

He sat at the edge of the bed, opening his legs so that she had better access.

She was tentative now, confronting his size—for the first time, he thought he saw some nerves in her eyes as she looked up at him—but she got over the shakes fast. A moment after she'd met his eyes, she had his balls cupped in one of her hands, her other supporting his shaft as her lips circled over his head, her tongue dipping out to taste him. He gripped the edge of the bed and pushed his hips forward, meeting her lips. Her mouth sucking at him felt like heaven, and just what he needed. He raised one of his hands to the back of her head, not pushing—yet—but prodding her forward and resting on her hair as if to encourage her to keep going. He looked down and watched her lips, stretching around him as she tried to take him all the way in and then pulling back when she realized he might be too much for her. Her eyes were closed, focused on sucking him off. When she opened them to look up, he saw she was about to pull back further, but caught her before she could.

He pushed forward instead, pulling her head in to meet him and enjoying the feel of her gasp on his cock as he stretched into her throat and she gagged around him before he let her pull back and catch her breath. Afterward, she was grinning up at him.

She came forward again and he held her red curls in his hand, reining her forward just a half-inch further than she wanted to come each time, until he sensed she'd had more than enough. Then he pulled her up by her elbows and landed her bouncing backward on the bed before he pulled a condom from his dresser and turned toward her. She was still out of breath, but her legs were spread lewdly, waiting for him, and she was wet and ready.

He landed on top of her and let his dick find her pussy immediately; even as his lips were finding hers and his hands were pressing her shoulders into the bed, his dick slipped into her and glided forward. She wasn't nearly as tight as he would have liked, but she was hot and wet and responsive, moving against him immediately and meeting him thrust for thrust. His lips on hers, he forced his right hand between their bodies and found her clit and squeezed as he pumped into her. He wasn't interested in taking it slowly, and doubted she'd really appreciate any finesse on his part anyway, she was so young and horny.

Holding her down, he felt her body buck against him as she screamed into his lips, and then he released her clit as he pushed into her as far as she'd take him, bottoming out hard and holding himself there as she screamed out her own orgasm; her cunt was spasming around him, pulsing with want, and her nails were digging into his arms as her legs held his waist, pulling him in against her as hard as she could.

When she seemed all but spent, he pulled out and then pushed in again as far as he could, faster and harder than he had before, and then he pulled away and turned her over. She was out of breath, but he wasn't. He knelt behind her with one hand beneath her pelvis, pulling her up to meet him, and he stationed the head of his cock against her ass; her pussy hadn't been tight enough for him, not with his mind still half-lost on Lauren, and the way this girl had been acting, he had to guess she was no stranger to anal play. Sure enough, she didn't protest when he pushed at her back entrance.

He put one of his hands down hard between her shoulder blades to hold her still and watched her hands clench into the bedspread, and then he inched forward;

the lubricant from her pussy and the condom was more than enough, and with a pop, he slid in quickly. She grunted in discomfort when he first came into her, but then she pushed back against him, and he only waited a moment before riding into her. She was yelling into the bed now, one of her hands below her body and playing with herself, and he leaned back, his muscled thighs spread on either side of hers as he kept pushing deeper into her, stroking back and forth, finally enjoying the tightness he'd been craving.

Closing his eyes, he let his cock dictate the speed and enjoyed the feel of the girl beneath him pushing back at him, goading him to take her harder until he pressed his hand heavily into her back and she whimpered with pleasure, coming on her fingers and spasming beneath him. He grunted with release when he came a moment later, jerking into his condom and the girl's passage.

Finished, he landed beside her and glanced to her; her lips were pursed with pleasure, swollen from his rough kisses, and her eyes were hooded with satisfaction. As he watched her, catching his breath, she licked her lips and practically purred at him, "I liked that a lot."

"Yeah?" David grinned at her, playing the flirtation he saw in her face back at her and appreciating the twisting of her body as she turned sideways to face him, and then landed her long fingers on his chest to play in his chest hairs.

"Oh, Danny, absolutely," she answered, smiling.

At least I don't have to feel bad about forgetting her name, David thought in return, already picturing what he'd do to her next.

Chapter 5

After another night spent tossing in her bed, Thursday found Lauren determined to change her situation—somehow. She had to get David out of her mind, and she had to get in touch with her mother's coven and see if they could help her, both with the 'promise' spell tying her to David and also with her magic. She wasn't getting anywhere by herself and trusting them seemed like the only option. It was a good few hours' drive to get to Mary, but her morning class had been cancelled because so many other students had the flu—getting an early start would give her enough time to be back for her evening class. If the coven couldn't help her win back her powers, she might or might not continue on beyond this semester, but she at least wouldn't give up just yet. Not until she knew for sure that the loss of her powers couldn't be counter-acted anyway. And, maybe, Mary could give her an idea of whether her mother's spell could be thwarted, even now that it had been activated.

After picking up coffee from a nearby gas station and hitting the highway, Lauren was finally able to relax; she enjoyed driving, and the souped-up sound system in her little Eclipse made it easy for her to get lost in focusing on the road and the brief drive. She knew the way by heart. Mary might be the youngest in the coven, but she was about the age of Lauren's mother; the two of them hadn't always gotten along, but Mary had been a regular babysitter for her when her mother had gone off the rails or needed her so-called space. As the weakest of the coven members, she'd often been the one to handle chores such as babysitting, but Lauren had been thankful for it. Over the years, Lauren had grown far closer to her than she'd been to her own mother, and had made this visit often enough—even after leaving behind the coven for what she'd hoped would be for good.

Driving up to the house felt comfortable, and for the first time in weeks, Lauren felt like things might actually work out. Even if the coven wouldn't come together to help her, Mary would find a way.

When the older woman answered her door, though, her face fell upon seeing Lauren. After a moment spent frozen, she leaned forward and hissed, "You can't be here, Lauren—I can't help you!"

Instinctively, Lauren put her hands up to stop the door from closing and pushed forward, keeping the door from shutting all the way. "Mary! I need ..."

"I can't help you, I told you," Mary said, glaring back at her and leaning into her door.

Lauren stared back at the older witch who she'd considered practically family for all of her life, and realized she might cry; this woman either knew something of what was going on with Lauren's life, or she knew something else that Lauren needed to know, and her expression was still totally closed off to her. "Please, Mary—ten minutes?" Lauren begged, pressing her face closer to the crack still left between the door and its frame. Watching her hesitate, she asked again, "Please? I don't have anyone else!"

Finally, the woman relented and backed away from the door. Lauren followed Mary into the kitchen. It wasn't as clean as usual—a sure sign that the woman was under stress.

"You shouldn't be here," the woman told her from her sink, pouring water into a tea kettle.

Lauren shook her head at the woman's back and took a seat at her island, pursing her lips. "Why not? I've been trying to get in touch with you for days, and ..."

"And you don't think the coven has been trying to get in touch with you? All of us, every other day at least, for weeks?" the woman answered, having cut her off and turned to her, stepping to the island. "Oh, Lauren, you've lost your powers, and we know it—there's no way none of us would be able to get through otherwise."

That's why she's saying I shouldn't be here? I'm cut off now that I've lost my powers? Lauren watched tears squeeze out of Mary's eyes and reached out to try to take one of her hands, but Mary backed away from her, practically trembling, she was so upset.

"Yes—I thought ...I thought they'd come back, but they haven't yet. Some men ...took me and took them. I didn't know it was possible," she said quietly.

"We'd heard rumors," Mary answered her, "that the government found something to do it, and we were afraid that's where you were, when you disappeared. The folks who engineered it were working with a witch, of course, if you'd believe it," she added before turning back to the sink and her kettle, muttering under her breath.

"And you ...the coven ...you don't know of a way to ...reverse it?" Lauren asked.

"No. That's why you shouldn't be here. There's probably a letter in your mailbox now, or it'll be there tomorrow."

Lauren blinked. "A letter?"

Mary put the kettle on the stove and turned to her. "You just came for help? You don't remember what this means?" she demanded, her eyes wide.

"No—I wanted to ask about this, and something else ..."

Mary shook her head and came back to the island, her hands clenched together in front of her. "Lauren, you know the coven's secrets. If you don't have your powers anymore, to protect those secrets—you *belong* to them. You're expected to get your affairs in order and then come back. Melania will place you somewhere, and you'll do the coven's bidding; nothing else. I thought you'd be running by now," she finished, her brow lowered and tight.

Lauren sat back, processing, and opened her mouth to speak, but then closed it again.

"You can't fight this, dear," Mary said gently. "You can run if you want to, and I thought you would be already, but it won't do you any good. Melania's as stubborn as your lost mother was, and she won't let this go."

Looking back at the other woman, Lauren suddenly felt like her other purpose for coming no longer mattered at all. If she didn't have a life, what did love or sex matter? "What'll the coven want with me, if I've got no powers to offer?" she finally asked.

Mary only shrugged. "It was spoken of some, last

night. They won't hurt you—Melania promised. I think, perhaps, you'll just ...be a servant, and help with the preparations for rites, or gathering supplies, maybe going through old books that have been collecting dust to see if there's something more that's useful, that's been forgotten." She shrugged again, turning her attention to her whistling kettle. "I don't know. You'll just ...you'll be with them, where they'll know you're not ..."

"Working against them," Lauren finished for her, her voice quiet. "I guess I should have known I couldn't just walk away, huh?" she half-laughed, suddenly realizing how absurd it was that she'd planned on spending three hours of her evening listening to a professor drone on about ethics in lab work.

"You'll be taken care of," Mary told her. "Perhaps it's for the best that you're here now. We can go to Melania's tonight and she'll see that you understand, want to cooperate."

"I have things I have to take care of—I can't just stay. But," she said quickly, when Mary looked up in a panic, "I'll come back. I just ...I can't stay now."

"The coven wants you here next week," Mary said, her voice hard again. "By the 30th."

The thirtieth. That's Friday. I have a week.

"That'll give you a week to clear your apartment; bring just what you need, alright?"

Mechanically, Lauren nodded back at her. What else could she do? The woman before her was clearly too scared to stand up to the other women; she'd always been the weakest of the group, and while Lauren had thought she'd help her, she'd never have imagined that the witch would go against her sisters to do so.

"You said you came for something else, also?" Mary asked, sipping at her tea.

"Yeah ...yeah, I wanted to know about getting help with counter-acting one of the spells Mom cast."

"Those ones she cast on you?" Mary asked knowingly, and Lauren nodded. The other woman shook her head. "She shouldn't have done that, I told her; hard spells, those are, to live under. But—no matter, since you'll be with us now. We couldn't countermand them anyway, but this way, with your powers gone ...well, it doesn't matter so much, does it?"

Somehow, Lauren made it through another fifteen minutes of what she would have been hard-pressed to call a visit. When she escaped to her car, she kept it together for a full ten minutes, until she'd gotten far enough away that she could pull to the side of the road and allow herself to break down in sobs.

This sealed it, that her powers were gone and that her mother's spells seemed to be for good ...but after a few minutes spent lost to angry tears, she realized she still had some small amount of hope. Josh Devlin and David Fredricks had taken her powers from her, but they'd admitted that they knew of her doing no wrong—maybe, if they realized what was at stake, they could give them back to her, if she could only convince them to give her a chance at staying good. Then, it would only be a matter of proving to the coven that she had them back, and then she'd have her life back. She'd just have to call them, and hope that they were so decent as they'd seemed at first, no matter what David had ended up doing.

This thought in mind, she headed for campus, and for her Thursday night class. She wouldn't give up on her life until she had no other choice. Tomorrow, she'd work on getting past David, seeing if she could find another man to take her mind off of him so that she wouldn't be so distracted by him if they met, and so she'd give herself just the day to collect herself before she called Josh on Saturday, and promised the man whatever she had to in order to get her powers, and her life, back on track. If she was lucky, maybe she wouldn't even have to see or speak to Fredricks again. At least, this was what she told herself she hoped for.

***

After attending her Friday morning labs, she managed a small amount of research at the library, and left with the feeling that at least she was getting her school life back on track. Now, it was just a matter of getting beyond thoughts of David—at least to the point where she could stand to see him and Josh, and ask for their help, or beg for it, if it came to that.

Back at her apartment, she readied herself to go out with some of the other girls. She hadn't bothered to go along for their girls' nights out in ages, but if anything could get her mind off of David, it would be a living man and not a fantasy of someone she barely remembered from high school. She dressed in a shirt dress that cinched around her waist and hugged her figure in all the right places. It was burgundy, and had three quarter-length sleeves—flirty because of its length and the top button undone, but not so much that anybody would get the wrong idea, hopefully. Assuming she didn't want them to, she told herself. After all, there was nothing holding her back now, right?

And then she was out the door, heading to the bus. Her friend Samantha would give her a ride home, and the bus was safe enough at this hour. Plus, it would give her a chance at getting rid of her nerves, and trying to forget that David even existed. As it was, it was hard enough for her to figure out why she was thinking about him. How was it she mostly remembered the moments when he'd been gentle, and that all of the roughness of his hands and voice had just been channeled into what she remembered of the pleasure he'd brought her? She told herself that she couldn't possibly have enjoyed the roughness, and his control ...it had just been an illusion, she told herself, brought on by the situation and wishful thinking. And then there was their night of flirting, before everything else, that she kept coming back to. It was driving her crazy, but he was hard to forget.

Walking into the bar, though, she was immediately distracted by her friends—all were clearly ready for a night out, dressed for the yuppie bar they'd decided to descend on for the night. It wasn't nearly a college hangout where they'd have to worry about meeting other students, let alone the students they coached through labs; this place was filled with folks who worked extended 9-5s and lived in their offices.

"Lauren, you look great," her friend Samantha greeted her, eyeing her black heels. "I'm going to have to borrow those heels after they get you a boy-toy."

"Right," Lauren forced herself to joke back, "and then I'll borrow your figure to get a new guy who doesn't care about shoes!"

Three rounds of Margaritas later, and stationed in a deep booth with two of the girls, Lauren was feeling more like herself than she'd felt in weeks. The hours of music were starting to make it harder to focus and hear, but her friends and the guys who flitted in and out of their circle were making the night go quickly, and enjoyably. As Samantha came back to the table with another round of Margaritas, Lauren noticed three men trailing behind her—all had tell-tale shadows suggesting they hadn't shaved since early that morning, and all had coats in their arms and wore dress shirts. Real estate agents, she thought, or maybe sales execs.

"Lauren, Jenny, meet the three architects!" Samantha chimed as if she were introducing a rock band. Two of them scooted tightly into the circular booth after Samantha and one pulled up a stool to the edge of the table and perched there. Lauren was directly across from him, her two friends sitting on each side of her.

The perching architect reached his hand across the table to Lauren even as Sam was making confused introductions. "Jerry," he told her, grinning, and her eyes caught the tribal tattoo reaching down his forearm from beneath his rolled-up shirt sleeve. *Of course he'd have a tribal tattoo*, Lauren thought, but she took his hand anyway. He held hers too long and too tightly, but she smiled back at him before going back to what her friend was saying about the latest X-Men movie, which Lauren hadn't seen, though it seemed everyone else at the table was able to follow along.

When next she looked up, Jerry's eyes were on her again, and she looked down to realize her dress' next button had come undone, revealing the band of her bra and far more cleavage than she'd usually have shown, given her curves; she was drunk, she realized belatedly, and felt herself blush as she hurried to slip the loosed button back into its hole. When she looked up, Jerry's eyes were still on her instead of his buddy, who was telling a story about some building she'd never heard of.

"You wanna get some air?" he mouthed.

Feeling flushed, and cramped in the booth, Lauren nodded thankfully and let him interrupt the story so that their friends would let her out. Excusing themselves, they headed toward the front of the bar and Lauren let him take her elbow to lead her outside, to the far corner of the patio.

"Mike'll go on about buildings forever with a captive

audience," he told her. "You want a smoke?" he asked next, offering her a pack he'd just dug from his jacket pocket. She hadn't realized he smoked until now.

"Uh, no, thanks, I don't smoke," she said, shaking her head as he waved down a nearby waitress and demanded two Margaritas. "I think I've had enough," she protested, but his raised eyebrow and the cocky smile on his lips were enough to convince her to let it go.

"So, you study ecology?" he asked. "I never did too well in science, but I worked on the zoo expansion a few years ago—we worked with some of your profs, I bet; they had university consults in some of the new buildings."

"Oh, yeah—that would be Doc Simon and Doc Bousper, I bet—I got here right after, but I saw the plans. You were in on that?" she asked, interested despite herself—these were architectural discussions she could find something worth engaging in, even if it was just to find out more about what the labyrinth of human passages within the zoo looked like.

Halfway through the next drink, their friends came out from the bar and announced they were heading out. Sam was hanging on her architect, though Jenny and the other man were separate enough that Lauren guessed they wouldn't be leaving together. "You want me to give you a ride home, hon?" Sam asked her, mid-giggle at whatever it was her architect's hand was doing—under her skirt.

Lauren smiled back, and only hesitated to nod for a moment in assent when Jerry jumped in to say that he'd make sure she got home safely. She was enjoying the conversation they were having, now that they were outside, and the fifth Margarita of the night had her floating pleasantly, and less concerned than earlier that her found date was a smoker who seemed slightly less than concerned about her own contributions to the conversation, as long as her eyes were on him. She'd passed the night in worse company, and after all, tonight was about forgetting David—and this man was the opposite of him, if anything. As Jerry flagged down the waitress for another round, she forced herself to note all of the differences she could, from what she could see.

David had been a fighter, all hardness and edges and muscle, and at least 6 foot. His skin had seemed naturally tan, and his nails had been rough. His hands had been rough in general—from work and labor and fighting, she had to guess—and his eyes had been a deep, heady brown. He'd had that scar on his hand, and worn a steel ring on his left middle finger. His face had been chiseled, his hair short enough that it could have been military style which had grown out into a conservative guy's cut, but well-trimmed, and she hadn't seen any tattoos. He'd had a kind smile when he'd flirted with her in the bar, and a bad sense of humor that she'd enjoyed, and ...she forced herself to stop thinking of him then, reminding herself that she'd only thought of him at all so that she could note how different Jerry was.

Jerry wasn't the opposite, but he was close. He was tall, but then, most guys were tall in comparison to her, and his eyes were also brown, if a lighter shade, but the similarities ended there. He was thinner than David had been, and had a narrower face that split apart with blindingly white teeth and an easy smile, but his hair was too long to be fashionable or really flattering. His skin was lightly tanned, and she'd guess it was from weekends at the lake or on a yacht, given that his hands were smooth—almost too smooth for a guy's, and with manicured fingers. The only thing marring his flesh that she could see was the end of the tribal tattoo coming down his arm, and the only jewelry he wore was a flashy watch.

Bringing her focus back to the present moment, he leaned forward and touched his lips to hers, pressing in. Lauren met him, tasting the salt and the liquor on his lips, and telling herself to enjoy it, but her undeniable instinct was to push him away. She didn't protest when his hands found their way above her knees, though, under her dress, and rested on her lower thighs, but she trembled when she thought about David's hands having been in the same spot, the thought coming to her mind without being invited and freezing her for just a moment. Jerry's hands were gentler—but they felt wrong. Lauren knew it was just the spell telling her what to think, but it bothered her. Actively, consciously, she pushed down the hesitation and leaned further into the architect, pushing her tongue against his lips and not pulling back when he bit down and held her lip for a second longer than she would have liked, one of his hands reaching further up her leg until she pressed her hand on his, through her skirt, to stall him.

When he pulled back, she gulped what was left of the ice and liquid in her glass, and breathed the night deeply into her lungs. Why was she suddenly tired, and nervous? She was supposed to be enjoying this, like Sam most certainly was right at this moment. Repeating the thought, she looked into his eyes and smiled, and when he asked her if she wanted to get going, she said yes. And though she had some doubts in the car, she didn't give any indication of them. Instead, she acted her part as well as she could, and he believed her.

Remembering how her body had felt electric with every one of David's touches, and how her skin had seemed to practically thrum beneath his, she'd thought that things would be okay, and she'd thought that a night with another man's hands and body on her would help. She'd thought that, though maybe she wouldn't enjoy sex as much, or come alive like she had, that it would be okay. And though maybe probably it wouldn't be nearly the same, it would release some of her stress and some of her worry, and let her know that the spell wasn't so bad as it had once sounded. Maybe it wouldn't be ecstasy with Jerry, but it would be something to take all of the nerves from her body and give her some relief. To tell her that she could have post-David relationships, and her body wouldn't stop her.

But as soon as they got to her room, she realized she'd been terribly wrong.

When Jerry kissed her, pushing her back toward her bed, all she tasted was cigarettes—it was as if all of the attraction she'd felt at the bar, what little of it there had been, had all been a trick just brought out by the atmosphere, and even the taste of him now was less pleasant with every pressing moment, now that they were in the intimacy of her studio apartment and the stakes had been raised. She put her hands against his chest to attempt to push him backward gently, but he leaned over her and pressed her into the bed so that her hands were trapped awkwardly between them as his hand found its way beneath her skirt.

Trying to speak against his lips, or slip sideways, she found that she was getting nowhere; if anything, his hands were becoming more persistent, and she could feel his cock growing against her thigh, through their clothing. She had to stop this before it went further, she realized.

Pushing against him, she tried to push at his legs and got nowhere as his hand slid further up her thigh, and then she felt two of his long fingers push aside her panties and slowly force their way into her, dry and hard, and forceful—insistent. She gasped against his lips and jerked back with the surprise of the penetration, suddenly sober and wondering how she could have let him inside of her apartment at all. Why had she thought this might be a good idea?

She turned her face sideways against his as he pulled his fingers away and then pressed them back into her fast. "I don't think this ...this was a mistake; I want you to stop," she said, pushing confidence into her voice even as she winced at the pain his fingers were bringing.

He kept his fingers inside of her and raised up, leering into her face. "I've been putting in time with you all night, baby, and you brought me here, into your room. What did you expect?" he asked, dropping his full weight back onto her as his other hand pulled both of her wrists up and over her head, landing them down against the mattress. She yelled into his shoulder just as Jerry pushed his fingers further into her, the rest of his hand digging into her most intimate parts, his expensive watch pressing hard into her skin, cutting her. She was dry, and felt more and more raw as he pressed against her; this was starting to hurt far worse than anything she'd experienced with David, and it occurred to her that she'd never felt this threatened by anything he'd done— panicked, yes, but she hadn't thought he would *hurt* her, or feared him like she feared the man who was on top of her now.

"Quit! Stop! No!" she told him, pushing back.

Suddenly, she couldn't even remember if she'd ever bothered to tell David no at all—she'd had doubts, but so much of them had come from the spell and the situation. She wasn't sure she'd ever really told him to stop, and tonight, it had never occurred to her that Jerry wouldn't stop if she told him to. "Jerry, I said no!" she yelled, trying to buck up against him.

"And I said yes," he insisted, biting her neck and pressing harder into her pussy. "Why the fuck are you so dry?" he demanded of her next, sounding angry, but she couldn't catch her breath to answer.

When he let her go and stood up, she lay where she was for a moment and caught her breath, listening to him rummage in her nightstand. Then, taking a deep breath, she lunged to her feet and toward the door, her one thought to get out of the apartment.

He caught her before she made it.

Swinging her around and pushing her back to the door, he overpowered her before she could even touch the lock. Her eyes found his just as his hand landed hard on the side of her face, blasting into her eye. She'd thought, before, that David's back-hands had hurt, but now she realized how much he had to have been holding back. Those hits had stung her cheek, but this made those touches feel like bee stings, if that. Jerry's fist had felt like cement with that hit, banging her head back into the door, and blinking twice still left things fuzzy.

Before she'd gotten her bearings, his hand slammed into her head again, and then again ...and then there was nothing.

When Lauren woke, she kept her eyes closed; everything was pain. Her whole head was throbbing, and her hands were twisted together behind her back, awkwardly, but she wasn't even on the bed—they were on the floor, and he was on top of her, his fingers forced into her raw pussy, pressing and moving back and forth. She groaned with the pressure when she felt one of his nails and opened her eyes. He was staring down at her.

"I was wondering when you'd wake up," he told her, and she saw that the man she'd brought home was both drunk and mean. She would have seen it earlier, if she'd been in her right mind and had her senses—she would have realized he was simply bad, like she'd somehow felt David was good, and she couldn't, even now, feel she'd been wrong about that. But this man was something else—he was all anger and narcissism, and she just hadn't noticed. Now, he was angry that she'd tried to refuse him, and that she wasn't responding, and she was stuck. Her head was throbbing, everything fuzzy. Finding her breath, she spit hard into his eye, and then screamed as his fingers inside of her curled up and pressed against her inner wall in response, a third forcing its way in a moment later.

"I've never felt a dryer bitch, but you're asking for this," he growled, and then he was off of her and pulling her to her feet by one twisted elbow. Holding her by the neck and by her wrists, he yanked her upward and slammed her into the tall footboard of her bed so that the breath was slammed out of her, and then he did it twice more until she thought she'd never breathe again, and she couldn't move, her ribs hurt so badly from the force of the hits against her wooden footboard. Her room was a blur in front of her eyes, her head facing the wall, and now her whole abdomen was screaming in pain as he pressed into her from behind.

She was barely aware of the sound of him tearing open a condom, but kept trying to squirm away. She couldn't breathe with the pain of what she was feeling, not enough to cry out for help and expect to be heard, and it seemed like her body was only becoming tighter, trying to keep him out, but at every moment she kept telling him no, consciously saying his name, again and again, until she felt his fist slam against her cheekbone from the side, even as she felt his member tearing into her.

When she woke again, he was gone, and she was lying on the floor by her bed, her whole body a mess of pain that throbbed out from her head, her ribs, and her vagina; she felt like he'd torn her open and beaten her with cement, and she wasn't sure that she wasn't dying. She wasn't sure she cared if she was, she hurt so badly. She just didn't want to feel anything else.

***

When she came to again, she lay still for a long time, aching.

She didn't do anything that weekend. She moved enough to put on a nightgown and get into bed, and only left bed for the bathroom and to try to lie in a bath, hoping that that would ease her aches. Even when she saw herself in the mirror, though, she didn't think about going to a hospital, and when going to the bathroom was so painful that it brought tears to her eyes, she still simply went back to bed, trying to deny the pain. Ever since she'd been a child and happened to see some horrific injuries while visiting a dying relative, hospitals had terrified her, and she'd never gone back. The few broken bones she'd had had been taken care of by simple healing spells, and a family doctor's office had taken care of her few other needs; for witches, hospitals were a last resort, and generally meant life or death situations.

Lauren was no exception to the rule, except in that she was actually terrified of them, and in that it seemed she was no longer a witch. Nevertheless, she couldn't face one. Maybe she would have reported the rape if she could have, but with everything else she was dealing with, attempting to get the police involved seemed less than desirable, no matter the arguments for doing it. And besides that, reporting it would require a rape exam, which required a hospital, and she was having such trouble staying awake and focusing that it all seemed like far too much effort to be contemplated.

Come Monday, she looked worse, and didn't feel any better, but she knew she couldn't lay in her apartment any longer. It hurt to breathe, though, and to move. She had a black eye, and the left side of her face was swollen, from her lower cheek up beyond her eye, to say nothing of her lips, which were wholly swollen and bruised. She didn't even look like herself. Her upper abdomen offered a kaleidoscope of bruises, as did her upper chest around her collarbone and into her shoulders. Seeing herself in the mirror, she now realized that David had been treating her with kid gloves. The bruises he'd left on her had been gone in a matter of a few days, and not really hurt at all once they'd been left. These throbbed constantly, and she knew she ought to go to a hospital, but she couldn't face it. And she was running out of time.

The letter Mary had spoken of had gotten to her door on Friday, as promised. Now it was the 26th, and they wanted her to report to the coven 'for custody' on or by the 30th.

After forcing herself to eat a half a bowl of oatmeal and sip some water, she picked up the phone to call Josh Devlin. And then she hung up, and dialed again, and hung up again. She couldn't even decide whether or not to ask him to come to her, or ask to meet him, or just try to talk on the phone, and her head was pounding, though she'd just taken another aspirin an hour before sitting down. How many had she taken in the last few hours? She wasn't sure, but nothing was helping and she wasn't getting better; she had to make the call, or lose the week to fuzzy consciousness and pain.

She picked up the phone again, and held it for a moment before she put it down all over again. She decided she had to see him to have a chance at convincing him to help her—especially since she couldn't quite think straight, and wasn't sure how convincing her words would be—and she thought that, if anything, maybe the state she was in would earn some sympathy help ...but that still left her staring at her phone, trying to get up the courage to pick it up and take a shot at her last chance.

Chapter 6

Devlin was sitting at his desk and going over potential cases they'd been sent for review. With nothing pressing, it was up to them whether or not to take a commission on something or take a few days off until they got called in, and he was feeling inclined to take the time off. The smallpox shit hadn't been what either he or David had signed on for, and while blowing off steam had helped take the edge off, they didn't need the money, and he wasn't necessarily anxious to jump into something without a few days off.

Plus, he had a date scheduled; he'd taken Claudia to Pinacelli's for Italian as planned, and their chemistry had been instant. Neither of them had had any desire to rush things, so they'd said goodnight at her door, but he was planning on picking her up again that evening so they could go to a local jazz club. The day, though, was his.

When his phone rang for the first time, he answered it without looking at the number, but the line was dead. The second time, there was silence, and then a hang-up when he demanded a response from the number he didn't recognize. Fifteen minutes later, when it rang again, he made sure to look at the number more carefully—it was unblocked, which was itself a surprise, but didn't bring up any of his contacts. Annoyed, he picked it up once more and determined that he'd turn the damned thing off for a while if this was another hang-up.

"Who is this?" he asked.

"Uh ...Mr. Devlin? Josh?"

The voice on the other line was shaky, and Josh didn't recognize it—he also never went by 'Mr.' anything. It was 'Agent Devlin' or it was his first name that got given out. "Who is this?" he asked again, rather than answering.

"It's ...sorry, it's, um, Lauren ...Merriweather. You gave me your card?"

He sat back from his computer. Her voice was trembling, stuttering, but now he recognized it; he just hadn't expected it. "Yeah, this is me," he said, standing and taking a step to his suite's entrance, closing the door so that his partner wouldn't hear the conversation if he happened by. "What's going on?"

"You said you guys owed me ...I didn't want ...I didn't want to call, but ...I need help. I was hoping, maybe, we could meet? I mean, if you meant that, what you said, about if I ...needed something."

Josh took a seat at his desk again, staring at his screen blankly. He had given her his card, but he hadn't really expected a call. If anything, he'd thought the call would be coming from a police station within hours of his dropping her off, but after a few days of hearing nothing ...

"What do you need?" he asked finally.

The answer was slow in coming, as it seemed all of her words were; even listening to her, he couldn't imagine what would have made her call. And her voice was muffled, so that he almost wondered if she was drunk, or stoned. "I ...it's complicated. I was just hoping ...I could drive to you?" she offered.

Her voice sounded like it was close to tears, too, and truth be told, Josh felt like they owed her quite a bit—the way things had gone with her hadn't sat well with him, or with David, for that matter. His partner still wasn't right about it or quite himself, and had avoided any mention of her, but he was drinking more and staying to himself more than usual, which Josh had to trace back to the girl on the other end of this phone. And curiosity almost always got the better of Devlin anyway. "You were thinking today, I take it?" he asked.

"Whenever you can," she answered.

Looking at his watch, he replied, "There's a diner called The Liberty Grill'n'Go off of State Road 34, running west from you; it should be about halfway between us. You want to meet there—say, an hour and a half from now?"

He heard her sigh across the line, in what sounded like relief, and then she agreed.

Walking into the diner just over an hour later, he wasn't sure what to expect. The place was mostly empty. It was 2:30, so the lunch crowd was gone and the dinner rush hadn't yet started. He took a booth in one of the far corners, and ordered two waters and a coffee.

When Lauren walked in a few minutes later, his eyes were already passing over her before he suddenly recognized her. She had an oversized beret-type hat pulled over her head, one side pulled low and holding her hair so that it covered the whole left side of her face in a style he would have equated with an angsty high schooler. She also wore a scarf, though the weather outside was fair, and she stepped into the place haltingly, favoring her right side. When she turned in his direction and took a step toward his table, it was all he could do not to spill his coffee, seeing some of the bruises she was trying to hide.

Lauren held onto the door, letting herself catch her breath before she approached the table. She felt dizzy. The drive had been hard, the seatbelt a bitch, and the thought of making the return trip made her want to cry. At least Devlin was here, though, and hadn't stood her up.

What the fuck? He stood hurriedly and came around the booth, and then ushered her into the seat he'd taken before so that the bruised side of her face would be to the wall and get less attention than what she'd gotten upon walking in. Up close, she looked worse, and he let her sip shakily at the full glass of water he pushed toward her before he said anything. She looked like she'd been beaten half to pieces. He didn't think anything was broken, though it could have been, but he was sure that the bruises went straight down to the bone, just based on the discoloration.

"You look like shit. What happened?"

"That's not what I'm here about," she said quietly, still not meeting his eyes.

Devlin stared at her, his hand twitching to call his partner so that they could go after whoever had done this. And yet, she came in looking like this, having said she needed help, and this wasn't what it was about? "You want coffee?" he asked. Upon her nod, he lifted his own coffee cup toward the waitress and gestured for two.

Lauren finally glanced up at him, her left eye bloodshot and nearly swollen shut, and her right eye skirting around his, taking him in, though it didn't seem like she was quite focusing on him or anything else. He watched her gaze wavering; no doubt, she had a concussion—he couldn't believe she'd driven herself.

"You're alone?" she asked.

He shrugged, still focused on her bruises. "Wasn't sure you'd want to see my partner, all things considered. You gonna tell me who did this to you?"

Lauren pulled a bottle of Aleve from her purse and drank two pills down with the water—now that she was seated, she wanted nothing more than to lay her head on the table and pass out. "I need your help," she said instead of answering him. "I need you, uh, to reverse the mix ...the one you guys gave me," she said, and winced as she tried to take a deep breath to continue, pain shooting through her ribs in reaction; it was worse since the drive she'd taken to get here. "I get that you guys were ...doing what you thought you had to do ...but I need to be able to cast at least basic spells. Like healing ones," she added.

Josh nodded at the waitress as she dropped their coffees and frowned at the girl across from him; if this was why she'd come, she'd wasted both their time. "I can't do it," he told her simply, and held her gaze when she looked at him.

"Can't or won't?"

"Both. Our boss gave us that mix—it's not like we put it together ourselves. And far as I know, there's no reversing it." He sipped his coffee as he watched Lauren close her eyes and take a halting breath—she wasn't breathing right, he noticed. "Have you been to a hospital yet?" he asked suddenly, eyeing the Aleve bottle now peeking from the pocket of her purse. He'd have expected a heavier pain killer, something prescription-level.

Lauren just shook her head, blocking him out. "If you had to, could you look into it, to see if there was a way of reversing it?"

"Depends why, I guess, but I'm going to ask you again, Lauren—have you been to a hospital?" Josh leaned forward, catching her downcast eyes. She was clearly afraid. Of whoever had done this to her, he guessed, but maybe him also. She was also swaying, even in her seat, as if she was dizzy.

"I'm afraid of hospitals. I'll be okay. The thing is," she went on, loosely holding his eyes, "I won't be okay if I don't get my powers back. That's why I called," she explained quietly. "My mom's coven—as far as they're concerned, I'm a liability if I don't have them."

"A liability?" he echoed, waiting for her to continue. Lauren took another breath, and Josh watched her do it, already wondering if he'd have to drag her to a hospital or if he could convince her, and which hospital he should get her to. Did she have anyone to come look after her at this point? They hadn't bothered to check, but there was no way she ought to be driving; he was surprised she hadn't crashed, just driving the straight road to get to where they sat now.

"They won't let me live apart from the coven; they'll ...it'll be like being a slave, Mr. Devlin. It doesn't matter that I'd left all that behind—and I had," she said, anger pressing into her voice for the first time since she'd come in. "If I can't show them that I'm still a witch, like them, they'll ...keep me. I'll be a servant to them for the rest of my life; I won't *have* a life. And I can't hide from them," she continued, her voice wavering less now that she'd gotten going. "I need to be able to cast basic spells. Even if I don't get everything back, I need *something*," she emphasized. "You two said you didn't intend to ruin my life, but right now, you have; I'm just ...I'm just asking for you to help me keep going, so that I can live any life at all. I deserve that," she finished, her voice cracking as she spoke. Then she leaned back, breathing jerkily, and letting her eyes shut for a minute, as if the brief monologue had taken all of the energy she'd had.

Devlin sat staring at her. So far as he knew, there wasn't a way to reverse the spell. And he also didn't have any reason to disbelieve what she was saying, though it certainly wasn't something they'd had cause to suspect would happen. He'd honestly thought that, by now, Lauren would have been back to her normal life of grad school and studying, and getting used to life without spells.

"What happened to you?" he asked again, if only to give himself time to think about what she'd told him already, and to keep her awake.

Sipping her coffee, Lauren hunched into herself, but her eyes appraised him. "If I tell you, you'll see what you can do?"

"We'll talk," he promised.

After a moment, she nodded. She told him, in brief, about the end of her week, and she told him more than she meant to. She told him about going to see the witch she'd been closest to, and being warned off and told to 'make any arrangements' she needed to and report to the coven. And about wanting to get her mind off of things, and going out with girlfriends, and meeting a man who she'd thought seemed decent. And about how her instincts for danger had been erased, with her powers, and that the decent guy turned into a monster, and that this was the first time she'd left her apartment since, he being the first person she'd spoken to.

When she stopped speaking, Josh edged her water glass closer to her, and pulled some napkins from the table's dispenser for her. It looked like she was fighting tears to stay calm in front of him, and her breath was hitching and paining her with the effort of it. "He raped you?" he asked quietly, but she didn't respond.

She looked away again before speaking in a way that told him the truth of things, hesitating. "I told you, he's not why I'm here—I'm here because I need help."

"Yeah, you do," he agreed with her before going silent again. "You can't lie, can you?" he asked after a few minutes of silence. He could see that she'd told him more than she'd meant to—he'd seen it in her face even as she'd been speaking, like she was too tired to fight the urge to just answer his question naturally—and her non-response to his last question had triggered something in him, to remember their time with her at the house; she'd never lied—she'd only not responded. Even then, when she could have bought herself time, she hadn't fibbed once. He'd wondered at it, but not at any length until now.

After a pause, she nodded. "A spell my mom cast on me."

"Jesus Christ," he muttered, and closed his eyes to think about everything laid out before him. "I'll tell you what," he offered after another moment, leaning forward. "You let me take you to a hospital, get you checked out, I'll see what I can do."

Lauren jerked up, her face going white with the sudden movement and the pain it caused, and Josh watched the panic run through her before he finally gave in to his instincts and reached out to cover her hand with his. "You need a doctor, Lauren. I'll see what I can do, though I can't make any promises, but I can't let you just get back in your car, the shape you're in. Fuck, I'm surprised you got here at all, the shape you're in."

"I can't," she said, shaking her head as her eyes darted back to the table and she wrapped both of her hands around her coffee mug. "They're ...they're too much. It's the only thing I'm scared of, besides the coven," she added. She couldn't even imagine walking into a hospital. Forget the questions that they'd ask and how much it would hurt to have a doctor prodding at her injuries, or the fact that the school-provided health insurance was such shit as to be nearly worthless.

She literally couldn't imagine getting up the strength to walk into an emergency room and ask for treatment. The thought of being alone in one of those hospital rooms, where she'd only seen people dying and suffering ...she couldn't handle it, even though she knew Devlin was right. She couldn't see straight, and she couldn't breathe without hurting, but it seemed like she kept seeing Jerry in the corners of her vision whenever she let her guard down, and the idea of being dropped off at an ER ...in a strange place, and alone ...it was too much; hell, she'd probably see him in the doctor who ended up treating her. And she'd barely gotten herself here. She'd die of fear before she could get treatment, she thought.

"I'll be with you," Josh finally told her, at a loss for what else he could say or do, short of dragging her out of the diner and causing God knew what kind of a scene to unfold. There was so much panic on her face, and her lips were fluttering with unspoken protests, but there was serious consideration there, too. She knew as well as he did that she needed a doctor; he didn't let himself think about how desperate or alone she must feel, to be willing to find comfort in his own presence being promised.

Finally, to his surprise, his final offer of being with her did the trick, and he watched her give a jerky nod from across the table, her hands still clenched around the coffee mug.

After paying the bill and escorting her outside, he opened the door to his Mustang for her and watched her gingerly recline into the bucket seat; her car would be fine here for the afternoon, and he'd find someone to come get it later, already realizing she wouldn't be able to drive home that day. Inside the car, he waited for her to buckle up before he pulled out, letting her stew in her own thoughts as he headed west, toward the hospital that was closest to the ranch house, and where he knew the ER nurses and could most easily get her seen quickly, and in and out without a fuss.

True to form, the small hospital's ER was pretty quiet, and his badge sped things up; within minutes, he'd signed off on the intake paperwork and she'd been settled in a private exam room, nurses flitting in and out to take care of her. Lauren had been drifting into a panic almost as soon as they'd come in, trembling and all but hyperventilating in a way that had made him want to panic, himself, but the nurses had been fast with some drugs to get her calmed down so that she didn't further injure herself. Then Josh watched the examination unfold, and wasn't all that surprised when the doctor lifted up her shirt to reveal dark bruising all along her rib cage and stomach that led down into her jeans.

While she was getting an X-ray and having her eye bandaged, it was the same doc who he'd watched examine her that approached him to ask about sexual assault and a police report. Knowing it had happened Friday night, though, Devlin realized that there wasn't much point in a rape exam, even if she'd have been willing to consent to it, which she'd insisted in the car wouldn't be the case. The police report was an easier conversation—since he counted as law enforcement, it was a simple matter to let the doctor know that that part was already taken care of and in the works.

An hour later, she was half-sedated in the hospital bed and he was sitting in a visitor's chair when the doctor came back.

"Well, it's a miracle nothing's broken, but we're not far off," he told them. "There's bruising to the cheekbone and eye socket, but no fracture—that's going to be painful, and the bruising will last a while, but as long as no further trauma occurs, it shouldn't require surgery. You do have two rib fractures," he said, facing her, and then turning to Devlin to deliver the rest of his news when it seemed like she was struggling to follow him, given the haze of the medications.

"And, as suspected, there's a serious concussion, which isn't any surprise, considering the bruise at the back of her head and the facial trauma; she may want to sleep a lot this week, and that's fine. She needs to be watched. We're going to give her a prescription for a pain killer for the ribs and her head that will also help her sleep, though the Aleve she's carrying should be good enough after a week or two, if not less. She needs to rest, and avoid getting worked up so that those ribs don't actually break. They will take a good 4 weeks to heal, but she'll be fine as long as she doesn't fall or get hit and re-injure anything. If she does fall or the pain gets worse, you bring her back here right away," he said, watching the girl close her eyes and emphasizing all of his words as he continued.

"She needs to be still to the extent that she can for two weeks, off her feet for at least one. And that bandage stays on her eye for five days. You know how to deal with the rib injuries, but that eye needs real rest also," he told Josh. "Does she have someone who she can stay with for a week or two so she can be on bed-rest, much as possible, or will you be around?"

Josh nodded without comment, noting that the girl in question was too dazed to really react; the IV they'd given her had done a number on not just her panic, but her level of awareness, as well. When the doctor had left, though, and Josh prodded her hand to see if she was awake, she proved she still had some of her attitude, at least.

"You're not going to tie me to a chair this time, are you?" she breathed out slowly, and Devlin allowed himself to chuckle in response, garnering what looked like a scared smile from her before she closed her eyes again. He knew she had to be drunk on pain killers to have made the remark, but it left him some hope that his partner was wrong, and that they'd not totally taken her spirit after all, as he'd feared.

***

With the doctor wanting to let the IV run its course, Josh slipped out to make some additional phone calls. The first went to Claudia, postponing their date to the jazz club and instead inviting her on a drive to pick up Lauren's car. The next call went to David.

"Hey, what's up? Where are you?" Josh asked.

"I'm at the house—where are you?"

Damn—so I guess I tell him now, after all. "You're going to have to hear me out on this one," he answered quietly, looking through the exam room's glass at the beaten girl he'd all but taken responsibility for at this point. "I'm at the ER, with Lauren Merriweather."

After a long pause, David's voice came back, tense.

"That's it? Am I supposed to know what to do with that?"

"Look, I'll have to explain later, but she needs a safe house, and she needs someone to keep an eye on her. I'm gonna bring her back to our place, maybe in an hour or so."

"And you think that's a good idea," David said flatly.

Josh didn't see what choice he had. "I think it's the *only* idea. I just wanted to give you a heads-up," he answered. "You good?" In reply, there was some murmured response that Josh couldn't quite make out, and then a click before the line went dead.

Back in Lauren's room, she barely reacted when he told her that he was going to take her back to the ranch house, where the coven wouldn't be able to reach her while they figured things out. More than ever, he was grateful for the sedative effects of pain killers.

***

At the house, David paced in the kitchen while he listened to his partner moving around and getting Lauren settled in the nicer of the guest rooms. He'd watched them come in on a security camera, and seen that she looked like she'd had a run-in with a fight club. She'd been stumbling along, with Josh half holding her up as he brought her in, clearly drugged, and with her face swollen up like a boxer's.

When Josh finally entered the kitchen, David took a seat at the island and simply stared, waiting.

"We need to get her car from the Liberty, and get some of her things from her apartment, as much as we can."

David waited, unblinking.

"What did you want me to do? Leave her at the ER?"

"That where you found her?" David asked evenly.

Josh took a seat after taking a beer from the fridge, glancing behind him toward the guest rooms as he did so. "She called this morning, said she needed help. I gave her my card when I dropped her off at her place last month, in case ...in case, I don't know what," he shrugged. "Figured this morning that I'd be gone for a few hours, take care of whatever it was without you having to worry about it."

David sat stock-still, staring at him and listening to the rest of the story, from what Lauren had told his partner on through the exchanges at the ER and her nearly comatose ride back to the ranch house after a stop at a pharmacy. "So what," he finally spoke up, "we need to clear out her apartment?"

"I figure I'll hire movers to box up her stuff and put it in storage. If you're up for keeping an ear out, Claudia and I'll go get her car today, and then I'll go into the city tomorrow and pack up what'll fit in a few suitcases, and maybe her computer. Claudia has the day off—I'll see if she can go with me again and help me figure out what she'll need. Kid told me today she's not going back to school this semester, so it's just a matter of taking what she'll need while she gets it together."

"Gets it together here, you mean," David answered, and Josh nodded. What else was there to say? If she'd called Devlin for help, it wasn't like they had much reason to believe she'd had anyone else to turn to.

Chapter 7

Lauren came to in the dark, with only a vague idea that she wasn't in her own bed. Her body felt numb, and there was a heavy blanket pressing her into the mattress where she slept in a comfortably cool room, but it didn't smell like the hospital. She didn't *feel* like she was in the hospital; she didn't feel scared. Blindly, she reached her hand out and found the side of the bed, and soon after that she found the base of a lamp and a switch. When she turned it on, she blinked until she could focus, feeling the bandage on her one eye that held it shut, and then she saw the room, and everything came back.

Josh had told her he planned to bring her back to the ranch house, where he and David lived, and that she'd be safe here while they figured out what to do about the coven. That it was warded, and they wouldn't find her here, and that he and David would pick up her car and some things from her apartment. And she'd been scared of the hospital, and lost in a daze of painkillers, and she'd agreed because she hadn't known what else to do, or even how to refuse. That had to have been around six, when they'd left the hospital.

What time was it now? Were the men around, or was she alone? And more importantly, could she find it in herself to get up and get a glass of water? Her throat was parched, and she couldn't quite think straight, she was so tired ...

Groggy, and moving slowly, Lauren raised herself up. She could feel the same ache in her middle that had been there before, but at least she could breathe now without being in so much pain; whatever the doctor had given her was still working. Inching her legs off of the bed, she kept her hands on the edge of the mattress for support as she stood up, getting her bearings. She felt unsteady, but not dizzy, which seemed like a good sign, but her mouth was desperately dry. The door to her room was open—that had to mean that she could wander, without them getting upset, right?

She blinked a few times, standing there, and then she slowly took her hands away from the bed. A glance in the mirror beside the door told her she looked no different than she had earlier, if slightly more rumpled, though her scarf had gotten lost somewhere along the way, and her V-neck showed the bruising along her collarbone now.

Going slowly, she stepped into the hall and leaned on the wall; she felt weak, but what sounded like ice hitting a glass drew her to the left. When she got to the point where the hall emptied out into the kitchen, she came to a jerky halt and let herself lean against the wall again, looking in. It was David, who she'd been hoping for weeks to never see again, while also hoping desperately that that wouldn't be the case. He was facing away from her, but his build and his hair were different enough from his partner's that there was no doubt of who it was. He had a hefty book open in front of him on the island, and a rocks glass of amber liquid by his right hand, his fingers running along the rim of the glass. Suddenly, she was thankful enough that there were enough drugs left in her system to be smoothing out the moment.

She wanted to turn around, but there was no telling when she'd be able to make herself get up again once she got back in that bed, and she was so thirsty ...

She coughed to announce herself, but should have simply said a hello; the contraction of her chest with the cough hurt like hell and jerked her sideways into the wall, which was even more painful. Before she had gotten herself together again, she felt David's hands on her arm and her shoulder, guiding her to a stool, and she couldn't help inhaling the cologne that she wished seemed less familiar.

Tilting her further into the kitchen, David wondered if he was imagining that she felt frailer than she had when last they'd met, and wondered if the bruises he saw on her chest were also on her arm and shoulder, beneath his hands. But he didn't know where to touch her without guessing and potentially hurting her, so he kept his grip on her until she was firmly settled on a stool, her hands on the counter to steady herself. Her nails were ragged now, bitten to the quick.

"You shouldn't be out of bed," he told her, hearing the growl in his own voice. He'd have to save the anger for Josh if he could, though—the man had to know he'd been trying to get this girl out of his head for the last two weeks.

"I'm sorry," she answered, blinking slowly as if she

were still waking up. "This wasn't—I didn't mean to, to end up here," she fumbled, closing her eyes with the words to try to get past the sudden dizziness that had come with the pain of her cough. "Can I have some water?"

Blinking, Lauren looked around the kitchen—it was clean, and comfortable, and the island she sat at had a warm wood top. She could imagine falling asleep here, right where she was.

"Right." David turned to the cabinet, wondering what he was supposed to do at this point. Josh was still off retrieving her car with Claudia, who'd been glad to help, and he hadn't expected Lauren to wake up any time soon. Earlier, he'd glanced into the room and seen her passed out cold, and gotten his first good look at the horror-show bruises on her face and along her collarbone, as well as her wrists. It hurt just to look at them, and he'd retreated to whiskey soon after seeing them. Especially her wrists reminded him of what he himself had done to her, and he dreaded the idea of checking her ribs later, to make sure she hadn't been further injured when she fell against the wall a moment ago.

Now, he passed water to her across the island and watched her sip at it. All of her moves were hesitant, and he guessed that everything was hurting her. "You can have some more pain killers at midnight, but we're not there yet," he told her, gesturing at the prescription bottle set on the counter with their salt and pepper shakers. "You okay?" he added, seeing her gaze slide sideways and then back as if she couldn't quite focus on even the nearby bottles.

She nodded, glancing fully up at him for the first time. He didn't look like he'd shaved today, and he could have been wearing the exact same jeans and t-shirt she'd last seen him in, for all the difference she could see. And God help her, but her body was humming, being back in his presence; she could almost still feel the warmth on her arm, above her elbow, where he'd gripped her to guide her to the stool where she now sat, and her shoulder ...Belatedly, she realized she'd been staring at him; the drugs were doing their work to the extent that she seemed only to be aware of sensations, whether pleasant or painful, and she blinked her eyes hard to try to bring herself back to the men's kitchen.

"Have you eaten anything today?" he asked suddenly. "Josh said you had some coffee with him, but he didn't know if you'd eaten anything else."

"I'm fine. I had some oatmeal, this morning."

"This morning, right." David turned away, glad to have something to do. He might not know what to say, but at least he knew how to scramble some eggs and get together a late dinner for her. "Think you can handle eggs and toast?" he asked her, already opening the fridge as he glanced to her for a response. She looked off-balance, but she nodded. "I'll have food up before you know it," he promised, slamming the fridge's door and turning to the stove.

"You don't have to ...do anything," she said helplessly, letting herself lean forward onto her arms. "I think I just need to sleep, and then I can go home."

When David didn't respond, Lauren let herself hunch forward on her folded arms and watch him move around the kitchen. She told herself she shouldn't be watching him like this, or feeling so comfortable—almost comforted—in his presence, considering what he'd done to her, just weeks ago, but she couldn't hold onto the thoughts, and closed her eyes instead to let herself just rest her eyes, for a moment. And then she was asleep.

David kept doing what he was doing, dropping eggs

in the pan in front of him even as he saw her eyes close. He knew it had been the drugs in her system doing the talking, and also knew that she didn't, at this point, have any home to speak of. By the time she was ready to go back to her apartment, the coven they had little method of tracking would be waiting for her, if what Josh had said was true. What she had was them, and the ranch house where her whole nightmare had started, with him.

Chapter 8

David had seen his fair share of concussions, and had two himself—one from high school sports, and a more recent one due to a scuffle in a case. For him, they'd meant a lot of fuzziness, and difficulty concentrating on anything, which had amounted to him sleeping for the better part of a week each time, and being a slug for a week after that. He'd seen others react differently, and his partner acted more like he was stoned than anything when he got a hard hit to the head, but it seemed that Lauren leaned more toward David's own tendencies. Essentially, she went into hibernation—much as a human could, anyway.

It had been something like two weeks now since they'd brought her to the ranch house, and for most of that time, she'd lain in bed, sleeping and healing. At first, David had avoided her. He'd let Josh and even

Josh's new girlfriend do most of the checking in, leaving food for her that she nibbled on when she woke and pushing her to drink more water. When a minor case had come up, David had even left to handle it on his own, leaving Josh to mind the house and babysit. Yet, after more than a week had gone by without much change, he'd started looking in more often. Before he'd known it, that had translated into him going out of his way to check on her, and even hanging out in the room when he drank his morning coffee in case she woke up and needed something. She hadn't asked for anything at all, as of yet.

The truth was, he couldn't figure out how he felt about her being there. He'd gotten over being angry at Josh for meeting her without telling him, and bringing her to the house—what else could he have done, after all?—but he wasn't sure what to do with the way things were. And, more and more, he was admitting that he was drawn to her, and had been since the moment he'd met her. He was running out of reasons to avoid her.

So instead of staying away, now he spent more time in the room than Josh. He worked on his laptop at the desk in her room and told himself he was there in case she needed something, and he let Josh have a break from the babysitting he'd been doing the last few weeks. He watched as Lauren's bruises faded from her face, day by day, and tried not to worry about the weight she was losing from not eating enough. Mostly, she'd been eating bananas and bagels, which he supposed was healthier than the cold pizza and nachos he'd lived on the last time he'd had a concussion. When she woke up bleary-eyed and half-asleep, he handed her water, and helped to steady her when she got up to head to the bathroom.

He never woke her. Claudia and Josh had woken her

a few times, so that she could shower when Claudia was there, in case she lost her balance in the shower and needed help, but otherwise they just let her sleep.

And, slowly, David could see she was getting better, more aware. The effects of the concussion were fading, though she still cringed when his phone rang and she was awake, or when the bathroom light or the hall light were switched on in front of her, each of which glared more strongly than the lamps they'd placed in her room. They'd had the doctor come by, as well, and he'd been satisfied enough with her progress, if not thrilled. He'd made them promise to make sure she ate, and kept taking one more pain pill per day at least to combat the migraines and the rib pain; if not, he warned she'd probably get a sudden pain while out of bed and fall, reinjuring herself. He'd assumed she wouldn't be leaving any time soon, too.

For his part, David had begun doing research on what could, or would, come next. He and Josh had come to the decision that the only way to help her was to get rid of the coven that wanted to wrap her up as their own. Everything they'd read backed up Lauren's story, that she wouldn't have a life outside of the coven now that her magic was gone, and they figured the only options were to track the witches in the coven and either eliminate them or treat them with the mixture they'd pushed into Lauren. They had a lead, right now, on two of them, each of whom had been recently asking around and trying to find Lauren. David was hoping that, assuming she'd support their conclusions, Lauren would be able to give them more names.

"David, you want a break?" Josh asked from the doorway, Claudia lurking behind him. They'd woken Lauren to shower much earlier in the day, but otherwise it had been David who'd been hanging out.

"No, you guys have fun. Pick up some beers if you think about it?" he added, waving them off.

A minute later, David heard the front door close and turned back to his computer, sighing and then taking a sip from his water bottle. Part of him worried that taking magic from more witches would just open up more problems that they hadn't before considered, as it had with Lauren. Now that he'd gotten to know her, to the little extent that he had, it was harder to think of witches as being criminals just for practicing magic.

Lauren blinked her eyes open slowly, squinting at the light by the desk and David's hunched form. He was almost always there when she woke now, working on whatever it was he was doing. She'd asked a few days before, but had fallen back asleep nearly a soon as he'd started telling her about a scientist they'd tracked down to arrest. She was always so tired, and though she knew it was her body insisting on healing time, and the medicine, it was disconcerting. She was down to taking one pain pill a day to deal with the pain in her ribs, along with over-the-counter pills, but medicine had always put her to sleep.

Helpless as she felt, though, she wasn't bothered anymore by David being there. After the first few times of waking up to see him working or drinking coffee and taking occasional glances her way, she'd gotten used to it. She wasn't afraid of him, or even worried he'd hurt her again. If anything, the few times when he'd had to touch her to help her get her balance or move, he'd seemed like he thought she might break to pieces if he wasn't careful.

Now, she winced as she moved slightly sideways, propping herself up enough that she could pull a pillow sideways and lean against it. She wasn't hungry, but there were fruit and bagels on the nightstand, and she knew she needed to eat if she was going to do anything other than sleep, ever.

David heard the bed shift and turned away from his computer; Lauren was pulling herself toward the headboard, gingerly. "You're awake," he said, twisting his chair sideways so that he could look at her. "Can I get you anything?"

Lauren shook her head and reached for an apple, wincing again when she twisted too far to the side. From the corner of her eye, she saw David begin to rise to help, and then settle back into his chair. "I'm okay," she told him, meeting his eyes for a quick moment before she bit into the piece of fruit and leaned back against the headboard.

"Hungry? I can make you something else," he offered, but she shook her head, as he'd guessed she would. They'd been through this the day before also, though she hadn't bothered to sit up then.

"No, I'm fine—I'm really not hungry. I just know ..." she shrugged, letting her words trail off. She wanted to leave her energy for eating, and then she'd go back to sleep. Each time she woke up and began speaking to him or Josh, it got harder to figure out what to say. It was easier to escape into sleep.

Lauren watched as David nodded and turned his head back toward his computer, his body still turned sideways, half toward her. But it was hard to ignore his presence. As always, he was in a t-shirt and jeans, a slight stubble showing along his hard jaw and his lips tight together, as if constantly holding back some comment, though he didn't talk all that much. He'd gotten a haircut since she'd seen him the day before—it was neater now, in that classic boy's style he wore, just a hint of bangs poking over his forehead.

Forcing herself to take the last bite of the apple, she

put the rind down on the nightstand and reached for the water, swallowing down two long sips before she sat back to take in a deep breath and try to give herself a few moments of waking relaxation before she passed out again.

"How long before I should take another pill?" she asked quietly, knowing half of David's attention was still on her and listening—the words on the computer screen had barely scrolled since he'd turned back to it, and her voice never surprised him when she spoke up.

David looked to his computer screen's bottom for the time. "An hour or so, but if you're in pain ..."

"No, I'll wait," she said. She'd tried not taking the pain pill, a few days before, but had awoken in the middle of the night in agony, having turned or twisted somehow and let the medicine get too far out of her system. She hadn't called for help, but by the time Josh had ducked in to find her in the morning, she'd been a mess, having lain awake for most of the night in too much pain to get out of bed, and too stubborn to call for help. She'd been so covered in sweat, and embarrassed enough that she'd decided she wouldn't skip a pain pill any time soon.

Now, she was taking one of the real ones at night, and taking a simple Aleve first thing when she woke up in the morning, and again in the afternoon if she had a headache. Truth be told, after the other night, she was scared to not take the real thing before she tried to sleep through the night, and figured she'd give it at least another week before she did. The doctor had told Josh she should keep using them for a month, and could use them for up to six weeks if necessary, though she hoped that wouldn't be the case. He didn't seem pleased with her ribs' progress, though, and had backed off of thinking that Aleve would do the trick sooner than later.

"You up to talking?" David asked, rolling his chair a few feet closer to her bed and watching her reclining back, water in her hand.

"I guess?" she answered, still thinking about the pills and wondering when her ribs would stop aching. Getting dizzy and falling a few days before hadn't done her any favors, she knew.

David edged his chair closer, examining the girl he saw in front of him. She bore little enough resemblance to the girl he'd first met in that bar, what seemed like a lifetime ago. She was pale, and there was a different quality to her eyes that was both more serious and adult, and more vulnerable. Even without the weight loss and the stiff movements, her eyes would have suggested to anyone who knew her before that she'd been through the ringer over the last month, and he knew he'd played a heavy part in that—there was no denying it, and more nights than not, it kept him up unless he drugged himself with whiskey to stop thinking about it. Each time he got close to her, he expected to see fear coming through, and found himself shocked that it wasn't.

"You told Josh there are ten other witches in the coven?" he asked finally, and watched as she blanched, her throat betraying a swallowing of nerves before she answered.

"Yeah...last I heard. It wasn't something Mom and I talked about," she said quietly, "but I think she would have told me if another had joined. You're going to look for them?" she asked, toying with the cap on her water as she did so. How did she feel about the prospect of them searching out the coven, and whatever Josh and David would do when they were found? There was a pit in her stomach, but she didn't know the answer. Maybe the hollowness was there because she didn't know the answer, she decided, finally meeting David's eyes. He looked sincere, and not at all deadly, though she knew he was.

"I don't think we have a choice, do you? You can't stay in hiding forever."

Lauren shook her head, acknowledging the point. "It wouldn't be forever," she told him, not looking up to meet his eyes. "They'd find me. I'd be with them now, if you guys weren't letting me stay here. I guess I owe you guys," she said, half-choking on the words.

David jerked to his feet and pushed his chair back to the desk, standing in front of it and glaring downward.

"Don't say that. You don't owe us anything," he growled eventually.

Lauren watched the man in front of her pacing back and forth across the room; he looked as if he wanted to punch something, but it didn't seem like there was much point in saying anything to stop him.

"I'm not saying we had a real choice," David finally said, stopping near the door to stare at her, "but that doesn't mean I don't know it's our fault you're in this position. We can't take it back...but the least we can do is try to fix it so you have your life back."

Lauren shrugged, wincing at the pang in her ribs when she did so. "You can't...I mean...you can't kill the whole coven," she finished helplessly. "Or take their magic. Plus, they'd never let you."

"You're saying their lives are more important than yours?" David came to the edge of the bed and sat at the foot of it, perching and waiting. He'd been wondering, knowing what he did of her, whether she'd support what they had to do, but neither he nor Josh had asked; this was as close as he'd gotten.

"I'm saying it doesn't matter," she told him, reaching one hand up to brush her hair backward, and then rubbing her forehead as if she had a headache coming on again. "You can't track all of them down, and as long as one of them is out there, I don't have a life, so there's not much point in you tracking *any* of them down, is there?"

So that's it; she thinks it's pointless. "You know the government keeps tabs on all of the covens out there, or at least tries to?" he asked, and wasn't surprised at the shock he saw when it came to her face. "Your mother's was somehow under the radar, but now that they know of it, their first priority is determining who's a part of it and what they're doing; what they've done in the past. The fact that they've stayed hidden over the years is enough to suggest that most, if not all of them, have broken the law, because there's no way they stayed hidden without trying, hard. Whether you were involved or not, one of our current projects would be to track them down and figure out next steps."

"Next steps?" she asked quietly.

"You know what I mean," David said, annoyance slipping through in his voice. "We had to get rid of your mother; there was no way around it. Others...maybe closing out the magic lines would be enough."

"Even if they've done nothing wrong?"

"Wanting to keep you as a slave isn't wrong? Is that what you're saying?" Leaning toward her, David knew he was being somewhat cruel—again. But he had to make her realize that, at this point, it was her or them. Didn't he? And, he wanted an answer.

Lauren looked up to him for a moment, but now she saw the danger in his eyes that she'd known was there. Maybe it wasn't being directed at her, but it was there. Instead of meeting it, she shook her head and inched down, further under the comforter, turning away from David's shape and closing her eyes. "I'm really tired," she said, remaining tensed until she felt his body rise from the bed. When she heard him walk from the room, she let out a shuddering breath and tried to ignore the fact that part of what she'd seen on his face had been desperation. Where it had come from, she didn't know.

***

He came back in an hour later with her prescription. Seeing that her eyes were open, he wordlessly twisted off the cap and shook one of the pills into his hand, holding it out to her even as she twisted up to take the water bottle from her nightstand. As there'd been the night before, there was a hesitating twitch in her movement when she took the pill from him, as if she didn't want her skin to touch his for even that briefest of contacts, but he tried not to be offended by it; he'd hurt her, and she had every right to shy away from any physical contact, slight as it might be.

"Night, Lauren," he told her quietly as she slipped back to the center of the bed and relaxed on the pillows; he knew from nights past that it would be only minutes before she was sound asleep—the pills knocked her flat.

"Night, David," she echoed, her voice at a whisper.

Turning away, he collected his laptop and turned off the lamps that had been lit, just glancing back to her for a moment from the door, but her eyes were already closed, her breath even and tired.

Downstairs again, he downed a half-rocks glass of whiskey before stripping and heading toward his shower. Inactive as he'd been that day, comparatively, it had been a long one, and he had little enough to show for all of the time he'd spent on the computer. With Lauren's reaction tonight, though—he wasn't hopeful she'd offer up more names, and he didn't have the heart to press her.

He adjusted the water temperature before stepping in and pulling the door shut behind him, and then leaned back against the wall and let the water wash down his body, hot enough that it was hard to stand and that steam was quickly filling up the small space. With his eyes closed as they were, it was hard for him to get beyond thoughts of the girl upstairs, and in moments like this when he was trying not to think about the stress of puzzling out the coven and didn't have anything else to draw his focus...his mind went to her.

The way her body lay under the blankets when she slept, and the way her breath shifted her hair when it had been washed but not brushed, and waved around her face. The way her curves filled out the yoga pants and light blouses she'd been living in since they'd picked her up, and the way that her lips glistened after she licked them or drank down juice. The way she half-hummed to herself in a little murmur when she was thinking of how to respond to something or searching for what to say. The way her pale skin made him want to touch her, and peel back the covers and her clothes, and let her know that he knew how to touch a woman gently, the right way, as he hadn't done with her before.

Without thinking about it, he let one of his hands move down to his dick and begin stroking it, letting it harden at the thought of what her body had felt like against his, and the way she'd moaned when she'd finally been forced to let go, shaking beneath him as he'd taken her like nobody else ever had.

His eyes closed, he turned and leaned against the wall, one of his hands bracing his tense body as his other jerked at his member, moving back and forth in memorized motions while Lauren's sounds and the sensations of their fucking rolled through his mind until his body jerked with the release of an orgasm he'd been craving all night, sperm shooting into the shower wall as he let his dick pump out his frustration in angry lunges that only drew his attention to the fact that he was alone in a shower, the vacuum of the space around him all he had to help him relax when what he craved was a floor above his apartment, as distant and essentially forbidden as if she'd been a thousand miles away.

Chapter 9

It was after midnight when Josh came in, having dropped Claudia back at her apartment. She'd made it easy for him to pretend that the tension at the house was less pervasive than it really was, but all of the calm he'd felt with her dropped away as he came back in and heard the sounds coming from Lauren's bedroom. He'd heard them for the first time a few days before, when he'd walked into her room and found his partner leaning over the desk with a glass of whiskey clutched in his hand, the girl on the bed behind him whimpering and arguing against some attacker she was fending off in her sleep. David had taken one look at him and fled the room, leaving him to wake her up, and they hadn't spoken about it.

He half expected David to be there again when he got to her room, but all of the lights were off. Going by the light of the hallway, he bent to a knee beside the bed and gripped her arm, trying for shaking her gently awake, but instead she pulled against him hard, jerking to the other side of the bed like she'd suddenly adopted him as an embodiment of whatever she was fighting in her dream.

"Lauren! Lauren!" Josh peeled her fingers from his arm with one hand, cringing at the way she was jerking in the bed—this was why she'd been more sore in the mornings, he realized, why the doctor had been frustrated by her lack of healing, and Josh suddenly thought that if anything they were lucky she hadn't fallen out of the bed yet. David's name slipped from her lips, freezing him for a moment before he leaned further over the bed and immediately had to block one of her hands from slamming blindly into his face. "Lauren!" he yelled out then, again, catching her face in one of his hands and pressing down on her forehead, hoping it would wake her.

It did. Lauren's eyes jerked open, foggy from the meds and terrified of whatever she'd been seeing, waking up and shifting away hard enough that the next sound from her mouth was a tight whimper of pain.

"Fuck," Josh sighed, leaning back on his heels. The girl in front of him was just staring back at him, wide-eyed and still working on waking. "That was worse than it's been," he muttered, more to himself than her as he took stock of her sweat-soaked clothes, and tried not to think about the fact that it had apparently been David she'd been fighting in her sleep. "Are you okay?" he asked, grimacing at the way her breath was hitching.

Glancing around her, bringing herself back, Lauren nodded, her voice caught in her throat. She'd dreamed of *him* again, on top of her in her apartment. What she didn't want to acknowledge, even to herself, was whose name she'd been calling out to for help. "Yeah," she nodded finally, taking a deep breath and suddenly realizing how much she'd managed to renew the pain in her ribs. "I...sorry, yeah," she said again, reaching down and holding her side, and closing her eyes to breathe gently through the pain like the men had coached her to.

"We shouldn't have put you in this room," Josh said, grimacing as he stood and pulled up the chair from the desk so that he could sit by the bed. An hour before, life had seemed easy; now it felt impossibly weighted.

Lauren looked to him, and then glanced to the packages she could see shadowed just at the door's entry—a case of beer and a plastic bag of whatever else he'd picked up. *He must've heard me when he walked in*, she thought, and then winced at the pain she received in return for reaching for her water.

"It's not the room...I just...I keep remembering; it's like I don't know how to turn it off," she said quietly, her heartbeat finally calmed even if her mind was still groggy from the pain pill she'd taken earlier. "I don't know why they only keep coming at night, but..." She shrugged, letting her voice trail off.

"Well, the room doesn't help. It looks just like...the other guest room," Josh said, thinking again that nothing he'd ever trained for had prepared him for what he was dealing with now, helping to house a traumatized girl who, in large part, was in this condition because of him and his partner.

It took Lauren a moment of wondering why he was focused on the room before she realized what he was thinking, and she didn't know whether she ought to be laughing or crying when she did. "No—Josh, it's not here...fuck," she muttered, interrupting herself when shifting sent another acute lance through her abdomen. "It's my apartment, the dream. It's...that guy," she whispered, seeing his face in her memory again.

Scooting forward in the chair, Josh leaned in and shook his head, scowling. "You don't have to make excuses, Lauren. I know what happened. And I heard it this time."

"Heard it?" she echoed, working to catch up with him. These guys couldn't read her mind somehow, could they?

"David. I heard you say David's name," he told her gently, reaching out to take the water when her wrist went limp on the side of the bed. Saying it, he'd never been angrier at his partner, for what he'd done to Lauren or for anything else, and he was all the more upset by the fact that, even still, there was nowhere else they could send this girl where she'd be as safe as she was with them, to recover and wait out whatever came next.

Fuck. Lauren blew out her breath and shook her head, closing her eyes. "I was calling to him for help," she whispered, looking away from Josh with the embarrassment of it. "I wanted him to help me."

Clenching her fists over the covers, Lauren kept her gaze from Josh's and tried to forget the memories that were still running through her mind. It didn't help that she felt drunk from the pain medication she'd taken earlier, dizzy from that and cold with sweat. And she didn't know how she'd ever get rid of the nightmares at this rate, but it certainly wasn't the room that was the problem.

"During the day, when you guys are around...I feel safe," she said quietly, knowing she wouldn't have been admitting as much if she weren't still doped up. "I can just sleep, and the room...it's fine. And then it's night, when it's dark and it gets quiet, and I know you guys are downstairs and are here if I need you, like you keep telling me, but...I don't know. I don't want to say I'm scared of the dark—I'm not, but I keep remembering waking up when it was pitch black, and he was... I just can't help getting scared at night, I guess, and tonight it was just...worse. I'm sorry I bothered you," she added, looking up finally and seeing that Josh was still shocked into silence, sitting beside her, squinting at her as if he was trying to determine whether to believe her, even though he knew perfectly well she couldn't lie.

"It's the guy you met at the bar that Friday who you're having nightmares about; not Dave?" he pushed. "You said tonight was worse?" he asked after she'd nodded, and he leaned back to re-assess his earlier thoughts, and figure out anew if there was any way to address the terrors she was falling asleep to.

"My fault, maybe, I don't know. We were talking, and then...I kind of shut down, I guess, so he left. After I took the pill, I knew he was going to go downstairs, but I was awake for a little while still in the dark and I guess it got to me, the quiet. You must think..." she shook her head, tightening her lips and thinking about how helpless, and silly, she had to sound to this man who'd been away at war, for Christ's sake, and here she was, acting scared of the dark like a four-year-old. And wanting a guy who'd raped her to come save her? Jesus. "I'm not usually scared of being alone, the dark, any of it...I don't know to fix it, though," she finished.

"Right," Josh acknowledged. "But it wouldn't be hard for one of us to stay around while you're falling asleep; we've been trying to give you your privacy, but hell, if that's making things worse..."

"I'm not a four-year-old," Lauren bit out, willing herself not to flinch at the hurt she saw cross Josh's face in reaction.

"No, you're not, but you are hurt, and you've been through a hell of a lot. There's nothing wrong with letting us do what we can to get you over it."

Letting his words sink in, Lauren shifted in the bed, noting the fact that even now, with the pain pill having just been taken a few hours before, the ache was so much worse than it had been, angry and throbbing. Whether she admitted it or not, these guys were the only things holding her together. That they owed it to her was beside the point—and her fighting against it was pointless. "It's embarrassing," she said quietly.

"No," David interrupted the quiet, his frame suddenly in front of them in the door. Lauren watched him come just inside the entry, blocking the light of the hall as he leaned back against the wall beside the door. He was shirtless, wearing sweatpants and in his bare feet, his hair rumpled. His hands dug into his pockets, he watched her for a moment and she didn't say anything. "What's embarrassing is how much I hurt you, and how little we can do to make up for that. Hell, we *can't* make up for it, obviously. But we can keep you safe if nothing else, and let you sleep," he added, a small smile coming to his face before he bit it back.

Lauren blinked, cutting her eyes from the muscles of David's chest back to Josh, who had an amused look on his own face now. *Fuck, I'm drunk,* she wondered at herself, realizing she'd remained silent and looked at David's bare chest for too long to go unnoticed.

"How much of that did you hear?" Josh couldn't help asking, seeing that Lauren wasn't about to get her voice back in a near moment.

David shrugged, crossing his arms. He'd heard all of it. "I heard you running, from my room, so I came running—got here as you woke her up, but—" Pausing, he took another look at the heavy blush on Lauren's face and thought perhaps he should have just walked away. "But I didn't want to interrupt, so I just stayed in the hall, case you needed me," he continued.

"And listened," Josh added, glancing to Lauren.

"I'm a curious bastard," he admitted.

Lauren looked up then, unable to keep from noticing the way that the man's eyes had crinkled around the edges with a small smile that she hadn't much seen.

"Can curious bastards get fresh sheets from the laundry room?"

David nodded at his partner and stepped backward, giving Lauren time to get her mind back on solid footing—or, what she could of it, given that the pain meds still had to be running through her system.

Having gotten his partner to give her some space, Josh turned back to Lauren. "You wanna change while you're awake?" he asked, and Lauren nodded back, already chilled from the sweated-through sheets and t-shirt.

"Yeah, thanks," she said, jerkily pulling herself up from the bed. She stopped there, shaking her head at the pain. She wasn't sure she could get up without help.

"Would you hit me if I recommended you take another pill, too? Your ribs are gonna be feeling that dream in the morning if you don't."

Lauren only hesitated for a moment. She wasn't ready to be off of them yet, so far as she'd pushed herself to be. And maybe now that the men knew, for better or worse, that it was being alone that scared her more than anything right now, she'd finally be able to take a step away from the nightmares and make a faster recovery, if anything. At least, she hoped that would be the case, and the thought of it, and of the outcome of David not slipping away so quickly at night, right when she needed him, was enough to somewhat quell the humiliation of having admitted that David was the one her subconscious had automatically been turning to for help.

***

Near on two hours later, David knocked at Josh's suite, having just heard him come down from Lauren's room and shut the door. It was coming up on 3 AM, but he wanted to know what the other man was thinking about what they'd heard.

Apparently unsurprised, Josh answered the door and gestured him inside before he headed to his fridge to grab them some beers from his personal stash. "Guinness or Yuengling?" he asked.

"Whatever," David answered, collapsing onto the black leather couch his partner had spent half-a-month's salary on. He wouldn't have spent the money, but he was glad to enjoy the comfort of it.

"You heard what she said? About calling to *you* for help?" Josh asked, handing him a beer and then taking a seat himself.

"Yeah—that's what's bugging me. How the fuck is that possible? You know what I did to her...you think she's lost it? Or what? Stockholm?" he asked, his brow creased. He'd been thinking about it for the last hour, but hadn't made any headway, and he didn't know what he was missing.

Josh shook his head. "She doesn't seem the type, and I've seen Stockholm—this isn't it. She's not trying to please you or me, or doing anything to suggest she's doing more than trying to recover. She's just scared."

"So what are we missing?"

"I don't know," Josh answered. "You ever get the impression she was scared of her mom? So scared that what you did would pale? I mean, she's scared of her coven, that's clear, but I don't know if that extended to family."

David thought back to wondering the same thing, back when he'd been interrogating her. She'd been scared then of something more than him. "Could be. What difference does that make?"

Shrugging, Josh thought about how embarrassed Lauren had been to admit she'd called to David for help, and how relieved she'd seemed when she gave in to the idea of letting them stay with her until she slept. "It's a longshot, but if that's the case, you saved her from her mom by making her give us her location. You forced her into it, gave her no choice; that's *one* less evil she has to deal with."

"No—we're missing something else. You said you realized at the diner that she *can't* lie, sure, but she ended up telling me the truth after...after I'd stopped, after she was in a bath and there was no indication I was going to touch her again. She didn't know we were working on getting rid of her magic. She was pissed at her mom at that point, I think, but if it had just been fear..."

"She never would have told you?"

"Right," David answered, trying to think how her subconscious could have done such a turn as to be looking to him as some sort of fucked-up savior. "Maybe she senses I like her?" he suggested quietly.

"I don't know that that would make a difference, do you?"

"What, jealous she's looking to me for help instead of you?" David joked half-heartedly. Truth be told, it made him happy that she was looking to him for help. He just wanted to understand it.

"Not really, no—I don't want the responsibility of liking her anymore than I do, not anymore than I wanted the responsibility of doing what you did," Josh added reluctantly. "She was pissed a few days ago, you know—one of those points when she was awake, in between medicine; you were out. She asked me what made us different, hurting people like her, than the folks we go after."

David closed his eyes for a second, gulping back a portion of his beer. "What did you tell her?"

"What else? Greater good. Her mom killed, what, forty-some people over the last twenty years, that we know of? You hurt Lauren to get to her, and who knows how many lives that saved?" Josh sipped at his own beer and shrugged. "I don't know how she felt about the answer—she went quiet, like you said she did last night when she shut down. Maybe that redirected some of the aggression away from you. And this guy who attacked her—he hurt her way worse than you, physically, and more recently. If she'd give us his name, I'd have gone after him before now," Josh added needlessly, knowing his partner felt the same.

David put his empty bottle down on the table, still bothered by it all. "Yeah, but that's the other thing—after what I did, shouldn't she have still been licking her wounds, staying in? It's not...something's not adding up."

"Man, you gotta give it up—one minute you're getting drunk and pissed at yourself for how much you hurt her, and the next you're wondering why she wasn't more torn up over it. Maybe she wasn't a virgin, after all," Josh offered finally.

"No," David replied, "she was. I...felt it, and there was blood like there wouldn't have been otherwise. And it made sense after the fact, with what she'd been saying, and with you finding out later on that she can't lie. There's something else we're missing here that's affecting her." Looking to his partner, he stood and shook his head. "Look, never mind; we'll worry about it later. Thanks for the beer," he said, heading toward the door.

"David?"

"Yeah, what?"

"Don't dwell on it. What's done is done. Next step, we find the other witches and we get this settled, it'll all be done."

Right, David thought to himself, heading back to his room. *It'll all be done, and she'll be gone.* "That's the goal, right?" he said aloud.

***

Although it went mostly unmentioned, David or Josh remaining in the room as she was falling asleep helped with the nightmares. Much as Lauren wanted to pretend that they, and their place, didn't offer some feeling of safety, she just couldn't. When the two of them both left the house, she felt it in her bones, whereas when David was nearby, she could somehow breathe more easily. And finally, she could really feel like she was healing; she hadn't fallen or jarred her ribs since that last bad nightmare, and the days of rest were adding up. She was also down to one pain pill per day again, with Aleve occasionally getting thrown in if some extra relief was needed, but she felt like there was a light at the end of the tunnel now—at least, in terms of her injuries.

She was sitting up in bed reading when the two of them came in together, David walking in a half-step behind his partner and carrying a chair with him to offset the one that was already in the room by the desk.

"How ya doing?" he asked, taking a seat near the chair his partner had settled into.

"I'm okay," she answered, meaning it. "But you want

to talk about something that's going to make me feel less okay, don't you?" she added, glancing from one serious man to the other.

"We found two names, and we know where the women attached to them live; we're just looking for confirmation," Josh admitted, and for the first time Lauren noticed that he'd carried a small notebook in with him. He glanced to it. "Chloe Draymond. Lalita Meyler. Either ring a bell?"

David watched a flash of something cross Lauren's face—maybe recognition—and leaned in. "They're members of your mother's coven?" he asked for confirmation.

Lauren closed her book, sitting back against the headboard. The women in her mind were, she thought, harmless. They sold love spells and trinkets, and although they could be accused of interfering with marriages and divorces and affairs, perhaps, they couldn't be accused of killing. They were in their forties, with kids and husbands, and she hadn't seen them in years. "What do you want to do to them?" she asked quietly.

Josh shrugged, answering first. "I don't know. We need to talk to them, get more names. Make sure they won't come after you. Given your mom's coven, the collective it is—that probably means requiring that they relinquish their magic. Especially considering that, if nothing else, they were protecting your mom all these years. We can leave agents with them to do the dosing, or more likely put them into protective custody for it. We're not planning on killing them, if that's what you're asking."

The last time Lauren had seen either woman, it had been at one of her mother's birthday parties. The two had come together and shown off pictures of their families; they'd been disappointed that, as of yet, their children weren't showing any sign of having natural magic in their bloods, which Lauren felt some comfort in now. And besides that, the kids would all be under 10—it likely still wouldn't have shown up in any meaningful way. If Josh and David took their mothers' magic or their own, they wouldn't miss it in any meaningful way. "They have kids," Lauren said simply. "You can't...not kids like me. Like, little kids, who need their mothers."

She looked up sharply when David barked out a laugh. His eyes were cold, looking back at her. "Like you needed your mom?" he asked. "When you were a kid? From what we can tell, she wasn't exactly parent of the month."

Lauren moved her gaze from David's and looked to Josh. "You can't hurt them," she told him.

"And we won't...probably," he said quietly. "But we need to move on this. Now, we've got their names— they've been looking for you, and so it wasn't hard to find them—but anything you can tell us about them will help. What they're like, what they care about, anything you remember."

"So that's it?" Lauren asked. "You just want me to tell you what I can...about them?"

"Unless you want to give us more names," David answered, but she shook her head.

"I don't even think I could have come up with *their* last names from memory—I just recognized them when you said them. For me, the women in the coven were all my mom's friends, first names only."

"You think they'll give us the others?"

Lauren only shrugged in return. She had no idea. "I don't want you to hurt them," she repeated.

David left his chair and paced to her bedside,

standing over her and glaring down, not letting her break his gaze. "They were looking for *you*, Lauren. You. These women were looking for you—it's how we found them—to take you back to their coven and *keep* you as some kind of indentured servant. You know that better than us. Protecting them doesn't make sense."

"You guys have to understand; if it were up to those two..." she trailed off.

"If it were up to those two?" Josh prodded, prompting David to move to the side so he could better see Lauren, and she him.

"I don't think they'd have bothered me, on their own," Lauren said quietly, but she knew there wasn't any confidence in her voice, and she knew the men before her could see that as plainly as she could feel it. The coven came first, and it always had and always would.

"But they're not on their own," Josh spoke up. "That's why we have to find them. Look," he added, "we got Mary's address from your car, but she moved; we told you that—it must have happened about as soon as we brought you here. That pretty much proves that all of these women are on the offensive, looking for you. These two women are the lead we've got now, and we're going to follow it."

David sat down at the foot of the bed, resting one of his hands on her ankle so that she jerked in response, looking up to him. "Lauren," he said, "these women supported your mother. The things she's done over the years—it should have been them who took care of it, before anyone else got involved. A coven takes care of their own, we get it, but you got hurt in all this because your mom's coven didn't take care of a problem when it came up. They let her kill, over and over again, when they could have stopped it. Now whether you help us or not, the truth is that they'd let another witch do the same, and they'll place their...what? claim? ...over you, before anything else. If you help us, it's not you being selfish."

Lauren started to interrupt, but David just shook his head at her, putting off the objection. "I can see in your eyes that's what you're thinking," he said. "But this is all just wrapping up what your mom started, and making sure that none of the rest of the coven hurts anyone else."

Chapter 10

She would have said, if asked, that she was out of tears. David and Josh had left early that morning, leaving her a note to tell her that they'd do their best to be back that night and to make herself at home, that there was food to re-heat in the fridge. She'd been getting up and moving back and forth between her room and the kitchen for more than a week—the only inconvenience on her end would be, embarrassingly enough, if they weren't there so that one of them could be nearby as she attempted to get to sleep. They'd offered to have Claudia stay over for her, with it potentially being the first time that they'd both be gone at night, but she'd waved them off.

But seeing the note they'd left, that they were finally heading out to question the two witches they'd ascertained were part of her mother's group, left her breaking down. She'd sobbed for more than an hour when she found it, left to her privacy. In her mind, she kept seeing the men threatening the women, torturing them, and then shooting them when they wouldn't give up the coven. With every fiber of her heart, she hated that she'd told them a thing about their lives, little as it had been and little as it had helped. David's assurances that they'd wanted her for the coven, and been actively looking for her, had been enough in the couple of days past to hold off the guilt, but with the pair of them gone to question the witches, she suddenly felt like she ought to have killed herself before giving them anything more in the way of information.

So when David had appeared at her door, and said simply, "They're alright, in protective custody now," she'd broken down, and he'd left her to it.

It was nearing midnight when Lauren ventured out of her room and into the kitchen, and David was waiting for her. He'd known for days that she was terrified they'd end up hurting the two witches whose names they'd gotten, and though he'd wanted to promise her otherwise, he hadn't wanted to chance a lie. Things had gone as planned, though. Faced with what they'd allowed to happen, the only thing either witch had cared about was protective custody for themselves and their families, which would last until their magic disintegrated and until the full coven had been collected; they'd offered up all of the names of the women in the coven.

Now, the two witches had a week to decide whether they'd want to enter witness protection after all was said and done, but Josh and David were done with that portion of things—they had the list of the eight witches whose names they hadn't had before, and plans to make, given that these two had been the weakest of the lot, and would certainly have been the easiest to find. Even having the names of the areas where the women lived, down to cities or towns or in two cases only a region of a state, meant that there was still work to be done in finding them, but the names would make it fast work if they went at it quickly.

Lauren's face said it all, of course, as it had the night before when the men had told her they'd leave in the morning. "They're really okay?" she asked even before she sat down across from David at the island, her eyes still wet from tears.

"Yeah, you have my word. In protective custody as we speak. Everything as planned, like we hoped," he said. "You want a drink?" he asked next, doubting himself for only a moment before he made the offer.

Lauren nodded; one drink wouldn't be the end of the world now that she was officially down to one pill per day.

David poured her a glass of whiskey and added some ginger ale to take off the bite, passing it across the table after he poured himself another short glass of the liquor.

"I trusted that you'd try," Lauren acknowledged with a nod, accepting the glass. She'd been so afraid all day that, now that the adrenaline was wearing off, she felt numb, and wasn't sure what more to say.

"I don't know whether you'll see them again, but you can talk to them this week if you want to. That's up to you. They have a week to decide whether they want to go into witness protection with their families—I think they might."

"I don't want to talk to them. It's not as if I knew them well," she added.

David gulped down the remainder of his drink. "We ate on the way back; did you eat?"

It took her a moment, to go from thinking of the

witches to the thought of food, but she shook her head when she'd caught up with him. "I was too nervous."

In a moment, David had risen to go to the fridge, telling her he'd fix her a plate. She sat and watched, struck by how odd all of this was. That he'd offered her a drink, and was making her food. Without considering what she was doing, she reached for the decanter of liquor that had been sitting by David's now closed laptop, and topped off her drink while she watched him.

Food in the microwave, he looked back to her. "Just be careful with it. You'd be surprised how liquor'll affect you after a concussion—even weeks after, and with you still taking the pills, it could knock you off your feet." He didn't stop her, though, figuring she needed the drink more than he did at this point.

Watching her eat once he'd put a plate in front of her, he thought about what his grandfather had used to say about his sister—that she ate like a bird. He'd never really known what he meant, until now. Lauren took small bites, as if she was considering each one and distracted, not sure how much she wanted even a moment after she'd begun eating. He knew the food was good, and that that wasn't the problem. His partner was an impressive cook—the leftovers in front of her, from just a night before, would be better than they had been, if anything. She ate slowly, though, and he didn't pretend to be otherwise occupied; he was too tired to bother after the day they'd had.

"You were waiting for me to calm down," Lauren said quietly, once she was done. She pushed the plate a few inches in, signaling she was done, and took a further sip of her drink. With the liquor heavier, the ginger ale was barely present, but the burn felt good on her throat, it had been so long since she'd had a drink.

"Just making sure you were okay," he answered her

before leaning over to take her plate and place it in the sink.

"I was going to do that."

"You sit. I can see the liquor you're drinking in your face. Relax," David told her, coming back to the island.

She frowned for a moment, but couldn't hide that she was feeling the alcohol. She'd been on pins and needles all day; that alone would have been enough to leave her exhausted, and things were catching up with her. "I'm trying to," she finally answered, and took another sip of her drink.

"How the ribs doing?"

She shrugged. "I took an Aleve this afternoon—haven't felt them since."

Letting the silence cover their tiredness, David watched her as she took the last sips of her drink, and then gave her another moment. "You ready for bed?" When her head jerked back up, he flushed and shook his head. "I didn't mean anything by it—it's been a long day."

Lauren saw the embarrassment in his face, at the way he'd phrased his question, and felt a smile come to her face. Slipping off the stool by way of answer, she stumbled, and was shocked at how quickly David appeared at her side, supporting her elbow, but she let herself lean on him. "You were right...I feel dizzy," she admitted. Suddenly, the room was spinning, and she had to close her eyes for fear of falling.

"Fuck, I got ya," David grunted, catching her as she leaned fully into him. *I shouldn't have offered her that drink.* When she didn't stand away from him after another moment passed, David gave up on waiting and bent down to pick her up. She was light, and unprotesting in his arms. Carrying her down the hall, it occurred to him that he could actually feel the weight she'd lost over the last month, even now that she'd gained some of it back after near on a week or so of mostly normal eating. Now that he thought about it, though, he realized she'd mostly been left to her own devices when it came to lunches, and wondered how much or how little she had been eating.

When he laid her in the bed, she held onto one of his arms for a moment longer than she might have, and then muttered an apology he brushed off. "My fault—I shouldn't have let you drink. Are you okay?"

"Yeah...yeah," Lauren repeated. Her heart was speeding in her chest, and she didn't know how much of that to attribute to her dizziness, how much to attribute to David's proximity. He was closer than he'd been to her in past weeks, sitting on the bed beside her with one of his hands resting on her forearm, his hip touching hers. Her skin felt warm, heated where it was touching his.

David kicked himself again for offering her a drink, thinking about the week's worth of pills she still had left, and which the doctor had all but ordered her to take. "You might want to save the pill for the morning, unless you wake up needing it."

"Yeah," Lauren said, and wondered why she couldn't seem to think of anything else to say.

David waited for her to speak, and then stayed still when she simply took another deep breath and then closed her eyes, seeming to deflate backward a moment later. After a second's thought, he got up to turn off the light, but then sat in the desk chair instead of leaving, pulling forward the other chair he'd brought in a few days before so that he could put his feet up. Leaning backward, the chair propped against the desk so that it wouldn't roll, he settled in for the night, telling himself it only made sense in case she woke up and needed a pill, or anything else.

***

Lauren lay in the living room of the ranch house, waiting for David and Josh to come in; they'd been gone all day, and she was anxious to have them back in the house. She was so relaxed, and felt more herself than she'd felt in ages. When she heard the Mustang pull up, she twisted so that she could look into the mirror on the wall—her makeup was perfect, her hair tussled like she liked it, as if she hadn't put any effort into it even though she had. She forced herself to sit back, and to look up casually when David walked into the room behind her.

She caught his eyes raking up and down her body, looking at her legs as they protruded from her skirt, and then up to her shoulder peeking out from her sweater before he caught her eyes and grinned a hello.

She didn't say anything, but he still seemed to understand what she wanted.

In a moment, he'd crossed the room and perched on the couch beside her, and was taking her body in his arms, pulling her up against his chest. She ran her hands along the muscles of his forearms, over his dress shirt, and then up over his bicep and to his shoulder, massaging his tight muscles as her hands moved. She heard him groan, and began consciously rubbing at his shoulder as their hug of greeting bled naturally into a kiss. Her lips met his, and he tasted like whisky. She let her other hand wander upward, into his soft, spikey hair so that she could hold onto him and make sure he didn't pull away. She let herself open up to his kiss, pushing her lips harder against his to encourage him.

"You taste so good, Lauren," he murmured against the edge of her mouth, and then he'd twisted her

sideways so that they lay together, his body above hers.

Suddenly, she doubted herself, wishing she hadn't encouraged him. What was she doing, with him of all people? She tried to pull backwards, down into the couch, but his lips and his hands followed her body.

She told him they couldn't—that she wasn't ready, and that she wasn't over him hurting her, and that this wasn't right—but then she stopped protesting when he kept gazing at her, his eyes projecting desire and making it difficult for her to find any reason to argue with his want.

She closed her eyes, listening to him tell her that she was beautiful, the only one he wanted, and that he'd been waiting to show her he could be like this, gentle and kind and hard all at once, just for her. She let her hands run along his muscles as he undressed himself and then her, dropping their clothes beside the couch so that he could rest his body on hers, his hardness against her thigh, and waiting, until her hand found it and began running up and down its length, feeling its size and its hardness and exploring even as she hated herself for encouraging him, wanting him.

His hands came to her breasts and she pushed up against him, reaching to nuzzle her lips against his neck and then reclining backwards when he finally pushed into her, opening her center that was already slick for him and waiting, pulsing with want.

She gripped his shoulders with her fingers when he thrust into her, slowly and then quickly, and called out his name with heavy breaths when he sped up, and then wrapped her legs around his thighs and held onto him with all of her might as he went deeper into her and she screamed in release...

And woke up, her eyes wide as she gasped. Swallowing, she peered around her into the darkness of what had become her room, noting that she was still fully dressed in the jeans and blouse she'd worn all day. And David was reclined across the room's two chairs, his hands clasped over his stomach, snoring slightly.

Chapter 11

David spun to his left as he crashed into the living room of the home, landing to the side of an ancient desk as a bolt of energy left nearby carpet smoldering. Gasping, he felt along his arm for any further injury. None yet, but the injuries he'd already sustained were making it harder to focus. He clenched his eyes shut, trying to collect himself as he heard the witch taunting him again from the next room.

"Mr. Fredricks, you won't want to be leaving yet, will you? Already? And here I thought..."

David twisted sideways away from the door he'd come through, using the desk as a partial shield as he raised his gun again and shot overtop of it, letting out a satisfied grunt as he dove back behind its cover when he heard the witch scream out, pain and anger coming through the cry in equal parts. He just wished he'd had the time to see where he'd hit her. Blindly, he raised his hand quickly and shot again, biting back a shout when an energy bolt threw a splinter of wood into his cheek as another splice of energy crashed into the furniture above his head. He pulled the sliver of wood from his skin and wiped the blood onto his jeans before shifting and calling out to the lone witch who seemed still to be fighting them.

"You can give up or you can keep getting hit!" he yelled without raising his head. "One of your friends is dead already and another dead or dying—do you want to add to the body count or get out?" he demanded, making a sudden move forward and scooting into the next room; this time, a line of energy grazed nearly the full line of his arm so that he dropped his gun, and then clenched his teeth hard against the pain as he shot out one foot to retrieve his weapon before he leaned his head back and cursed under his breath. She wasn't giving up, and it was only the two of them left standing in the fight at this point, to the extent that he was even on his feet.

Unsure whether he could use the arm she'd just hit, he did his best to ignore the new pain and adjusted his other hand's grip on his gun, reminding himself that this was why he practiced shooting with even his non-dominant hand. Chancing a look around the corner, he saw that the witch still hadn't entered the room he'd just occupied. That meant she was in the hall or the kitchen since the layout of this place was a circle—he needed only to cross the room and look through the other entrance to this dining area, and he'd be able to see her.

Crouching, he stayed low as he moved, and took a deep breath when he reached the opposite wall. He was now an open target if she followed the path he'd come along. Keeping low, he spun sideways into the kitchen area and fired shots as he scuttled forward to land behind the island, just beside the body of the witch that Mark had managed to kill before he'd been shot out of the window; the operative was a good man, with a family, and David hoped to God he was alive, but he couldn't chance rising to look out the window. The witch he was still after was screeching in pain, caught again by one of his bullets; his own fight was almost over here, one way or another.

He chanced a look up to see her vanishing into the next room, that he'd occupied just moments before—he'd taken too long to pull himself together after his move into the kitchen.

Now he balanced against the back of the island, his gun rotating back and forth between the kitchen's two exits. He just caught himself from jumping when her voice echoed in his head, filling all of his awareness even to the point that his injuries became echoes.

"Well played, David Fredricks. You've won my retreat."

"NO!" he yelled, flying toward the nearest exit, but he arrived only in time to see the last vestiges of her form disappearing into thin air. "Goddamnit," he spat out, leaning back against the wall. She was gone.

Knowing she wouldn't have left like that unless she truly meant to take the time to recover from her own injuries, considering the spot she'd had him in, he holstered his gun and stumbled toward the sink, looking out into the yard. Mark lay where he had to have landed when he'd been thrown from the window, but there was no telling how hurt he was from this distance. Meanwhile, David could still hear Josh upstairs, clambering against the door of whatever space this last witch had managed to shut him into. Mark's partner, David knew, was dead on the front porch—they'd seen AJ blasted backward as he and Josh had come in the back, and there wasn't any coming back from a hole of energy boring through your chest.

Jerkily, he made it to the stairs and pulled himself up. He had energy burns scattered along his torso and his back, along with the major one on his arm and some splinters digging into the skin of his shoulders, chest, and cheek—every one of the lacerations was burning more and more with each second, and their own house was two hours away, no sanctuary closer.

Finally reaching the top of the stairs, he saw that a gigantic bureau had been pushed against the door he could hear his partner banging on—the witch had thrown it there before she'd turned her full attention to David again, but he hadn't been able to take advantage of the distraction, he'd been so jarred by one of the energy hits. He shook his head at the thought of the way things had played out, now trying to get his breath back from the climb up the stairs—they'd come in expecting one witch, and found four, and four people against four witches wasn't near any stretch of even he could think of.

"It's me!" he called out, leaning onto the piece of furniture and giving it a futile push.

"David? Where's Mark? Did you get her?"

"Mark's down, outside—I haven't checked on him yet, I don't know," David grunted as he gave another push to the bureau, which barely budged. Groaning, he let himself collapse in front of the hulking furniture and begin yanking out drawers, all of which were full to the brim with blankets and gemstones—no wonder the thing had been so fucking heavy. "She got away after I hit her a few times; must've decided she was too injured to keep coming at us," he added, pulling out another drawer. "Yours?"

"Dead in here," Josh answered, throwing his

bodyweight into the door again so that the bureau bounced up a few inches before landing back where it had started.

"Hold on," David growled, "before you crash the thing on top of me. I'll have it in a minute."

With the last two drawers discarded, David dragged himself to his feet and took a moment to lean against the wall, grimacing with the pain that was now lancing its way into his bloodstream.

"Try now," he grunted, pushing weakly at the bureau.

Josh ran at the door from the other side, jarring the furniture backward with a smash that left a gap which was large enough for him to force his way through. He reached out and caught David's forearm as the other man started to slip down the wall, only Josh's grip holding him steady.

"Can you walk?"

"Yeah, I'll make it. You go—check on Mark," David said. His partner gave him a doubtful look, but then sprinted down the stairs. At least one of them was uninjured.

David glanced into the room Josh had been locked within; the witch Josh had chased up the stairs lay dead, her throat all but cut off by what had to have been three or four bullets. She was the one of the four witches they'd expected to find here, and one of two that they'd managed to take down. Based on description, he was sure she was the one named Moriah. Combined with the dead one downstairs and the ones who'd already surrendered, they'd taken care of six members of the coven now. That left four, including the two who'd just escaped them.

He turned from the room and nearly fell as a shooting sting ripped through his back, but he caught himself on the bannister. Then, step by step, he made it to the bottom of the stairs and came to a shaky halt, sitting heavily on the bottom stair; it had to have taken him longer than he'd thought just to get this far—he could hear Josh re-entering the kitchen already.

"Mark's okay—stunned, and he's got a few broken bones, but he'll make it. We gotta get you to the house, get him to a hospital."

"You call a clean-up crew yet?" David muttered, letting his partner heft him to his feet.

"I'll do it in the car. Come on."

***

Josh forced himself to keep the car slow as he turned into their long drive—both David and Mark were in a lot of pain, and bouncing them along for two miles of dirt road wouldn't help matters. He took a fast glance into the rearview and saw that David was still hunched sideways, baring his teeth and clutching his right arm to his chest. Mark wasn't much better, leaned back in the passenger seat and apparently trying to ignore his broken leg, and what Josh guessed were a few broken ribs and a broken wrist to boot. He was worried there was internal bleeding also. The window he'd flown through had had a height of a good fifteen feet over the ground outside, and the force of magic behind him had pushed him twenty feet out into the yard; it had been a hard fall.

"We're almost there. We'll drop David off, get him set up, and then get you to the hospital."

Mark grunted an affirmative, and Josh kept his eyes on the road. He was hoping he could corral Lauren into helping David—he didn't think his partner could manage much on his own at this point, despite what he'd claimed would be the case—but if not, he'd have to stick around long enough to make sure the wounds didn't go untreated. Otherwise, the pain would rip through him and burn up his bloodstream until his heart gave out, and there'd be nothing left of him to treat by the time Josh got back from dropping off Mark at the hospital that was another thirty minutes down the road. He could have dropped Mark off at one closer to where they'd been, but Mark had insisted on getting back to home base, closer to his family—Josh figured part of the insistence had come from knowing that broken bones could wait, but David's wounds couldn't, and no hospital would know how to treat him so that he'd heal. That was where their own training came in.

Unfortunately, Josh now suspected that neither man's injuries could wait, and that meant he needed Lauren's help.

Pulling into the garage even as the door was still rising above them, he opened his door at the same time as he threw the car into park. He turned and pulled his seat forward then, reaching in to his partner.

***

Lauren was in the laundry room when she heard Josh's Mustang rumble into the garage. One of her shirts stilled in her hands, it took her a minute to place the sound, and then another moment to realize why it bothered her. She'd heard the men pull vehicles into the space to work on them or clean them, but other than that ...Lauren dropped the shirt and headed toward the garage at a dead run. The only other time they'd used the garage when coming home, since she'd known them, had been when they'd dragged her back from that bar.

She skidded to a stop in front of the door just as Josh pulled it open from the other side. "We need your help," he said.

Lauren stepped forward and looked past him; she saw Mark in the passenger seat of the Mustang, his head thrown back and his eyes closed, and then she saw David at the back of the garage, seated on the worktable built into the back of the space and cradling his right arm against his chest, his head down. She looked back to Josh, suddenly noticing the bloodspatter on his clothing and how filthy he was. "AJ?" she asked of Mark's partner.

Josh shook his head. "Can you help David? It can't wait, and if you can do it, I need to get Mark to the hospital."

Lauren blinked back at him, licking sudden sweat away from her lower lip as she felt nerves rush through her. "Tell me what to do?"

"He's got energy bolt burns—you know what those are?"

"Yeah, but I've never—"

"That's okay; he can tell you what to do. You need to boil water and get some cloths out of the closet so he can clean the wounds, and he might need help to get his shirt off. Make sure he gets all the soap off before he puts the cream on, but they *need* to be washed, okay? Give him whiskey if he wants it for the pain, but nothing else—his system's already got too much to handle. And just soapy water, okay? No peroxide—it'll be too much. The energy-pulling cream that he'll need is in the back of the fridge there," he said next, gesturing to a fridge in the corner that she'd never noticed before. "He'll need that as soon as he gets the wounds cleaned. You understand?"

Josh had so spoken quickly, jumping back and forth around what was needed, that Lauren took a moment to process it all before she nodded back at him and took another glance at David, who looked like he wouldn't be able to help himself at all.

"Listen—I'll call once I get Mark settled. Call me if you need to, and answer David's phone when it rings, alright?" he pushed, his eyes on hers.

Lauren nodded, and gasped when Josh suddenly pulled her into a fast bearhug she hadn't been expecting. "Thank you," he whispered hard into her ear before he let her go and hurried back to the car.

Lauren didn't wait for him to leave—Josh's hug told her more than his words that too much time had already passed. She spun on her heels and ran back toward the kitchen to put water on.

Josh nodded at David from the front seat as he began to pull backward, taking some comfort in the fact that his partner was aware enough to return the gesture; Josh just had to trust that Lauren would help him. He'd gotten more and more worried that Mark was dealing with internal bleeding—neither he nor David could stand more of a wait for treatment, so this was the only option. He just had to trust that Lauren's goodness would win out and that she'd take care of his partner, no matter what they'd done to her in the past. It was all he could hope for at this point.

***

The large spaghetti pot filled with water, Lauren put it on the stove and turned the heat to high before pouring a rocks glass mostly full of whiskey and then moving to the laundry closet for fresh cloths.

David was where they'd left him, and she paused for only a moment to collect herself before approaching. He didn't look up, though, even when she came to within a foot of him, and she had to reach forward and touch his knee to get his attention before he finally seemed to process her presence. His eyes were unfocused, his pupils dilated, and his whole face was tense with the agony of the energy running through his body, based in the cuts. Lauren could feel it thrumming off of him like a mild current or shock, even through his jeans.

"The water's on. I brought you this, if you want it?" she offered, holding out the whiskey.

It took a moment, and then he nodded; she saw him start to move his arm and then wince with the pain, and then she stopped allowing herself to think about anything. Carefully, she leaned forward and put the glass to his lips, tilting it so that he could take a long sip, her other hand on his shoulder for either her own support or his, though she couldn't have said which as she tried to ignore the feeling in her own skin when his jaw touched her hand.

She brought the glass down so he could breathe, and then tilted it back up when a quick jerk of his chin told her he wanted more.

When she took the glass away this time, he swallowed twice, heavily, and then finally spoke. "Thanks. Listen. I need you to help me...get out of this shirt—I tried to move my arm up to do it, but..."

"No, it's okay, yeah," she said. "Just tell me what you want me to do."

"There's a knife strapped against my calf."

She looked at him for a minute, and then shook her head. "A knife?"

"You can cut it off."

Lauren closed her eyes for a minute, helplessly flashing back to David cutting her own clothes off. Not to mention the fact that she'd never used a knife in a situation anything like this—she'd be bound to add to the injuries he was already dealing with. "I'll get the kitchen scissors," she told him quickly, and then turned before he could protest, running back toward the kitchen.

David watched Lauren flee the room, hunching forward as he cradled his arm. Each time he moved a muscle, the poisonous energy in his wounds seemed to renew itself and steal his breath. He'd known Josh had to leave to get Mark to the hospital, but he wasn't sure he could do this himself—he wasn't even sure he could bring himself to move his injured arm away from his body at the moment, let alone get to the fridge for the cream and paste it over the lacerations. Worse came to worse, that would be all he could do—there was no way he'd get himself to the kitchen for hot water, or even clean his cuts if the water were brought his way.

For a moment, his eyes glazed over as he tried to make a move to stand, and he fell back against the table rather than chancing a fall against his arm; his knees nearly buckled with the pain that rushed through him in response to the brief attempt, and he tried not to think about how far away that fridge was. It occurred to him that he could slide to the floor, and then slide to the fridge, if he couldn't stand without being too dizzy to stay upright, but just thinking about the agony that would bring was enough to make him curse and close his eyes, wanting just to pass out.

Lauren came in a moment later.

Right away, she saw that he'd turned somewhat, one of his legs grounded on the floor and his body diagonal to the table—he was swaying as if he might fall, and she rushed forward, putting her hand on his uninjured arm before she could stop herself. She could still feel the energy coming off of him, and there was a horrifyingly inappropriate rush of desire thrumming through her own blood as she touched him, but she managed it without wincing away; his eyes were only half open when he nodded at her in what seemed like relief. Instinctively, she realized what the look meant—he'd thought she was deserting him.

"I wasn't going to leave you," she said gently, holding up the scissors she'd retrieved. "You sure you want me to cut this shirt off?" she asked, forcing an evenness to her voice that she didn't feel.

"Yeah—have to. Undershirt, too," he muttered.

Lauren grimaced—she could hear how the pain had deepened from the strain in his voice, and see it in the way he was clenching his arm against his body. Shakily, he turned sideways further so that she could better access his back, and for the first time she saw the scorch marks in the back of the shirt, long and jagged—two bolts of energy must have grazed him, she realized—and there was another along his side, which she hadn't seen before because it was hidden by his injured arm. Without thinking about what she was doing, she pulled at the hem of his shirt and held it away from his body so that she could work the scissors around it, and then began cutting upward. It took no time at all for her to reach his neck, and then she began again at the bottom of his undershirt, until his back was exposed.

Trying not to touch his skin, though she knew she'd have to eventually, she gently pulled the left portion of the ruined shirts sideways and helped him tug the fabric over his uninjured arm, in a fashion that allowed him to stay as still as possible. Yet, she couldn't help hearing the whimpers snaking out of his breath, and noted that his lips were tight, biting back anything more.

Now it was down to his injured arm. She traded looks with him and he nodded, and moved the arm slightly from his body with a pained grunt, bracing it with his other arm. Carefully, Lauren took hold of the main shirt at his shoulder and peeled it downward as gently as she could, wincing at the way it had to be tugged away from the actual wound that ran the length of his arm as she went. She could feel David fighting the instinct to jerk away from her—his whole body was tensed, his knuckles white where they were clenched into fists.

Finally, she was able to tug the shirt fully from his arm and see the angry burn that ran deep along his limb—by far, this was the worst of the lacerations. At least the running energy was keeping blood loss to a minimum, but this one should have had stitches, clearly, though she knew without asking that no doctor would know what to make of the energy or how to help him.

Another minute passed, and she had the undershirt removed, having peeled it painfully away from the injury along his rib after she'd cut the remaining strap so that his arm could remain stationary.

"Whiskey," he muttered to her roughly, and she picked up the glass and held it to his lips, letting him swallow the last of it before she took the glass away.

"I can get you some more," she said quietly, eyeing the wounds that needed cleaning. With his shirts gone, the damage was clearer. Along with the two wounds she'd noticed on his back, and the one on his side and the other along his arm, there were slivery wounds all along his upper chest and shoulders, where she guessed that sparks of energy had to have hit him and burned through to his skin. There were signs of splinters, too, that she could see in his hands, and one even close to his ear, below his left cheek bone. The gashes were larger than the bits of wood she saw, so she guessed the larger pieces must have been removed in the car or just after he'd been hit with them.

"After," he said. "Whiskey after."

"The water should be boiling by now. I'll be right

back," Lauren promised him, meeting his gaze and willing the man to believe her. His eyes were unfocused again, his pupils still over-large, and she tried to pack reassurance into the look she gave him before turning away.

In the kitchen, she split the boiling water between two large bowls—one container for soapy water, one for clean, she told herself, working to keep herself calm and thinking about things step by step.

Moving through the garage door, she saw that David had his eyes clenched shut, his body getting wracked by violent muscle spasms as he kept his injured arm hard against his chest, his other hand clenched on the table's edge to keep himself upright.

Lauren hurried. She'd seen energy bolt burns before, but only small ones. This was beyond her, and she felt the pressure of knowing that David couldn't do it without her, but even that didn't change the fact that she desperately wanted to run away screaming and just hope that the situation would resolve itself. Instead, she forced herself to place the bowls far enough out of David's range that he couldn't spill them if he jerked away from her touch, and then she steeled herself to grip onto one of his hands.

Touch against touch, skin against skin, she felt some of the electricity running through his body from the witch's blows, but even more than that, she felt her own skin reacting, wanting more contact. She had to bite back a moan and then blink her eyes hard to hold herself back from running her other hand over his naked chest, knowing he had no idea of what her own body was experiencing, and understanding that it was a perfect opposite to the pain he himself was fighting.

"David," she said, gripping his hand hard so that he looked at her. His eyes were wobbling, out of focus.

"We have to clean the cuts. I'll do it, but you have to let me."

Another heavy shiver ran through his body, and he clenched his arm harder against his chest, eyeing the soapy water Lauren had brought. This was going to hurt. He nodded jerkily, shutting his eyes as Lauren released his hand and grabbed a cloth.

When she first touched it to his back, he pulled away so violently that he would have tumbled from the table if she hadn't caught his arm to help him balance. He heard her gasp for breath at the same time, and wondered how bad the wounds looked—still, he couldn't do this without her help. "I'm okay now," he muttered. "Wasn't expecting it."

Tensing his body, he steeled himself for the extra sting of the soap, and managed to stay mostly still when it came. She was gentle, but fast, which he was thankful for. He felt her running the cloth twice over the cuts on his back, and then nudging his uninjured side so that he understood she needed more access. He shifted slightly, holding himself upright by sheer will, and used his good arm to move his right bicep away from his chest so that she could run the cloth down along the wound in his side. She backed off for a moment, and he heard her put the cloth back in the bowl. A moment later, she was back with a clean cloth that was hotter, running what he guessed was just clean water along the cuts and getting rid of the slickness and sting of the soap before he heard this cloth also getting discarded. Then she was back in front of him, pushing against his leg to get him more evenly and firmly back on the table, his back to the wall.

Now Lauren could see that tears had squeezed from his eyes in reaction to the pain of the soap on his back, but she tried to ignore them. There was blood leaking from his lip also, where he had to have bitten it, but that was the least of their concerns. She ran the soap over the cloth again and then ran it twice over his chest, holding the cloth to his body even when he flinched, and taking care to not let her own skin touch his. Next came his arm. She met his gaze and he nodded once, hard, and she saw him grasp the table's edge with his other hand, bracing himself.

"Do it," he told her, nodding at the cloth she held.

She nodded back, and moved gingerly to his shoulder. She had to touch him now, and did that first, knowing she had to work through the desire she couldn't help feeling, inappropriate as it was. She braced one hand on his shoulder, in back where the cut didn't reach, and then held onto him to keep him as still as she could when he involuntarily jerked away as the soap touched the upper reaches of the cut. Evenly, she ran it up and down his arm, covering the deep laceration twice and then going over it for a third time to be safe. She knew the soap was seeping into the cut, and hoped the cream they had would have some ability to close it up like stitches would have. When she finally stepped away, the bloody cloth in her hand, she heard David release a deep, pained breath.

"That's the worst of it, right?" she asked as she moved to exchange her rag for the clean one. She didn't really know, after all, whether the cream would be worse, though she hoped not.

"That's the worst," he agreed shakily.

The next stage went fast—after the soap, the clean water offered more relief than pain, though contact still hurt. Getting rid of the last of the soap, Lauren was finally able to steady her own breath, and found herself taking stock of the scars that specked David's torso, which she hadn't noticed before.

There was a puckered wound along the side that

wasn't now injured—clearly an old one, and round, and she thought it might have come from a bullet, though she couldn't have based the guess on anything but movies. Then there was a longer wound, diagonal to his belly button, that had to have come from a blade of some sort, and a small scar that she guessed would have come from him getting his appendix out at some age, and a round birthmark not far from that. Even as she finished running the clean water along his injured arm, she found herself wanting to catalogue his scars with her fingers, and had to fight the urge; he'd think she was nuts if she did, not to mention the fact that putting off the cream could endanger his life further; the energy was still in his blood, even if its sources had been removed.

David felt all of his muscles spasm again, the electricity in his blood spiking as he bit his tongue and grunted with the pain. Beside him, Lauren flinched in surprise so that one of the bowls spilled, but she grabbed onto his arm in time to help him keep from falling. Another spasm came on the heels of the first, kicking his leg involuntarily into the table below him as he cursed aloud; he was lightheaded now, nothing existing but the hot pain in his bloodstream and along his skin, and Lauren's hands on his leg and his arm, trying to hold him steady.

She worked to catch his eye, squeezing his leg as the last of the sudden seizure stopped in order to get his attention.

"The cream in the fridge—it's labeled?" she demanded quickly, and he gave a jerky nod.

She ran, and opened the fridge to find that it wasn't full of beer as she might have expected, but jars and bottles of creams that she mostly recognized as basic potions and healing creams—all telltale signs that the partners hunted witches and had to deal with their spells and weapons on a too regular basis. Putting aside the thought, Lauren dug through the creams until she found a clear jar holding a grayish cream, labeled 'Energy-Puller'.

Turning, she went to hold it up for David's approval, but saw that he was slumped over, barely upright on the table.

"David," she demanded when she reached him, gripping onto his knee again for attention. His eyes opened against hers, wandering, and she held up the cream. "This? This is it?"

When he nodded, she fought the top of the jar for a moment before getting it pulled loose, and then instinctively dipped her fingers straight into the cream without giving a thought to what she was doing. As gently as she could then, she ran her goop-covered fingers along the long burn on his arm, from his shoulder to midway down his forearm where it stopped, making sure the cream covered the wound thoroughly and evenly, and dipping her fingers back into the jar twice to make sure the wound was covered. She could feel his body relaxing beneath her hand as she worked, and knew it was helping already. Her own body was reacting to the contact also, thrumming with desire, and she fought to ignore it.

She reached beneath his arm, slathering a thicker dosing along the laceration on his rib, knowing his arm might rub some of it away. She heard him groan in response, and made doubly sure not to push her fingers into him, just grazing his skin with the cream and checking for coverage. Then she moved to his chest and shoulders, and ran her fingers along the latticework of wounds there, dabbing the cream at the various burns. She could feel him breathing more evenly beneath her hands now, which made her more aware of what she was doing, and how close they were, so that she didn't look up at all now to meet his gaze. When she took a step back, he moved without help, shifting slowly so that she could reach his back.

Lauren dipped her fingers into the sticky gray concoction again, and covered the wounds on his back. He was sighing now with the relief of it, and she could feel the tension leaving his body. When she finished, he turned back so that he could face her. Covered in the gray cream as he was, he looked like he'd been splattered with wet cement that had gotten smoothed down over his skin, but there was real life in his face, and he didn't look stunned anymore, as he had since she'd first entered the garage.

"That would on your arm needed stitches—will the cream do anything to hold it together?" she asked.

"It's supposed to," he answered, reaching up to wipe sweat from his face.

"I didn't ask if I missed any, washing," she said quietly, twisting the top onto the cream rather than meeting his eyes. Once again, she was incredibly aware of how close they were, and how her fingers had felt running along his skin.

"No, you got them all. I owe you," he answered, stretching slightly. Awareness coming back to him, he could still feel the stinging of the energy in his blood, but it was receding—what had been unbearable was now painful, but nothing he couldn't work through, and he knew that even this pain would be nothing more than a dull ache in his body and some extra fatigue by the time 72 hours had passed.

Watching him stretch forward, Lauren stepped forward without thinking. Now that his eyes were examining the drying cream on his arm, she'd lost focus on keeping herself separate, together. Without thinking, and still running with adrenaline, she reached to his shoulder and ran her fingers along his uninjured bicep so that he froze in front of her. Feeling him still with the touch, she gulped back whatever asinine thing she'd been about to say and sought some excuse for touching him again.

"You've still got some splinters we have to get out," Lauren said too quickly, too loudly, forgetting that now he was probably capable of doing that much himself, and didn't need her any longer. "Do you have tweez—"

They both jerked in surprise when his phone rang, and David was able to move to answer it, fishing it out of his jeans and answering his partner's call even as his eyes stayed glued onto Lauren's. As soon as he spoke into it, though, Lauren realized she'd been watching him awkwardly like some deer in the headlights, and she rushed to grab the cream again, practically running it to the fridge.

Lauren was back and grabbing the bowls to head toward the garage door even as she heard David reassuring Josh that he was okay, and correcting his partner to tell him that it had been Lauren who'd taken care of everything. She fled the garage and leaned against the hallway's wall, the door closed behind her, taking a shaky breath and feeling as if she might go limp.

Swallowing, she moved toward the kitchen and put the bowls in the sink, and only then went to wash her hands of the sticky cream she'd been working with.

"You look as much a mess as me," David spoke from behind her, and she whirled to see him leaning on the doorway into the kitchen, eyeing her.

"Yeah?" Lauren asked, looking down at herself. He was right. She'd been wearing light-colored jeans and a tan blouse—both were now splattered with gray goop, water, and hints of pink that she knew had to be left from wiping away David's blood and then re-using the towels after washing them out. At least she'd worn a tank beneath the blouse, she thought, so that she was still decent.

David watched her over-examining herself, and felt again like she was going to pains to not look at him. He no longer knew what to think. As his wounds had calmed and she'd covered more of them with the cream, he'd been more aware of her, and more aware of her hands on his skin. More aware of her shallow breathing, which he was telling himself had to have been adrenaline, but which hadn't felt like it. Now, he let himself observe her re-pulling her hair into a tight ponytail, and then wiping her hands on her jeans before she finally looked up at him.

"You okay?" she asked, and he nodded.

"I'm about to get the tweezers—I should be able to take care of the splinters myself," he added, and watched her blush.

Lauren forced herself to nod. Even covered in what looked like wet cement, the form of his body's muscles was impressive, and now that she had some distance from his injuries, she could practically feel them back beneath her hands, heating her own blood. She made herself look him in the eye, and saw that he was examining her. Spinning back to the sink, she began plucking the dirtied cloths from the bowls and wringing them out. "I'll take care of this and then get a shower, then, if you don't need me anymore," she told him.

"Fair enough." David stayed watching her back for a moment longer, thinking about how calm her words had sounded, and how un-calm she seemed. Only when he walked away did it occur to him that she'd not even asked about the fight they'd had that day, or whether any of the witches they'd faced had gotten as good as they'd given.

Chapter 12

Unsure what to make of her nervousness, David tried to give Lauren the time and space he thought she needed. He really did. After he left her in the kitchen, he tweezed out the slivers of wood that had been left behind in the skin of his shoulder, along with one from his cheek and another from his hairline. Then he covered the cream Lauren had applied in gauze, and used a hand towel to wash away what sweat and blood he could from his skin and his hair. And it all took longer than it should have, sore as he was.

Dressed in fresh clothes, he then scarfed down a sandwich before sitting down at his desk to make a shopping list of the ingredients they needed to make more of the cream. That done, he attempted to write up a report of the day's fight, though it left him with such a headache that he left the computer in favor of bed.

And he tried to sleep. He lay there, thinking he should be sleeping off the day and letting his body rest, but his mind kept going back to Lauren. The way she'd stopped hesitating and flinching away as it became clearer he needed her help, as his pain had progressed, and the way that, when all was said and done, she'd come close again, to run her hand along his arm. Like that had been normal. Like that wasn't the way you touched someone when you wanted more.

When he heard Josh moving around upstairs, he gave up on sleep. His partner had brought sandwiches, and was coming back from delivering one to Lauren when David got upstairs. She'd elected to eat in her room instead of joining him in the kitchen, and he'd left it at that.

"How's Mark?" David asked, sitting down across from Josh and pulling a sandwich out of the bag he'd brought in.

"Out of surgery," Josh replied, his mouth full of food. "He'll be okay, but they're gonna keep him for a few days, maybe a week. You?"

"Okay, out of surgery, ready to rest for a few days or maybe a week," David echoed, biting into the turkey sub his partner had brought him. He'd eaten less than two hours ago, but he found he was famished anyway.

"Glad you can joke," Josh told him after gulping down some water, eyeing the gauze covering David's upper chest and arm. "So you and Lauren did okay?" he asked.

David shrugged, nodding. "She didn't say anything?"

"Seemed to want to be alone. Why I'm asking," he added.

Instead of responding, David kept eating, prompting Josh to do the same. When the sandwiches were gone,

Josh rose to pour them both refills of water before he sat down again, and then he stared hard at the man across from him. Like Lauren, he was withdrawn—there was more about him that was off than the injuries. "Something happened, between the two of you," he finally said. "You told her we had to kill two of the coven?"

Drinking down some water, David thought again about how he'd left Lauren. "She didn't ask," he said quietly, and then looked up to meet Josh's confused look. He felt the same.

"She didn't ask what happened—how you and Mark got hurt, what happened to the witches ..."

"None of it." David shook his head.

Josh stared out the window over the sink for a minute, trying to make sense of it. She'd been so concerned when they'd gone after those first two witches, and less so when they'd left on each successive trip to find the coven members, one by one. But she'd seen the results of today's trip—she had to have thought about who would have been on the other side of those wounds. "She asked about AJ," he finally said, recalling the way she'd looked panicked when she'd seen only Mark in the car.

"Yeah?" David asked. He'd been trying not to think of the other man. None of them had known what they were walking into—it could have been him or Josh who'd died just as easily.

The plan had been simple enough. He and Josh had approached from the back while Mark and AJ had gone to the front, AJ taking lead. The other men had been coming in the front as he and Josh came in the back, just in time to see the witch they guessed to be Johanna Wilkins take a direct shot at AJ, blasting a six-inch ball of energy straight through his chest like she was a fucking rocket launcher. Then it had been chaos.

Mark had lunged and taken out Kelly Shacovin in a second when she jumped in front of Wilkins, who'd disappeared in a flume of dust. Josh and David had both been occupied by the highest up of the ones who'd been present—Nell Everett—leaving Moriah to blast Mark out of the window, at which point they'd split up out of necessity, Josh chasing after Moriah and David working on dealing with the already injured Nell.

The names and the witches and the day's events flooding his mind, David finally realized he'd been glad that Lauren hadn't asked about any of it. Maybe she'd decided not to after hearing they'd lost AJ—he didn't know, but he wasn't sure he cared about the reasoning, now that he thought about it.

Josh's voice interrupted his thoughts. "You think she could've warned 'em?"

"Huh? What do you mean?"

"Man, there were *four* of them. We were ready for Moriah, maybe Mary also since we knew they were close friends, and she wasn't even there, but four of them?"

David shook his head—the thought was beyond him, and unreasonably, he felt his blood heated by it. "She wouldn't have."

"What, cuz she's loyal to us? Man, I gotta tell you...I felt pretty sure she'd help you when I dropped you off today, I swear to God I did..."

"But there was a part of you that wondered," David finished for him. He shrugged when Josh nodded, grimacing.

"Sorry. I didn't know what to do, but hope she'd help. I thought she would, but I knew Mark needed..."

"No, don't apologize. You did what you had to, and it was fine. I would have figured it out if she hadn't helped me," he lied.

"We have to ask her," Josh said after a moment. "Right?"

"I'm telling you, man, she wouldn't have warned them. Hell, how would she even have done it? Why?" David rolled his shoulders backward and then forward absently, thinking again of the intimacy he'd felt between them that afternoon. That hadn't hinted of betrayal—not for a moment. Fear, maybe, but not betrayal. "I'm not blind here," he said quietly. "She was uncomfortable helping me, *maybe*, and I can't even tell you why unless we just go with the obvious, but I swear to God she was surprised I needed her help. She thought today was just another day, like last time, when we'd come in and tell her one of the coven had joined up with Witness Protection and rolled."

"You didn't tell her we were going after Moriah, ahead of time?" Josh pressed, staring at him.

They both knew the difference, after all. Moriah had been the first witch they'd gone after who *didn't* have a family outside of the coven. If they'd been about to hit a wall, they'd known it was going to be there. And none of the four witches who were left now had any family to speak of, beyond each other—things weren't about to get easier, David knew. But, no. He shook his head adamantly. "I didn't—I wouldn't have. You?"

"No, I didn't."

David stood from the table and paced back and forth before stopping up in front of the fridge and grabbing a beer. "I'm not gonna do the asking. You wanna accuse her of selling us out after she helped save my life today, you do it."

Josh watched his partner move to the sink to stare out the window, a beer in his hand. "Well, not tonight. I just need to crash. You need anything?"

"Nah, I'm good. We gotta get to the store tomorrow, though—I made a list. Figure we ought to buy enough shit to replace the energy-pulling cream I needed, and stockpile some, just in case."

"Yeah, maybe carry it along with us in a fuckin' cooler next time, too," Josh answered, groaning as he rose. "Fuck, I'm sore. See you tomorrow," he said before turning toward the stairs.

David stayed where he was for another few minutes, nursing the beer in his hand and staring blankly into the darkness outside. Josh could think what he wanted to, but David was sure about what he'd felt coming off of Lauren. For whatever reason, she'd cared. She'd been all nerves and fear and adrenaline, all of which he could make up excuses for, but nothing about the way she'd acted or reassured him or taken care of him had suggested—not for even a moment—that she could have caused the day's catastrophe. It had never even occurred to him.

What *had* occurred to him was that what he'd felt coming off of her, for whatever reason, had been want...maybe even desire. He'd already known she felt safe with him, for no good reason he'd been able to figure out. And he'd already known that they'd grown some odd sort of intimacy between them. As if they were comfortable when both of them forgot that that was the last thing they ought to feel around each other. But he hadn't been able to reason out any of it, and he was tired of wondering. From the moment he'd seen her washing out those bowls in the sink, he'd known without a doubt that she wanted space, and that she wanted him to leave her to her own thoughts, and he'd thought he could. But he'd also thought she'd emerge from her room to eat, or at least open the door like she usually did after she'd changed and was ready for one of them to lurk nearby as she tried to get to sleep.

But he hadn't heard her re-open her door since she'd accepted the sandwich from Josh, and it was getting later. Swallowing down the last of his beer, he moved to the fridge to grab two more and then head toward her room. One way or another, he was tired of waiting on answers, and if Josh was going to push the issue by accusing her of selling them out, he needed to find out what was going on sooner than later.

***

It only occurred to him after he'd knocked that he should have put on a shirt—after all, he'd been in bed and trying to sleep before coming upstairs—but it was too late by this point, so he simply waited with the beers in hand.

Lauren opened the door to find David standing awkwardly before her, bare-chested but for gauze and with two beer bottles clutched in one hand. The sight was so unexpected that she froze with her hand on the door for a moment, nothing coming to mind.

"Brought a peace offering," he told her, holding up the beers. "Care for one?"

"A peace offering?" she asked. "Were we fighting?" Of course, as soon as she asked it, she knew what an absurd question it was—they were never at peace and they were never fighting. Whatever was between them was in some gray area that she doubted any two people had ever attempted to define. Sane people, she thought, would have run away from it.

David held up the beers again, and she finally took one from him, stepping back so he could enter the room. He took a seat in the chair by her desk as he usually did, and then took a swig from his beer as he looked her over. She was calmer than earlier, her hair still damp from a shower and pulled back tightly. It had gotten longer since they'd met, and the goth black he'd hated had faded some. She'd dyed her roots with some hair dye she'd requested they get her, but the one he'd picked up had been a more natural black than what she'd originally sported. And either he'd gotten used to the darkness against her pale skin or it was growing on him, but he didn't mind it as much as he once had.

Tonight, in jeans and a light sweater, she looked a lot like the girl he'd first met, if with longer hair and a bit skinnier. "You saved my life today," he told her, when it seemed she was content to sit on her bed and watch the rug rather than speak. "I told Josh I could take care of things when he left; I thought I could. But I would've been dead on the floor by the time he got back."

Lauren kept her eyes on the area rug below her feet, following the swirls of the gray and blue as they tangled together. "You would have figured it out, but I appreciate the beer." She took a breath, leaving her hands both clenched around the bottle he'd given her. "Listen...I meant to tell you earlier, I'm sorry about AJ. He seemed like a nice guy," she added quietly, finally looking up to meet his eyes.

"Yeah...it was...there was nothing we could do," he said simply, thinking about the call he knew Josh had made from the hospital, to the man's dad. "You didn't ask about what went down," he added to change the subject. "I wasn't thinking straight enough earlier..."

"I figured, I mean...you must've gotten Nell Everett, right? Killed her, I'm guessing, since there must have been a real fight. I mean, those energy burns..." Lauren shrugged again, looking over the ragged gauze David had plastered around his body. "They look like what she'd do, and with what happened to AJ and you, I just figured..." she trailed off absently, thinking of a bolt of energy she'd once seen the woman punish a sister witch with after some indiscretion.

"Yeah, these were her work," David said, grimacing. "But she got away. There were four witches—she and Johanna split before we could—"

Lauren jerked to attention, processing what David had said, and he stopped speaking in response. She felt her body tensing, the desire she'd felt at seeing David paling beside the realization that they'd been lucky to survive at all. What the hell had they been thinking?

"You went after four of them at once?" she demanded, emotion pushing her to her feet. "What, you guys are suicidal now?" Lauren moved toward David without thinking about it, and grabbed a hold of his wrist before she could stop herself, lifting his arm and turning it awkwardly before him so that he could see the full line of its injury. Ignoring the warmth she could feel running through her body in reaction, she glared at him, and shook his arm, knowing he was probably dealing with a dull ache by now, at worst. "*Four?*" she asked again.

David jerked his wrist away from her fingers and leaned back. She was close, again, and this wasn't the reaction he'd been expecting. "We didn't *know*, Lauren. We were going after Moriah," he told her, leaning back. Suddenly, she seemed to realize how close she'd come, and perched beside him on the desk, staring at him. When she didn't say anything immediately, he went on, "Kelly Shacovin and Johanna Wilkins were the others there. Wilkins was the one who took down AJ, soon as he came in. She disappeared, and...Shacovin took a shot meant for her and went down."

Lauren shut her eyes, not really surprised. Maybe she'd been thinking that they'd killed Nell—four men against that witch had seemed about right—but none of the witches left of the coven, she felt pretty sure, would be surrendering. "And you went after Nell, and Mark and Josh..."

"It was chaos," David answered quietly. "Moriah took Mark out of the equation. Josh went after her; I went after Nell. Moriah didn't make it either, but Nell got out." David stayed still, watching the girl stationed beside him and letting the quiet speak for itself. Lauren might not have been what she'd call friends with the women who'd died that day, but she'd at least known them.

Lauren slid back, easing herself fully onto the desk so that she could stay seated beside David, her feet dangling above the floor. The thought of Nell, and even Johanna, scared her—enough so that she'd been trying to avoid thinking of them at all. When she'd thought about going back to the coven, she'd thought about trying to stay near Mary or Kelly, or the two witches with families who'd first been picked up by David and Josh. But when she thought of Nell and Johanna, and of Melania also, she just felt cold, and scared. All three of them had capacities for cruelty. That meant that, of the four women left who she had to worry about, three had been the most powerful and terrifying to start with. And now they were angry, to top it off.

"Johanna..." she started to say, and then paused for thought. "She and Melania, they'll sacrifice the others if they have to, to get away. Nell might, too, I don't know. Mary wouldn't. But Nell and Melania are the most powerful, the ones who you should try to...not face when they're together with the others. And Johanna— she can be mean. Cruel. It'll be worse than today, if you do try to take them on together again," she added.

David slipped his hand onto her knee and felt her

twitch in response, but he kept his hand there until she finally looked to meet his gaze. "What am I missing here?" he asked.

"Missing? What do you mean?"

Grunting, David leaned toward her and set his beer on the desk, rolling sideways so that he was in front of Lauren, looking up at her where she sat. "I mean, what am I missing about you? What are you...thinking? When I told you there were four witches today, you were pissed at *us*, me and the guys, for making the mistake of going up against them like that. And you're right," he cut her off before she could interrupt. "We wouldn't have even gone in if we'd known there were three, forget four; we were careless, and should have watched to be sure—that won't happen again. But that doesn't change the fact of how you're acting."

"You're not...That's...It's..." she stopped correcting herself, searching for words. "I'm, I'm scared of them," Lauren finally stammered, leaning back from him. What was she supposed to say here? That she didn't want him to get hurt?

"Yeah, you are." David reached out and gripped her hand as she set it on the edge of the desk as if to slide down from her seat, holding it loosely in front of him. He was watching her, and he could feel the nerves coming off of her, but he wouldn't let this go. Not after the reaction she'd just offered. "But there's more than that. You're not just scared of the coven. And you're not scared of me either, are you?" he asked. "I thought that's what it was—and you'd have every right to be—but it's not that either, is it? So what is it?" he asked, tugging at her hand to get her to look at him.

"You should go," Lauren said instead. She was staring at his hand covering hers, feeling her blood heat with desire, and trying not to look at the rest of him, sitting in front of her. The feel of him being so close...it was driving her crazy. Like there was some drug in her system just pushing her to lean forward and drop into his lap like some wanton ragdoll. It was pitiful, and yet she knew she'd do it if she met his eyes, and he'd probably be so shocked that he'd either laugh at her or run out of the room. And why wasn't he wearing a fucking shirt, anyway? "Seriously, just...just go, okay?"

David shook his head, keeping hold of her hand. "Nuh uh—not this time. I want to know what it is you haven't been telling us." He reached out for her chin when she still remained silent, and tried to tilt it up so she'd meet his eyes, but she tugged away instead, leaning backward so that it was only his one hand holding hers that connected them. He could feel her practically quivering in front of him. He just wanted to know why, for fuck's sake.

"You're trying to humiliate me?" she bit out quietly. "Is that it? Because I don't know what to tell you."

Lauren reached for David's beer after taking the last gulp of her own, and took a sip from his without asking, her one hand still held in his. His grip was rough, and warm, and too comfortable.

"Ya know, I haven't told you...every day since Josh brought you back here—I swear to God, Lauren, every fucking day—I've wished we could have met some other way. That there'd been nothing planned, and I wouldn't have known who you were or been thinking a damn thing about witches or killings or any case that could have a goddamned thing to do with you. Every fucking day," he added, waiting still for her to meet his eyes. "But we didn't, and now...I guess I feel like you're wishing the same thing. And maybe you're too embarrassed to admit it. And I get it, after what I did," he said, taking his beer from her loose grip and taking a sip before he handed it back to her. "But if that's what this is...it'd be nice to know," he finished.

David waited for another minute for her to say something. He felt like he'd trapped her here, the way she was on the desk and the way he was sitting in front of her, holding her hand, but this had all made sense earlier. Getting an answer, figuring out what she was feeling toward him...it had made sense. Now, he just felt like an asshole all over again.

Sighing, he went to stand, letting go of his grip on her hand, and he was before her and pushing away the chair he'd been sitting in when he felt her hand catching his again, and holding on. When he looked back to her, her eyes were searching for his, and her lips were parted, and there wasn't anything to think about—not with the way she was looking at him, anyway.

Lauren leaned up helplessly, shutting off her brain and letting the heat in her blood push her. She wanted to feel safe, and heated...and complete. She wanted to forget about the coven, and the past, and magic altogether. She wanted things to be okay, and easy, for a little while, to where she didn't have to think.

So she slid forward toward him and let her knees part around his thighs as he stepped directly up to the desk, his arms slipping down around her back so that he could hold her, and it felt perfect.

David dropped one of his hands to her lower back and leaned into her, meeting her lips with his. He waited on her cue, opening his lips when she did, meeting her tongue with his when she reached out, and then he let himself pull her body closer. Her lips were warm and slick, exploring his, and he felt a whimper of desire just as much as he heard it when he pressed his tongue briefly between them and let his other hand rest on her thigh, and then hold onto it.

Lauren wasn't thinking—she couldn't. Much as she knew this didn't make any sense, she couldn't help just wanting to be with David, everything else be damned. More than she had since her magic had disappeared, she could feel a life in her blood that hadn't been there lately, as if all of her nerve endings and all of her cells were reacting to him and the way he touched her. With one of his hands on her back and one on her thigh, she couldn't help reaching out so that one of her hands landed at the back of his neck, her fingers in his hair and pulling his lips into hers. Her other hand was on his left bicep, and all of her skin seemed to tingle where it was touching his. When she felt his tongue press again between her lips, she sucked it in and heard the groan of pleasure that came from him in response as her back arched against his hand.

David slid his hand beneath her sweater and she whimpered again, her hand gripping his arm and holding on. He didn't know where this had come from, and didn't care. Kissing her, he explored her skin with his hand beneath her sweater, forcing himself to keep his other hand just holding her thigh. Every instinct in him told him to pick her up and take her to the bed and let things go where they might, but whatever was happening here, he knew he had to understand it first— and after what he'd done to her, he owed her not just that, but something more than fast lust.

With his fingers wandering along the strap of her bra in back, Lauren pulled her lips from his and tried to catch her breath. She felt him kiss her forehead then, gently, and the gentleness of it undid her.

I can't do this, she thought, and pulled back so suddenly that she nearly tumbled sideways off of the desk, his hands having dropped from her instantly when she moved. "I'm sorry, I'm sorry," she muttered, shaking her head and clutching the edge of the desk. "I shouldn't have..."

"Stop apologizing," David interrupted her, and he moved sideways so that he was standing in front of her again. He didn't touch her now, but waited instead for her to say something.

"You should go," she told him again, her eyes clenched shut. Maybe her body wanted him, but she couldn't—she wouldn't let herself. She was more than this stupid spell of her mother's, and despite the fact that she could still taste him, she had to remember that.

"Yeah? That's what you said before you kissed me." Gentle as he kept his voice, he was frustrated. She was shivering in front of him after having practically thrown herself at him, and his dick was hard in his jeans with wanting her. He'd *been* wanting her, and wanting answers, and all he constantly got was more questions.

"I can't, David, I can't, don't you get it?" she asked. She took a deep breath, holding herself still, and locked her hands to the sides of the desk before she looked up. "I know I'm not making any sense, okay? Not to you, I get it, but this...it's not right," she told him. "Don't you get that?"

She watched him take a shuddering breath and shake his head, closing his eyes for a long moment as if to gather himself. "I don't know what to do here, Lauren," he finally said. "Forget everything else—I want you, and you seem to want me. So what's going on here? Is it what I did? Tell me if that's it, and I get it, I do, but you have to give me something here so I know what the fuck's going on."

Lauren shook her head and raised one hand up to her forehead, touching her skin where he'd kissed her, and then she met his eyes. "My life is a mess," she said. "And I don't *want* to want you, okay?"

"But you do, and you're fighting it..." David sighed, turning away and pacing across the room before he came back toward her, and then retreated to take a seat at the chair left near her bed. "It probably sounds grotesque for me to say it, to you, but I'm not a bad guy, Lauren. I hurt you when I pushed you into bed with me, with all those questions, not giving you time to say no, but that...that wasn't something I'd done before. I wouldn't do it again to you or to anyone else, if that makes a difference."

Does it? Lauren didn't know. She couldn't decipher what her body was hoping for versus what her mind was saying, what her logic was telling her, and it was driving her crazy. When she'd seen David injured today, she'd been scared, right away, but had that been her body wanting him, or her brain knowing he was a decent guy who didn't deserve to be hurt? She didn't know.

"I'm gonna go. I'm not up to...whatever we were about to do, anyway. After today...I just wanted to talk," he added.

"Yeah, sorry—"

"Stop." David glared at her, now standing, and waited for her to look at him before he continued. "Stop apologizing. It's a fucked up situation, I get it, and we need to talk again...but not tonight. Just...sleep, okay? Get some rest. I'll do the same. Nothing'll change tomorrow. Josh and I aren't going back out for a few days—I need the rest. There's time."

"Yeah. Okay," Lauren answered. "I should have asked how you were feeling, when you came in," she added, blushing as he turned away at the thought of all of the other things she'd said and done, without really thinking about the obvious.

David barked a laugh, glancing back at her as he put his hand on the door to leave. "I'm okay—just sore.

Tired. I'll be fine," he added. It was good to see her blush when he understood the reason.

Lauren nodded. "I'm glad."

"Lauren—you know where to find me, you need anything. You good with me crashing?"

"Yeah, of course," Lauren nodded, and felt her body untense as she watched him leave.

It wasn't as if she could ask him to stay to watch her fall asleep after all that had just happened.

Chapter 13

He'd had every intention of asking if she'd alerted the coven to their next move, somehow, but when Josh saw Lauren nursing her coffee in the kitchen, he lost the heart to do it. "You sleep at all?" he asked instead.

Lauren took another sip of her coffee and went to speak, but then shrugged instead, yawning as she motioned to the coffee pot in open invitation. "Did I wake you?"

"Nah—I'm not used to crashing by ten like I did last night; couldn't help waking up early," he answered, taking the cream from the fridge and pouring a heavy dose into a mug before he added the coffee itself. "So how does it work, the whole not lying thing?"

"Huh?" Lauren blinked back at him—she'd barely been paying attention to him, truth be told, tired as she was. What was it, 7 AM, and he wanted to talk about that?

Josh took his cup to the island and sat across from her. Considering the circles under her eyes, she looked like she needed to be back in bed instead of sipping coffee. "Just then—you wanted to tell me you'd slept, and then you shrugged off the question. Because you couldn't even lie about that, am I right? I hadn't gotten around to asking whether you could lie about little things," he added when she was still blinking back at him rather than answering. "You know—polite conversation? Saying things are okay or that someone looks fine—all that."

Lauren stretched, trying to wake herself up enough to have a conversation; she'd expected another hour to herself before either of the men woke. "How about I trade you a real answer for breakfast, if you feel like cooking?" she asked after taking another sip of her coffee.

"Any requests?"

That's easy. "Banana pancakes like you made last weekend?"

Josh grinned and stood. "You got it." He took a gulp of his coffee and began moving around the kitchen, taking out what he needed as well as some bacon—she might not have requested it, but he and David would want it, and he knew she'd snack on it if it was offered. "So spill it," he told her as he worked. "The whole lying thing, the spell—how does someone get by when they live in that Jim Carrey movie where he can't tell even the slightest fib?"

"You get used to it; you saw a moment ago—it's automatic now. Mom cast the spell on me...God, I guess I was twelve? Somewhere in there. I'd gotten into the habit of lying about little things. Meeting friends at the mall instead of to study, keeping some of the change for myself when she sent me to the grocery store for something...kid stuff, ya know?" she asked, rising to get herself more coffee. Thinking back, she watched Josh slicing bananas, and thought about the breaking point in everything. "Then I lied about meeting a boy I liked...we actually *were* studying, but I'd told her I was meeting a girlfriend to study. She was always so paranoid about guy friends, I hadn't wanted to tell her. And you know he was actually gay? I didn't tell her, though; figured she wouldn't believe me anyway."

"Did you ever tell her?" Josh asked after a minute, dropping some bacon into the frying pan as he took a quick glance at her; this was the first he'd heard her talk so freely about herself.

"I...I don't remember. I know I thought about it," she added, her gaze far away. "Anyhow, she said the spell was for my own good," Lauren answered, just catching herself from saying *spells* instead of *spell*, singular. *I'm too tired to be talking about this*, she thought, but sat down again as she stirred some sugar into her coffee.

"Anyhow," she began again, "I got used to it. I mean, omissions are still okay. Sometimes it gets hard on the phone, but I'm not much of a phone person. Other times, I can usually get away with changing the subject—"

"Or with a shrug," Josh finished for her.

"Right. Or a shrug," she agreed. "It did make me fail a paper once," she said after a moment. "I was in English Comp...we were supposed to write two short papers, taking opposite sides of an issue. It was a good assignment, actually—I really enjoyed hearing everyone struggle through it," she said more quietly. "But I couldn't do it. I got the one paper done, but our teacher had told us to pick a subject we cared about—something that mattered to us—and hadn't told us what was coming. So we all wrote the first paper, stating our case and our opinion, and turned it in. Then she turned around and told us we had to take the opposite side, and make it personal."

Josh waited a few beats, and then prodded her, "And you couldn't do it?"

"No...not at all. I tried, too. But I either couldn't write it, or the words came out to the side I'd already argued. I thought about getting someone else to write it for me...but that could have led to me failing the class, assuming I'd even been able to turn a plagiarized paper in. I don't know if the spell would have let me, but I'd have caved if the teacher asked about it, so I figured the one F was a safer bet."

Glancing over his shoulder at her, Josh didn't have a hard time imagining the girl in their kitchen as a freshman in college, struggling with a paper for nights in a row. "What were you writing about? What subject did you choose?" he asked.

"Hmm? Oh, biodiversity...I...I like plants," she said quietly. "My first paper argued that we couldn't afford to lose anymore rainforests to logging, clear-cutting, pollution...because we needed them for us as much as for the planet."

"Fair argument," he answered, turning to watch her as he let the bacon cook and waited to flip some pancakes.

"Yeah, well...it's easy to write about stuff you care about, right? I mean, that was the whole point maybe, to show us that and then get us to think about both sides. But anyhow, yeah, that was the hardest not lying was until..." she trailed off then, her voice dying out rather than going to the next logical spot.

"Until here," he said, "with us."

"Yeah." Lauren sipped her coffee and rubbed her

eyes for a moment. Maybe she should just go to bed.

"I guess I shouldn't have brought it up," Josh said, turning back to the stovetop. "But I'd wondered...what me and David do, we have to lie some; there's no way around it."

"No kidding?" Lauren saw Josh tense at the sarcasm in her voice, but didn't take it back. She didn't hold what they'd done against them, though she probably should have, but that didn't mean she had to be okay with it.

"You're thinking about David lying to you at the bar? Or something else?"

Lauren shrugged. "I don't know—that, I guess, yeah."

"Did he?"

"What do you mean?"

Josh turned back to face her. "Did he lie to you at the bar, when you met?" Truth be told, he doubted his partner had. He'd been attracted to Lauren from the first—he'd admitted as much when they'd first brought her back—so although Lauren might have assumed he was lying...maybe it was only fair that she knew he hadn't been.

"I..." Lauren stopped. Had he? She'd simply figured he had, but now that she thought of it...they'd been flirting, and he'd told her she was pretty, and they'd talked about music and movies, and then he'd offered her a cigarette..."I don't know," she said, realizing it for the first time. Somehow, she'd been assuming he'd been lying to her from the beginning.

Josh turned back to the stove. "Ya know, yesterday...man, I was pissed. About AJ, about everything. David told you what happened?" he asked.

"Yeah. He did, last night."

"I figured—he didn't come downstairs right away

after we ate, so I thought he might. But yeah, I was pissed. And I thought—it occurred to me that maybe you somehow warned them we were coming."

Lauren nearly choked on her coffee, and covered her mouth as she forced herself to swallow it down. "You thought I warned them?" she asked.

"Yeah, I don't know," Josh answered. He glanced behind him, though he didn't have to—the shock in her voice was real, as had been the sound of her almost spitting out the coffee in her mouth. "The point is, David said there was no way. Didn't even consider it a possibility. Said you wouldn't 've if you could've."

Lauren swallowed, thinking about it. "He was right," she said quietly. "I guess...last night he was asking me why I was upset with you guys for going after four at once—I mean, when he told me, I thought you guys did it on purpose, and I was mad—I couldn't...I can't...I don't know," she said helplessly. "You guys are saying that my loyalties shouldn't be with you or them, I guess?"

"I guess," Josh echoed, pulling some finished pancakes off the pan and pouring in some more batter before he added some sliced bananas into the frying pan to cook into them. He'd heard what she'd said about being upset at them for going after four at once, on behalf of them, but he couldn't process it now—it would be something to figure out later. "I was just thinking, after I left David here, that maybe you could have tried to trade us for your safety, freedom, whatever. And that I wouldn't have necessarily blamed you, for putting yourself over us," he added. "What you know of us, all things considered. I don't think anyone would blame you."

"But me," Lauren answered before she could stop herself, and then froze under Josh's glance when he looked back to her. "I mean...I couldn't do it, is what I'm saying. Maybe that's silly, or crazy. It probably is. But I don't owe the coven anything," Lauren told him, thinking about the fact that it never would have occurred to her to try to trade their skins for her own. These guys didn't deserve that—nobody would. "And they wouldn't have taken the trade anyway," she added, forcing a flippancy into her voice that she didn't really feel. "Melania and Nell...they're stubborn. I'd never trust them to set their minds on something and then trade for something else."

"You're saying they would have killed us and taken you anyway if you'd tried to offer us up in return for you going free," he commented. It was the same conclusion he'd come to that morning, though he'd planned on looking for confirmation from her anyway.

"I don't know them well...I'm not saying I do. I'm just saying I wouldn't trust them."

Josh flipped the pancakes and mixed some bananas into the last of the batter beside him, letting the quiet last. "You wanna get plates out while I go wake David up? He'll shoot me himself if we eat all of this without him."

Stretching, Lauren nodded agreement and stood to collect place settings while Josh headed downstairs. Tired as she was, the conversation had left her feeling somehow better than she had earlier that morning. Like the air was more clear. And with Josh's cooking to look forward to...well, it was easier to put aside the night's nightmares, and put aside whatever the next few weeks would bring, and just try to focus on the moment. *Pancakes, and then a shower. One thing at a time*, she told herself.

***

Soon after breakfast, and finished with a shower and a round of fresh cream and gauze, David parked himself in front of the television to watch baseball without any intention of moving in the near future. He'd DVR'd two Orioles games from earlier in the week, and he figured live coverage of the next game would be on by the time he watched-slash-forwarded through the saved games. Despite the fact that Josh made fun of him for the fact that he tended to erase more games than he got around to watching, it was days like this when he was thankful that he'd bothered to set the recordings. He'd felt fine the night before, if sore and tired, but a night of sleep had left him aching, exhausted, and overly warm—as if he'd gotten a bad sunburn the day before.

Really, there wasn't much he had the energy for beyond staring at the tube, and with Josh out to run errands and Lauren parked in her room with a book, he figured he might as well try to lose himself in sports.

Four innings into the first game, though, he felt himself dozing off, and gave in to the urge without bothering to pause the game. It was too early in the season for there to be much at stake, anyway. When he woke, he could hear Josh moving around the kitchen, and soft music coming from what he guessed was the sound set-up in Lauren's room. 4:48 PM blinked up on the cable box, the television long gone silent. He'd slept away most of the day.

Sitting up, it seemed like he could feel every one of his muscles—even the ones that hadn't been touched by the witch's energy. And he was so fucking warm, though he could hear the air running. Someone had placed a bottle of water on the table for him, and he gulped the whole of it down before he stood and stretched, and then made his way to the kitchen to find Josh shaping burgers on the island.

"Mornin' again. How're the burns?"

"Hot," David answered, fishing another bottle of water from the fridge. "You were right about me needing a few days down—I feel like a fucking burnt zombie."

"Yeah—I got some bad energy burns when I was still in training and I was down for a few days. You'll be back to normal soon enough. I made some more of the cream, by the way."

"Thanks. Any new developments I oughtta know about?" he asked, taking a seat at the island and nudging the pepper shaker toward his partner—far as he was concerned, he never put quite enough pepper in the burgers he grilled.

"Man, between the errands and the cream and deciding I felt like us doing an old-school cook-out, I barely checked email today. Figured the other side's recovering, too, so I'd take a day off with ya," Josh answered, shrugging. Truth be told, he was out of ideas for how to next track the witches who were left, and thought a day off might push a new lightbulb into his existence if he just stopped trying to think about things so constantly. They had to figure out how to get to them while the witches were still licking their wounds.

"Claudia's coming over around six; figured we could fire up the grill and eat outside if you're up for it."

"Long as I get to stay in the shade," David answered slowly. "And Lauren?" he asked.

"What about her? You think I'm not gonna feed her, too?"

"The wardings—they're stronger in here. You think we're okay eating outside?" David pressed, taking a quick glance behind him to make sure she hadn't approached. Since they'd brought her to the house, she hadn't *stepped* outside, and that had been on purpose. The house was, without a doubt, safe. The land probably was also, but outside of the walls...

"It'll be fine. She needs to get outside, and we'll just be on the patio. You don't think it's safe?" Josh asked after a moment, looking up as his partner shrugged.

"I don't know. But she's scared of the witches who are left—I get the impression from her that we're done taking out the easy ones, maybe with the exception of the Mary chick. I just don't want to take any chances."

Josh nodded after a moment. "Okay, so we won't. I'll call Barry and invite him over, get him to double-up the wards we've got on the patio and pay him with burgers."

Makes sense, David thought. It wouldn't take much. Barry was their resident expert on wards, and hadn't failed them yet. "Fair enough. You need help with anything for the cook-out?" David asked.

"You could shuck the corn, you feel like it."

Lauren slipped behind David just as he was going to rise, shaking her head as she moved and giving a quick smile to Josh. She looked tired, but refreshed, and David had to figure she'd just come from one of those long baths she enjoyed. "I'll do it; you rest," she answered for him, already pulling the corn out from the fridge.

"You like burgers or hot dogs?" Josh asked.

"I'll take whatever you're cooking," Lauren answered easily. Settling at the island a stool away from David, she started pulling the silk from an ear of corn. She'd been fighting to keep herself awake today, and was glad to have something to do that was useful. She wanted to sleep that night, which meant she didn't want to nap. "How are you?" she asked, glancing up to David. She found that he'd been watching her, and looked back to her hands quickly rather than acknowledging it.

"Alright. Hot," he admitted, shifting on the stool.

"Claudia's coming over—figured we'd eat on the patio and have a real cook-out, nice as the weather is," Josh said after a moment. "She's been bugging me to have all of us hang out—now that you're better," he added. "Shoot," he interrupted himself. "David, you wanna call Barry?"

"Huh? Oh, yeah." David pulled away from the island and stood, pausing when he saw the questioning look Lauren was shooting him. "He's gonna double-up on the patio wards so you don't have to worry about being outside. It should be fine anyway, but just in case."

Lauren nodded, but part of her heart was in her throat. She had no idea if the witches had a way of tracking her, but as close as they'd been to her mother and her mother's magic, it wasn't out of the question. Still, it would be nice to be outside for a while.

****

Sitting back in one of the patio chairs, David felt more relaxed than he'd felt in weeks. Barry had brought his usual life to the gathering, and though he'd never met Lauren or Claudia before, he'd had them laughing and joking with him within minutes. Now they were inside the kitchen with Barry's newest girlfriend, a lanky basketball-player-tall girl named Cara he'd met only the night before, mixing up a second round of frozen Margaritas.

"For the men of the house!" Claudia announced as she came through the door with two overflowing drinks in her hands for Josh and David. Setting the drinks down, she took her own drink from Lauren, who'd followed her outside. "We're gonna sit by the pool if you boys wanna join us," she added, tipping her glass at

Josh and offering a wink. He just grinned and leaned back, watching the two women walk away.

As the girls hung their legs from the patio into the water, David took a sip of the drink they'd brought him. "Strong," he commented. "Think they're okay over there?"

"They're fine," Barry answered from behind them.

David looked up to see that the other man had joined them, even as his date headed over to the side of the pool.

"What is she," David asked, "ten years younger than you?"

"No idea," Barry answered, grinning and taking a seat. "But look who's talking, right? Josh here's the only one who's got a date that's near his own age."

"Lauren's not a date," David growled, catching Josh's smirk from the corner of his eye. "Protective custody, remember? The whole reason you're here?"

"Doesn't mean there can't be more than one reason, mate. Just sayin'," he added, waving his drink around dismissively. "But hey, yeah, they're fine. I don't know if they could be tracking her anyway, or how they would, but they'd have to lock onto her thoughts, if anything. I've got wards around this whole property, and her feet dangling outside of the immediate wards doesn't make a damn bit of difference, I guaran-damn-tee."

"Yeah, well, these Margaritas are strong enough that those girls are gonna be stripping down and jumping in the pool if we're not careful, so I hope you're right," David commented. Drinking down more of the frozen drink in his hand, he watched them at the edge of the patio, and thought about how weirdly normal this felt. What Claudia knew of Lauren was simply that she needed a safe place to stay and was in protective custody for a while, and as someone who was closer to his and

Josh's age, she'd seemed to adopt the younger woman as a sort of younger sister. He could see Lauren wasn't used to it, and it made him wonder how solitary she'd been. She hadn't told him much about her life prior to their meeting, and he hadn't felt like it was his place to ask, but on a night like this, where it really did feel like he was a part of three couples getting together for an evening of relaxing and passing the time...

He stood fast enough that what was left of his drink spilled across his pants leg when what had seemed like joking by the pool suddenly ended in Barry's date, Cara, playfully shoving Claudia and Lauren into the pool before diving in after them. "Fuck," he muttered, moving toward the pool until Josh caught his hand.

"She's fine—don't lose your cool," Josh told him quietly as Barry passed them by to start fishing the girls from the water.

"Why is the pool so cold?" Barry's date complained, and for the life of him David couldn't even remember her name. She seemed younger by the minute.

Lauren met David's eyes nervously as Josh grabbed her hand to help pull her out of the pool. She was biting her lip again, and David felt the same. Probably, she was safe anywhere on the property, but they'd planned on staying on the patio; he'd just reminded her of it when they'd finished eating, in fact. Barry's whistle brought him back to the moment, and back to the obvious.

Lauren had been wearing a light cotton skirt and a thin cotton top; he'd been watching her curves walk back and forth in them all night. Now, the clothes were plastered to her, the clear outlines of a lace bra and panty set showing through the clothes and what little she could cover with her hands. Meanwhile, though Lauren had had reason enough to climb out, Claudia was protesting that she wouldn't leave the pool until Josh got her a towel—she was in the same bind now, clothing-wise.

Blushing, and giving up on Claudia, Lauren hurried past with an embarrassed wave toward Barry as he cat-called again, and David followed her as Josh went to the patio's ottoman, where he'd finally remembered that they kept extra pool towels.

Inside, David followed Lauren to her room and knocked.

"I'm changing!" she called through the door.

"I know—I'm not coming in. You okay?"

"I...yeah? Wait a second?" she asked, stuttering through the words as he listened.

When Lauren came out, she'd changed into jeans and a loose top—the veritable opposite of what she'd worn before, both in how the clothes covered her skin and hid her figure. "Hey," she said nervously, opening her door as she combed fingers through her hair.

"Hey. You alright?" he asked from across the hall where he'd been leaning on the wall, waiting for her.

"I guess..."

"It should be fine," he answered the question hanging between them, despite the hollow in his stomach. "We don't even know if they could have a way of finding you now, and there are wards on the whole property."

"You told me to make sure to stay on the patio—so did Josh and Barry. I didn't mean—"

"Yeah, I know, and it's fine. Try not to worry, alright?"

Josh came around the corner then, his lips pursed. "Lauren, you got some clothes Claudia could borrow?"

"Oh, yeah, of course," she answered, already ducking back into her room. "You want some for Cara also?" she called backward.

Josh shrugged at David, rolling his eyes. "I don't

know if she cares, but why not? Thanks."

True to Josh's guess, she didn't care, and didn't actually seem to realize that she'd caused any awkwardness at all, which Lauren supposed made things easier. Cara was the type of girl she'd never been comfortable with—so carefree and joking that it was as if she'd never had to deal with bad news or stress in her whole damned life. As if she was on some different plain of existence that didn't acknowledge any of life's difficulties. All was forgiven, though—Lauren had to take the guys at their word and trust that a moment's dip outside of the patio's borders wouldn't have made a difference.

Soon enough, she was seated beside David and drinking down a third Margarita. Cara was actually in Barry's lap, and Lauren could only imagine what she was whispering into the man's ear, but it provided some amusement for the rest of them while they pretended toward focusing on a conversation built more around when it would be warm enough to *enjoy* the pool, and how good Josh's cooking had been. It was easy, soon enough, to sit back and stop worrying about what might have happened, or might not have happened. And, there was the way David had looked at her to distract her.

When Josh had pulled her from the pool, she hadn't actually realized how see-through her clothes had become—she hadn't even considered it until Barry had whistled, truth be told, and then she'd been shocked when she'd seen herself in the mirror in her room. David's look, though...on the heels of the shock and worry she'd seen in his face when he'd first approached the pool, mirroring her own emotions, the look in his eyes had been shaded over by all-out desire when she'd suddenly been standing on the pool's edge. He'd looked like he'd wanted to sweep her up right there and continue where they'd left off the night before; that had been why she'd fled inside, coupled with how clear the warming in her own blood had been in response. It had been what she'd wanted, too.

Most of the way through her third drink now, she realized she was leaning toward David, her body signaling its attraction whether she intended it to or not. Her free arm dangled over her chair's edge, toward his, and her legs were crossed, one tilted toward him. And his posture mirrored her own. Noticing it, Lauren let her gaze be caught by Claudia's as the other woman smiled and shot her eyes toward David knowingly. She let herself offer a small smile in response, but her heart was speeding. Snuggling further back into her chair, she looked out over the landscape of the property, and then up to the stars, and tried to focus her mind there. She could relax if she didn't think about how comfortable she felt right now, and what that meant.

Chapter 14

ulled from bed, from sleep, Lauren moved sluggishly, following along behind David and Josh as they led her to the door. Her limbs felt heavy, as if she were wearing weights on her limbs, and each step came at the cost of a labored breath. Blinking, she leaned against the wall near the kitchen, and looked up to see both of the men staring back at her, angry and silent, their jaws set in frowns.

"I don't know what I did," she murmured, but again got no answer. Instead, David crossed his arms and nodded toward the front door.

Shivering, Lauren struggled to keep her eyes open and take another step. They hadn't even given her time to change, to put on shoes. Now, she was cold, and felt as if her lungs were full even when she breathed out. The men hadn't turned on a light, and were shadows ahead of her. At the door, they stepped to the side and waited for her.

"I'm sorry," she whimpered. Even her brain wasn't moving right, she realized—she couldn't focus enough to decide upon any one train of thought that might prove an answer as to why they were kicking her out in the middle of the night. Had the drinks been that strong? But more importantly, why they weren't speaking to her? And they looked so hard, almost as if she were suddenly a stranger all over again, or an enemy. She stopped suddenly, leaning on the back of the couch for support as she reached the middle of the living room, swallowing what had felt something like a sob, and something like stopped-up air. Her body felt so weighted. It was getting harder to breathe, too, as if she were breathing smoke and her body was fighting it, but the men didn't seem to notice. She closed her eyes, panting, and tried to ignore the heaviness in her limbs. She just wanted to sleep.

There were tears on her cheeks now, but her arms felt too heavy to try to wipe them away, and so she took another step forward, and then another, and then another, until she was standing before the door, leaning on it with the men to her side. They hadn't actually told her they wanted her out, she suddenly realized, but she knew that was their intention. And, they'd led her to the door.

She looked at Josh's face, and then David's, and saw nothing more than hard recognition. "Okay, so I'll leave," she said to herself more than to them.

Lauren turned the door's lock, and tugged, but hit a barrier. Slowly, she raised her face and saw the deadbolt she'd forgotten about, thrown solid and holding the door closed, at the top of the door. Her arms were too heavy, she thought, but she finally reached a hand up anyway. Even leaning against the door, she couldn't reach it.

She slid down against the wood, her back to it, and

looked to the scowling men. "I can't reach it; you'll have to let me out."

Instead of moving to the door, though, they both stood still, glaring at her. Lauren closed her eyes, willing herself to stop crying. The tears were more from exhaustion, and from the weight of her body, than the fact that she was being chased off into the night, but they were making it hard to focus, and she was so tired...

"I can't reach it," she said again, letting her legs splay out in front of her.

David grunted, and the sound stirred something in her, but she couldn't tell what the sound meant. He headed toward the back door to the patio, and she rested her head back on the front door. "There's one there, too," she said.

They know that, she told herself. And then, *If they want me gone...why do they want me gone? ...But if they do...they do, right? ...Why won't they just release the deadbolt?*

Lauren swallowed again—she felt somehow desperate for air, and incredibly cold. Opening her eyes, she looked at Josh, who was still frozen above her in that hard stance, glaring down at her. For a moment, she thought he might kick her. And then...he flickered.

Blinking, she tried to focus—he wasn't moving. She looked beyond him to David, who'd turned to look at her and now stood unnaturally still, himself, and suddenly she realized their heights were wrong. In front of her, walking, they'd been the *same* height.

And that wasn't right.

Was she dreaming? What was happening? Lauren felt her body lighten momentarily, and then grow heavier than before so that she felt as if she were being pressed to the floor as both men suddenly began walking toward her, Josh reaching her first and bending down in front of her.

"You're body's asleep," he told her, but in a voice that wasn't his—it was robotic, and almost feminine. "Pity that your mind didn't stay asleep, and this wouldn't have been so difficult."

Lauren shut her eyes, willing herself to wake up as she felt Josh's freezing-cold hand land on her wrist and pull her upward, turning her toward the door. Her body hurt all over, aching from the cold and the weight she was feeling in it, but he was lifting her. She wrapped her other hand around her arm, tightly, into the crook of her elbow, holding it curled to her chest so that her hand wouldn't reach above her shoulder level. She thought he'd give up, and let her go, but then she was an inch off the ground, his hand wrapped around her wrist and lifting her curled fingers toward that deadbolt, pressing her up against the door.

All of her strength was in trying to hold her arm down, away from that lock, and he was struggling to pull her body upward against the door, but he was doing it. She balled her fist, but she didn't have the strength to fight back against his body; she could only hold onto her arm and try to keep herself unyielding. *They're connected to me, not the house*, she realized. *I can't let them take me out of the house. I can't throw that bolt.*

Feeling herself pulled upward another inch, her feet dangling—she was halfway there now—she packed every bit of energy she had into a scream, and yelled out as the phantom lifted her another inch from the ground, stretching her arm and wrist so that it felt as if her elbow would be pulled apart, or her arm broken. She didn't know how loud she was, but she thought she heard her voice echo backward, and the sound of it was cavernous in her mind, calling out David's name as if her life depended on it, which she thought it did. She couldn't gather air again, though, and suddenly wasn't so sure that her scream had been loud at all. *Maybe, with Mom's spell...maybe that connection...*Focusing all of her concentration into one thought, she imagined David, and imagined him hearing her, and screamed in her mind as loudly as she could, willing him to hear her, and hoping.

***

David jerked up from his bed. He'd *heard* something—and for the life of him, he thought he'd heard it both from the air around him and from inside of his brain. The room was silent, but his head was pounding as if there were a noise echoing within it.

Going on instinct, he pushed back the covers and rushed from his room without bothering to dress, only grabbing his gun as he moved. He had to get upstairs, check on Lauren, and make sure things were secure; maybe it was the tequila in his system, but he was wide awake and pounding with adrenaline, as well as a headache that felt like it had come from a cement wall more than liquor.

He heard what sounded like shuffling when he reached the top of the stairs and froze; it was coming from the front entrance. Whirling to the sound, he ran, and then skidded to a halt. At the door, Lauren was suspended in mid-air by one of her wrists, the arm curled against her body so that it looked like she was hugging herself, only one hand and wrist showing above her shoulder as she slid up the door—dragged by a flickering image of his own partner. A matching, unreal image of himself stood nearby, staring at the struggle.

The shuffling sound had been *her,* her feet already dangling six inches from the ground, brushing at the door.

Dropping his gun, David ran at her, recognizing the phantom visions of himself and Josh for what they were and blasting his body through them so that they disintegrated on impact with contact from something other than their focus. He wrapped his arms around Lauren from behind and yanked her backwards, away from the door and the residual cold.

The two of them landed on the floor together and Lauren curled into David's chest, suddenly awake and sobbing. The weight she'd been feeling in her body was gone, though her arm ached and her wrist had gone numb with the cold grip of the phantasm that had been holding her up.

"What the fuck, what the fuck," David muttered, holding Lauren beside him and staring at his door. He'd seen her *floating*, for fuck's sake. Phantasms being projected into the space were one thing—this had been something new. "Are you okay?" he demanded, and clutched her tighter when she just nodded into his chest.

"I followed...I followed them; I thought they were you, you and Josh," Lauren stuttered. "They were trying to get me to leave, but then I couldn't reach the lock. When they couldn't open it, I realized..."

David swallowed down frustration and shifted so that he could pull Lauren over one of his legs and wrap the whole of his body around her shivering frame, and just hold onto her. Running his hands up and down her arms, he could see where ugly bruises were already forming at the elbow and wrist of her right arm, where she'd held onto her own body and where the thing had gripped her to try to get her to the lock.

"You're okay, I've got you."

Lauren breathed in, trying to focus on the heat she felt coming from the man holding her, and the heat in her blood that was slowly starting to respond to him, and starting to wake up. She was still so cold, though—and those things had been so close to getting her outside. "I didn't recognize them as spirit matter," she whispered. "I would have thought...I would have thought I'd recognize things like that, but...I thought it was you, and Josh, telling me to get out. But I couldn't figure out why, and then I couldn't reach..."

"Shhh. It's okay," David said again. "You're not going anywhere. We wouldn't tell you to get out, you know that. You're okay," he repeated, to himself as much as to her—and then he thought of the fact that the coven had managed to pool energy, into matter that had been solid enough in form to lift Lauren from the ground even inside of a warded space, now that they knew where she was—and with that realization, he knew they were out of time.

***

Nell sat back from the circle of women, waving her hand at them to gesture for silence. She needed to think. The man's presence had of course cut through the pool of energy she'd drawn into the area for her phantoms, but how he'd known to get there, and why there'd been those traces of residual magic in Lauren's aura...that didn't make sense.

"Mary, you spoke to her—you said her magic was essentially gone, that you couldn't sense it at all. She came to you because of the magic, but did you speak of anything else?"

Mary shrugged, leaning back from the small circle with a scowl. She'd thought tonight would be the end of things. "She asked about breaking that affection spell Phillippa put on her when she was young—the one to tie her to a man who she slept with. You remember—it was when Phillippa's husband was having that affair and she...lost control," Mary said delicately. "For the first time. Lauren came to see if we could help restore her magic or break her mother's spells, though she seemed less concerned with the one about lying." She paused, going over the scene they'd observed being projected in their circle. "You think that man could be the reason she was asking? The man who interrupted things?"

"It seems far-fetched, doesn't it? But...you said some men took her; that that was how she lost her magic. The timing—for her to be concerned about her mother's spells suddenly, right as that would happen—it would fit, wouldn't it?"

Melania interrupted them by standing and stretching, a scowl laced across her thin face. She'd been against this plan from the beginning. Better if they'd just waited at Mary's new place, planning an ambush. If they'd found Moriah's house, they'd know where to find Mary's soon enough. "It doesn't matter if the man with her now is the one she chose to sleep with or not. There were problems with this plan and we knew it. We'll be on to the next step now. Self-preservation first, and then we'll deal with Lauren's running away from the coven. What's left of us," she spat.

Mary looked hesitantly between the other witches. Johanna sat grimacing across from her, still angry after their retreat from Moriah's. Nell was poised and thoughtful, but just as dangerous. The only think Mary had going in her favor was the fact that there were only four of them left—none of them wanted an internal disagreement to cause a further weakening of their coven. "If Lauren retains some magic, as we saw just now, doesn't that make all of this moot, at least in terms of bringing her back? If she's got magic..."

"It's residual," Nell answered with a shake of her

head. Her mother's spell is in her blood, and active if she's that close to the man she's tied herself to. That must be the case. When she's separated from him, when he's dead, the magic will fade. I doubt she even realizes it's there, weak as the glimmer is."

"But with that spell..."

"Mary, don't be an imbecile," Melania interrupted. "The man can't live after what he and his partner have done to our coven, and the bit of residual magic Lauren seems to be giving off is nothing."

"She must have called to him mentally, though," Mary answered quietly. "That's how he knew to come and break our entrance, isn't it?"

"Perhaps. I don't see how it matters, however. Lauren's broken the rules of the coven, and these men have torn our group apart, killing two of our number and convincing the weak of the group that a life outside of magic is preferable. We won't ignore that. Not any of it," Melania finished, meeting the eyes of the other three women each in turn.

***

It wasn't hard for David to convince Lauren that she needed to stay in his rooms for the night—they both needed sleep, and it wasn't safe for her to simply go back to the guest room. Maybe if he'd wanted to sleep on the floor in the hall, but he didn't. Plus, her being downstairs put extra space between her and the door, not to mention offering the extra warding and security that they had in place between the upper floor and their suites. But her footsteps stopped when they got to the bottom of the stairs.

"You coming?" he asked, his hand already on his doorknob. She was just in front of the staircase, still wearing the light cotton pajama pants and tank top he'd found her in upstairs. The fear, though, had been replaced by nerves. She nodded at him now, but she didn't move forward. "You can take my bed and I'll take the couch," he offered finally. It wasn't what he wanted, but more than anything, he just wanted sleep; the adrenaline had worn into exhaustion, and now he was afraid he'd have to go about convincing her she needed to be downstairs all over again.

"No, it's fine," she said quietly, finally stepping forward and following him into his rooms.

It wasn't what she'd expected. She'd thought, perhaps, they each had bedrooms downstairs, but what she stepped into was more of an apartment. Coming downstairs, she'd felt more and more like she was crossing some boundary—which she had been, between their professional world and their personal world. And she'd known that; she just hadn't expected to feel the rush of intimacy that had come to her as she'd descended. Now it was worse. Instead of the hotel-room-like atmosphere she'd expected, there was what looked more like a bachelor pad before her.

There was a kitchenette to the side which essentially amounted to cabinets and a small fridge, along with a counter, and the space was otherwise a living room set-up with a threadbare recliner, an old couch, and a large-screen television. There was an extra wide armchair stationed under a reading lamp to one side of the room, an e-reader beside it on a table, a jacket thrown over the chair. Closer by, some empty beer bottles sat on a coffee table beside David's truck keys. The space looked lived-in, and comfortable.

"Bedroom's through here," he interrupted her examination, and she followed him down a short hall with only two doors leading off of it. "Bathroom," he told her, gesturing to the right, "and bedroom," he finished, opening the door that had been mostly open already. David stepped inside, and Lauren followed him to the doorway. There was a large bed to one side of the room, and Lauren could see a stack of folded laundry taking up the one chair in the space. There were two doors, one of which she could see opened into the large bathroom he'd already pointed out from the hall, and the other to a closet that he was already standing before, pulling down extra blankets.

"It's okay," she told him awkwardly, "you have a big bed."

David eyed her—she was still standing in the doorway. "You sure?"

Lauren nodded. She'd seen his couch, and doubted he'd get much sleep if he went back out there. Without a doubt, his feet or his head would be hanging off if he did. And the bed was big, she told herself, ignoring the fact that there was more reasoning than that to her wanting him to stay in the room with her.

"I don't want to kick you out of your own bed," she said. "If you're okay with me..."

"Not a problem on my end," he assured her, already pushing back into place the blankets he'd been getting from the closet.

Lauren went to the side of the bed where it looked like the covers had been less disturbed, guessing that David normally slept near the nightstand where his phone lay, and gingerly pulled back the covers. He watched as she sat down and then tucked herself into the bed, nearly as close to the edge as possible, before he went to the other side and returned his gun to his nightstand.

"It gets pitch black in here—not like upstairs where you have the property lights shining in the windows some. You okay with that?"

Lauren nodded, but was still jarred by the utter blackness that descended when he switched the light by the door to turn off the overhead. "It's okay," she heard him say, and then his footsteps came back toward the bed, and the mattress shifted beneath her as he settled on the other side, the covers moving beneath her arm when he lay back and pulled them up. "If you need anything..."

"I'll tell you," she replied quietly. "Thanks."

"Not a problem," he answered, a yawn taking up the last of the phrase. "Just...I'll probably wake up, but don't go upstairs in the morning without waking me, alright? And use anything you need in the bathroom."

"Thanks," Lauren repeated, willing herself to relax.

She knew she was imagining it, but it seemed as if she could feel the heat of him through the mattress, inching into her own body and warming her blood. She could feel the desire coming on, too, as she'd known it would if she stayed close to him even after the evening's terror wore off. Laying on her side, facing outward, she felt for the edge of the bed and held onto it—trying to station herself to the present and not to what her body wanted, trying to stay still, trying to push herself into slumber by snuggling deeper into the bed, beneath the blanket.

"You comfortable?" he asked from behind her. He could feel her shifting. Hell, he could feel her nerves from across the bed, eating at her. His own nerve endings were driving him crazy in return, sleep suddenly far off and fading.

"Getting there," she answered.

He felt her turn over, re-situating, and fought the urge to turn to her. He was laying on his back, as he usually did, but there was still plenty of space between them, he knew. She had personal space. He had to let her keep it. But then...she'd kissed him back before. And he'd seen the recognition in her eyes at the way he'd looked at her earlier, after she'd stepped from the pool and shown just as much of her figure as if she'd been wearing a bikini, what with her clothes soaked. And he'd felt what was between them when they'd been in the garage, too.

"It's up to you," he started, "but if you're still scared...if I'm holding onto you, I'll wake up when you move again, if you do," he said quietly, willing her to accept the invitation. So be it if he didn't sleep.

"You don't mind?" came the answer.

He nodded before he realized she couldn't see the gesture, and then turned sideways so that he could reach for her. "Not at all," he said just before his fingers came down on her arm, and though he felt her gasp at the touch, she moved backward, sliding in against him naturally so that they landed in the middle of the bed. He pulled the pillows inward. He didn't know what he'd been expecting, but he hadn't quite expected for her to just slide back and spoon herself against him. The softness of her body pressed against the length of him was something he'd thought about often enough, but the feel of it was something else.

She was almost demure against him, her legs tight together in front of his, but her ass was round and full, and he could already feel his dick stirring in response. Trying to think of something other than touching her, he tucked his arm beneath his pillow and then let his other arm rest over the covers, overtop of her body and her arm so that it snuggled the covers down around her waist. After he settled, he felt more than heard her release a deep breath, and her body untensed beneath his arm.

"You smell good," he couldn't stop himself from

telling her, and then he felt her huff out a smothered laugh.

"You don't have to say that, David. I'm just...I'm glad to not be alone. Upstairs, it was like I was confused at first—when I was asleep, I guess—but once my brain woke up...once I realized what was actually happening, I mean...I was terrified. I don't think I've ever been that scared," Lauren said quietly.

David shifted, letting his lips land gently at the back of her head to press down, offering her more of his presence. "We're gonna figure this out," he said again, knowing he didn't have a way of backing up his words at the moment. Feeling her press back into him, he realized again that holding her so close hadn't been a good idea. Here she was, scared and just wanting human contact, and his dick was waking up like it was being offered a helluva lot more. "Lauren, you're so warm, and God, I like holding you," he said gently, "but maybe too much."

Lauren caught her breath at David's words, and froze as he tilted backward so that he was laying on his back again, just beside her. She'd thought, when she'd been laying against him, that she'd felt him stirring in his sweats, but had told herself it was only natural, and was just that—a bare stirring, and not a signal of more. But she'd felt more when he'd pulled away from her, as the angle he'd moved at had allowed him to press into her, for just a moment. Turned away from him in bed now, her body was screaming for him after just the brief bit of contact, and she couldn't deny it. Her pussy was already soaked, begging for him.

Turning over, she let herself roll against him so that one of her legs landed just over his, and now she could really feel him, against her thigh. Her hand landing tentatively on his bare chest, she let herself hide in the darkness, glad that she couldn't see the look on his face as she let her hand run lightly over him, exploring the smattering of hairs on his chest, around the gauze, and landing at the scar she'd noticed before, tracing it.

David coughed, clearing surprise from his throat. She'd rolled with him, instead of scuttling to the bed's edge like he'd thought she might if she realized he was getting hard. He stayed still, feeling one of her hands trace the scar he'd gotten two years before. "I got shot there—that's what you're feeling," he told her.

"I saw it, in the garage, and figured," she said, her breath hitting his nipple so that his body tensed, his dick growing harder.

"Lauren, I'm sorry, kid, but you're gonna drive me crazy, being this close."

He listened to the silence, but instead of backing off, she let her fingers trail to the middle of his chest, and run up and down so that he had to bite his lip to keep from groaning at the sensation. Did she know what she was doing to him?

Lauren took a deep breath, feeling the weight of his member resting against her thigh, and the warmth at her center that was begging for him. She'd been aching for him, for weeks, whether she'd wanted to admit or not. And now that she felt like he'd been tempted by her also, and now that he was so close..."What if...what if I decided I'm okay with that? With us driving each other crazy tonight? After everything that's happened...if it's what we both want?" she asked.

The invitation hung in the air while Lauren waited, wondering what he had to be thinking of her. But she knew she was right, that he wanted her as much as she did him, and the shame was all hers at this point, wasn't it, anyway? Maybe just addressing it, just tackling the desire head-on and dealing with it, would lessen that, and allow her some control over it. Or at least, she thought, allow her to enjoy it for one night.

David felt her hand stilled, resting on his chest, and wished he could see the look on her face. It was pitch black in the room, though, and he only had her heavy breaths and still form to go by, along with his own heated blood. "If we start...I don't want to stop and start and us keep teasing each other. You say the word, right now, I'll go sleep on my couch."

"I don't want you to sleep on your couch, David," she answered, and he didn't hear any hesitation on her voice. Instead, he just heard the same want he'd heard the night before, when he'd allowed himself to think for a minute that this was where they were heading.

Swallowing down the voice that told him this was a mistake, he lifted one arm and moved it to the breast grazing his abdomen, cupping it with his hand and hefting it, playing gently with the hard nipple he could feel through her tank so that she gasped at his touch, but leaned further into him, encouraging him. "This is what you want, Lauren?" he asked quietly. "You're sure?"

When she said, "And more," he squeezed the breast in his hand and shifted, bringing his other arm out from where it had rested beneath his pillow. He moved slowly then, rising onto his side and finding her face with one hand, guiding her to his in the dark. She opened her lips on contact, her mouth letting his tongue slip inside and then pull back so that he could suck her lips between his own one by one, listening to her moan soft encouragement. His hand still on her breast as he kissed her, he gently pushed her backward so that she was on her back and he could straddle her.

Lauren lay back beneath him, her hands holding onto David's ribs for purchase on the moment. In the pitch black, her blood was burning, pleading for this man to be even closer, inside of her, and she felt more alive suddenly than she'd felt in weeks. Kissing him, she could almost imagine the spell heating her blood was her own magic, and not just what was left of her mother's, begging for release. She pulled his tongue into her mouth, holding him there as she felt his hands cupping and squeezing her breasts, his rough fingers twisting around her nipples.

Pulling up, David let go of her and moved his hands to the bottom rim of her tank. He left his hands there, touching skin and fabric and waiting for just a moment, giving her time to protest before he went ahead and skimmed it off of her so that they both now only wore the pants they'd gone to bed in. He ran his hands up her abdomen, along her sides, feeling her body shiver beneath him. When he heard a little mew of need, he lowered himself to one of her breasts and sucked the nipple into his mouth, playing with the hard bud with his tongue and teeth, remaining gentle but insistent as one of his hands found her other breast and his other reached around her to slip into her sweatpants and hold onto her ass, gripping her and sandwiching her body between his hand and his hard dick, pressing into her thigh.

Lauren let out a whimper as David's teeth came down lightly again, sending another spike of need running through her blood. One of her hands was in his hair now, holding onto him, her other on one of his forearms, running up and down his muscles. His hand on her ass was only a reminder of what she wanted, and she arched into him, hearing him groan in response just before she lifted her hips beneath him, pressing her body harder against his. He was holding his weight above her, keeping himself from pressing down into her with all of his bodyweight, and that meant there was too much space between them, so far as she was concerned.

David slid up her body, his lips landing at the base of her neck. "I want you," he told her, only half-listening for the response. Everything he needed to hear from her was being broadcast clearly, in every mew of need and whimper of response coming from her lips, and every tremble that was running through her body at his touch, her hands exploring all of the skin of his body that they could reach as he kissed her, wanting to make sure that she remembered this for all of the right reasons, and knowing he had a fair bit to make up for.

She gulped when she felt him fully against her; she'd forgotten how large he was, somehow, and now that his face was alongside hers, his lips teasing her earlobe, his dick was hard and long against her crotch, pressing into her through her pants. It was a reminder of what she wanted, what her body was craving, but also of pain, how big he was, and that scared her. She wanted him, but feeling the reality of him against her, she couldn't help remembering how she'd felt like she was being torn apart, ready as she'd thought her body was for him.

David felt her tense beneath him, and was suddenly glad he hadn't bothered to get up and turn on the lights. Maybe it was better if they were in the dark right now— he wasn't sure he wanted to see the look on her face at the moment, guessing as he was at what she was remembering. "I'm not going to hurt you," he whispered into her ear, and felt a shiver come from her in response. He steeled himself, letting his hands come to a rest on her, stilled with one on her waist and one wrapped around her, cradling her shoulders against him. "You trust me?" he asked.

Lauren nodded against him, pushing down the traces of fear. She did trust him, for better or worse. "Just go slow, okay?" she whispered into his neck.

"You got it, baby," he promised, kissing along her

neck and then over her lips, his hands massaging her skin once again, exploring her. He hadn't been able before to really enjoy the smoothness of her body or the sweetness of her curves, and that was what he'd been thinking about for weeks now.

Sliding down her body, he pulled her pants down, shaking the covers off of the two of them in the process. He wished the light were on, so he could see her below him, but there was something to be said for the way touch heightened when another sense was shut down. He'd been straddling her before, but now he gently took hold of her legs and guided her to spread them so that he could kneel between them. He let his hands run up and down her thighs at first, trying to gentle the shivers he could feel coming from her, until he felt one of her hands reaching out, touching his abdomen and then exploring upward. He stilled for a moment, letting her, and then he put his own hand over hers and gripped it, grinning at the way she accepted his touch without flinching now.

"Relax," he told her, laying her hand to the side of her body and then moving his hands up to hold apart her thighs. When his tongue first touched her, he felt her shudder in response. This, he remembered—how wonderfully responsive she was, and this wet desire that soaked her pussy, just for him. Taking his time, he lapped at her, taking in her sweetness slowly and enjoying the whimpers that came from above him as he did. One of his hands was on her thigh, gripping her and holding her leg far to the side so that she lay open for him. His other hand was on her breast, and he could feel both of her hands on his forearm, running up and down and tensing with his movements. He pulled his hand away, sensing her moving her hands to the side so that she could hold onto the sheets.

He'd been darting his tongue into her, but now he moved his lips to her clit and sucked lightly so that she yelled out; he could hear her trying to muffle the cry by biting her lip, and smiled against her. Shifting, he moved his hand to her opening and pushed in one finger. God, but she was tight. He added a second, and felt her gasp, getting accustomed to the pressure. "Just this for now," he whispered up to her, kissing her lightly above her clit and then licking at her so that she sighed out need as he let his fingers move, back and forth, slowly. She was getting used to him, and he added a third finger, moving even more gently, entering her by centimeters and letting her wetness soak his hand as her walls pulsed around him. By the time she'd taken the fingers into her, she was breathing heavily, but he was able to move smoothly, and his dick was hard as stone, begging to be next.

"Am I hurting you?" he asked quietly, running one hand up her body and along her breasts, tweaking her nipples. Her hand came down on his, holding onto him, pressing his palm into her skin.

"No—you feel—you feel really good," she breathed out.

David grinned, letting his fingers pound harder into her for a moment so that she groaned aloud, and he felt the shiver run through the whole of her body. Then he moved his lips to her clit, and sucked hard as he pumped his fingers harder into her, once and then twice, fast, and she bucked beneath him, screaming out the release he'd been working her toward.

Lightening his pressure, he stopped moving his hand until her body had slowed its quivering, and then he ran his slick fingers along her thigh and took another slow lap with his tongue that pushed another tremble through her skin before he rose up and again took one of her breasts into his mouth, cupping the other and playing with her nipples with tongue and fingers alike.

"David...I want you...inside of me," she panted from below him. Lauren ran her hands over his shoulders, relishing the feel of his skin and the aliveness running through her body already. This was all she'd been wanting. She raised her hips against him, biting her lip. Her blood was burning for him. "Why are you still dressed?" she complained softly, and then he moved up her, and began kissing her once again. She could taste the sweetness of her own juices on his lips, the slickness of desire, and pushed her tongue into his mouth, prodding with her hands and encouraging him.

With his lips at hers, she stretched one of her hands down, fighting through her nerves so that she could reach to him, to the part of him that her body was begging for. She slipped her hands beneath his waistline, and felt his rough pubic hairs against her skin as she explored further, and then found him, thick and hard. He groaned into her at her touch, and she took it for encouragement, wrapping her fingers along his thick shaft. He lifted, and reached down to help her, resituating himself so she could reach more of him, and his hand landed on her wrist, guiding her as she explored his dick, moving up and down his shaft.

"Tighter," he whispered gruffly, and she allowed herself to hold him more firmly as she ran her hand up and down along his length, enjoying the weight of him. Her finger landed at his head, and rubbed at the pre-cum leaking from him, circling him as he nibbled at her neck and she caught her breath at the newness of what she was doing and feeling, her body pulsing beneath his.

"I want you inside of me," she groaned again, into his neck, but this time he listened.

Pulling back, David kicked off his sweatpants and

then reached blindly for the nightstand, pulling out a condom. Kneeling above Lauren, he let himself enjoy the feeling of her hands on his thighs and his dick for a moment before he tore open the condom, and rolled it onto his dick. He could hear her breathing below him, and feel her hands trembling their way along his body as he moved himself against her, pressing his cock to her slit. He felt with his fingers, and finding that she was as soaked as she'd ever be, he pressed his head into her, stopping just inside and finding her breasts as she gasped, her body stretching around him and reacting.

"Tell me when," he whispered, lowering his body overtop of hers and holding himself in check, waiting for her say. He could feel her breathing heavily now with the pressure, and he needed to make sure that he didn't hurt her, whatever he did. He only wanted her to remember pleasure when she woke up in the morning.

Feeling the head of his cock in her entrance, her labia and pussy pulled open to accommodate his girth, Lauren rolled her head back and let her hands find David's shoulders, then his arms, and hold on. He was so big, but the ache she felt was secondary to the pleasure of finally having him taking her again. His cock was hot and hard inside of her, and her pussy was pulsing for him, all want and wetness. David's lips ran along her collarbone as one of his hands toyed with a nipple, and then she felt him massaging her shoulder and her neck with his other hand, running gently along her skin. His cock was still, waiting and promising, and she finally pressed her hips upward slightly, enough that he caught his breath and breathed into her ear, "Lauren?"

"Yeah, yeah," she panted. "I'm ready, David..." her words trailed into a whimper of need as he pressed into her, inching inside of her until he stopped again, waited, and pulled back out before he pressed in deeper. Lauren let her lips lock onto the spot of his shoulder that was nearest her mouth, needing something to muffle her cries, her own hands clenched into his back. She could feel her body stretching around him, accommodating him and wanting more, pulsing and aching for whatever he'd do next.

When David pressed in again, he allowed himself to go further, focusing on the burn of Lauren's fingernails in his back to slow him down, to keep himself in check, understanding he had to go slowly; and knowing that her previous experiences were not only weeks in the past, but dangerously painful, he didn't want to chance scaring her, or allow her to think that he might lose control with her. He wouldn't. Pressing in again, he gasped at the feel of her pulsing around him, her hips thrusting up gently to meet his own pumps forward.

"You feel fucking amazing, Lauren," he said, slowing his movements to near a standstill a he licked at the sweat along her collarbone, enjoying the whimper of need she released at the feel of his lips on her skin. He took his hand from her hip and slipped it between them, resting it on her clit and barely pressing at the slick button of need, but still he felt her squeak in surprise and jump with sensation beneath him so that he had to catch himself from slipping in too far, hurting her. He lifted his hand from her clit when one of her hands found his forearm.

"Too much," she gasped. "Too sensitive, for now...I just want you," she said a moment later, and he felt his dick press forward, instinctively reacting to the want in her voice, the naked need there.

He moved his hips sideways as his lips found hers, rhythmically moving in small circles, knowing what it would do to her pussy, and enjoyed the gasps that he elicited as he did, his dick staying pressed into her now, barely moving out before he pressed it back in, his hands kneading her body beneath his as his lips devoured her. God, but she was tight and warm, and driving him crazy.

"You okay?" he whispered against her ear, and then he nearly bit her earlobe in surprise when her reaction was to arch, pressing her hips and pussy hard into him, pulsing and wanting. "Okay," he gasped, before beginning to speed up, allowing a heavier rhythm to develop between them as her hands held onto him, gripping his sides as he pumped into her, enjoying the exertion and the burn in his muscles as she mewled beneath him and then finally wrapped her legs around his, holding onto him, her pussy now trying to hold onto him each time he pulled away, only to press back home, harder and more insistently with each thrust.

Lauren held onto him, closing her eyes to take in the fullness she felt, with him buried inside of her and wanting more. It wasn't like anything she'd felt before, and the aching pleasure of it...she felt as if her whole existence were focused into her center, pleasure thrumming out in waves and running through her whole body as if David's every breath and move were being transferred into her blood, livening her and gentling her all at the same time. She couldn't think, for the sensations and the pleasure, and she could feel her body beginning to heat toward climax yet again, feeding off of his thrusts and the way he was moving inside of her, pushing her.

Her gasps against his chest told him she was about to come again, and he sped up, allowing himself to hurry as one of his hands reached down to grasp her ass, holding her to his body as his other arm wrapped around her, hard, gripping her so that he could hold her to the rhythm he'd set and kiss her at his will in the dark.

When she came, she screamed out his name, bucking against him as her pussy spasmed, her whole body quivering suddenly and feeding into his sudden explosion as he let loose, grunting out his own release and pushing hard into her, coming inside of her with a yell that was barely muffled by his lips pressing into her hair, his hips locked to hers and his dick buried inside of her, spasming with release.

"Jesus," he groaned, leaning up from her, feeling her body cling to his by instinct as he withdrew some, propping himself up on his elbows—his cock still mostly buried in her depths, her pussy still pulsing around him. Kissing her, he pulled the sweat from her lips and sucked each of her lips gently between his, exploring her now that their heartbeats were slowing as one of his hands ran up and down her side, enjoying the smoothness and the quivering of her body as she came down from her orgasm. "Jesus," he said again, finally lifting from the kiss, and wishing the lights were on so that he could see her. He could feel the emotion coming off of her, and the heat of her body in the way she still clung to him. He didn't need to see her to know she was high on the sensations, and swimming in pleasure still, regretting none of it.

"Yeah," she finally breathed, and ducked her lips up to run along his neck, breathing out so that his skin trembled beneath her lips in response.

***

David had woken to his alarm earlier, but then set it back a few hours, considering the night they'd had. Instead of getting up, he'd texted Josh that Lauren was with him and that they'd be up later, and turned off his phone to avoid any questions that might follow. Then, feeling Lauren against him, he'd just pulled her closer, and fallen back asleep as she murmured some assent to the extra warmth. One of the benefits to their underground rooms was that darkness could be maintained at any hour, so the morning didn't itself offer reasoning for an early wake-up.

When he woke again, Lauren was still nestled against him, but his brain was already churning. Disengaging from her, he slipped out to crack the bedroom door and turn on the hall light so that she'd have some illumination when she wanted it, and then retreated to the shower. Under the water, thoughts of the girl in his bed quickly focused more toward what came next. Josh had sent a text in response to his—he knew where Mary was, or at least where her new home address was. And they couldn't afford to lose more time since it seemed that the coven had somehow found a way to track down Lauren. Whether they knew where to find the ranch house or not, they could reach her, and that was enough.

Dressing, he let Lauren sleep. He needed to talk to Josh, and he didn't relish what was coming. Upstairs, though, he found that little explanation was needed.

"Should have figured you'd already be on the security feed," David commented, looking over Josh's shoulder at the stilled image of the two of them, holding Lauren against their front door.

"Yeah, for what good it does. You saw them in person—anything you can add to the record?"

David shook his head. The stiffness in the figures was clear, there on the computer screen. And they'd seen projected phantoms like this before, after all. Just not in their own house.

"How's she doing?" Josh asked, looking at him knowingly before rising from the kitchen's island to stir whatever he had cooking on the stove.

David ignored the look and instead glanced to the clock—it was already past noon. "She's sleeping. Scared. You think it was that dip in the pool that did it?"

"Honestly? Not really. Remember, after the fact, we wondered whether Wilkins could have disappeared to the outside, put a trace on our car before she really disappeared? I gotta figure that's what happened. Should've known she wouldn't panic and get out that quickly," Josh muttered in conclusion, still focused on the stove. "What about you?" he asked, turning. "You up to hitting another house today, or do you want to hold off till tomorrow?"

"What is it, a few hours away?"

"Something like that," he answered.

David thought about it, but wasn't sure they had a lot of choice. It had only been forty-eight hours or so since the fight, but if the witches had a way of finding Lauren..."Yeah, I'm up for it," he answered. "Let me get Lauren up. We'll eat, and then we'll go. You wanna call in some back-up?"

"Three teams, you think?"

"Yeah, sure, or four," David answered, already heading back down to his rooms.

***

Lauren sat heavily on the couch as soon as David and Josh were out the door. She was tempted to stand at the window and watch them leave like a forlorn puppy, but her self-respect wouldn't allow it. Everything in her told her that this was wrong. That they were headed into a trap by going to Mary's house—especially by going so soon. Maybe if they waited a week or two, but now?

Sure, she understood the ticking clock they'd harped on. Between the fight at Moriah's and the intrusion on the ranch house, of course she did. She was at the heart of it, wasn't she? But there had to be somewhere, she thought, that the three of them—maybe even with Claudia—could have disappeared off to until things cooled. But it was like they were desperate to have this done, and part of her wondered whether that was Josh, at least, being anxious to have her out of the house. After the night they'd shared, she was certain David didn't feel the same...but she'd understand it if that had only added to Josh's wanting her to be gone.

There was something else that was holding her back from being so sure of things as she might have been, though. She could feel something still in her blood. She'd felt her blood responding to David every time she'd been near him, but the sex itself had amped up everything, every sensation, as if her body had suddenly felt like itself for the first time in weeks. In the moment, she'd not had the time or the focus to give it much thought. But now...some 12 hours after they'd been together, she could still feel it in her blood, lurking. Not as magic that she could use, maybe, not like it'd been before she'd come here, but it was there. More than it had been.

She couldn't come up with an explanation, and wasn't sure she needed to, but instinctively...she felt like there was still some magic in her blood, waiting to come back to life if she just made the right choices, the right moves. And that was the one thing that made her grateful for the space she had now, at least until Barry showed up after a few hours to further the wards leading downstairs, where she'd stay the night through while Barry stayed up here.

She could use the time to think. Because it wasn't just the fact that she felt sure the men were headed into a trap that was bothering her. It was also the lingering question now, now that she felt so connected to David, that she couldn't help wondering about. If there was really something between them, something more than the spell which she had no way of breaking anyway, then how could she disappear? And if that was the case...what would he do if he realized that her magic wasn't so gone as they'd all thought?

Chapter 15

Mary's house lay midway down a state highway, forty miles from where they'd found Moriah's house. In this case, the road was mostly surrounded by single farms and cropland—there weren't many off roads, and only two directions in. David was driving north toward her home, with plans to stop before they reached the dirt drive that Google Maps had shown actually led to her residence. Then, he and the men with him would cut across the land on foot, making the half-mile trek in through the hilly terrain that surrounded her house. Josh and the operatives riding along in his Mustang would come from the other direction.

All told, there were eight of them, and David had worked with the men in his truck before. All of them had been warned of what was coming and were riding in silence, the plan in mind, when David's ringtone cut through the air.

Josh's name flashed on the truck's display as David hit the connection button to accept the call through Bluetooth.

"We got set back as we came in; we're behind an hour," Josh's voice broke through the truck.

"You what?" David asked, taking his foot from the accelerator. He glanced to Mike, the man in his passenger seat, but saw confusion there also.

"We were a mile out from the turn-out, and then, I swear to God, we were back on the highway, practically back where we started from. I'm detouring now to follow your way in, but we're behind. They must have had a trap on the road to look out for the Mustang."

We knew there'd be something. It was why they'd split up, guessing that the Mustang would be the vehicle to draw attention if one of them did, and wanting to have a separate vehicle with someone who'd already faced the witches. That was why the Mustang was more heavily armed, spell shields in place. It hadn't occurred to them that a spell might lift the whole damned thing into another space entirely. "Fuck," David muttered. "You guys may need to change cars."

"Yeah, we're heading to the Maines house now; Carheart said he'll loan us his ride. What do you wanna do?"

David looked in the rearview mirror to gage what the other operatives in the car were thinking. It was Hawkes who spoke up. "You guys said you got hit by four witches when you expected one. Assuming we get where we're going, smart thing is for us to start surveillance; we'll be there when you get there, yeah?"

David nodded, though there was a pit in his stomach. "Simmons, Mike—speak up if you disagree." After seeing shrugs from the others, he re-focused on the road. "That's the plan, Josh. We'll see you guys when you get there. You gonna come around from our side?"

"Yeah, just in case it's the road and not the car. You guys be safe," he finished, and the display showed that the call had ended, reverting to the satellite radio rock that had been playing before.

"Well, hey, I would'a been disappointed if we got through the mission without seeing a single goddamned spell anyway," Simmons joked from the back, and David forced a grin in response. He didn't near feel the same, but thought that the parlor trick of shooting the Mustang off track was at least a sign that the spells they'd first run up against would be deterrents more than shoot-to-kills, which was something enough to be thankful for. Assuming, he thought, that the Mustang's own wards hadn't been at work after all, and made the spell less dangerous than it might have been otherwise.

There wasn't time, though, to worry about it. The turn-off they'd been heading toward was approaching. It was time to park, and move in.

***

Nell watched the men through the woods, noting that it was the one who she'd fought, the one who'd rescued Lauren at the house, that was leading this group. When the Mustang had disappeared, they hadn't known who'd been driving it, or even been sure that a second vehicle would approach—until there'd been encroachment from the road. Now, she was stationed between the men and that road, watching them settle in to watch Mary's house. What they hoped to find, she couldn't guess, unless they were simply waiting for their friends or thinking to determine numbers.

It didn't matter. Mary and Johanna were both inside, well aware of their presence, and they wouldn't be waiting for the men to go on the offense. They were just waiting for full-on darkness. Her only disappointment here was that the men hadn't brought Lauren along—she hadn't particularly expected them to, but thought they might if they were aware she still had some strands of magic at her will. Would she have told them? Nell imagined she would have at least told Fredricks, the man who'd rescued her. Perhaps, she thought, he was such an alpha that he would have refused, either way, to put her in danger. That wasn't outside of the realm of possibility.

Leaning back into the branches of the tree she'd cradled herself into, she pursed her lips and focused on the men. All had wards painted into their skin—there wouldn't be an option of reading their thoughts, or of taking control of any of them, but she'd expected that. Observation was fine. Fredricks was clearly the most focused. He was close to the ground, his eyes trained on the house, his body unmoving. The smallest and leanest of the four was eating his second granola bar since they'd stopped, crouched behind a tree and also watching the house. One of the others was staring intently at his phone, a hand around it to cover any light that might otherwise signal their presence to the house. The fourth looked younger, and less sure of himself than the others; he was tensed, crouched behind a log and fingering his gun as if the fight were imminent.

In order of importance, in order of kill, she decided her first target would be the man with the phone. It was possible he was reading email, but it was also possible he was studying something more pertinent. The younger one's death would be a distraction to the others, and he'd be easiest to kill, but he was also likely the least dangerous of the four. Unless one of the three strangers separated themselves and made an easy target of themselves, it would be the man with his phone who'd be first, she determined.

David, she wanted to keep alive, and she'd told the others as much. She wanted him to suffer for the scars along her skin, brought on by the spelled bullets in his gun, and because he'd made a near joke of their last attempt on Lauren, far as Melania was concerned. And, of course, any suffering he underwent would be added punishment for Lauren, for running, if the girl cared for him as much as she seemed to. This thought, at least, made Nell smile. She was looking forward to having the upper hand again.

***

David had barely grunted in acknowledgement when Simmons had mentioned he was backtracking into the woods to relieve himself, but he took more notice when Hamid put down his phone and rose, announcing that he was going to find the youngest of their group. Hawkes glanced backward from his own cover, catching David's eye with a frown. "He gone more'n three minutes?" he asked.

"Five," Mike Hamid answered, already unholstering his gun.

David looked to his watch; it was getting dark, and Josh and the others were still likely thirty minutes out. "You wanna go with Mike?" he asked, but Hawkes shook his head.

"I'll keep an eye on our six."

From where they were, the house was some fifteen yards distant, and mostly dark. There was light coming from two of the lower rooms, and he'd seen a silhouette pass by a few times. They were too far out for the operatives to know whether it had been the same person, or whether there was more than one woman wandering the lower floor of the house, but only one vehicle was parked outside. Of course, David knew, there'd only been one vehicle at the house where they'd last run into trouble—it wasn't as if witches necessarily relied on them.

Minutes more passed with no sign of either John Simmons or Mike Hamid returning from the woods, and no sounds to announce obvious trouble, but David could feel his pulse quickening with every passing second. It had become too calm, and he was about to tell the man beside him that they should decide to either attack the house or retreat to find out what had happened to the other men, when suddenly the air grew thicker.

He took a breath to speak, but it was as if his lungs were being slid into slow motion; a glance to Hawkes told him the other man was having even more trouble, and that there was a mist around him, circling him. David reached for his gun automatically, but although his mind was commanding his muscles, they weren't obeying at normal speed, as if they'd been disconnected somewhat from his intentions—a delay installed between his mind and his movements. Still working to reach for his gun, but already realizing there was little point, he watched Hawkes beside him, seemingly sinking inward, his throat convulsing, and saw that the other man wasn't getting any breath at all. Whether it was his lungs moving too slowly or his throat imploding, oxygen wasn't available, and his face was turning unnaturally smoky in color.

Instinctively, David attempted to gulp down air, as if his would also be cut off momentarily, but although his muscles had slowed and he felt his body responding only sluggishly, from his fingers down to the depths of his lungs and his heart, he could breathe, and he could also watch as Hawkes was suffocated, sitting still and alone just a few feet away as it grew darker.

When the other man had gone fully still, David's hand finally reached the holster of his gun, and there he felt the air grow thicker around it, so that it was held still even as the rest of his body could move, however slowly. It took what seemed like minutes for him to turn his head, sideways, to where he'd sensed movement on the periphery of the small gap in the trees where they'd taken up surveillance. He wasn't much surprised to see that Nell Everett was standing there, in black jeans and a forest green turtleneck, smiling languidly and leaning against a tree as if she'd come for a picnic instead of a killing.

***

Lauren was lying in David's bed when she heard a knock on the suite door, the sound immediately followed by its opening, and Josh's voice calling for her.

Instinctively, she wished she were dreaming. If it was Josh coming in to find her, that meant that David couldn't. When Barry's voice joined with an echo of her name, she sat up and pulled herself from the bed and the land of wishful thinking. She was already dressed to meet them.

"What happened?"

Josh's voice was flat, his expression more so. "My car got way-laid and the house was empty when we got there; they took David, and the others are dead."

Lauren just stood for a moment, processing. Josh's hands were clenched at his sides, but he was looking at her as if he expected some answer. Barry stood behind the other man, grim-faced and staring at his phone.

"I don't understand," Lauren finally answered, "I

thought you guys were together."

Josh shook his head, turning on his heel. He didn't know what he'd been hoping for in waking her, though she obviously hadn't been sleeping. Here, she just looked shell-shocked as she followed him back toward the living area, and he wondered again if there was anything more to be found at the emptied-out house. They'd stayed for hours, searching, and found nothing but the bodies of Simmons, Hamid, and Hawkes, laid out on the front porch and waiting for them.

"I was driving and David was driving, from different directions. He was able to get there as planned; the Mustang got...repositioned, an hour back, and we had to switch vehicles. Whatever happened was done when we got there," he finished, collapsing onto his partner's couch and staring blankly at the door. "House empty, David gone, the others dead." *We should have waited longer, caught them off-guard,* he kept thinking, but it was too late. They'd had good reason to go in. But they should have gone in with larger numbers, he realized now, and not attempted to stall for partial surveillance instead of just going all-out as they'd done before, when they'd at least found marginal success. And a lower body count, on their side. Now, three men were dead, his partner was unaccounted for, and the only lead they'd had had ended up being a trap.

Lauren bypassed Barry, who seemed to be frantically texting back and forth or searching for something on his phone, and moved to sit at the other end of the couch from Josh. Her head was swimming. She'd thought about the men getting killed, or injured, but it hadn't actually occurred to her that the witches would disappear with them. She wasn't sure now whether it made sense to be grateful that David wasn't among the dead, or fearful of what that meant for him.

"He must be alive, right?" she asked quietly. "I mean, they wouldn't have taken him, otherwise, right?"

Josh nodded, still facing the wall. Like her, he wasn't sure whether that was a good thing or not.

***

He woke to heat, and to artificially clean and filtered air like you found in the far lower reaches of a bunker where fresh air couldn't quite penetrate. Before he'd opened his eyes, this was what he noticed, and silence.

David shifted, as if he were still asleep in case anyone were watching. The flooring he was laying on was hard rubber, like you might find in a gym, and his limbs weren't bound. But he was stiff, as if he'd been lying still for hours, and not dropped in the spot gently either. His head was pounding, but he felt uninjured—just hot.

"I can tell you're awake, Fredericks. Your breathing changed."

The words had come from Nell Everett, David knew immediately, and suddenly he remembered the last of what he'd seen before he'd passed out for lack of oxygen—her smiling, hanging out on the edge of that small gap in the trees and...waiting for him to go unconscious. He opened his eyes and forced himself to sit up without pausing, gritting his lips against the stiffness he could feel in his muscles so that a groan didn't slip out. The room he was in was bare and gray, and Nell was sitting on a bench against one wall, lounging with her legs crossed and wearing that infuriating smirk. The heat and the heaviness he'd sensed in the air were coming from an even clearer source—he'd been lying in the middle of a square that was built from lasers, running from floor to ceiling in lines of lavender that were less than three inches apart, forming a three-sided cage of energy that ran up against a concrete wall which formed the fourth wall, an open doorway there that he could see led to a spartan bathroom.

"I don't think you'd survive powering your way through the bars, but you could try and see," Everett offered, leaning forward from her perch as if she thought he might.

"The other operatives who were with me?" he asked quietly, staying still as he attempted a mental inventory of his own body—he felt uninjured. Just sore, and hot from the energy surrounding him and the thick air.

"Dead," she answered. "We left them for your partner. Let him know what might be in store for you," she added, finally standing to step nearer to the bars running from floor to ceiling.

David didn't bother to rise; he was an open target if she wanted to do something, and he didn't have any recourse as long as the energy was in place. Plus, she could have killed him already if she'd wanted to. "Nice decorations. A little pastel, all this energy, and a window would've been nice." He watched the slight witch move around the cage, examining him, but pushed himself to breathe evenly. Whatever was going to happen would happen whether he panicked or not, whether he stood or not, whether he said anything or not.

"How long do you think you'll be here?" she asked, examining the perfectly manicured nails on one of her hands rather than bothering to look at the operative on the floor. She was impressed with the calmness he was exuding, though she wouldn't admit it.

Rather than answering, David lay back on the floor and forced himself to take a deep breath. The air was heavy, but didn't seem toxic. "And I'd be able to answer that because…"

"Because we sent word to your home, of course. As soon as Lauren turns herself in to us, you'll be free to go. You must have guessed that's all we've wanted."

Right, and not revenge. "Not to sound like a cliché, but you don't actually expect me to believe that?" David forced his body to relax into the ground, which was cooler than the air. He could almost pretend he was comfortable.

"Mmmm," she murmured. "I am curious…how long have you been sleeping together? It must have happened soon after you met." David's head jerked with surprise, his eyes dancing up to meet hers. *Gotcha,* she thought.

"What makes you think we're sleeping together?"

Crouching outside the cage, Nell cocked her head, watching him. He'd broken out in a sweat, and she didn't think it was the air. "You are," she said simply. "That's the only way Phillippa's spell would have come to life, the only way Lauren would have been able to call to you the other night when she was half asleep. You let her tie her blood to yours. I'm curious—was it before or after you killed her mother? Or was that someone else, and you just took the spoils of war by seducing her?"

David's stare hardened on her, and she flushed despite herself. "Who did it, Fredricks? Did you seduce her, and trick her into giving herself and her mother over, or did she seduce you to keep a hold on some magic while you were taking it from her?"

What the fuck is she talking about? David was struggling to catch up, but he refused to let it show in his face. Somehow, this woman knew he and Lauren had been sleeping together, and what's more, she claimed there was still magic in her because of it. But if that was the case…why had they ever begun looking for her? And what did their sleeping together have to do with her having been able to call for help?

"Jesus," Nell muttered, leaning forward. "You don't know about it, do you?"

Forcing himself to turn his eyes back to the ceiling, he stayed silent. She was doing enough talking for the both of them.

"Just tell me—who seduced who?"

"Fuck off," David grunted, clenching his fists at his sides despite wanting to appear unaffected. Whatever she was talking about, he was at a disadvantage in not knowing. Instinctively, though, he realized that whatever she was hinting at was what Lauren had been hiding all this time.

Nell watched him close off from her, putting shields up against showing reactions. That was fine. She could deal with that.

Delicately, she pulled a baggie from her side pocket and waved it in the air. "Clippings of your hair. If you won't tell me, I'll read it," she whispered sulkily. Focusing on the task before her, she plucked some of the strands out and dropped them to the rubber before her, only allowing herself a small smile of humor as she saw the trapped operative in front of her self-consciously reach to his head and run his hands through his hair, as if to retrieve the strands. She hadn't taken enough for him to feel it, but she'd taken enough. Murmuring to herself now, she clicked her tongue and touched her fingers to the hair on the ground, and then struck a match and dropped it, inhaling the smoke, and closing her eyes to watch what she sought.

Inside of the cage, David had risen to a sitting position again, to observe. He could guess what the witch was seeing as her lips tightened before she gasped aloud, and then grimaced. It was minutes more before she opened her eyes, and snarled, "You raped her. You raped her, by never giving her any option to say no, and without even knowing what you were doing, you bastard imbecile."

He held off the witch's gaze with his own. He'd come to grips with what he'd done—a woman like this, a witch like this, wouldn't make him feel further guilt for it.

"And she hasn't even told you what you did to her," Everett growled, and then spit at him, her saliva reaching through the cell's bars as far as his pant leg.

"She told me she was a virgin," he answered despite himself, suddenly realizing that, absurdly, he wished he were having this conversation with another man.

"But not what it *means*," she whispered in return. "Do you want to know? Do you want to know how much you hurt her, how badly you ruined her? Even if we weren't bringing her into the coven, she'd be ruined for anyone else. You understand that?"

Finally, David let emotion show, sneering back at the woman. "This isn't the eighteenth century, Everett. Deflowering a virgin isn't the end of the world. You telling me you've only ever slept with one man, or what, you haven't gotten around to sleeping with anyone?" He pushed himself to chuckle, even as he realized he was missing something. There was something here he still wasn't getting, that she wasn't telling him, and that Lauren hadn't told him.

"No, but rape has always been rape," Nell answered, standing. "But I'll tell you what you did, because what I saw just now tells me you've managed to get to care about her. So maybe *this* will hurt *you*," she hissed, leaning down toward the bars so that David could have reached a finger through to touch her, if he'd dared.

The look on her face being what it was, though, it was a struggle for him to stay his ground and not back toward the other side of the cage. He wasn't imagining this—she wanted to kill him, now, and was just holding herself back.

"Her mother cast a spell on her, Mr. Fredricks. To tie her body to the first man she slept with. Any other man who touches her will only hurt her, from here on out. You want the details? She'll be dry and unresponsive and disgusted by any other man's touch, and if she tries anyway, the spell will turn into an aggression in the man that will leave her regretting it—he'll end up hurting her, badly, simply because she tried to move on from you; her mother would have liked to leave that part out, I imagine, and maybe she meant to, but obviously she didn't. So that's what *you* did to her. And when she gets near you? Her blood heats in reaction to your touch; her body *pushes* her toward you. She can't even think, I'd be willing to bet, she's probably so torn up by desire—and how, Mr. Fredricks, do you think that makes her feel? That she knows what you did, and can't help wanting you?"

David choked on a response, pausing the witch from her rant. "Why?" he asked after a moment. "Why would any mother..."

"She thought she was protecting her, in some demented way. From giving herself over too soon. She cheated on her own husband who cheated on her, and her personal life was a disaster. She wanted better for her daughter; misguided, obviously. And she didn't plan on *you*."

David realized Everett's eyes had been somewhere else as she'd responded, and that her guard had been down with him, if only for a moment. He'd have to find more moments like that, but now..."There's something wrong with your theory, in any case," he made himself say, considering everything she'd said, and remembering the one-night stands he'd had since first taking Lauren. They might not have been meaningful, but he'd gotten pleasure from them. He wasn't as tied to her as Everett seemed to think. "I've *been* with other women since that first time with Lauren. It was the same as always. I'll buy that there's something between us, but..."

"It only affects *her*, you dolt," Everett whispered. "This isn't about you. The spell is about *her*. *Her* being faithful and tied to one man. *Her* capacity for love, for commitment. *Her body*. She could have never seen you again after you raped her, and you would have gone on with your life, without ever knowing what you did. She, on the other hand, would have been aware of it every time she thought of kissing another man. You want the truth? She was probably dreaming about you, even before the bruises you and your partner left on her had healed."

His breath caught, David could feel himself paling beneath the witch's words. The anger there ...It was impossible not to believe her, and if all of it was true, he couldn't begin to imagine how much he actually had tortured Lauren, without ever even realizing it. Suddenly, he wanted to block everything out, from the witch to her words to the world around him, but she'd already decided to keep going.

"That's why her blood called to yours the other night, why she can't resist you—why there was enough magic for you to *hear* her when she needed you, and why *you dying* will mean she'll be alone, forever. So, yes, sure, feel free to hate the coven for planning to keep her, so that we are safe, but her life is over whether we do or not, without her magic and without the capacity for love...You think she'd have a lot to look forward to, lonely as she'd be without us and you? Jesus. You didn't just rape her, David Fredricks—you made it utterly impossible for her to ever find pleasure from even the kiss of another man. *That's* what you did," the witch hissed, and spat again through the bars before jerking to a stand and stalking away, toward the room's one door.

Staring after her, David wanted to argue, but he'd suddenly gone cold. He'd heard the truth in every bit of anger that had dripped from her lips, and although a small part of him wanted to believe, still, that she was lying, the whole of things suddenly made sense. Jarring his eyes shut and sitting forward to fight back the sudden nausea he felt, he thought of the way Lauren's skin always thrummed beneath his, reacting to him. The way, from the moment she'd come back to the ranch house, she'd flinched away from his presence even as she'd admitted it made her feel safe. The way she'd seemed to fight her attraction to him even after she'd begun giving into it.

She's under a fucking spell, he thought belatedly, closing his eyes again at the thought of her touch, and how helpless she always seemed to be around him. It was because she *was* helpless, whether she wanted him or not. There'd never been any question of forgiveness or love or anything he else he might have imagined showing up between them. And it didn't matter what he felt, because anything on her side was false, forced. He'd raped her once, and because of it, he might as well still be forcing her to feel everything she experienced around him, just the same as he had that afternoon. Any other explanation was just semantics. What she felt, if she felt anything for him at all, as he'd been starting to believe...It all simply came from a spell that he'd set off, and which he had no way of taking back.

Chapter 16

Nell joined Melania, and dipped her eyes and her figure both in traditional greeting before moving to the circle. Mentally, she was still working out how to shift Melania to her way of thinking, and so she let the silence linger before Melania's voice issued her name, prodding her to give her report on what she'd learned from the captive operative in the energy cell.

"We were right—they've formed a bond that's being nurtured by Phillippa's spell. I think...I do think Lauren will come, for him."

"If not for herself," Melania grunted, eyeing the woman across from her. "You look as if he put you on edge," she commented lightly, a twisting sneer belying the fact that the idea was more humorous than believable. "What else?"

"I read the memories he has of her, to see which one of them initiated...to see if she seduced him in order to perhaps sustain some of her magic through her mother's spell..."

"And?"

"And—I learned he handcuffed her to a bed and teased her until she couldn't say no, and then he took her. That was the spell's initiation," Nell said quietly. Instinctively, her fists clenched in the fabric of her jeans at the admission, and she looked up to see Melania biting back a rare show of emotion. *I'm glad she's angry also*, Nell thought. *Mayhap she'll listen.*

"He raped her?" Melania asked, the words coming slowly. It hadn't occurred to her that Lauren hadn't initiated the spell in some desperate attempt to either retain her magic or gain the man's help. One or the other, she'd thought, had been a given.

"From my perspective? Yes. For information...they were trying to learn where Phillippa was hiding; I suppose they were trying to break Lauren's spirit, though the memory felt...off, in that regard. The emotions were too complicated to read, probably because of the relationship he's formed with her in the time since. But the original intent was information."

Melania looked up suddenly, catching the younger witch off-guard and leaning forward. "She *gave* him Phillippa's location, didn't she? That's what you're not saying. The little slut gave up her own mother?"

Nell's silence was enough of an answer—this was what she'd feared telling, and what she'd been so floored by. This had gotten under her skin, not David. It had been one thing to think that Lauren would betray the members of the coven who, truth be told, she'd barely known, and always feared. That she'd betrayed her own mother was nothing they'd really considered. Still, knowing what Phillippa had been doing...Nell was torn, but she knew from the look on Melania's face that the other woman's only thought now was of punishment. Any suggestion of leniency that Nell might have hoped to make, based on the fact that Lauren had been raped, skewing her judgment, and all she'd gone through since...it wouldn't be heard. The best to be hoped for was that they could use her, more than they'd expected.

"I was thinking, Melania," Nell began, "that with her magic coming back...we could nurture it. She'd be a more useful slave, with some power rather than none."

It took another moment for Melania to nod, and Nell breathed a sigh of relief when she did. She'd rarely seen the older witch with so flat an expression as she'd been wearing for the last few minutes—it had been terrifying.

"We'll see what happens, but I can't argue with that. With the man contained...it's possible we could keep him longer than we'd planned, to give her magic some stability before we kill him. She needs to be punished, though. No matter what happened before, what she's done since is inexcusable. I want her to suffer." Turning her eyes back to Nell, Melania pursed her lips. "Your impressions from what you saw—she's in love with him?"

Nell considered the scenes that had played through her mind, and the emotions of them, but could finally only shrug. "She at least thinks she is...but it could be the spell. She could also think it's the spell. Oh," Nell startled, realizing what she'd left out. "He didn't know about it, by the way—the spell. I told him. He was...disturbed," she finished, a smile coming to her lips for the first time since she'd entered the room. No matter that the women couldn't agree on how best to deal with Lauren; there was no doubt that they wanted David Fredricks to suffer for what he'd done to their sisterhood.

"Hm," Melania grunted, rising to her feet and

wandering to a sidebar to pour herself some tea. She took her time, spooning in sugar and then stirring it slowly. "So he'll be doubting her emotions, wondering how much of what they've shared is the spell. We'll use that. I just have to think on how. For now...let's plan on having that sycophant servant of Mary's pick up Lauren on Sunday, and expect that she'll be there. And you...visit him again later. Groom him to take suggestion so that he'll do our bidding when we ask, will you?"

Nell nodded, already considering her options. He was prepared for spells, which could have made things more difficult, but they had time on their side, which was far more important. Not to mention energy.

***

It felt like she'd gone backwards in time, to staring at that first letter the coven had sent. She remembered when she'd first received it. Even expecting it, she'd sat on her couch and simply looked at it—first at the unopened envelope, and then at the frighteningly clear words, directing her to give up her life and turn herself in. And now, here she had another one.

Barry had answered the messenger's knock, and stayed with her when she'd opened it in the kitchen, suspicious of what it contained since nobody was meant to know she was even there. Now he was on the phone with Josh, who'd gone off to some meeting, and she was here...once again staring at a letter from her mother's coven. Barry had taken away the photo that had been included—a glossy shot of the three men who'd ridden with David to the house, dead—but it didn't matter. The image had been burned onto her retinas at the moment she'd seen it. It had been meant to scare her, and it had.

Dear Lauren,

We're deeply disappointed that this is the path you've chosen to follow, but we understand you've been scared, and had little trustworthy guidance. Understand that, from the beginning, we have had your wellbeing in mind. It is our hope that present circumstances have led you to think differently of your decisions. If not, we regret that it has come to this, but lacking any alternative and considering where you've placed yourself, we've been left with no choice but to punish your acquaintances and demand that your paramour remain with us until you've understood that joining the coven is your only choice.

Should you join us, we'll release the man you've chosen to take as your lover, and allow that the men already killed should be a just return for our lost sisters, this being adjoined by your full surrender and the understanding that your sacrifice will also be made in recompense for the hostility we've faced, despite having engaged in no crime beyond self-defense.

I regret the fact that our sisterhood has been reduced to threats, but we do not seek an all-out war with the men you've chosen to align your interests with, and nor do we believe should you. Should you care to have any future at all, and/or should you care at all for Mr. Fredricks, this is your last chance to present yourself.

You'll be expected inside the East entrance of Overhead Park this Sunday at 4 PM. Come alone. Do not be late. This is our coven's last offer of mercy, and I sincerely hope that you'll take advantage of it.

Sincerely,
Melania

It didn't matter how many times Lauren re-read the letter. What came with it were images. Images of the dead men who'd been alive last week, who David and Josh had called for help with the coven. Images of David's energy burns from the aftermath of his run-in with Nell. And finally, images of that phantom Josh's hand, wrapped around her wrist, holding her to the door.

A small part of her wondered what would happen when the coven realized she had some bit of her magic left, but at the same time, she wasn't confident that it would last if she were separated from David for any length of time. Realistically, there wasn't any way to know. She could feel it now, if she searched, but barely, and after all she'd done...the witches would want someone to punish for their time and for their losses, and despite anything the letter insinuated to claim otherwise, that punishment would land on her if she turned herself in.

But of course, none of that mattered. No matter what David had done to her in the past, he was someone else to her now. And even if he hadn't been...well, it wasn't as if she could have brought herself to sacrifice anyone at all, just to give herself a better shot at things.

Her shots were over anyway, she figured, one way or another.

***

David rolled onto his side, grunting with stiffness. What time was it? Hell...what day was it? Light was always the same, and the food and water meant nothing—whenever he ran out of granola bars or fruit or water, they brought more. And while he'd thought at first he could gauge the time based on his hunger, he'd realized quickly that that wouldn't work—not with his body still fighting off the effects of the energy burns he hadn't recovered from before setting out again, and not when the boredom he faced had no distraction but bodily needs. He wouldn't have been surprised to find he'd spent three days in the energy cage. He also wouldn't have been surprised to find out it had been five or six.

"What are you doing?" he growled at Everett. She was at it again, walking the outside perimeter of his cage, sprinkling some dust or another. He couldn't feel anything from it and he didn't recognize it.

"Preparing things, I told you," she answered, a lilt in her voice. She was wearing loose jeans and a black tank top today, and didn't bother to look at him when she spoke.

"I'd like to wash," he told her. "With more than that," he added, jutting his chin to the small adjoining bathroom that only offered a toilet and sink.

Nell Everett finally looked up at him, narrowing her eyes. "You want to wash? You kill our sisters, steal magic from one of our own, *rape* one of our own, and you're worried about luxuries like showers? You should be glad we're feeding you," she commented, taking her eyes back the dust trailing from her fingers. It was grayish, but had a sparkle to it. Not knowing what it was was driving him crazy.

"What day is it?"

"Two days before we get your precious Lauren back into our fold," the witch answered. And then, her chore done, she turned and stalked from the room, leaving David to scowl after her. Lacking anything else to do, he took up another apple and a bottle of water, and parked back in the middle of the cell. He could only wait.

***

Lauren didn't bother arguing with Josh and Barry—she could go to the park alone or accompanied, but the result would be the same. Whoever Melania sent would have a homing hold on them, and Lauren had no doubt that she'd disappear with them as soon as they were within touching distance. It was the way the witches would operate something like this. Josh had wanted to plant a homing beacon on her person, but they all knew that the likelihood of something like that working after she was vanished, to be re-homed somewhere else, was nearly nil. Now it was Friday, with less than 48 hours left until she needed to be at the park, and Barry had come up with something even more outlandish.

"You want to tattoo me?" she asked flatly, her eyes veering between the two men to find the joke.

"I think I can track the symbol with this ink I've developed. We've talked about using it on operatives and just hadn't tried..."

"So I'm the guinea pig?" she asked. "And you want to tattoo metal into my skin?"

Barry looked to Josh, shrugging. "It'll be like a normal tattoo. It's not like we're talking about mercury. But if we make the pattern large enough and distinct enough, yeah, we should be able to find you. It might not be quick, but it'll give us a chance."

Lauren closed her eyes and tried to breathe deeply. She'd never had any desire at all to have a tattoo. "What do you mean, large enough?" she finally asked.

"I was thinking...maybe up your arm, like a long line?" Barry traced a line along his own arm from wrist to shoulder, ending in a circular pattern around his shoulder. "We'd make something larger at the top—there's a lot of room for you to tell us what you want. I know a tattoo artist who said he'll make room for us tonight, and he's already got the gun for this ink on hand; we got it to him a few weeks ago."

"You want me to get a sleeve?" Lauren asked, grimacing.

"No, no...just, something?"

"What about a quote?" Josh asked. "Or, like, a cat at your shoulder, and the tail goes all the way down to your wrist?" he tried.

Lauren stared hard at him for a moment until he looked away. He wasn't joking. "Unless the cat's as big as my back, the tail wouldn't be that long," she told him.

"It's a tattoo, Lauren, it doesn't have to be realistic," Barry put in. "What about something tribal?"

"Do I look like a frat boy?" she growled, her mind invariably going to the tattoo she'd seen sported on Jerry's arm, and shivering with the memory. Still—they were right that there was nothing to lose at this point.

"Song lyrics?" Josh asked quietly, and Lauren shook her head, thinking.

"No." She bit her lip, her eyes running along the line of her arm. "Would a vine do it? Like, a thin vine with some leaves?"

"Yeah, absolutely!" Barry said, clearly excited—this was apparently one of his pet projects, she realized.

"And you could have anything anchor it. The important thing will just be that it's got something larger, up by your shoulder. Should I call Parker?" he asked.

Still looking at her arm, Lauren finally nodded. An hour ago, she'd thought she had no chance at a future; hinging any hope she and David had on a tattoo seemed a step beyond crazy, but it was something.

***

Lauren leaned back into her seat, self-consciously

turning her arm so that she could look again at the delicate vine running up her arm. This was supposed to save them?

"You don't have to do this," Josh offered quietly. His eyes were on the dash, but he was being honest. He didn't like the options in front of them. It was less than an hour to when Lauren was supposed to be meeting whoever was coming for her in the park, and they were stationed on a nearby street, his Mustang parked and quiet but for the rain outside of the windows.

"You don't think the tracking system will work?" Lauren asked, forcing a lightness into her voice that she didn't feel. Her stomach was in knots, watching the minutes tick by.

"Barry says it'll work, it'll work," Josh answered, unclicking his seatbelt and leaning back, staring ahead at the park entrance rather than at the girl beside him. "But it might not be fast. It *won't* be fast enough for any guarantees. It'll be another two days before he's ready to upload the software, and they're rushing development as it is. After that? Best guess is that it takes a few days, four or five, to track you. That's a week, Lauren."

"So, I just have to con them into not doing anything drastic for a week. Then you and the cavalry swoop in and rescue David."

"And you," Josh commented after a moment, when it became clear she hadn't meant to say more.

"Right," Lauren acknowledged, but she didn't look at him. If she was being honest with him and with herself, a week seemed like an awful long time. Maybe she could convince them to let David go. Maybe. But convince them also to let her remain as she was, without zombi-fying her into someone who'd be good for nothing but doing their bidding? After she'd mostly lost her magic, and then run from them on top of it? That was a harder sell, and she knew it. If she were lucky, she thought she might be able to give David a chance at getting away before her mind was lost. But that was all. Maybe Josh would be coming for her, if the tattoo worked like it was supposed to, but she doubted he'd know what to do with whatever he found that was left of her.

"Listen," she said after a moment. "If you get to finding me, and I'm...not myself, you should just get David out, if he's not already."

Swallowing down nausea, Josh looked sideways at her again. He knew what she was risking here—they'd talked about it, both on that first day when he'd met her at the diner and taken her to the hospital, and more recently, since the last letter had come. This wasn't the kind of slavery you walked away from.

"You have to put them off, Lauren. You're a smart girl—you'll figure it out. Tell them...tell them you need time to write down your mother's life story, or spells she told you, whatever. Give us a week, we'll get you out."

"Or a little longer," she said quietly.

"David wouldn't want you to be making this trade, you know," Josh told her. "Tattoo, tracking, whatever...he wouldn't sign off on this."

"Yeah, I know." Lauren glanced to the clock on the dash again. They had a half hour left.

Chapter 17

Something was wrong. Not just with the situation, not just with him being trapped—something was wrong with his thinking.

He'd known it for hours now, since before he'd last slept. The anxiousness and boredom he'd been feeling had been bleeding into anger, and aggression. Like all of the time he'd spent learning to control his emotions and impulses was ebbing away from his experience. He literally ached to punch something, as if throwing his fist into something would change anything.

Every time he'd dozed off lately, he'd dreamed of violence. Fact and fiction. He'd relived fights with criminals, physical training, and yeah, even what he'd done to Lauren. And he'd dreamed of other things that he'd never done—beating faceless men to pulps, hurting and raping women who he'd had wholly consensual relationships with, and shooting to kill. At first, he'd thought the bloodlust was confined to his dreams, eking out the frustration of being held like some kind of a circus animal in a cage. Now, he was less sure.

Now, the aggression was with him even when he was awake. And what really frustrated him, what was starting to scare him, was that it wasn't just directed at the witches who were holding him. It was anyone. He wanted to hurt *anyone,* to punch *anything. He wanted to cause pain.*

He wasn't stupid—he knew it wasn't natural, that this was coming from something the witches were doing. Something in the air or in his food, or even in the circle of powder that Everett kept refreshing around the cage. But knowing that didn't change it.

He'd stood to pace when Melania entered the room, and now he stopped to watch her. Unlike the other witches he'd gotten used to seeing, she always had a loose smile on her lips when she came in. Like there was an endless train of inside jokes, running through her mind to amuse her. Seeing it now, he felt his hands clenching to the point where he wouldn't have been surprised to find creases in his skin from his ragged nails. He wanted to hurt her.

"Looking more dangerous today, Mr. Fredericks," she commented. "I'm glad to see it."

"What have you all done?" David asked. He was pleased to note that his voice was solid, flat without being desperate. He didn't feel weak physically, but losing control was itself a form of weakness, he knew well enough. And he wasn't far from that edge—or, at least, he wouldn't have been, if he'd had anything to take out his aggression on.

"Done?" she asked. Stepping toward the energy cage, Melania leaned in until her face was only a few inches from the bars. The man inside was tensed, primed for violence. He was denying it, but of course, he wouldn't be for long. "We're only feeding the person you are, David, that's all. You're a violent man with violent tendencies; you can't deny that. We're just going to have you offer us your services, that's all."

Turning from the lead witch, David paced backward and stood facing away from her, swallowing down the rage that made him want to sling his fists through the energy to get to her. He knew that would be suicide, however tempting it might be. *I'm in control. I'm me,* he repeated to himself. *I can beat whatever this is. It's just a fucking spell, fucking with me. Fuck.*

Melania grinned, and then called toward the door. "Mary, bring him in!"

David turned to see Mary escorting in a man who was bound in zip-ties, his body floating along two inches above the ground as he struggled against the invisible bubble holding him. He had a long scar running down the left-hand length of his face, and close-cut hair that was mostly grey. His features were Mediterranean, but his eyes were a bright blue, suggesting some other lineage. His image had long been burned into David's mind, also—this was a serial hit man utilized by criminals in six different countries. He wasn't just among the FBI's most wanted, but that of a number of other agencies, as well. Sneering, the criminal spit toward Mary. "He's angry," she commented emotionlessly.

David looked from the felon to Melania, and then to Mary as the other two witches slipped in the door behind them.

"What would you like to do to this man, David?" Melania asked, her Cheshire cat smile fuller now, teasing. "He's killed government operatives like you, hasn't he?"

The man's eyes widened at the comment, his focus

now on the man in front of him, frozen behind the energy bars.

"Max," Melania said, "meet David Fredericks, government operative extraordinaire. General do-gooder and rescuer, occasional murderer and rapist, and aggressive alpha...behind bars," she added, her lips twitching.

Nell stepped forward, sending a dismissive wave sideways that sliced away the zipties which had been holding Max Rollyson's wrists and ankles together. A moment later, before he'd recovered from the surprise, a few words from her lips had placed him in the cell with David.

Breathing heavily, David watched as latticed metal appeared between the interior of the cage and the energy bars, scrolling up from the floor out of nowhere—now either man could press the other into the cage's edge, and there'd be warm metal there to hold them, instead of energy set up to shred them. "What do you want?" he asked, his eyes on the man who stood sizing him up.

"Oh, we've already explained it to Max; I guess we ought to explain it to you," Melania commented, making a gesture that moved the few supplies that David had had from the inside of the cage to just beyond the bars, leaving nothing but empty space around the two men. "We want to see a fight with one survivor," she hissed.

Melania curled daintily to the ground, crossing her legs beneath her and perching her elbows on her knees, her eyes on David. The other witches followed suit, Nell leaning against the wall as Mary and Johanna took seats on the ground, forming a small audience.

David turned to Rollyson, attempting to ignore both the women and the aggression he could feel curdling within him. "We don't have to do this," he told the other man.

Before the words had fully left his lips, though, Max was on top of him, and there wasn't any holding back after that.

Max's first kidney punch slammed into David's side, doubling him, but the aggression in his blood more than overcame the pain. He'd wanted blood for more than a day now, and with first contact, the instinct was insurmountable. He turned into the other man's body and tackled him backward, bringing one of his fists up in a tight punch to the side of his skull.

The men grappled, one of David's forearms landing across the other man's neck as he leaned in and punched him twice in the gut, the other man reduced to defensive posturing. Rollyson brought his legs up and managed to kick David away then, rising almost immediately to follow and land on him with blows, but David was the more experienced wrestler. Before the other man knew what had happened, David had pinned him fully so that he lay on his stomach, one arm twisted behind him as David let loose a dozen hits, rotating them between his kidneys and his head. When the man struggled beneath the blows, David didn't hesitate to twist the arm he held so that the other man screamed, animal-like, in pain. The arm twisted from its socket, David re-focused and reached for a wrist, breaking it without a second thought so that the man stopped struggling and began to cry, begging to be let up as he writhed beneath David, who'd only grown more violent as the seconds passed, his grip digging in as his punches came down hard and fast.

When the man had stopped moving, and had stopped pleading, David swung him over so that he could deliver two crushing blows to the front of his face.

Some small part of him acknowledged that the man's eyes were closed now, blood leaking from his lips, his nose, and his ears, but he stood and began kicking at his body, enjoying the thump of his foot against the broken man laying before him. He grunted with the effort of kicking Rollyson hard into the cell's bars, and then landed on him to offer more blows, to his gut and then to his head.

It was Melania's clapping that finally stilled his fist, and then the body was gone and David was panting for breath, covered in the other man's blood and on all fours. Alone again, within the cell, he stared at the beaten felon who lay outside of the bars as the metal latticing of the cage disappeared. The man outside lay unnaturally, one of his arms folded limply beneath him. None of them—not the witches, and not David—could question whether the man was alive or dead. He'd stopped breathing minutes before the brutality had ended.

As Melania clapped, David stumbled backward, acknowledging that the bloodlust in his veins was still pumping, still wanting to do more damage. With the thought, he tripped toward the bathroom, falling before the toilet and vomiting up what was left of his aggression—horror at what he'd just done, and what he wanted more of, burning through him. Only vaguely did he hear Melania's voice.

"Good," she was saying. "Now, perhaps, dial back the violence, up the cruelty, and he'll be ready."

***

Lauren sat frozen, numb and suddenly exhausted. She was in a small room, no larger than a small walk-in closet. She rested on a small circular bed that she suspected had originally been manufactured as a large dog bed, and was wrapped in the oversized men's sweater that Josh had given her off of his own back to ward off the rain coming down when she'd headed into the park. She pulled it tighter, staring at the blank screen in front of her.

A moment before, it had played back the most gruesome fight—if it could even be called that—that she'd ever witnessed. She'd watched David beat a man to death, unable to turn away from it. There'd been no sound, which she was thankful for.

She'd told Melania that she wanted to see him, to know he was okay, and then Johanna had brought her to this room, and this screen. It had switched on suddenly, and she'd seen him standing there...and then there'd been another man with him. And they'd fought. And she'd watched. The screen had gone blank after the second man's body was removed from the cell David occupied, and after he'd stood up, covered in the other man's blood, apparently uninjured himself but for a few bruises.

Turning from the screen, Lauren numbly curled into a small ball at the center of the pad she'd been offered, her eyes on the door in front of her. She'd known he was a fighter, sure...and maybe she'd thought she knew what he was capable of. But the violence she'd just seen—that had been like out of some movie. There'd been nothing in his eyes but violence, anger...aggression, like there was nothing he'd wanted more in the world than to see the man dead. And whatever he'd done, he'd been punished ten times over for it. Assuming he'd done anything at all, Lauren thought, suddenly shuddering all over with the idea that he'd been innocent, just someone picked up for the pleasure of a beating.

Had the violence been for her benefit or the witches', or had they wanted to punish someone? And how...why...had David kept going, even after he was still, and dead. She shut her eyes, but the images were engraved on her eyelids now—the blood spattering away from his face as David had landed those last few blows. She'd been so anxious to see him, to know he was alright, and now...Now there was a part of her wondering which David was real. The fighter who she'd just seen beat a man to death, who hunted criminals and who'd raped her in order to find out what she knew. Or the man who'd been protective of her, and who she'd thought deserved at least her loyalty, if not her love.

When the light above her went out, she welcomed the darkness, and pulled the sweater yet tighter so that she felt it pressing around her like a cocoon. She didn't want to sleep, knowing nightmares would come, but she wished she could find some blankness. At the moment, losing herself, and losing all of her memories, seemed less fearful a prospect than it had at any time before.

***

The video replayed intermittently, and more often than not, Lauren couldn't resist watching.

Sometimes it would come on when the room was wholly dark otherwise, and sometimes the light would be on. Sometimes, when the video was playing or when it wasn't, a snippet of David's voice would play from a speaker, somewhere above her. She knew the phrases were chosen to jar her, and they did.

I killed him. I'll kill you. Give me a chance and I'll rip you apart. You don't deserve my sympathy. I'll kill you. Fuck you. I don't give a shit about you. I'll kill you. The sentences didn't come together, and it wasn't hard for Lauren to imagine that David would have said them to Nell or any of the other witches. But out of context, with no other conversation to back them, and with the malice coming through in his voice, when it wasn't simply flat...the phrases got to her. She feared his voice over the speakers more than the video now.

At first, she'd tried to rationalize why he might have killed the man, and in that fashion, once she'd gotten over the shock of it. And when the nightmares started, so that she wanted to sleep as little as possible anyway, it became a game—keeping herself awake by numbering out and listing different scenarios, different things that that man might have done, different reasons David might have had for being so violent...and yet, she never came up with anything really satisfying.

There were other games she played to stay awake. Trying to remember the details of their conversations, since his voice was the one foremost in her mind anyway. Trying to figure out how long she'd been in this little room, let out only for unpredicted bathroom breaks and time to shower. She could swear she'd once been told to shower twice in a span of only five hours or so, just to mess with her. And given two meals within two hours—again, just to mess with her. She had no sense of time anymore, and the emotion she was closest to was fear. She feared the video and David's voice over the speaker, and she feared sleep, because it brought nightmares.

When Melania told her after one of her bathroom breaks to dry her hair, she did as told without thinking about it, accepting the dryer that was handed to her. And when the witch gave her fresh clothes, she put them on. She didn't know what was coming, but the shift dress and sweater was a welcome change from the clothes that had gone smelly and greasy with her sweat and fear, and this was a change of routine to put off sleep for a while, if nothing else. Besides this, she was so tired...fighting such simple requests didn't deserve consideration at this point. Anything to stay out of the closet.

Following behind the woman, she ran her hands along the thin dress, pulling the hem down. It was too short, coming halfway up her thighs. Given the option, she normally would have worn it over jeans. And the sweater was lacy and insubstantial—something she wouldn't normally have chosen for herself at all. It made her wish she'd been allowed to keep Josh's sweater instead, dirty as it had been. There wasn't any cold to fight off, but there'd been some comfort in that garment, and this one made her feel nothing less than vulnerable, light as it was over the short dress.

Melania led her through a maze of corridors, and then down some stairs. There was nothing familiar in the space, and since Lauren hadn't been invited to speak at any point, she didn't bother. What was there to say?

When Lauren followed Melania through a final door, though, she recognized the room they'd come to. Or, at least, she recognized what lay within it. To the side, centered against one wall, was the cage she'd seen in the video, but without the metal that it had held in the fight. David was at its center, sprawled out on his back with one knee cocked up, a light snore coming from his chest. One of his arms lay to his side, the fist clenched, his other hand resting on his bare stomach. He wore only jeans, and his hair had grown out. She could see the shading of facial hair over the side of his jaw. She guessed he'd discarded the shirt he'd worn before because of the blood from the fight, but the sight of his naked chest still jarred her.

Hearing a light chuckle come from Melania, she turned sideways, coldness running through her blood. "What is this?" she asked quietly. "What do you want?"

"It's not about what I want. It's about what your body wants, Lauren. What your *magic* wants. That's what I want *for* you."

And in a flash, Lauren found herself standing within the cage, a few feet from David, watching as Melania flashed her signature smile of cruelty, and then backed out of the door they'd come through, shutting it behind her.

***

As had become his norm, David put off opening his eyes. Nothing would have changed. He could feel it in the leftover images from his dreams, playing out violence, in his hands that were sore from being clenched, and he could sense it from the hard rubbery floor beneath his back and the smell of his own sweat and body, still being warmed by the energy cage. But then he smelled something else—sweeter, almost flowery—and he sat up.

Leaning against the little bit of wall space by the bathroom, apparently asleep, Lauren was curled into herself, just a few feet away. Most of her legs were showing, smooth and familiar, from beneath a too-short ruffled dress, and seeing them was enough to stir his blood to want to touch her. To want to *grab* her, in fact. Biting back her name, he stayed where he was and let his eyes roam over her. She looked healthy, though there were circles beneath her eyes, showing even as she slept. Over the dress, she wore a light sweater, and she had her arms crossed over her midsection, hugging herself. The pose and the dress showed off the tops of her breasts, and his eyes lingered there. Her lips were moving, barely, and he knew she was dreaming.

Swallowing her name, he bit his own lip to bring himself back to where he was, trying to remember himself. His breath was coming faster, his dick hardening at the sight of her, and his fists were clenched.

She looked vulnerable, and that should have given him pause, but it didn't—it just fed into the things he wanted to do to her, none of which were gentle. Instead, he sat and watched her, his whole body tensed and wanting, only a small, sane part of his mind dreading the point when she'd wake up.

We're fucked, he considered, and the part of him that was still good, still grounded, cringed and forced him to turn away from Lauren. For too long now, he'd been blood-lusting, wanting violence, and feeding off of the adrenaline left over from killing the convict the witches had thrown to him. Maybe there'd been more cruelty than killing in his dreams over the last few hours, but that was little enough of a change. And Lauren had been in his dreams, too, a sort of temptress to keep him occupied with sex instead of death. Now that she was here, though, the desire to dominate her was overwhelming. To punish her for lying to him, for not telling him about the spell. For bringing him to this point, intentionally or not.

He knew the witches had dressed her like this for him, on purpose, presenting her to him in his fucking cage like she was some delicacy. The way the dress showed off her figure, even curled up like she was, and that film of a sweater...she was a study in how to balance innocence against seduction, and she'd already been his weakness. He couldn't imagine their reasoning and didn't want to, but he knew they expected him to beat her or fuck her, if not both; their way of punishing both of them, he had to guess, but knowing this didn't make it any easier to resist touching her.

His blood had been running hot with violence and lust for days, and there was no turning it off now. He could stare at the opposite wall, but he could also *smell* her, and see her body in his mind's eye, bending and whimpering beneath him as she'd been doing in his dreams for days, like a doll that was his for the taking. And now she was here, and it was only a matter of time before she woke up.

Shutting away the image of her as much as he could, he closed his eyes and worked to clear his mind. He couldn't—he wouldn't—let himself hurt her again. That meant he had to shut down the part of himself that had been awakened by whatever spell the witches had circling this room. Whatever violence and lust was in his blood, and wherever it was coming from, there was no choice but to move beyond it.

He put his hands on his knees, forcing himself to take deep breaths, cross-legged in the middle of the room. First, he tried picturing the woods where he spent time hiking, when he could get away, attempting to pace himself down the various trails in his mind. As they kept stalling out, he gave up and moved on to attempting some plan that could allow them out of the den they'd found themselves in, but there was nothing new to consider, beyond Lauren's presence, and that only brought him back to the girl slumbering behind him, and back to his clenched fists and his stiff dick, reminding him what he'd tried to move his thoughts from to begin with. When he began trying to figure out how long he'd been in the cell, and how much time had passed since they'd been ambushed at Mary's house, he already knew he was fighting a losing battle.

The best he could do would be to try to take control of his desires, and act on them while he had some control, instead of waiting until the spell had more power over him than anything. Right now, at least some of the violence running in his blood had been sated with the fight from a few days before. Maybe if he focused on the lust...maybe he wouldn't hurt her. This was what he told himself, at least.

Moving to stand beside Lauren, David for a half a second wondered whether this was the same girl he'd left behind at the house, or if the witches had taken her will like they'd threatened. Taken her memories, and her desires, and all that made her the woman he'd begun caring so much for over the past weeks. Kneeling beside her, he realized he didn't want to know. Not yet. Nothing would change the aggression in his blood, or the lust. And he didn't want to make love to a shell of this girl anymore than he wanted to hurt or fuck a shell of her. If she wasn't herself any longer, it wouldn't change anything, but to make him feel worse in the moment, if anything.

In a single move, he covered her lips with his own and took her upper arms in his hands, breathing in the gasp she let out as she awoke and relishing the smell of her as he moved her sideways, laying her backwards quickly, without his lips ever leaving hers. Her hands were on his own forearms, holding on tightly, and her body had tensed—was tense—beneath him. He took his mouth away from hers but didn't look in her eyes, just leaning sideways to whisper into her ear, "Don't fight me."

It was all he could do, working to be gentle, and he knew he wasn't being gentle enough as his hands held her arms down, his lips at her neck, drinking in her scent as he kissed, and then nibbled, relishing the quivering skin beneath his hands and lips, soft and smooth. Lauren hadn't said anything yet, but she was tense, stiff, so that he was doing all he could to loosen her up, at least somewhat, before taking things any further. He wouldn't be able to hold himself back once they started, and though part of his brain wanted the roughness, and the power, the smaller and more authentic part of him wanted a continuation of what they'd had before, and an avoidance of any pain at all. Still, he couldn't help biting down on her neck, hearing her gasp, and letting his hands stray to groping her breasts, squeezing hard and enjoying the firmness through the dress, and the way she whimpered in response.

As soon as he felt her hands loosen on his forearms, one of his hands moved further down. The dress hung loose on her—it took only a moment for him to lift enough that it was pulled high, bunched above her breasts, and now he realized she'd only been wearing panties, with no bra, and took his mouth to one of her nipples even as she moaned beneath him, one of her hands weakly pushing at his shoulder.

"Don't fight me," he growled again, grabbing her wrist and roughly pulling it to the side, re-focusing his mouth on her breast and biting down before he could help himself, so that she called out, pleasure mixed with pain and fear as her other hand gripped his bicep.

Lauren could barely breathe, and couldn't think. Waking up to David's lips had stunned her—it had been the last thing she'd expected—and the way he was acting now, it was like he was possessed. His lips were rough, his teeth coming down harder on her skin than they had in the past, and his hands were everywhere at once. She took a deep breath, flexing her hand beneath David's grip—he was holding her wrist so tightly that she thought he was close to cutting off circulation—and then arched beneath him with a gasp when he bit down on her breast again.

"David, not here..." she groaned when he backed off enough to focus on sucking at her nipple, the hand that wasn't holding onto her wrist suddenly finding its way into her panties, to her wet slit, and rubbing against her. Lauren could feel him, rock hard within his jeans and pressed against her thigh, and her body was reacting to him, pleasure running through her blood and wanting more even as he held her wrist so tightly that her whole arm was immobile above them. But goddamnit, he was hurting her—she didn't want to be responding to him like this, and not here of all places, but she bit back another protest as he seemed to let out an actual growl, the rough stubble of his facial hair rubbing against her breast as he did. And suddenly she knew that had been on purpose—the *pain* he was causing was on purpose.

"Here," he answered simply, a full minute after she'd spoken, and then he finally let go of her hand, but he moved his fingers to her face, holding her jaw and letting one of his fingers push inside of her mouth, forcing her lips apart.

Knowing what he was demanding, Lauren sucked on his finger, and then on an another when he pressed it between her lips, his hand on her jaw in a way that told her, clearly enough, he didn't want to her to say another word. He was watching her accept him, his eyes boring into hers and reinforcing the dominance she could feel in her every muscle. Shutting her eyes against his gaze, she tried not to think of where they were, and the way she must look to the witches who she knew had to be watching, with David above her, holding her helpless— with his mouth now torturing her breasts, one of his hands pressed against her mouth and digging into her, keeping her gagged, his other exploring her below, offering another sort of torture that her body couldn't help but surrender to.

David pushed a second finger deep into Lauren's wet snatch, working her so that she was already panting as he sucked at her breasts and used his other hand to keep her from speaking. His dick was painfully hard, and anything she said would take his focus away from maintaining some control over what he was doing to her, and her body before him. God, but she was tight. He pressed his fingers in harder, exploring her, and let his thumb find her clit a moment later. He felt a shudder run though her. Jarring himself backward, he yanked her panties down her legs with one hand while undoing his jeans with his other, pushing them and his underwear down to his knees as he knelt beside her and then shaking them away from his body as he went back to her.

Lauren hadn't caught her breath yet, David had moved so quickly. Even as she realized she could pull her dress down and regain some of her modesty, she saw David's hard member pointing at her, and he was back, staring into her eyes and positioning himself above her as he pressed her thighs apart and moved between them, his eyes on hers, full of aggression...this was the man she'd come to fear over the last few days, the man from the video who she'd watched give himself over to killing. She felt the head of his cock against her thigh and tried to push backwards away from him, but he caught her by her hips and held her so that she couldn't help but stare at him, already shaking her head. One of her hands went to her dress, trying to at least cover her breasts, and her other landed on one of his hands, trying to peel his fingers away from her body.

"David, not here, please," she whimpered.

In a breath, though, he was fully on top of her, the head of his dick just pressed into her, and she thought he'd never felt so big, so demanding. "Here, Lauren. Stop fighting," he growled, his eyes on hers as he let his weight press her body down into the hard floor.

David felt his hands gripping her hips hard and tried to take a deep breath, shifting so that his lips could come down on her neck. There was fear in her eyes, and she was trembling and stiff; he couldn't not hurt her, the way she was, but at least she was wet, because he couldn't wait any longer.

In a hard push, he pressed his dick all the way into her, letting the weight of his body carry him into her as his teeth nipped at her neck and she gasped beneath him, her hands clenching against his sides as she called out. He could feel her pussy already trying to accommodate his size as he moved, pressing back and forth along her channel. She was shaking beneath him, and he could feel wetness on his shoulder from crying that he hoped was more embarrassment than pain. Roughly, he grabbed the fabric of her bunched dress with one hand and pressed it further upward as he kept thrusting, so that the fabric was just a line of material over her collarbone and no longer covering anything. He brought his mouth down to one of her breasts, using his hips and legs to hold her down for his pleasure as his hands explored her skin roughly, possessively.

Lauren was moaning—she couldn't help it. David was like an animal on top of her, and she barely knew if he was aware of who she was or what he was doing, but her body didn't care. Her blood was humming with being close to him again, and there was more pleasure than pain, despite the hard floor beneath her and the soreness along her hips and arms where he'd held her still. Suddenly, he gripped one of her thighs with one of his hands, pulling her further open so that he could lunge against her, thrusting harder and deeper, and her body arched beneath him, spasming, the climax forcing a scream from her throat that he bit off with a bruising kiss, his dick buried inside of her. She'd still been working to get used to him, and the stretching of her muscles, alongside the pulses of her body around him, were almost too much to bear. For a moment, she was sure she'd pass out, deep as he was pressed into her as he bit down on her upper lip, and then he was moving again, his hand moving now from her thigh to her clit and pushing down so that she bucked against him.

"That's it, baby, that's it," he growled into her ear, and for a moment she thought he sounded like the man who'd made love to her at the ranch house, when they'd last been together, but then his thumb pressed harder into her, no gentleness to be found in the touch, and her body went white-hot with pleasure and pain as she spasmed against him again, writhing, tears forced from her eyes with the sudden violence of it.

A moment later, she realized his cock was spasming into her, erupting with seed and rocking her, and her pussy was milking him for it, the one part of her that was still wanting him, still ready for him and pulsing with desire.

David gripped her hard, his whole body jerking with the release into her, letting it last, and then he lay heavy on top of her for a moment, his dick still rock hard inside of her. He caught his breath, listening to her whimper and pant beneath him. Her body had been wracked with pleasure already, bruised by his need, but he needed more.

Lifting himself from her after a moment of rest, he muttered, "Turn over," and pressed her sideways so that she rolled to lay on her stomach. She was barely aware of what he was doing as he moved behind her and between her legs. Absurdly, her sweater was still on, covering her back, a lump beneath it at the top of her shoulders where her dress had been bunched. From between her thighs, he reached for the neck of the sweater and pulled it backward, listening to her moan as her limbs moved to accommodate the fabric's pull.

He watched it reveal her shoulders, and saw the raw

tattoo she'd gained as he pulled it down and then twisted it so that it bunched around her wrists. Disconnected from what he was doing, barely aware of the pain he was causing to the girl squirming before him, he kept twisting the fabric tighter, holding her wrists tied together as he examined the tattoo and enjoyed his power. It was delicate—a twining of dark leaves and vine work running from her shoulder to her wrist, where it looped in a braided bracelet. At her shoulder, it went from being a single braided vine with occasional leaves to a latticework that erupted into a small tree, foreign in species, that covered not just the ball of her shoulder, but the back of it.

For a moment, it made him doubt this was Lauren, but he pushed the thought away; he'd ask about the tattoo later. For now, it was enough to see it—it was fresh and gorgeous, and he'd make a point of trying not to touch it now that he knew it was there, but still, for now, he needed more of her beneath him, around him. He twisted the sweater, pulling her limbs closer together.

Shutting out her whimpers, he leaned into her wrists so that he could whisper into her ear, again, "Don't fight this, baby—just accept me. I want you to lift up, alright?"

Lauren was barely aware of what David was saying; her wrists were aching, and she'd thought that his pulling away her sweater and revealing her tattoo might have given him pause and made him stop for a moment to realize that he was hurting her, but his voice was still gruff with need, and his dick was hard against her thigh, wet and pulsing. She shook her head against the floor and pulled at her wrists as she felt his hand come down between her shoulder blades and press, holding her against the floor as his other hand and his thighs nudged her lower body forward and repositioned her, moving her forward until her breasts were pushed hard into the floor, her face sideways, but she was on her knees before him also, her ass in the air.

She felt his fingers groping her, and then she felt his dick again, pressing into her pussy from behind as he nudged her knees further apart. She groaned beneath him, her body instinctively reacting to the new angle as he pressed in harder, deeper, and then began to ride her, one hand on her back and one hand on her hip, supporting her and pulling her against him to meet his hard thrusts.

Gasping at the new angle, Lauren's every instinct was to get away from him. He was rubbing against her wet channel in a way she'd never felt before, and she was already tender from cumming beneath him. But here she felt her body stretching to take him all the way in, further, her pussy lips clenching around him with each stroke, each move of his body against hers, his balls hitting her skin as he pulled her against him roughly, making sure she met him thrust for thrust, and her writhing on the ground wasn't doing any good. She gave up, knowing there was nowhere to escape to, and tried to lose herself in the pleasure more than the pain as he grunted above her, and she couldn't help groaning in return, moving helplessly in response to his need, his pleasure.

Letting herself be used, Lauren felt every inch of the rippling heat of her blood reacting to him, pressuring her to climax yet again. She was sore, from inside to outside, but at least her wrists were forgotten with the pleasure of the way David's dick felt with her, demanding and large, pressing her open. Her body was focused there, in her center, the rest of her body a dull ache centered on that desire. It was enough that he'd stopped twisting the sweater, and that now the garment was only a loose tie to hold her arms immobile as he directed her body, using her, pressing her to let him take her however he wanted to, as roughly as he wanted. She gasped as he seemed to suddenly go deeper, yet again, and then her body was spasming beneath him, shaking with another wracking climax as he lunged into her, harder and faster, grunting with the effort of it, his hand against her back slick with their sweat.

When the height of Lauren's climax subsided, and she was only shaking from the remnants, David moved his hand from her back and leaned away from her to catch his breath, both of his hands now clasped around her hips and ass as she quivered beneath him, gasping, his dick still buried all the way inside of her folds; her pussy was pulsing around him, warm and tight with desire. He didn't know whether Lauren was whimpering more from pleasure or pain, but her body wanted this— it wanted him. Holding himself still against her, he reached with one hand and pulled away the sweater, pushing her hands to the floor.

"Hold yourself up," he told her, clenching his teeth upon hearing the harshness in his own voice. She didn't seem to hear him, but when he pressed her hands to the floor and then reached below her, grasping a breast and pulling at her, she took the direction and found the strength to support herself so that he could grip one of her breasts, playing with the nipple as he caught his breath, his other hand stroking up and down her back, calming her, working to gentle her, letting her catch her own breath.

When his dick jumped inside of her with the adrenaline and aggression still running in his blood, he realized he didn't want to wait any longer.

With a jerk, he pulled her hard against him and

renewed his efforts, feeling her body tense as her arms gave out beneath her and his hands went to her hips, holding her hard. He gritted his teeth at her whimpers, and at the sight of her hands clenched against the floor, scrambling for some purchase to allow her to move away from him. She was writhing now, trying to get away from the sensations he was forcing upon her, but he couldn't let her. He held her against him still, knowing now that he was bottoming out against the end of her channel with each of his thrusts, shaking a fast, gasping yelp from her each time.

When he came this time, he found her clit at the same moment and she screamed beneath him, bucking beneath his body with her back arched as her pussy milked him, pulsing with warmth and desire. He hadn't come directly into a girl, no condom, in years, and the pleasure of it kept him going, hard within her passage and pushing at her, demanding every sensation of pleasure she could bare before he finally stilled, panting behind her and watching her shudder.

He felt more himself now—more himself than he'd felt in days—if laced with guilt for what he'd put her through, and for the fact that his dick was still hard, still wanting. Releasing her, he leaned backward and felt her sigh with relief as he left her channel, and she rolled sideways, curling into a loose ball.

Lauren was too exhausted to fight for her modesty now—her whole body was pulsing with pleasure and numb from exhaustion, heated and bubbling over with sensation. She couldn't catch her breath, or understand what David was saying to her, but she was thankful that now his movements finally seemed slower, less primed to erupt, and she didn't fight him as he moved beside her and then pulled her body into his, one of his arms snaking beneath her tattooed arm and going around her stomach.

His dick hard against the back of her thigh scared her—the idea that he wasn't yet satisfied was too much—and she shut it out, but she came back to herself when his hand began moving, toying with her nipple.

"David, no, please—I can't take anymore," she whispered, turning her face up and trying to find his sight, to find some mercy, but then she shut her eyes when she felt his fingers tighten, pulling more insistently on the already diamond-hard nipple and reminding her of how he'd bitten down earlier. She took a deep breath at the pain that came with his tugs, and pushed her head back into his chest, shaking her head. "Let me pull down my dress, please," she whimpered, the sound of her hoarse voice begging unrecognizable to her own ears.

"We're not done, baby," David replied, knowing even as he said them how cruel the words were, and how he was torturing her. *Only a little more*, he promised himself, *and then I'll be myself, and can leave her alone for days. Better to get it over with now.* He could feel it—he was close to being satisfied, close to getting out of the reaches of the spells of lust and aggression that had had him on edge for days. He just needed a little more from her, and the way her body responded to him...he couldn't resist taking it. And besides—he wanted to sleep. He was close to being satisfied, and hadn't had real, peaceful sleep in days; he knew that, with a little more time, he'd be able to get it.

She was too weak to fight him as he began playing with her body, for the first time able to take the time to appreciate what the spell her mother had cast did to her. He'd thought he understood the idea of a girl being putty in his hands, but this was something else. Knowing what was happening, he couldn't see how he hadn't realized it before. Even as he caressed Lauren, holding her against him so that he could play his hands along her abdomen and her stomach, her breasts and her thighs, he found himself realizing that he was angry with her, for not telling him about the spell. Her whole body was tensing and quivering in turn as he moved his hands, and she was too weak to do more than murmur protests that he barely heard. Instead, he focused on what he could do to her, and on the firmness of her breasts and the slickness of her slit. He could practically feel her blood shuddering in response, her whole body beginning to tremor with need again as he stroked her and teased her, his dick still hard against her thigh.

"Why didn't you tell me about the spell, Lauren?" he asked finally, his voice gruff, and then he asked again when it seemed like she hadn't heard.

"The...my mom's spell?" she asked haltingly, and then gasped when he ran one of his fingers along her wet thigh and then lifted it, circling her juices and his semen around a nipple. And then he did it again, and she squirmed against him, helplessly pushing back into him as if that would allow her some escape from the sensations. He'd trapped her hands between their bodies now, and she was open to him, helpless. Her whole body was on fire with want all over again, shaking, her pussy as wanton as it was sore.

"I didn't know how," she gasped, feeling David's lips suckling at her neck.

He nibbled at her skin, and then licked, feeling her shudder. "You didn't want to give up control," he whispered huskily. "You didn't want me to know you couldn't say no to me," he added, moving his lips to her ear and licking along her earlobe.

David no longer could have said what was driving him—his own need or her reactions to what he was doing. As she nodded in acceptance of what he'd said, he shifted up so that he could kiss her, pressing in hard and allowing himself to enjoy the whimper that came from her bruised lips as her wrists pressed into his forearms now, arguing for space, or time, or both. This was like a drug, though. Being able to feel her blood heating in response to his touch, and feeling her shudder with each brush of his skin...it was like a new level of desire he'd unlocked, and now had time to enjoy. Before, he'd known she wanted him, and wanted his touch. Now, he knew she'd had enough, and was sore enough that pleasure had crossed into pain, and yet she still couldn't say no; her body didn't even want her to.

He ran two of his fingers against her wet slit, feeling her swollen labia—she was aching for more, but also raw and sore. He kept spreading her moisture, slicking it along her folds and then bringing his hand up, forcing her to taste herself, and her need, and teasing at her nipples. Her body was already primed for more. He bit down into her shoulder and then licked, listening to her whimper and feeling her twitch against him, her soaked pussy gripping his scissoring fingers with the shock of the bite.

"Once more, baby," he whispered then, grinning into her shoulder as he felt her shiver. Sliding to the side and pulling her body into him from behind, he reached down, and lifted her leg upward so that he could nudge forward, positioning himself again at her opening.

Lauren was too weak and too stunned to fight him. One of his hands was still toying with her breasts, his lips on her neck, as she felt his other hand lift her leg, pulling it backward so that it rested over top of his before he shifted his hips, his leg now holding her open for him; then she felt his dick at the lips of her opening, and tried to pull away, but he was holding her tight to him, pinned, and there was nowhere to go.

She groaned as she felt him slide into her yet again, stretching her open and filling her; she'd grown sore and swollen from their earlier couplings, and now he only felt bigger, somehow, as he pressed into her firmly, moving back and forth against her in slow, knowing thrusts. She almost wished he'd go quickly, so that it could be over with, but he was taking his time.

David used his legs to keep her lower half tangled against him, her one leg pulled back to allow him deeper access, and moved his hand up to her belly, pressing in rhythmically and dipping down to brush her clit at odd moments as she shuddered against him. This wasn't a violent climax like she'd had before—he was pulling tremors from her, slow and steady, and she was pulsing around his dick, moaning with each slight move he made. Now he had the control back so that he could go slowly, and coming within her earlier had taken most of the edge off; his dick was still hard, but there was no urgency on his part, and he wasn't sore. "You belong to me," he muttered to her when she gasped again beneath him, shaking with want that she couldn't deny as he pushed into her again.

Tweaking her breasts as he held her against him, he began pressing down on her belly each time he thrust into her, feeling her body accommodate him as she whimpered with each new thrust, each new push. She was shaking now, begging for him to stop, but he kept going, licking the sweat from her neck and enjoying the way her skin trembled in response each time he moved his hand between her breasts or along her abdomen. Finally, he felt himself wanting more, and moving to a last climax; Lauren was barely conscious against him now, her body simply reacting to each sensation as it came, but her pussy was pulsing around him, meeting each of his thrusts and tightening, shuddering.

"Come on, baby, one more time," he grunted into her ear, biting down so that she gasped, and then he sped up, shifting so that she was half beneath him, less beside, and so that he had more leverage. He found her clit with his fingers and her body jerked against him as he came again, spurting into her what was left of his need as he grunted into her shoulder, his hands caressing her breasts and her belly as he came down from the high and she shuddered beneath him, her body still quaking in reaction and his dick still within her, but finally softening.

When he'd caught his breath, he slipped from within her. He pulled her dress down, and then he pulled her underwear up her legs, trying to ignore how slick with sweat and need he'd left her body. She was laying on her back, and he retrieved her sweater and spread it over her, covering her upper arms. He watched her then for a moment, lost to exhausted sleep, before he retrieved his own clothes. He discarded his underwear that he thought he might as well have discarded days ago, and simply pulled on his jeans before he lay beside her. After a moment, he turned sideways and rested one arm over her belly; when she didn't react, he pulled her body into his and turned her, cradling her against him, landing her head on his chest as he lay back on his back. She shuddered once at the contact, but didn't awaken or say anything, and he knew they'd both sleep.

Chapter 18

"**S**ay yes to me."

Lauren could feel herself trembling at the request, shaking her head even as her body leaned backward into him. This wasn't what she wanted, but she also didn't know how to say no to him—not anymore, not with what he knew and where they were.

She was cradled in a crouch against him now, with her back against his chest, her eyes shut. Both of David's hands were caressing her thighs, running up and down her skin gently, kneading and stroking. Her hands were trapped behind her, between her body and David's, clenched to keep herself from touching him automatically and giving in to what he was asking. His own back was leaning against the frame of the door leading to the bathroom, and the cage's bars glowed around them, hot and deadly.

She'd woken slowly that morning, and though she'd woken up wrapped in his arms, she'd moved away and he'd let her. She was sore from yesterday, her lips and her pussy swollen from his attentions, and now her body was reacting to his touch yet again, but it was the last thing she wanted. Her blood was pulling her toward him, reacting to his skin against hers, but she also knew that more contact could only lead to more pain than pleasure.

"Not yet, David," she whispered. His heart beat faster. Were his hands becoming harder, more insistent? She could feel his stiff rod against her ass now, through his jeans and the thin material of her dress. "Please," she added, "yesterday was too much. I need more time before..." she trailed off helplessly and closed her eyes as she felt his chest inhale heavily against her, his breath on her ear, heavy and warm.

David's hands only paused for a moment, and then they were pulling her thighs apart so that she moaned, whimpering what she knew sounded like defeat. One of his hands tugged harder at her thigh, sideways until her leg was propped over his own, and then he raised his knee, and did the same to her other leg so that she was slouched against him, trapped and wide open with her legs straddling his. She gasped when one of his fingers thrummed lightly against her wet panties. God, but she wanted him even now, when just the thought of sex brought as much pain and attention to soreness as it did wetness and thoughts of pleasure.

"Relax," David whispered, and then he sucked her earlobe between his lips and bit down lightly as he ran his fingers along the outline of her pussy, and then inside of her panties and along her swollen lips, along her soaked slit, toying with her. He could feel her body pulsing with energy, hot and responsive. He'd thought yesterday that he'd still be satisfied at this point, happy to let her rest...but he wasn't.

Ever since he'd woken, he'd been thinking of nothing but taking her.

He wanted to punish her for withholding the truth of the spell and her attraction, and more than that, he wanted her to admit that she was his. For as long as they were together, and even when they weren't, she'd belong to him. And since they were trapped here, she was also his one distraction, which he planned to take advantage of. If it kept holding off the aggression he'd felt before, that was what mattered. That's what he told himself, at least, as he felt her gasping for breath and fighting to close her legs even as her pussy clenched down on his fingers, wanting more.

He pressed his fingers deep into her, simultaneously raising his legs some so that her hips suddenly angled into his hand at the same moment, and she let out a high yelp that bled into a groan. She was quivering against him now, and he sucked on her earlobe as he let his thumb find her clit, playing her orgasm out of her until she was mewling in his arms, her voice barely recognizable in its hoarseness.

When he thought she couldn't take anymore without passing out, and she was left gasping for breath, he lowered his legs so that her own fell over his, her body limp. She didn't fight as he turned her sideways on the ground, finding her eyes with his. They were dazed, a sheen of sweat glistening on her skin. The vulnerability there, for a moment, undid him, overriding the cruelty and lust he felt in his blood so that a sudden bolt of guilt rode along his spine and stabbed into his gut. He swallowed it down. If he wasn't going to hurt her with violence, he knew instinctively that he had to allow his lust to get its fill and tire out his muscles.

He held her gaze, leaning forward so that their foreheads nearly met. "You have to trust me."

The gruffness in his voice made Lauren's blood practically shiver in response—his desire for her was naked, almost torturous in how present it was, and her body wanted all of it, raw and used as it was. She let her head fall back as David's hands went to the hem of her dress, pulling it upward and then over her arms so that she was naked but for the soaked panties clinging to her hips, reeking of sweat and pleasure. She heard herself whimper when David's fingers tugged those down also, but didn't fight him when he moved overtop of her and nudged her legs apart with his knees, lowering his cock to her slit so that his head grazed her, and then pushed inward.

"Let me in, baby," he whispered against her neck, feeling her body tense. She was so wet that it did little to hold him apart from her, but he wanted her to be with him on this. He felt her take a deep breath and he rose enough to see her eyes, searching out his.

She looks scared. The thought jarred him, but didn't stop him. He willed his gaze to gentle as he pushed forward, one of his hands holding to her shoulder and the other on her breast, feeling her hard nipple at the center of his palm, betraying her body's want. "I've got you, baby, let go," he told her, pushing forward again and opening her hips to him, willing her to respond. She was struggling still, squirming beneath him in a way his dick was responding to, her pussy squeezing him as she whimpered, her eyes shut against his. He leaned closer to her ear, whispering, demanding. "Lauren, you've got no choices here; you want me, you know it. Relax and let me do this." His voice was a growl, but he knew his demands, coupled with his hard body over hers, were making a difference—she couldn't have enough energy to keep struggling for too much longer.

And then, it was as if all of his patience was sapped—he wanted her, and she was his; he shouldn't have to wait, he thought, cruelty spiking in his blood. "Stop fighting!" he finally barked out when her body tensed once again as he pressed forward, more than halfway into her.

She did. Lauren froze at the violence in his voice, her breath sucked up by the danger there, and she let herself go limp beneath him, a sob escaping her throat with the fear she couldn't help feeling.

And he felt the moment when she gave in, her body allowing him in with a release of her breath, accepting that he was going to overpower her whether she wanted him to or not. He felt the moment when her will broke, and he saw it in her eyes, and then he kept going, forcing himself deeper and enjoying the clench of her pussy around his dick, pretending he hadn't seen how his finally yelling at her had broken her.

When he bottomed out, he felt her body clench around him as a whimper left her lips, her nails digging into his arms, and he pounded into her again, and again, closing his eyes as the thrusts worked both of their bodies toward a sharper pleasure, Lauren mewling beneath him with each movement.

Despite herself, Lauren closed her eyes and felt her hips rising to meet David's thrusts, her pussy as wet and wanton as ever as she found herself panting beneath him, letting his strength guide her to meet his want. His hand was firm on her breast, squeezing, and his dick was as hard as ever, filling her in a way that she'd never imagined could feel so completing, so pleasurable...so compelling. Her body wanted his—she couldn't deny it even in this situation, where she was shamed by where they were, and who she knew had to be watching, and the fact that she didn't want this right now, or in this fashion, but had no choice. And her body didn't want her to have a choice.

Each move was tinged with pain now—they'd been together too many times in the last 24 hours for her body's desire to be able to make up for all of the friction, all of the rough use—and the moisture between her legs wasn't enough to take away the edges of rawness. It hurt, but her body still trembled as David moved over her, craving more even as she began gasping that she needed him to slow down, please, begging him to try to be gentler...but she wasn't sure whether he even heard her.

David pressed in deeper, bottoming out hard so that she screamed out below him, and her hands found his hips, trying to slow him, to hold him back, but he took it for encouragement, putting more force into his thrusts and pressing in harder, firmer, so that the rawness of her channel burned and she squeezed her eyes shut against the pain, biting her lip until blood came. *I don't want this; I don't want him like this*, her mind yelled, but her body kept going, meeting him until she was climaxing again, violently, bucking beneath him and shuddering in his hands until he sped up roughly, biting down onto her shoulder as he exploded inside of her, pushing deep and spasming, his hands gripping her hard, demanding she keep up with the jarring want that was rocking him, and shaking her body in return as he found release.

When he pulled away and his dick left her body, he saw how swollen he'd left her, how red and raw her lips were, and how her whole body was trembling. She was covered in sweat, and her pussy was soaked, but this time had hurt her badly—he'd felt her trying to push him away, but he'd needed her.

He hadn't had any choice, and she'd wanted it, too.

And when his blood wanted her again, he'd have to take her, no matter how tired her body was, or he'd end up doing worse. *They have to get here, to get us out of this. Josh has to be on the way*, he told himself as he covered her with her dress, laying it on top of her; she was already passed out again, and he didn't want to wake her to feel the aftermath of their fucking. Instead, he just pulled the dress out to cover as much of her body as it would, and then turned away to clean himself up, pull on his jeans, and hope something changed. Something had to give—he could only hope it would be in their favor, or at least in hers. She'd become nothing more than a doll for his lust, but until something changed about where they were, or she was taken away from him, there was nothing he could do to help her, or himself.

***

Melania and Johanna watched the security video together, and they saw what David saw—Lauren suddenly deflating beneath him, her struggles stopping cold when he lost control and yelled at her. Johanna looked to the lead witch and nodded—there was more cruelty in his blood now than violence, but it had been that little bit of violent anger that had done the trick. They had what they wanted.

"We'll give it another day to make sure, but I think that did it," Melania commented. "You can begin mixing up the ingredients for the spell and we'll use it tomorrow night, midnight. Once her will's gone, I plan on letting Nell kill Fredricks, less you or Mary object. She's too tired to feel it now, but the way he's been on her, her magic is probably peaking; we want to freeze it soon, at this level."

Johanna watched David covering Lauren with her

dress in the video and scowled; she didn't want to see any kindness or pity from him at this point. She wanted this over with. "No objections," she answered.

***

David pressed his hands into his forehead hard, and then down the rest of his face, washing in the ice cold water from the faucet for the fourth time in a row. The lust was worse when he'd just woken from the goddamned dreams, and he was determined to stay awake now. He was exhausted, but another short sleep would leave him unable to control himself—not with Lauren so close, smelling of desire, and with her lips so puffy from their kissing that it was impossible to look at her and not think of sex.

Leaning into the sink, he stared at his reflection. The weight he'd lost had made the angles of his face leaner, and his hair was too long. There was still a bruise healing on his cheekbone from the past week's fight also, and the overall effect was, he couldn't deny, that he looked meaner. There was anger all over him, bleeding off of him, and he'd seen in Lauren's face that morning that she was scared of him now. Even when he wasn't near her, when she was covered and they were both seated, feet apart, she was simply afraid of him. Like he'd expected her to be when she'd first come back to the house.

He turned on the faucet again and swiped water across his arms and upper body. He felt like he stank of sweat and sex and Lauren, and smelling Lauren on him wasn't going to help him stay calm around her.

Wiping his hands on his jeans, he stepped out of the bathroom and moved over to the small basket of provisions, picking up an apple and a granola bar before he took a seat. Lauren was on the opposite side of the cage, back in her dress and sweater, sitting cross-legged and staring out at the door, waiting for whatever came next.

"You eaten anything? Drank anything?" he asked as he took a seat and ripped into the granola.

Lauren felt herself jump at his voice; she'd been expecting his touch—a grab, or a pull—more than words, though she hadn't known when it would come. "An apple, and some water while you were asleep," she answered after a moment, keeping her eyes focused on the door. She didn't want to look at him. Her whole body was sore—especially her center. Using the bathroom earlier had been agony, and her voice was hoarse from begging him to stop yesterday. She didn't even think he'd heard half of what she'd said.

Logically, she knew what the line of powder surrounding the cell was doing. It was heightening his aggression and his lust, and no matter how much he fought it, he couldn't fight off the effects entirely. He hadn't hit her yet, but she thought it had to be a matter of time, and at this point...she wasn't even sure that a beating could be worse than more sex, assuming he could stop himself from killing her. Yet, knowledge couldn't keep her from being frightened of him. The way he'd reacted when he'd been above her—his moves had been punishing, cruel. That had to have come from somewhere within him, and she hadn't thought he was capable of the hurt he'd already caused her; she didn't want to know what might come next.

"Everett said you have some magic left...that the spell your mom cast kept it going. Can you feel it?" he asked, his voice flat.

Lauren glanced up to him, a flush in her cheeks and her eyes wide. "I...yeah, a little. Mostly, well...mostly when we're...together," she stumbled. "But it's not..."

"Not enough to get us out of this?" he finished for her. At her nod, he didn't know whether he felt relieved or not, but it wasn't worth thinking about at the moment.

"It's not strong. It's like...it's there to react to you, to what's around me, but I can't find it to hold onto it, to do anything with it. I started feeling it again after...after we slept together at the house. I didn't know how to tell you."

"Or whether you should," he added, thinking back to the way she'd reacted when told that her magic was gone permanently. "I'm glad it's back, Lauren, for you...I've been thinking for a while that we shouldn't have done that to you. But if they know that...hell, why are you here?"

Lauren shrugged. "I don't think there's enough magic to matter at this point, after everything. I guess."

Or, they just want to punish you like they want to punish me. And they know me hurting you makes it worse on you. Still, the thought gave him some hope that maybe her punishment would end at some point, and she'd be given another chance. Left alone to have a life.

When she didn't say more, David leaned his head back with his eyes closed, trying to stretch the tension from his muscles and wake himself up. He'd have given anything for coffee, for a mainline of caffeine or even just a soda. With no other choices, he rose to retrieve another granola bar and some water. Finishing the rest of his meal, he tossed the trash over to land in the bin near the snacks, and then began stretching more earnestly, working to stay awake. He watched Lauren as he did, the way she was doing her best to ignore him, to give him space. It killed him that she was back to being afraid of him—more afraid of him than she'd been at any point in the past—but he understood. It was only the next morning, and he'd bet she could tell from looking at him that he was aching to take more from her, and exhausted and just holding it off.

When he finally stopped stretching, she still wasn't looking at him.

"I wasn't expecting the tattoo," David said finally. He couldn't think of what else to say, but he wanted them to communicate. He wanted to stay awake, and he needed her help to do it. For a moment, he thought she was going to ignore him, but then he saw her shoulders shrug, her head tilting sideways like she wasn't sure what to say.

"It was Barry's idea," she answered quietly, her voice just loud enough for David to hear her. She doubted the coven would be able to take anything from knowing his name—the tattoo looked like a tattoo, after all, right?—but she didn't want to chance them being suspicious about it.

It took a moment, and then he realized what her words signified. *The metallic ink. The fucking metal's there.* David's mind spun, thinking about the experimental tattoo ink they'd been discussing and trying to figure out how fast Barry might have been able to finish the tracking software. He couldn't ask—Lauren had been right to give him a bare bones answer like that, for fear of the witches getting suspicious. What would they do if they knew? Skin her arm? Cut her arm off? He didn't want to know.

He ached to ask to examine it, to look at it closer and see if he could find the metal in the design or tell from sight that it wasn't a normal tattoo, but he held his tongue. He didn't need to be close to her right now. For now, it was enough to know that there was some hope—some real hope—that there was help on the way.

Lauren glanced back to him quickly, just to see if

he'd understood her. She could see from the way he was looking at her that he had. But his eyes were still dark, cruel, and she could see from the way his hands were clenched that he was struggling to keep himself in check. She turned back toward the bars and shut her eyes.

***

When David woke, he didn't take time to hesitate or to think about what he was doing. When sleep had been inevitable, he'd made his decision. His best bet was to use the dream to help him move more quickly. If he could act like he'd never left the dream, and just finish what had been started there...it would be quick. Trying to fight the urges would only give his body time to amp up its want, and need more.

Even as his eyes were opening, he was taking stock of the room. Nobody else was there with them, as usual. In another moment, he'd rolled to his feet, and he was on top of Lauren before she had time to speak.

"I'm sorry," he growled, pushing her forward out of her cross-legged position so that she landed on all-fours, gasping from the surprise.

Lauren kicked backward at David's leg as she tried to squirm forward, just realizing what he was doing. *I thought he was asleep, I thought he was asleep*, her dazed mind repeated as she fought to get away, twisting beneath him.

His lips were practically against her ear when she heard him repeat that he was sorry, but then he was pulling her dress up and she found herself begging, flinging her arms backward to try to hold him away from her body.

"David, stop! Stop!" she yelled again, but then his

hand was in her hair, arching her neck back so that her eyes were forced into meeting his, wild and angry. The look on his face froze her from fighting, and she let herself go limp. He didn't have to say anything; he had to do this, and she had to let him.

David stared hard into Lauren's eyes for another moment, letting all of the cruelty he felt come through in his expression and in his hard grip on her hair and on her hip. He needed her to understand that she had to stop fighting him, and this would be easier.

Trying not to think about what he was doing to her, he pulled her dress far up her body and let his hands run along her sides as his cock found her entrance. He could feel her blood warming to him already, but she wasn't wet this time, not yet—just swollen, and raw. Roughly, he dug three of his fingers into her at once, stretching her, barely hearing her sobs as he began pumping his hand, two times and three times and then four, until he felt her body's natural juices begin to respond; apparently, his constant use of her had begun to wear out even the spell's automatic arousal of her skin against his, but it was coming back. She was wet now, and moaning. He bent to suck at her earlobe as he reached below her to knead her breasts and his cock found her slit again.

"Okay, okay, David, just try to go slow," she murmured, her hand on his wrist to try to slow his movements, until he pulled away and she bit her lip as she felt his cock find her pussy yet again, ready and unyielding.

He pushed in hard, pressing forward with all of his weight and closing his eyes at the choked breath he heard coming from her lips; she'd begun begging him again to stop as he pushed in, but he needed to finish quickly this time, and be done. He clenched his eyes shut and pictured the wanton Lauren he'd fucked in his dream, who'd bent to his punishments and begged for more as he fucked her, and so he pressed harder into her, biting into her neck and then reaching to cover her mouth with one of his hands, cutting off her yells.

She was so tight, and so warm, and he could feel her pussy beginning to quiver around him again, pulsing with the want that he found so addictive. Her body was soaked for him, even through the pain of having been so thoroughly used, and he took advantage of it.

Leaning back, he pressed her thighs apart further and pushed in balls-deep, slamming into her again and again until she was gasping for breath and convulsing around his cock, and he was sweating with the exertion of man-handling her into submission, holding her down for both their pleasures. When he was close to release and she'd long passed her first climax, he gripped her ass and began yanking her body back against his own, ignoring the fact that her hands were scrabbling at the floor, her body squirming with both desire and fear of him.

When Lauren felt him begin rocking into her in the frantic rhythm that suggested he was close to coming, she couldn't help going all but limp beneath him, worn out from pain and desire as she let her body's instincts take over, her hips rocking against his in the tight grip of his fingers, her own hands clenched against the floor. And then he slowed down, as if to show he'd been teasing her toward another climax, but wasn't ready to be done with her yet. *Fuck, I'm going to cum again*, she thought with shock, gasping for breath.

The burning of him pressing into her again and again was unbearable, but her clit was aching and pulsing along with her pussy after another forced release. When she came, she couldn't help screaming, and he kept working her body as she climaxed, pressing harder and more insistently as she came down from it, and then speeding up again, his cock seeming to want to punish her for her pleasure. Her blood was still warm with the power of the orgasm, but the pain was stronger now as his movements inside of her became frantic once again, and she found herself repeating his name over and over again, whimpering beneath him instead of offering anything intelligible. She just wanted him to stop.

And he finally came, shooting his release deep into her, and Lauren let out a choked sob as she felt him collapse on top of her, gripping her hips still as his dick pulsed within her and her body instinctively milked out what was left of his semen. Trembling beneath him, her body still gripping him, she lay still and hoped he was done.

***

He sat apart from her, thinking about what he ought to be doing, or saying.

There were a lot of things David wanted to say to Lauren. He wanted to be able to tell her not just that he was sorry, but that he wouldn't hurt her again. That he wouldn't touch her again unless she wanted him to. But he also knew that telling the lie of any of that would be far crueler than just staying silent. He couldn't make her a promise, knowing he'd probably have to break it, so he stayed silent.

They'd traded places from where they'd been when he'd first woken to find her in the cage. He'd braced himself against the wall by the bathroom, his whole body tensed against the desires running through him. He'd hoped so much that attacking her once, as soon as he woke, would be good enough to keep his lust at bay, but he'd been wrong. Now, the best he could do was to try not to think of it, and to avoid coming close to touching her, but he was practically shaking with the tension in his muscles and the want, his dick aching for more of her. For her part, Lauren was just as tense, curled up in a tight sitting position near the center of the room. He'd been able to feel the heat coming off of her when he'd taken her the last time, and guessed that she was burning up, between the heat of her own blood in reaction to his, and the heat of the bars. He wasn't even sure her blood had had time to really cool down between their last couplings; she'd looked feverish from the moment he'd touched her, and she still did.

When Melania walked in, Mary following her, it took a moment for either of them to notice, lost as they were in their thoughts. Melania was within a few feet of the cage when David's face jarred upward to meet hers, a snarl on his lips. Lauren looked, but as if from a haze, which made the witches smile all the wider.

"David, dear, you're practically vibrating with trying to stay away from our pretty Lauren," Melania purred, stepping to within a foot of the cage to observe him. He looked to be sweating from the exertion of holding himself in check, and his eyes were dark when they returned her gaze.

"What the fuck do you want?" he growled, his fists tightening so that his nails dug hard into his skin. It had been taking everything he had to stay away from Lauren, and now every instinct he had told him to attack Melania—but with the bars in place, that would be suicide. Maybe that would be better, it occurred to him suddenly, but he wasn't ready to take the step yet.

"I want to thank you for breaking her heart, for one...for breaking *her*," the witch added quietly, her eyes now on Lauren.

David watched Lauren shake her head, but she didn't

look back to him.

"She's not broken," he answered, but even he could hear that his words were flat. He could see it in the way she was curled in upon herself, refusing to look any of them in the eye. Hell, he'd felt it, the last few times he'd taken her. The contradiction was in front of him, and now it was just a question of whether she'd come out of it.

"Well then, we'll just wait until she is, won't we?" Melania offered, and David's eyes moved to Mary, who looked upset and now stood back against the room's outer wall.

"Seems like all we've been doing is waiting," he commented tightly.

"Then a little more won't hurt. Whenever you're ready, David, that's fine."

David looked up to meet Melania's gaze, but her cruel smile was focused on Lauren.

"If he takes you once or twice more, I think that will be enough. And he'll give in soon now," the witch announced.

Lauren curled tighter into herself. She could hear the small whimpers coming inadvertently from her own chest now, her own throat, but she couldn't stop them—no matter that she knew they were what Melania wanted, and knew that they probably hurt the man behind her, if he was still capable of feeling hurt. She was so warm, and so sore, she couldn't imagine being able to take anymore, or how her body could survive David pushing her like he had been. Even in the last few moments, just the sound of his voice had been enough to make her wet with want for him, but she still ached, and just the idea of him taking her again was enough to bring tears to her eyes. She couldn't handle more.

David watched Melania's words push Lauren further

into herself; she was whimpering quietly, crying, and there was nothing he could do. Melania was right—he couldn't refuse to touch her for forever, and he was close to losing control, again.

Clenching his fists, he knocked his head back against the wall behind him and took a deep breath, trying to still his mind. Melania began giggling soon after he'd closed his eyes, but he ignored her, blocking out her words when she began speaking to Lauren, and trying to sink into himself and go blank. If he could just forget where he was, forget the tension in his body that wanted to attack, forget his hard dick and his desire to feel Lauren beneath him, struggling, then maybe he could hold off. Maybe he could just stay here, ready to explode, until someone came to rescue them. It was what he'd been thinking since he'd first jumped Lauren, when he'd first woken to find Lauren in the cage with him, and that had to have been days ago...but it was all he could do. He just had to hold on to what control he had left.

***

Johanna and Nell were observing the scene from the security room when they heard the back door to the warehouse being eased open downstairs. When a quick look at the relevant security picture showed no change, and no movement, Johanna eased forward toward the dirty window that overlooked the warehouse floor, and froze at the sight below. What seemed to be a small army of men was swarming in silently, taking point positions around the room. Two men in combat gear, warding clearly painted along their arms and facemasks, were already poised at the foot of the staircase that would lead up to where she and Nell stood, with a line of others spreading out and preparing to enter the hall that led to the bulk of the warehouse's space, both at floor level and below.

"How the fuck did they find us?" Nell spit from behind her.

Johanna shook her head. There'd been no tracking device on Lauren, she was positive. And they had jammers set up on top of that, not to mention the wardings. "I don't know," she growled.

Just then, the men began moving both up the stairs and into the hall below. Johanna's mind flashed to the fact that she still had time to get to her own room and retrieve the few items she'd brought to the space, if she hurried.

"We can't take all of them; you want to try to warn Melania?" Nell asked skeptically, already eyeing the door at the other end of the room and thinking that Melania wouldn't be bothering to ask on their behalf; she'd just be keeping herself safe.

"You can if you want to," Johanna answered after a breath. "But she wouldn't risk her ass for ours. I'm getting out," she said as she tapped hurriedly on the keyboard before her, having already decided that erasing the computer files and retrieving her own personal items were far more important than ensuring the four of them all got out.

By the time the men had entered the room to clear it, both women had disappeared.

***

Josh moved into the doorway and took in the scene in a moment—Melania and Mary were standing in the room, both focused on the energy cage that held his partner and Lauren, both of them sitting and looking ill, shivering even in what felt like an absurdly warm room. He brought his weapon up and kept his eyes on Melania, feeling four more men slip by him and into the room as he covered the lead witch. At the moment surrender was called for, her hand came up toward the cage and he took his shot, catching her in the back of the head before she could cast whatever spell she'd been about to throw toward the cage. A moment later, he saw Mary attempt to pull something from her pocket as she was shot down by the partner of one of the men her coven had already killed.

Pulling his facemask up, Josh moved toward the space where the energy cage met the wall, eyeing David. "You okay?"

"Devlin...you need to get us out of this."

Josh froze, and looked more closely at his partner. His voice had been strained, stilted and gruff. Not with pain or sickness, but with anger. Now he noticed that his fists were clenched, his arms crossed across his body like he was holding himself together. Josh looked to Lauren, and saw that she'd barely looked up to the men who were now spread around the room—himself and four others who were talking on radios and searching the witches' bodies. The girl was wrapped into herself in a way that reminded him of the day they'd met at the Liberty Diner before he'd taken her to the hospital, and he saw her face was wet with tears. His gut clenched, and he looked back to David, thinking there was no point in trying to talk to her at the moment. "We'll have an energy bar spreader here within the hour, set up in two," he began.

"No, Devlin, now. You need to get her out *now,*" David growled, swallowing down frustration at the thought of another hour. He couldn't wait that long.

Another use of his last name. His partner wouldn't be

using it unless things were desperate, but there was no way to break through these bars with the equipment they had. "Her?" he repeated then, realizing his partner hadn't said 'us' in his second request.

"The powder," Lauren whispered now, "can you scatter it? That might help?"

Josh moved toward her, and saw that one of her fingers pointed to the thin line of powder running along the outskirts of the cage, which he hadn't noticed before. It was a solid line of lavender and gray stuff, spread along the whole of the cage's outside.

"Devlin," David growled again, shaking his head. "Get her out."

Again...Get her out? Not us? Josh took another look at David and saw his bloodshot eyes, his gritted teeth; whatever was going on, they didn't have an hour to wait.

"Aveen, take care of getting rid of this shit—scatter it as much as you can and then find a way to get it up; just erase the line first," Josh commanded, keeping his eye on his partner, who offered a jerky nod. He turned tail and moved back to the hallway then—he couldn't get to them through the bars, but the ceiling might be an option.

Back in the hall, he paced down past the point where the room within would end and then kicked his boot at the wall, scuffing it to mark the distance he'd measured out. He was in a warehouse—there had to be a ladder somewhere, and while a twelve foot ceiling might have kept David from being able to get out of that cage without more help, it wasn't anything they couldn't overcome with a ladder and rope.

***

Lauren glanced gingerly around the room, wondering

where Josh had gone to. She'd looked to David a minute before—he was close to losing control. She'd seen it in the way he was trembling, with his eyes clenched shut and his teeth gritted as if in pain. She thought that if anyone could stop him from losing it again, it was Josh. And the idea of David attacking her while these men were here to watch...she didn't know what she'd do, what they'd do. Josh had to get them out before that happened.

One of the men came up to the cage's edge to speak to David—from the sound of it, he knew him well—and she bit her lip. She thought their best bet was to leave him alone, but she didn't want to say anything. She knew, from what David had said earlier, that he was doing his damnedest to forget she was there, and though she knew she was curled up like prey, like a victim waiting for him to attack, it still seemed like the safest option. Listening to the man trying to get David to respond to him, though, to say something, she found her tears coming more quickly and pushed her head down into her knees to muffle the sound of them. She'd never known what it felt like to shiver in heat when you didn't have a fever, or to shiver from terror. Now she did.

"BACK OFF!" David barked from behind her, and Lauren heard the man stumble backward in surprise. She choked back a louder sob. Then she heard a sound that she thought was David hitting the wall, and then it came again, and again, and she sensed the men outside of the cage backing off. She cringed inward, hearing the sound again. Getting rid of the powder hadn't helped much—it had been too little too late.

When a new sound came after another minute, she kept her head down at first. The sound was coming from above them, like a rough buzzing or cutting. When she did finally look up, she thought she was imagining it at first.

Near where David was, there was a saw blade cutting down through the ceiling, sawing out a rough oval. Another minute went by, and she heard Josh's voice yell for them to move out of the way. She was far enough away already, but she watched as David jerked to his feet and backed into their little bathroom just before the oval of drywall came crashing down, breaking into pieces as it hit the ground.

***

Within an hour, David found himself pacing in front of the warehouse, a dozen yards from anyone else. He'd wrapped his bloody hand in a shirt that one of the other men had thrown at him, and guessed he'd broken a few bones with hitting the wall in the cell before Josh had been able to offer an escape route, but for now he just needed to be away from people, to make sure he didn't hurt anyone else. As it was, he'd had to hold himself back from decking the guy he'd watched Josh hand Lauren down to, for no good reason; it wasn't as if Josh could have handed her to him, after all.

After Josh had dropped a rope down, David had scrambled up first, offering no explanation but knowing he had to put distance between himself and Lauren, which Josh had thankfully seemed to understand. Then Josh had gone down the rope he'd tied off, and helped Lauren to get up and through the ceiling before following.

Out in the hallway, David had watched Josh help Lauren lower down to the six-foot ladder that was not just unsteady, but a far bit down from the ceiling, Sam Aveen being there on the ladder to help her get down and then to the ground. Seeing his hands on her, even helping, had been hard to watch—especially when she'd cringed away from his help as his hands found her knees. She didn't want anyone's touch anywhere near her, and David knew that was on him.

Now, it was all David could do to try to stomp out his aggression and breathe himself back to some semblance of normalcy. From where he was, he could see Lauren sitting on the back tailgate of Aveen's pick-up, shaking her head to whatever Josh was asking her and still hugging herself. Someone had at least given her a coat from one of the trucks, so she had something more than the slight summer dress to cover her. It was warm out, though it was past sunset, but there was a solid enough breeze that it was bringing a chill on, he was so covered in sweat; after being hot in the cage for however long he'd been in there, he found it welcome.

By the time he heard Josh approaching, he'd slowed down and managed to calm some of the emotions running through his blood. He backed off when Josh moved in to offer a hug, though, just as he'd backed off quickly when Josh had tried to grasp hands with him in the ceiling space—he didn't think contact was a good idea yet.

"Some kind of aggression spell?" Josh guessed quietly, standing a foot or so away from his partner.

"Yeah," David sighed, coughing the hoarseness from his voice before he spoke again. "How long...how long was I in there?"

"Twelve days; we didn't have any leads until Lauren went in."

"The tattoo," David said flatly before turning away, staring back at her where she was still perched on the pick-up, leaning against its side with her head resting in her arms. "Man, how the hell did you guys let them get to her? We knew they had a bead on the ranch house..."

"Get to her? She didn't tell you?" Josh caught himself just as he reached for David's arm, and pulled his hand back, running it through his hair instead and shaking his head. "Man, she insisted. The coven sent a letter—demanded she surrender and they'd let you go. We told her she shouldn't do it. *I* told her she shouldn't do it."

"She came in for me?" David looked from his partner back to Lauren, going back over the last few days in his head. Swallowing down nausea, he thought about the bruises that were visible on her arms from where he'd held her down, and the dark hickies he'd left on her neck and shoulders, drawing out her whimpers and her desire.

"Listen, man, I don't know...I don't know what you guys have been through. You need a hospital for your hand, though; I know that much. Nice move, beating up the wall, by the way," he tried to joke. "Does she need a hospital?"

"I don't know. I don't...I don't think so, but you should ask her," David added. "I'll ride with Aveen—I owe him an apology. You'll get her back to the house, or to a hospital, or wherever she wants to go?"

"Yeah, but, look, David—they weren't all here. We got Melania and Mary, but Johanna and Nell split; we never saw them. Lauren said they were here, but..."

"They were here," he said quietly. "Alright, so you bring her to the hospital or the ranch house. I'm riding with Aveen. Lauren doesn't need to be around me," he commented quietly. Taking another glance at her, he then nodded at his partner and headed off toward the men left standing outside of the warehouse entrance.

Josh watched him go before heading back to Lauren, and he stood in silence beside her for a moment before speaking; she looked exhausted, and scared.

"Lauren, do you need a hospital?"

"I just need to sleep," she answered quietly.

"I'll take you back to the house, if that's okay," he answered. He didn't think Nell and Johanna would come after her at this point, they'd already lost so much, but he didn't know. And if he was being honest, he didn't want her to disappear. Instinctively, he couldn't feel like that was the best move for either her or his partner, or even for him, no matter what had happened in that warehouse; she'd become like a little sister over the past weeks, and after being willing to sacrifice herself to get David back...he couldn't think of why it would make sense to have her anywhere but at the ranch house. One way or another, they all were going to have to move forward, and for better or worse, that seemed to mean that she was tied to them for a while longer. When she didn't answer immediately, though, he perched on the truck's tailgate beside her. He thought about reaching out to touch her knee, or her hand, or something, but didn't.

"I don't know...I don't know what makes sense," she finally said. "And already, everything you guys have done...I mean..."

"Whatever you're about to say, this isn't about anything but what you want," he said. "And know this—David's my best friend. He's a good guy, he's my family, and we wouldn't have found him if you hadn't been brave enough to put yourself out there with just that tattoo as a lifeline. You put yourself on the line for him; I can't repay that. You're family now, Lauren. Whatever you need, we're here."

Lauren shook her head, but pulled the arm of the jacket up so that she could take a look at the tattoo. Somehow, she was glad it wouldn't be disappearing. "I'm not brave, Josh. I'm...I can barely think right now. I just feel—I just feel scared," she whispered, shrugging and pulling the jacket sleeve back down.

"I can see if you could stay at Claudia's for a few days," he offered quietly after another moment. "She's been worried about you guys, too. But, Lauren, after everything—hell, you're like a little sister to me at this point. As long as you need it, the ranch house is open to you. But Claudia has a guest room, and I don't think she'd mind."

Lauren shook her head; even the warmth of Josh's saying she was like family felt distant—the comment would have thrilled her, two weeks before, but now she was numb. She didn't know what the answer was, either, or what made sense at this point...but she couldn't chance putting someone else in danger, on the off chance that Nell and Johanna were just mending their pride before coming after one of them again. "No. If you really don't mind, yeah, I'll stay...I think, I'll stay at the house," she answered.

"Alright then," he sighed, relieved. "You ready to go?"

"Yeah," she answered, slipping off the tailgate and moving toward the vehicle that Josh indicated. When he opened the passenger door, she glanced up from the ground, to him and then around them.

"David's getting a ride to the hospital," he answered, seeing the question on her face. "His hand needs to get looked at."

"He was hitting the wall."

"Yeah, well, I guess it had it coming, right?" Josh said, his voice gentle as he watched Lauren climb into the car and then pull up the seatbelt. She wasn't meeting his eyes, but the fact that she'd asked about David seemed, at least, like a good sign. He didn't want to think about what would happen if she just disappeared now, after the way David had acted before he'd really gotten to know her, back when she'd been out of their lives the first time. And Josh himself wanted her back at the house, truth be told; he'd been as worried over her as he'd been about David over the last week.

Lauren nodded belatedly as Josh closed the door and walked around the vehicle to get into the driver's seat. She didn't need to be told, or say aloud, that David had been hitting the wall in order to refrain from hurting her. No matter how scared of him she felt now, she knew that mattered, and she had to try to remember it, whatever came next.

About Your Author

Michaela discovered Stephen King and Piers Anthony when she was in fourth grade, and there was really no going back from there. She penned her first full-length novel in 7th grade when she fell in love with *seaQuest* and passed the time between seasons by coming up with her own adventures for the characters; now, she knows to call it fanfiction, but back then it was for her the beginning of a life-long writing passion, and the stories were as real as anything else in the world. From the beginning, her stories ranged from horror to science fiction and fantasy, and involved danger, passion, and character-driven nightmares.

A constant reader and writer, she grew up in Virginia, spending most of her time in the backstage area of her high school theater or wandering the woods near her home, wondering what it would be like to cast spells or meet a vampire. Eventually, she moved to South Carolina and her escapades expanded to sipping whiskey and skinny-dipping in dark lakes where she'd still like to believe monsters lurk.

Now, she lives and writes in southwest Florida, where she works as a full-time book editor specializing in horror, dark romance, suspense, fantasy, and anything at all involving the paranormal. Her own writing always takes dark turns, but tends toward character-driven stories which blur genre lines and ask the questions that she believes we sometimes even hide from ourselves. *Spells in Waiting* is her first full-length published novel, and she jokes that she didn't mean to write it… but, in the end, it demanded to be written, and its sequel is now complete and 'coming soon' since the characters in the book aren't people she's quite found a way to walk away from just yet.

If you'd like to contact her about her works or get in touch for editing, you can email her at MichaelaLCane@gmail.com or follow her on twitter, where you'll find her @MichaelaLCane.

Other HellBound Books Titles
Available at: www.hellboundbookspublishing.com

The Southern House

There are some places that lie where the barrier between worlds is thin and growing thinner. These corridors are as old as the Earth itself, hidden in dark and forgotten places, waiting to be found. There is a being who stalks these places and travels between those worlds. He was given the name Mr. Shift by generations of children and madmen.

Just as Hickory Grimble hits rock bottom, he inherits his grandparents' farm and believes his luck is changing. He soon finds he inherited more than money and land.

Haunted by his own inner demons, now he has new problems. He begins to see strange creatures on the dark, sprawling acreage, animals that have no business living in middle Tennessee. He also discovers a decrepit, abandoned house in the forest that never seems to be in the same place twice.

Balanced on a razor's edge between, addiction and fate, Hick is now face to face with an ancient evil that has returned once more to claim more of the town's children.

Them

Ray Sanders returns home from Florida to bury his mother.

Soon, the supernatural evidence behind his mother's demise begins to surface in the form of dreams and mysterious happenings.

During all of the madness, Sanders must face his destiny and vanquish the generations-old evil that has plagued his family since the 1800's…

In 1854, Louis Sanders, with the help of Elias Atkins, dug a well to provide water to the family farm. What they did not anticipate was the water to be infested with Odomulites - ancient sins. These malevolent beings - were trapped in our world on their way to the spirit world - formed a pact of protection with both Sanders and Atkins; the families would serve as guardians of the Odomulite nests and in return, a blind eye would be cast when the Odomulites took host bodies to inhabit and feed upon. It was this pact, which in 2016 would propel Sanders and Julie Fontaine - a young woman with a special connection to the Spirit World - into the heart of the last active nest to rid the town of its insidious Odomulite population.

Blood in The Woods

Based upon true events...

For Jody, growing up in the late eighties and early nineties in the small Louisiana town of Hammond with his best friend Jack was filled with wonderful childhood memories.

Time spent playing in the woods, shooting pellet guns, blowing up mailboxes, fighting at school and upon the dawning of interest in the fairer sex, their carefree lives typical of children with few responsibilities and no worries beyond the next pop-quiz or getting to second base. As they grow older together and experience the joys and pains of life, love, family and friendship, they uncover a grim secret that their home town has kept, and through little more than an innocent, idle curiosity, Jody and Jack stumble upon something horrific in the woods and their lives quickly take a most sinister and dangerous turn as they find themselves hunted by an unspeakable evil...

Schlock! Horror!

An anthology of short stories based upon/inspired by and in loving homage to all of those great gorefest movies and books of the 1980's (not necessarily base in that era, although some do ride that wave of nostalgia!), the golden age when horror well and truly came kicking, screaming and spraying blood, gore & body parts out from the shadows...

This exemplary 80's themed/inspired tales of terror has been adjudicated and compiled by one Mr Bret McCormick, himself a writer, producer and director of many a schlock classic, including *Bio-Tech Warrior*, *Time Tracers*, *The Abomination*, *Ozone: The Attack of the Redneck Mutants* and the inimitable *Repligator*.

Featuring stories from: Todd Sullivan, Timothy C Hobbs, Mark Thomas, Andrew Post, James B. Pepe, Thomas Vaughn, Edward Karpp, Jaap Boekestein, Lisa Alfano, L. C. Holt, John Adam Gosham, Brandon Cracraft, M. Earl Smith, Sarah Cannavo, James Gardner, Bret McCormick, and James H. Longmore.

Worship Me

Something is listening to the prayers of St. Paul's United Church, but it's not the god they asked for; it's something much, much older.

A quiet Sunday service turns into a living hell when this ancient entity descends upon the house of worship and claims the congregation for its own.

The terrified churchgoers must now prove their loyalty to their new god by giving it one of their children or in two days time it will return and destroy them all.

As fear rips the congregation apart, it becomes clear that if they're to survive this untold horror, the faithful must become the faithless and enter into a battle against God itself.

But as time runs out, they discover that true monsters come not from heaven or hell…
…they come from within.

Demons, Devils and Denizens of Hell: Vol, 2

The second volume in HellBound Books' outstanding horror anthology fair teems with tales of Hades' finest citizens – both resident and vacationing in our earthly realm…

Compiled by the inimitable P. Mattern and featuring:

Savannah Morgan, Andrew MacKay, Jaap Boekestein, James H Longmore, Stephanie Kelley, Ryan Woods, James Nichols, P. Mattern, Marcus Mattern, Gerri R Gray, and legion more…

Shopping List 2: Another Horror Anthology

Once again, HellBound Books brings you an outstanding collection of horror, dark, slippery things, and supernatural terror - all from the very best up and coming minds in the genre.

We have given each and every one of our authors the opportunity to have their shopping lists read by you, the most wonderful reading public, and have the darkest corners of their creative psyche laid bare for all to see...

In all, 21 stories to chill the soul, tingle the spine and keep you awake in the cold, murky hours of the night from: Erin Lee, The Truth Artist, John Barackman, Serena Daniels, M.R. Wallace, Isobel Blackthorn, Alex Laybourne, Jason J. Nugent, Josh Darling, Jovan Jones, Nick Swain, Douglas Ford, Craig Bullock, Craig Bullock, Jeff C. Stevenson, PC3, David F Gray, Sergio Palumbo, Donna Maria McCarthy, David Clark & Megan E. Morales

**A HellBound Books LLC
Publication**

http://www.hellboundbookspublishing.com

Printed in the United States of America